warrior

Other books by Bryan Davis

Dragons of Starlight series:

Starlighter

Echoes from the Edge series

1 | *Beyond the Reflection's Edge*

2 | *Eternity's Edge*

3 | *Nightmare's Edge*

Dragons in Our Midst series

1 | *Raising Dragons*

2 | *The Candlestone*

3 | *Circles of Seven*

4 | *Tears of a Dragon*

Oracles of Fire series

1 | *Eye of the Oracle*

2 | *Enoch's Ghost*

3 | *Last of the Nephilim*

4 | *The Bones of Makaidos*

Dragons of Starlight

Warrior

Bryan Davis

ZONDERVAN

Warrior

This title is also available as a Zondervan ebook.
Visit www.zondervan.com/ebooks.

Requests for information should be addressed to:

Zondervan, *Grand Rapids, Michigan 49530*

ISBN: 978-0-310-71837-6

Cover design: Jeff Gifford
Cover photography or illustration: Cliff Nielson
Interior design: Carlos Eluterio Estrada
Interior composition: Greg Johnson, Textbook Perfect

Printed in the United States of America

11 12 13 14 15 16 17 /DCI/ 22 21 20 19 18 17 16 15 14 13 12 11 10 9 8 7 6 5 4 3 2 1

warrior

one

Cursed by blindness, Zena shuffled on her knees—reaching, groping—a beggar stretching out empty hands into the hated void. Oh, yes, it was blindness, but not the indiscriminate shackling of innocent eyes by a careless creator. Hers was a wretched, calculated blindness inflicted long ago by the accursed Starlighter, the selfsame Cassabrie who had delayed the arrival of the prophesied hatchling … until now.

The black egg lay near. Its presence—close, warm, alive—beckoned. The prince within the stony shell called with an inaudible voice, a plea that rode the winds of sensation, a yearning for intimacy. She would provide sympathy, as always. Souls trapped in darkness often cry out for the solace of another lonely prisoner, each one hoping for the day of liberation. Perhaps her role as comforter would reap rewards even beyond the benefits she sought.

Her fingertips brushed a dimpled surface. Chill bumps raced across her skin as she purred, "There you are, my darling!"

She reached for the velvet case in the pocket of her silky gown, withdrew the Starlighter's finger, and set the tip on the shell. Ah! The connection brought a new icy chill. Such joy! It was just a finger, to be sure, but it meant so much more. That vile girl had paid for her deed, and she had paid dearly. The great Starlighter had lost her precious perfection and now lent her missing digit to a dragon who was prophesied to be born handicapped. What a delicious irony that her finger provided the means to instruct the unborn prince about the history of Starlight and inform him of his glorious future.

The chill continued, in spite of the heat in the Basilica's cavernous incubator room. Five paces away, a circle of fiery fountains soared up from the floor and splashed against the marble ceiling high above—a protective fence of flames that whipped the air into a hot, whooshing swirl.

As Zena held the finger in place, the cold sensation eased, replaced by a surge of warmth that sizzled into her body, the sign of connection with the dragon youngling inside. Her blindness faded, and the black shell came into view, reflecting her ivory skin, slender face and hands, and long black dress. Propped on a nest of soft pillows, the egg shifted, giving evidence of the life within.

"My prince," she whispered, "can you hear me?"

The finger quivered for a moment, then became still. As she waited for a response, the shadow of a dragon enveloped her in winged darkness. Zena resisted the urge to tense her muscles. Magnar's visits had become more frequent, and his silent approaches had too often given him the advantage of catching her off guard. The noise from the flames masked the sound of his wings, and his ability to pass through the fountains unharmed had proven him to be the most powerful dragon in the world. His cooperation remained essential.

Keeping her focus on the egg, Zena spoke with a steady voice. "I will have news in a moment."

Magnar thumped his tail on the floor, impatient, as usual. Zena let her lips stretch into a satisfied smirk. Or perhaps he was uneasy about the finger she had cut from the Starlighter's hand so many years ago. For all the bravado he displayed as king of the Southland dragons, he did not cope well with trivial reminders of the death sentences he had ordered.

When the quivering resumed, a low voice rode the Starlighter's bone-thin finger and penetrated Zena's mind. *I hear you. Is everything prepared?*

"All is ready," she said out loud. "Magnar is here to witness your emergence, and once he verifies that you are, indeed, the prophesied king, he will abdicate as planned."

Magnar's skepticism is excusable. Very few kings are willing to relinquish power to a promise.

Zena lifted the finger and set it back in its case, gazing at the wrinkled skin's almost imperceptible glow. Another precious moment of clarity had been spent. How many more remained before the finger's power died away and permanent blindness set in? Fewer than before; that was the only certainty.

She blinked, still able to see clearly. This brief view of the visual world would soon fade, but likely not before the historic birth of the next dragon king. Seeing him emerge had dominated every dream, and now all her years of service would finally bear fruit. The triumph of his kingdom would bring her restored vision. The prince had promised it, and she would do everything in her power to see his rule expand throughout all of Starlight.

The black egg tilted to one side and leaned for a moment before rocking upright on its nest. A slight cracking sound reached her ears, barely audible amidst the rush of flames.

"The time has come." Still on her knees, Zena closed the case's lid and slid it into her pocket. She then opened a panel in the floor and turned off the fountains. As the flames shrank away and the breezy rush settled, she caressed the egg's shell, pausing on a tiny crack near the top. "The king will hatch soon—perhaps minutes."

With a beat of his wings, Magnar scooted closer, extended his long neck, and sniffed. "The crack is deep enough to allow his scent to escape. It will not be long now."

"Have you decided whether or not to tell his mother?"

"She must not know until I give the order. Her exile is deserved and will remain intact. If this prince is indeed the prophesied one, it will not be beneficial to have another powerful dragon as his ally."

"If that is your wish." Zena wrapped her arms around the egg, making her loose sleeves ride up past her elbows. Intertwining her fingers on the opposite side, she laid her cheek on its surface, letting her hair drape its reflective shell. As she bathed in its purple aura, she sighed. "For centuries we have waited. The day has finally arrived."

"You never lost faith," Magnar said, "though many others have."

"True. I am not shy about my own loyalty. I deserve accolades." Reaching out a hand, Zena stroked Magnar's claw. Years ago, he would have recoiled at her forward manner, but now he didn't even flinch. His scales felt warm, reflecting their fiery appearance. With her vision still somewhat intact, his elegant draconic form stayed in view. His long, sleek neck curled like an adder ready to strike, and his ears, short and pointed, rotated as if searching for a lost sound. His backbone spines bent slightly toward his lengthy tail, giving the appearance of swift movement, as if blown back by the wind.

"What do you think?" she asked. "Will his handicap be obvious? Perhaps something so crippling that other dragons will be loath to accept him as their new king?"

"If the prophecy is true, he will be able to quell any uprising of potential usurpers among us." As he drew his claw away from her hand, his scaly brow dipped low. "Or human invaders."

Zena looked into Magnar's eyes—scarlet, pulsing, furious. His anger over the release of Jason and the new Starlighter still scalded his temper, and his desire to pursue the escaped humans consumed him. He was a beast lunging against the bars in a cage of his own making. "Have you tested the barrier recently?" she asked.

"Less than an hour ago. As long as the Starlighter remains to the north, she is out of reach."

"When the prince emerges," Zena said as she lifted her cheek from the egg, "he will provide guidance concerning the Starlighter. Since Koren threatened to kill the youngling, perhaps he has given up on luring her into servitude. If the prince orders her execution, then it might be safe for you to travel beyond the great wall and bring her to justice."

"A guess is all you have." Twin plumes of dark smoke rose from Magnar's nostrils, and his voice deepened. "If you are wrong, and the Starlighter ruins our plans, my wrath will be speedy and furious, beginning with a certain priestly dragon and ending with a hatchling prince and his blind guardian."

Zena raised a rigid finger. "Stay your fury for another few hours. If your faith remains steadfast, you will be given what you have coveted for so long."

"Again, a guess on your part. Every moment we wait separates us further from the Starlighter and her companion. If she arrives safely in the Northlands and finds the star, all could be lost."

"She is ignorant. Without the prince, she can neither harm Exodus nor resurrect it."

"The star reveals its own secrets. She might be ignorant, but she is not a fool. It will not take her long to piece the puzzle together."

"Fear not. We still have time." Zena petted the top of the egg. "Do not be shy, my love. The shell has cracked. You need only to break through. Then you will be able to assume a throne of power from which you will rule this world."

After a few seconds of silence, the egg vibrated in time with a pecking sound. The crack lengthened, then widened. A sharp black claw protruded near the top of the egg, almost invisible against the shell's surface. It disappeared for a moment before breaking through again at a lower point. Soon, a jagged-edged fragment dropped to the pillows, and the two halves of the egg fell away from the center, revealing a black conglomeration of scales and twisted body parts.

The bundle swelled. Ever so slowly, a pair of wings unfurled, and a head emerged from a coil of neck and limbs. A pair of scaly eyelids blinked, briefly veiling two blue eyes, clouded and without defined pupils. They glowed as if embedded with a phosphorescent dye. As the newborn dragon scanned the room, the glow passed across Zena, then returned to hover over her. Again he spoke to her mind. *Greetings, my friend.*

Smiling broadly, Zena extended her hands. "Shall I carry you, my noble king?"

Not yet. I must test my abilities, including my voice and motor skills.

With every phrase, the youngling's mouth had remained still, yet his words came through clearly, even without the Starlighter's finger. Apparently the shell had hindered his telepathy powers, and now he could communicate freely with her, a benefit of their spiritual attachment.

When the young dragon stretched out, Zena looked him over. He appeared to be of normal size for a newborn, perhaps five feet long from the tip of his tail to the top of his head. His wings were well-formed, as were his forelegs and hind quarters; no sign of handicap in his body structure at all. He differed from other younglings only in color, jet black instead of reddish brown, with blue eyes instead of yellowish orange.

"I am ..." The newborn's voice squeaked as he spoke in the dragon language. He coughed twice and spat out a wad of thick liquid before trying again. "I am Taushin."

"A lovely name." Zena clapped her hands. "You are draconic perfection."

"He has an impressive form," Magnar said. "Classic dragon beauty in every way. Yet it is his handicap that will prove his kingly right, and I see no obvious deformity."

Taushin swung his neck. His light beams drifted across the bigger dragon and toward his face, halting at his eyes. For a moment he appeared to be deep in thought, then his ears perked up. "I have found a new sense of perception and am now comprehending my surroundings through Magnar. Why do I not have this ability myself?"

"How strange." Zena looked into Taushin's glazed eyes. Even though her own vision had already dimmed, the truth was evident. "You are blind."

"Blind?" Taushin repeated. "You have mentioned this label in describing yourself."

"Sometimes I can see shapes and shadows," Zena said, "and sometimes I am totally without vision, but I have overcome my lack of eyesight. My other senses are more acute."

Blinking, Magnar turned away from the probing glow. "So that is his handicap—blindness. Truly this is severe enough to fulfill the prophecy."

Taushin's expression turned sour. "Zena, you feared a bodily deformity of limbs or wings, but I suspect that this is worse. Still, I would not be blind if I had a different companion, one who could see. I could look through her eyes."

"I can only beg your tolerance," Zena said. "I promise upon my life to serve you with every skill and talent I possess. If not for that Starlighter …" She tightened her jaw. Her eyesight had been stolen long ago by Cassabrie, but Cassabrie had paid the price with great suffering and death. There was no use airing once again a story that never failed to make her boil.

"Yes, you told me about Cassabrie." Taushin lowered his eye glow to the floor. "You have also mentioned Koren. She is a Starlighter as well. She could serve as my eyes."

Zena stroked his neck, pressing her fingers in as deeply as his armor would allow. "Serve as your eyes? But, my liege, only hours ago she threatened to kill you."

"An empty threat, I assure you. When I call for her, she will return."

"She is dangerous," Magnar said. "She has the power to hypnotize any dragon who watches her stories come to life."

"So I have been told." Taushin blinked again, momentarily shutting off the blue rays. "Perhaps a dragon who cannot watch her stories will be immune."

"I see your point. An intriguing advantage." Magnar averted his gaze and appeared to be looking at the hole in the ceiling, an exit for flying dragons. "If you are the prophesied king, then you have been born with a message for me. When you deliver that, and I deem it to be adequate, I will be satisfied and abdicate my throne."

"As if you could stop me from taking it." Taushin smiled, exposing two razor-sharp fangs. As his lips relaxed, hiding the fangs, his voice altered to a deep register, mysterious in tone and bearing a hypnotic cadence. "Fear not, Magnar.

As your father promised, the key to the portal will come to you, carried by a girl from Darksphere. Yet, beware. Although she appears to be nothing more than a ragged refugee, she possesses great gifts akin to those of a Starlighter. You must not underestimate her." After a short pause, he added, "Zerrod has spoken."

"Zerrod?" Magnar's ears perked up. "How could you know my father's name?"

"Perhaps now you are convinced that I am, indeed, the new king." Taushin's eyes shone bluer and brighter than ever. "Before you leave, I must ask you to do something for me."

Magnar bowed his head. "As always, I am at your service."

"Call for a gathering of dragons and humans alike." Taushin sat up high on his haunches with a wing bent across his chest. "I will present myself to them this very evening at the Zodiac. Dragons and humans alike will welcome the dawning of a new day, an era that has no need for slaves."

"Perhaps. At least until they learn what those words mean." Magnar looked up at the hole again. "Our search for the dragon assassins should be complete by then, so everyone will be available." After bowing again, he flew upward in a tight spiral and through the opening.

As soon as Magnar disappeared, Zena stroked Taushin again. Nearly blind once more, she sighed. "Are you certain of your decision to call Koren? Are my services insufficient?"

He arched his back, apparently enjoying the strenuous massage. "You are a benefit beyond all estimation, but you cannot give me sight."

She thrust her hand into her pocket and withdrew the velvet box. Both hands trembling, she snapped it open and grasped the Starlighter's finger. Her eyesight immediately began to clear, as always. "Look through me now," she said, unable to keep her voice from shaking. "You will see. I can serve you as well as Koren can."

Taushin looked into her eyes for a moment, then turned aside. "Yours is an aided vision that will eventually fail. Why should I rely on the recipient of light when I can have the source?"

She brushed away a tear. "I … I understand. You must have the best servant possible. Yet, if I may be so bold, there is no substitute for loyalty. She of the green eyes and red hair will not soon be persuaded to worship you as I do. Cassabrie could not be tamed, so I expect the same from Koren. And Cassabrie may yet create a stir. I have not told you this, but her spirit lives on. I saw it myself."

Taushin's ears flattened, and a reddish hue tinted his eyes' glow. "I assume you have not yet found the body from which you cut that finger."

"Not yet." She caressed one of his wings. The leathery texture felt good against her skin. "I have not been able to prove my theory, but I strongly suspect that Arxad knows where it is. If you question him, he might—"

"There is no need to question Arxad. From what you tell me, he would never reveal secrets that will bring harm to his precious humans. I will locate Cassabrie's body myself. Even now I feel its presence. It is close, perhaps even within these walls. If we are able to obtain it, we will have the ultimate bait to lure the spirit of Cassabrie into our grasp. With her and Koren working together, nothing can stop us from resurrecting the Northlands star or from dominating every inhabited world."

"Two Starlighters?" Zena said. "How can we restrain such power? How will you coerce them to do your will?"

"Koren is easy prey. I have read her mind, and I know her weakness, a soft spot we will have no trouble exploiting. Cassabrie, however, will not be so easily persuaded."

Zena held the finger in front of her eyes. "Trust me. Cassabrie longs for restoration. Even if we never find her body, we can lead her to believe that we have it. With this bait, perhaps we can control her as well."

Taushin's blue rays penetrated Zena's eyes and reflected back at the finger. "As you said, there is no substitute for loyalty. Who else could conjure such a deceptive scheme?"

Zena smiled, her lips trembling. "And our schemes have only just begun."

Balancing on vine-tied logs, Jason pushed a steering pole into shallow water and guided his raft toward a moonlit bank on the right. Koren slept curled on her side, in spite of the northbound river's quickening current. A few hours earlier, they had anchored their rickety craft using a vine and stone and then dozed atop the river, hoping the water offered protection from any wild beasts that might be roaming the shores. Although those hours passed without incident, Jason had awakened many times, pain from the head wound Magnar had inflicted throbbing in time with his heartbeats, and his hypersensitive ears alerting him to every strange noise. After the fifth time a loud owl-like hoot sent his hand flying to the hilt of his sword, he decided to get up and try to make some progress in spite of his weariness.

He touched the wound with a finger. The bleeding had stopped, but the pain raged on. Like a seasoned warrior, he would have to ignore it and press forward.

Koren, on the other hand, seemed undisturbed. With her head resting on her hands and her Starlighter cloak covering her body from neck to ankles, she appeared to be as comfortable as if she were lying on a feather-stuffed mattress and satin sheets. Even when an occasional splash misted her hair, she merely fidgeted. This Starlighter, as she called herself, had clearly exhausted every ounce of energy.

When the front end of the logs bumped against the shore, Jason gave the pole a final shove, pushing them higher on the sandy bank and making the raft tilt toward the river. Even then, Koren didn't budge.

He knelt close and listened, trying to tune out the sounds of running water behind him, a talent he had learned from his brother Adrian. As Koren drew breaths in a steady rhythm, her eyelids twitched, making tiny droplets glisten on her delicate lashes. The bright moon, Trisarian, had passed its zenith but floated high enough to illuminate her features—a small nose on a face as smooth as silk, hair so fiery red it seemed that the mist should sizzle on contact, and thin lips posed in a slight pucker, somewhat dry and peeling from her slave labors in the heat of the day.

He set his hand inches above her hair. It seemed a shame to wake her, especially after witnessing the deeds that had spent her energy. Her amazing storytelling gifts allowed her to create ghostly characters who acted out a tale that recalled the capture of humans from Jason's home planet, Major Four.

In the story, the humans' brave leader, Uriel Blackstone, resisted enslavement, escaped, and returned home through a portal deep within a mine where slaves drilled for pheterone, a gas that dragons require for survival. Back on his home planet, Uriel tried to mount a rescue, but no one believed him. In fact, the authorities accused him of killing the Lost Ones, as Uriel called them, and they confined him to an insane asylum where he spent the rest of his life.

Because of Koren's storytelling, Magnar, the dragon who had captured the Lost Ones, became hypnotized, which allowed Jason to purloin a key that unlocked Koren's chains. After some shrewd negotiating, Arxad flew them to this river, and, after providing counsel to travel to the Northlands where a helper awaited, he returned to the dragon village, leaving them on their own.

Jason moved his hand away from Koren's head. It would be better to let her recharge her dragon-charming gift. If not for her ability, they would both likely be dead. They could wait a little while longer, at least until—

Koren sucked in a breath and shot to a sitting position. Holding her hands against her heaving chest, she stared with wide eyes. "I can ... I can feel him ... like a fire burning inside."

"Him?" Jason met her gaze. "Who?"

After taking a deeper breath, she swallowed. "The prince. The dragon in the egg. I hear his voice. I feel his presence."

Using a cup he had fashioned from leaves, he dipped out a little water from the river and handed it to her. "How do you know it's the prince?"

After taking a drink, she slid her hand into his and clutched it tightly. Her green eyes looked like copper fire in the moonlight. "While I was chained next to the black egg, he spoke to my mind, almost like he was inside me. It's the same now."

"What's he saying?"

Koren withdrew her hand and looked southward toward the village, separated from them by countless miles and the great wall that, with aid from a mountain range to the south, hemmed in the dragons' realm. Her tone altered to a stretched-out, ghostly cadence. "Come back to me, Starlighter. I am Taushin, the newborn prince and soon-to-be king. Together, you and I can break the tyranny and help your people find liberty."

"Taushin?"

She nodded. "I've never heard that name before."

He jabbed the pole into the ground. "No matter what he says, he's a dragon, so he's not on our side."

She shifted her gaze to her lap where she threaded the leaf cup through her fingers. "I know, Jason. I know."

He bent lower to catch a glimpse of her face, now pensive and confused. "You don't *want* to go back, do you?"

"Of course not. It's just that ..." She let out a deep sigh and looked up at the moon. "If he really does want to help us, we'll never find out."

Jason stood upright and reached for her. "Better to stay the course for the Northlands and find the person Arxad mentioned."

When she grasped his hand, he pulled her up and helped her step to solid ground. She nudged the raft with the toes of a bare foot. "Why did you bring us to shore?"

"Arxad mentioned a waterfall. I think I hear it, and the water's getting rougher." He picked up a pumpkin-sized cloth bundle, food Arxad had supplied, and walked out onto a dry grassy field. He stopped and scanned the moonlit expanse, a fairly flat terrain. "We'll have to go on foot."

Koren joined him, yawning and stretching. "Did you get any sleep?"

"Some. A hooting bird kept waking me up." While attaching the food bundle to his belt, he looked back at the river. "But I had a strange feeling that something else lurked out there, something that watched us, waiting for us to come to shore. So I decided to forget about sleeping and ride the river until that feeling went away."

She slid her fingers around his arm. "Then we'll have to find a safe place to sleep, maybe in some bushes."

"Not yet. We'll sleep during the day. March while it's night. We don't want a dragon patrol to spot us."

Koren looked up at the moon. "Trisarian is so bright, if the dragons sent a patrol, even at night they would probably see — " Her head tilted to the side. "How strange!"

"What?" Jason followed her line of sight. A cloud bank drifted close to the moon, the leading edge reaching toward it with gray fingers. "The clouds are strange?"

She wrinkled her brow. "It rarely rains in the lowlands, so clouds are usually confined to the mountains. I have seen them veil Trisarian before, but not until later in the cool season."

"Then we're in luck. The darker the better." Turning slowly, Jason scanned the area again. Soon, the landscape would be shrouded, so he had to take in as much visual information as possible. Now his confident remark about darkness seemed premature. The feeling that something lurked returned, pricking his senses. It was out there somewhere. Would darkness embolden the creature? Give it an opportunity to attack?

As a breeze kicked up, Jason inhaled the air, moister than before and carrying a variety of odors—grass, mold, and … and something else, something wild and bestial. Closing his eyes, he allowed his sense of smell to hone in on the wild odor's source—to the east, out in the field, maybe a stone's throw away. If only he had his father's amazing sense of smell. He and Adrian had inherited a portion of it, but no one could identify a scent as well as Edison Masters could.

Jason opened his eyes and looked in the odor's direction. Now darkening with each passing second, the field resembled a dim ocean, with the tops of the grass stalks undulating in the wind. Dozens of small trees dotted the landscape, and many of them swayed as well. Any one of the stationary shadows could be the stalker. Perhaps a carnivorous beast lay low in the grass, relishing the opportunity to taste human flesh.

Jason grasped the hilt of his sword with one hand and reached for Koren with the other. "Let's go," he whispered. "We'll get as far as we can while it's still light enough to see."

With the river on his left and the field on his right, Jason hurried toward the north. His sword whipped his leg, and the food bundle bounced, forcing him to travel slowly. After a minute or so, he released Koren's hand, hoping to secure his baggage and quicken his pace, but she soon began to fall back, limping.

He halted at a copse of bushy trees and waited for her to catch up. Although she was only a few steps behind, if not for her white dress and flowing cloak she would have been invisible in the failing moonlight.

The river's roar increased, signaling their nearness to the waterfall and forcing him to speak above a whisper. "Are you hurt?"

She lifted a leg and showed him her bare foot. "There are sharp stones in the grass. I think it's bleeding."

"That's not good." He knelt and held her foot, small and narrow, with rough calluses on the sole. Blood oozed near her heel from a thumbnail-length cut, but its depth was impossible to determine. "I'd let you wear my shoes," he said, "but they're way too big. Maybe I could wrap it with something."

"That would be helpful."

"Let's duck under the trees." He led her into the copse, nothing more than a tight semicircle of tall shrubs.

She sat on a patch of grass, her leg extended. "What do we have to wrap it with?"

Jason scanned the field beyond the shrubs. If a predator crept out there, it could approach without being seen. "We have this." He unfastened the food bundle from his belt and sat next to her. As he spread the cloth out on the grass, he kept glancing at the field. Maybe if they ate their fill and left some for the creature, it would be satisfied. Then again, it might follow them in search of more. Perhaps it could track the scent of Koren's blood.

"Let's go ahead and eat," he said, trying to keep his voice confident. "We need the energy, and I can use the cloth to wrap your foot."

"I suppose you're right." She winced, as if her own words scraped her senses.

"What's wrong?"

"Taushin. His call is more urgent. He says I'm in mortal danger. If I come back to the great boundary wall, a wolf pack will guide me safely to him. Then I can choose an attendant and give her an easy life. I will live as a princess in the Basilica without any labors."

Jason kept his focus on the cloth as he spread out an assortment of fruits, raw vegetables, and dried meats. "Did he mention me?"

Koren shook her head. "I don't know why. Zena knows you're with me, so he probably knows, too."

"He plans to cook me at the stake. That's why. He doesn't want you to know."

She laid her hands over her ears. "He's getting so loud I can barely hear you."

"Can you use your gift to drown him out? Maybe tell a story?"

"That might work."

"Go ahead and eat first." Jason drew out his sword and laid it next to the food. "Choose what you want, and when you finish, I'll bind your wound while you tell a story — that is, if you can wait that long to squelch the prince."

"I think I can," she said as she lowered her hands. "It's already a little better."

While they ate, Jason glanced between Koren and the field beyond the shrubs. With clouds fully enveloping the moon, and trees blocking its muted light, her green eyes seemed to be the only visible objects, like little emeralds floating in the dark air.

Jason concentrated on their surroundings, again tuning out the river's noise. Outside their refuge, the grass rustled in the breeze, and every creaking sound and popping noise gave Jason a start. It seemed that the stalker lay just beyond the copse, watching with hungry eyes.

Jason picked up his sword and the cloth, leaving a few meat strips on the ground. "Let's go to the river and wash the cut before I wrap it."

"Good idea." She rose and brushed off her dress.

"Is Tau-what's-his-name still talking?"

"Taushin. Yes, the same message over and over."

"Have you tried talking back to him?"

She shook her head. "I'm not sure if I can, and I don't want to give him the satisfaction. Maybe he doesn't know he's been able to reach me."

"True. But if you decide to answer, tell him I said to go back into his shell and shut up. It'll take a lot more than a scaly parrot to get you away from me."

Koren covered a smile with her fingers. "I'll think about it."

Following the sound of falling water, they passed through the tree boundary and walked to the river. As they stood at the edge, Jason surveyed the scene, barely visible in the veiled moonlight. The river rushed past their feet and, about ten paces downstream, tumbled over a cliff and fell into depths unknown. Beyond the falls and to the left, the spilled water flowed westward. To the right, the grassy field extended eastward and northward, acting as a precipice for the gorge.

Koren sat at the river's edge and hiked up her dress, revealing short trousers underneath. "I can wash it myself."

"No. Let me." Jason set a knee on the sand and a boot in the shallows. He moistened a corner of the cloth and swabbed the sole of her foot. As he continued dipping and washing, she winced with every touch. "Is Prince Persistent still bothering you?" he asked.

She cocked her head. "That's strange. I don't hear him anymore."

"Good. Maybe not answering was the right decision." He wrapped the cloth around her foot and tied it at her ankle. "Let's see how it feels."

Holding her hand as well as his sword, he helped her limp toward the trees. "What's the verdict?" he asked.

"I can walk but probably not very fast."

When they arrived at the center of the copse, Jason stooped and felt for the meat. It was gone. He sniffed the air. The wild scent had returned, stronger than ever.

"Koren," he whispered, still crouching. "Don't ask why. Just climb up on my back. Do it now."

"Okay." Her hands gripped his shoulders, and her trousers brushed his sides. Soon, she had mounted and settled on his back.

"Are you ready?"

"I think so."

Jason slowly straightened, holding her wrist with his free hand. "Just hang on." Leading with his sword, he burst from the trees and ran into the field, heading northward and keeping the river and waterfall to his left. As long grass whipped his legs, he listened for a pursuer, but the river drowned out all other sounds.

He couldn't look back. Every step held a potential trap—a hole, a gulley, or even a plunge into the river's gorge. With only a few feet illuminated in front of him, even one second of carelessness could cost them their lives, or at least a painful tumble.

"Jason!" Koren yelled. "Something's following us!"

With his own heavy footfalls shaking his voice, he shouted, "What does it look like?"

"A man!"

"A man?" Jason slowed to a halt and turned to face the pursuer. As he stared at a dark form creeping toward them, he readied his sword, whispering, "Get down."

Koren slid off his back and stood at his side. "He's slowing."

"Who are you?" Jason shouted.

The form stopped. As Trisarian peeked through a gap in the clouds, the human frame clarified. He stood with a hand on his hip and something long and pointed in his other hand. "I had planned to ask you the same thing." The man's voice was gravelly, yet dignified in tone.

Jason inhaled through his nose. Yes, the stranger carried the bestial odor. "If you are a friend who will help us," Jason said, "we will introduce ourselves. If you are here to harm us, I will introduce you to the point of a sword."

The man let out a genial laugh. "Since you left food on the ground, I assumed it was for me and that you considered me a friend. Perhaps it was an ill-advised assumption, but my stomach said otherwise. I have not had meat in a long time. In fact, I had been thinking about trying to catch a fish in the shallows. The roots, berries, and field potatoes in this land are not very filling."

As the man drew closer, the moon shone on his face, dirty and covered with a thick, choppy white beard. He halted within striking distance and dropped a sharpened stick. "You talk as a free man would. Where are you from?"

Jason sheathed his sword. "I am Jason Masters. I have come from Major Four—"

Koren jerked on his sleeve and hissed, "Don't tell him everything! We don't know him yet."

"It's all right," Jason said. "He's human, not a dragon."

Her voice dropped to a whisper. "You can't trust every human, especially one who isn't a slave."

"If he was an ally of the dragons," Jason replied, also in a whisper, "he probably wouldn't look like a homeless beggar."

Koren's skeptical expression softened. "Do what you think is right."

"As I said," Jason continued, turning back to the man, "I have come from Major Four, the world of humans, in order to rescue the slaves and take them home." He nodded at Koren. "And this is Koren, one of the slaves."

The man pointed in the direction they had been running. "If you think home is that way, you had better think again. You will find only snow, ice, and a castle filled with ghosts."

"Ghosts?" Jason half closed an eye. "As in disembodied spirits?"

"Exactly, young man. I have seen them myself."

Koren stepped forward and offered a half curtsy. "Pardon me, sir. Jason told you our names. Will you tell us yours?"

"I apologize for my rudeness, Miss." The man gave her a formal bow. "I am Uriel Blackstone."

two

Elyssa skulked along a deserted street, following Wallace, the one-eyed boy who had promised to be her guide in the dragon village. Cloud-obscured moonlight spilled over the landscape, and an occasional lantern illuminated the small, one-story structures. Towering over them, enormous cathedral-like edifices—spires, domes, and a belfry—cast an array of long shadows.

Wallace used his borrowed sword to point at one of the larger buildings. "That's the Zodiac." With a dozen spires encircling a domed roof and marble columns supporting a portico in front of massive double doors, the Zodiac emanated white radiance, as if energized by a land-bound moon harnessed within. The spires shone with a silvery paint that glowed in spite of the lack of outside light.

Keeping his back bent, Wallace scurried toward the closest column. Elyssa shadowed him step for step. When they reached the column, they stooped behind it, out of sight of any human or dragon who might pass by on the cobblestone street.

"What's the Zodiac?" Elyssa asked.

Wallace looked at her, his single eye blinking as he brushed an insect from his chest, visible through his open shirt. Although he was probably only twelve or thirteen years old, slave labor had sculpted the muscles of an older teen. "It's where the priests study the stars and get prophecies. One of the priests is Arxad, a dragon who might be willing to help us find Jason and Koren."

"Might be willing?" Elyssa sighed. "If we have a choice that doesn't include trusting a dragon, I'd like to hear it."

"No other choice comes to mind." Wallace nodded toward the empty street. "It's strange. Normally the night-duty slaves go from place to place in preparation for morning, to get meals ready for their masters or to collect supplies for daytime laborers. Between this and what we saw at the cattle camp, it looks like something terrible has happened. Everyone must be in lockdown."

Elyssa gave Wallace a questioning glance.

"A lockdown," he said, "means that all slaves are supposed to stay in their homes. If any are caught outside, they are killed. The dragons do it when they're searching for an escaped slave."

"I see."

"So we'll have to watch for Wardens," Wallace added.

"Wardens?"

He set his hand about a foot from the ground. "They're like round little dogs, and they spit out a strange light like a dragon shoots flames. It feels like a million needle pricks, and it will knock you flat. Wardens can even hurt dragons, so they don't use them very often. Maybe they didn't have time to get them out of the kennels."

"If I see one, I'll stay as far away from it as I can." Elyssa laid a hand on the cool, smooth column and leaned toward the street. A shop of some kind lay to the right, dark and void of activity. Far to the left, a cactus-adorned patio separated them from a much larger building, one with a fence of black iron bars guarding its massive inner courtyard. Something large moved within the dark railing, perhaps a dragon.

Earlier in the evening, when she and Wallace journeyed to the cattle camp, she had expected to see such a guard within the camp's stone walls, but nothing stirred inside. All lay still, as if death itself had stalked the grounds. In fact, from their vantage point atop the wall, it seemed that a dead dragon lay on the ground near a stream. A shudder rippled through her body. Something wicked had left its mark.

Before their visit to the camp, she and Wallace had sent a group of slaves home to Major Four, accompanied by Randall and Tibalt. To that point, everything seemed to be progressing well. Now with the specter of death hanging over the world of dragons, her spirits sagged.

She reached into the pocket of the trousers she had borrowed from the lumber camp house at the beginning of her journey and felt the crystal, a two-finger-length peg she had found in the mining pit, the key that opened the portal leading home. Its smooth surface eased her anxiety. As long as it stayed in her possession, she always had a way to escape this horrible place.

"What's that building over there?" Elyssa asked, pointing. "The one with the black bars. I see something lurking."

"The Basilica. That's where the Separators decide where the slaves go, and it's guarded by a dragon. Humans aren't allowed in there unless they're being separated, and only then if they're drugged."

"Drugged? Why?"

"I'm not sure. I don't remember ever going there. Maybe I did, and the drug kept me from remembering. Or maybe my Assignment didn't need approval." Wallace shrugged. "I guess I'll never know."

Elyssa turned to the Zodiac and stared at its closed doors. With an arched top as high as the tallest dragons and a breadth as wide as five human body lengths, if someone opened the wooden doors, a dragon could easily fly in or out. Light from within seeped through the crack at the bottom, an alluring glow that promised answers to her many questions.

She focused on the crack and used her Diviner's powers to probe beyond the doors for any sign of life, dragon or human. The space within felt empty, void of movement, yet energy radiated from something inside.

Rising, she signaled for Wallace to stand. "Lead the way."

"Lead the way to what?"

"Sorry. You're not used to me yet." She gestured with her hands as she explained. "I often skip steps without telling why, so it's hard to keep up with me. You didn't offer any other choices, so finding Arxad is the only one we have. If he is in the habit of consulting the stars, then it stands to reason that if some kind of crisis is happening, he might be inside right now, trying to get a reading before dawn. But the early hour means no other dragon is likely to be there. Get it?"

Wallace gave her a firm nod. "I get it. It's now or never."

"Right. And since you have the sword, you're supposed to lead the way." She tiptoed to the door and laid a hand on the rough wooden panel. "I'll push it open, and you go inside."

He readied the sword. "Let's do it."

Elyssa pushed, but the door didn't budge. Bending her knees, she leaned her shoulder against the massive slab of wood and shoved with all her might. The door swung open slowly, letting out a creaking sound as it scuffed against the floor.

She halted the door's swing and waited for any reaction on the other side. As light poured through the narrow gap, Wallace peered in. Leading with his sword, he walked through, whispering, "I think it's safe."

Elyssa eased away from the door. It stayed in place. "Perfect," she whispered to herself. "A way out."

She tiptoed behind Wallace through a huge hallway, trying to keep her shoes from squeaking on the marble tiles. A line of lanterns, mounted on protruding iron rods along each wall, sat dark in their frames. At the far end of the corridor, maybe a hundred paces away, another set of double doors blocked escape in that direction.

On the left wall, a mural displayed a life-sized dragon aiming a jet of flames at a radiant sphere. In the midst of a background of star-studded darkness, the dragon flew toward the sphere, fury evident in his ruby eyes, scaly reddish brow, and toothy, wide-open maw. A woman cowered behind the sphere, apparently hiding from the dragon. Long auburn hair dressed her delicate head and draped her petite frame.

Elyssa stepped toward the wall to get a better look. The sphere's glow washed over the woman, as if offering a veil of protection, but how could an aura of light provide a barrier to that torrent of flames?

Rubbing her fingers together, Elyssa felt the air. Particles of radiance streamed from the wall, as if the painting itself emitted light. But how could that be?

On the opposite wall, a redheaded girl stood within a semitransparent spherical aura that acted as another source of light in the corridor. Wearing a long white dress and a dark blue cloak, she looked upward, her mouth open as if in prayer or song. Her green eyes glowed, giving her the appearance of a prophetess or …

"Or a Diviner," Elyssa whispered.

Behind the girl, a woman dressed in black approached, clutching a dagger in her bony fingers. With a gaunt pale face, black eyes, and thin gray lips, the attacker looked like a corpse come to life.

Elyssa called with a loud whisper. "Wallace, do you recognize anyone in these paintings?"

He stood in front of the redhead. "This girl looks a little like Koren." Narrowing his eye, Wallace took a step closer. "It's strange, though. Magnar called Koren a Starlighter, and that reminded me of a story one of the elders, a man named Lattimer, told me. A Starlighter is someone who can make stories come to life, and Lattimer said to be on the watch for a redheaded girl who could do that."

"I only got a glimpse of Koren before the dragon took her away." Elyssa stared at the girl's soul-piercing countenance, so passionate, so riveting, as though her green eyes could actually see those who admired the painting. "Do you think Koren is really a Starlighter?"

"I wasn't sure back then, so I didn't mention her to Lattimer, but when she and I were in the cattle camp together, she helped me get food. Since I'm missing an eye and I was so small, I couldn't compete for the bread the dragons dropped from the sky. Koren and I sometimes sneaked out together, and she helped me beg in the village streets. Her ability to tell stories made people feel sorry for us, so we stayed pretty well fed, and that helped me grow strong enough to get transferred to another Assignment. It was a lot easier for Koren. Since she has red hair and green eyes, the dragons think she's a good-luck charm, so she was picked up by the Traders, and Arxad bought her."

Elyssa reached up and touched the glowing aura. Somehow an attachment took hold between herself and this mysterious girl, this Starlighter. Maybe their gifts were related. Bringing stories to life seemed similar to reading invisible realities in the air.

"Shouldn't we get going?" Wallace asked.

"Sure." Elyssa followed Wallace to the end of the corridor. She pressed her ear against a sliver of a gap between the doors, closed her eyes, and allowed her mind to sweep through. Inside lay a circular chamber with a high ceiling. The upper boundary clarified in her thoughts, a curved shape with a small hole at the center. An observatory? Probably. Arxad might be studying the stars at this very moment.

Letting her mind probe sink to the floor, she surveyed the open expanse. Something stood at the center, dark and indistinct. Elyssa squeezed her eyelids tightly shut and concentrated. The object appeared to be a short column with a sphere mounted on top. Could that be the observation device? A sky scope?

Before she could delve into the sphere further, the air around the short column quivered, as with an exhale. Something odd lay nearby, a large living mass that breathed slow, shallow breaths. It was too large to be a single human. Maybe a group of slaves or …

She pushed her thoughts toward the center of life energy, a singular source rather than many. It seemed morose, despondent, defeated, as if imprisoned and waiting to die. Its size and intelligence could mean only one thing—a dragon.

Opening her eyes, Elyssa stepped back and looked at Wallace. "I'm going first this time. There's a dragon inside, and I think my gifts will be better than a sword."

"I don't think any dragon is going to be impressed with your gifts," Wallace said. "Unless the gifts make him laugh so you have time to run away."

"This dragon isn't in any mood to fight. Trust me."

"If you say so." Wallace leaned against the door and pushed. This one swung much more easily.

Elyssa padded toward the central object, a crystalline sphere atop a column-like pedestal, also made of crystal. The sphere pulsed with a dim white glow, like frost reflecting moonlight, plenty of illumination on this obstruction-free tile floor.

Indeed, a dragon lay close to the pedestal. With his neck curled and his head tucked under a wing, he appeared to be asleep.

Signaling for Wallace to follow, she closed in. A heavy chain and an iron manacle bound the dragon's back leg to the pedestal. Long scratches covered his wings, and a gouge divided two scales on his neck. He appeared to have been scourged and then shackled, a prisoner left here alone, but for what purpose?

As she drew even closer, she penetrated the sphere's glow. A buzzing sensation burned her skin. She raised a hand, signaling for Wallace to stop, and stepped back. She rubbed her forearm. The light from the orb carried a sting.

Pulling Wallace close, she whispered, "Do you recognize the dragon? He looks like he's been flogged."

"I can't see his face, but I'm pretty sure it's Arxad, the high priest. I have no idea what happened to him."

"Hide the sword," she said. "I'm going to talk to him."

After Wallace laid the sword on the ground behind him, Elyssa walked within a few paces of the dragon, cringing as the stinging sensation returned. "Arxad," she called. "Can you hear me?"

A low rumbling voice rose from the body, muffled by the wing. "I have heard you ever since you intruded into my domain. The Zodiac is off limits to slaves who have not been invited, especially during lockdown."

"You appear to be a prisoner," Elyssa said, "yet the chains seem inadequate for a dragon of your size. Does the orb weaken you?"

"I find it irritating that an intruder would ignore my warning and go on to conduct an interrogation." He withdrew his head from under his wing and glared at Elyssa with throbbing scarlet eyes. "To answer your question, I am physically strong enough to escape, but I have vowed to my captors that I would neither break my bonds nor lie to the Reflections Crystal to darken its light."

Elyssa studied the prisoner. Since the dragon slave masters were likely his captors, perhaps it would be safe to reveal her purpose. How else could she get the information she needed? And if this Reflections Crystal, as he called it, darkened with the telling of a lie, the situation could work to her advantage. Still, she should test it first.

She cleared her throat and spoke directly to the orb. "My name is Jason Masters."

The crystal darkened to gray, then to black. With the stinging light now gone, she marched up to Arxad and knelt beside him. She laid her hand on the manacle and rubbed her palm across the surface. Arxad emanated concern, perhaps fear. Her gifts weren't quite enough to know if he could be trusted completely. "Does the crystal detect any lie?"

"Do you want me to answer and risk the return of the light? I am willing to suffer further, but I doubt that you are." He moved his head in front of her and gazed into her eyes. As he stared, his pupils faded from deep scarlet to grayish red. "You are not an ordinary slave, are you?"

"I am not a slave at all. My name is Elyssa, and I came here with Jason Masters to rescue the slaves and take them home to Major Four."

The sphere brightened and cast its stinging glow across her body. As she cringed, she grunted, "But I hate Jason. I hate him with all my heart."

The sphere instantly turned black again.

Elyssa waved for Wallace to join them. "Come over here and tell lies to this oversensitive ball while I talk to Arxad."

Wallace picked up his sword and ran to the crystal. "I don't have a sword," he said, smiling at the orb. "And I have two eyes. It's just that one is embedded in the back of my head."

While the sphere stayed dark, Elyssa focused on Arxad. "I hope we don't confuse your lie detector."

"You need not worry. It is not fragile." Arxad glanced between Wallace and Elyssa. "Why have you approached me? Surely you know that I could kill you both with a blast of fire."

"I didn't know," Wallace said. "I have never seen a dragon before in my life."

Elyssa smiled at Wallace's antics. "We have a saying in my world. 'An enemy's prisoner is an ally indeed.' I assumed you would be our friend."

"You assume too much." Letting out a sigh, Arxad lowered his head to the floor. "Yet, if you really consider me a friend, then have the young man plunge the sword into my belly. It would be better for all if this duplicitous dragon were to die."

Wallace gulped. "Uh … I really want to do that, Elyssa. I have killed dozens of dragons. It won't be a problem to kill another."

"Duplicitous?" Elyssa said. "Have you betrayed someone?"

"My own species. I have deceived my king and aided humans in their quest to escape slavery. Although I pity their bondage, if they depart before we can set up an alternative survival apparatus, then I will have contributed to the doom of my race."

"I see." Elyssa glanced at the hole in the domed ceiling, a large enough gap for a dragon. "You vowed not to break your chains, but if you would help me locate the key, I could unlock them. Your vow would be intact, and we could fly away."

"You lack understanding. I do not wish to escape. I wish to suffer the punishment and humiliation I deserve. Not only that, I am not one to parse words in order to escape my vow. I believe in the spirit of truth, so I will not be a slave to literal renderings."

As the orb brightened, Elyssa shot Wallace a glare.

"Oh, right." Wallace raised a finger. "I understood every word Arxad said."

When darkness veiled Arxad again, this time the gap between them seemed denser, as if a curtain of gloom had fallen. Still, his red eyes pierced the dimness, though they pulsed more weakly.

Elyssa rubbed her fingers together, feeling the air—saturated with melancholy and hopelessness. "Can you at least tell us where Jason went? I don't think I can rescue the slaves alone."

"You *are* alone," Wallace said. "I'm going to desert you the first chance I get."

Arxad offered a weak smile, revealing two sharp teeth. "I sent Jason and the Starlighter to the Northlands. They will be safe there, and they will find the dragon king of the North as well as a friend they do not expect. If the king decides to send them here to destroy every dragon in this domain, I am content. He is the Creator's greatest prophet, so his word is both law and spirit."

Elyssa nodded. "Then Wallace and I should go to this Northlands place immediately."

"I think we should unchain Arxad," Wallace said, "and fly with him to Trisarian."

"You're right." Elyssa extended her hand. "Give me the sword."

"What? You're not going to let him go, are you?"

"Just give it to me." Elyssa reached and jerked the hilt from his grip.

As the orb began to brighten, he shrugged. "Okay. You said you skip steps, but I wish I knew what you're thinking."

"You'll see. And don't tell any more lies until I say so." She rose to her feet and set the tip of the blade near Arxad's eye. "You will take us to Jason, or I will gouge your eye out."

The sphere darkened again. Elyssa tensed her face, trying to hide a frown.

Arxad sighed. "I understand your motivation, young lady, but it is impossible to make a false threat in the presence of the crystal. Even if you believe your own words, it is able to test your resolve, which is apparently lacking. In any case, I welcome the injury. As I said before, I deserve punishment."

Elyssa let her arm droop. The orb's glow strengthened and began to sting. Clutching the hilt more tightly, she ached to whip around and smash the fool thing with the sword. As she imagined shards scattering across the floor, she looked at the dragon's face. His visage brightened, as if his heart were tied to the crystal's energy—an odd response to pain.

Elyssa returned her gaze to the sphere. What did this peculiar torture device mean to the dragons? With its prominent placement in the observatory, it had to be more than a lie detector. It was a treasure, perhaps even an object of worship. And that made it a point of vulnerability.

Grimacing as the pain increased, Elyssa reared back with the blade, ready to strike. "You will take us to Jason, or I'll smash your precious crystal!"

"You will not!" Arxad shouted.

"I most certainly will."

As Wallace retreated a few steps, the sphere brightened even further, sending sharpened darts of energy into Elyssa's body. Setting her feet, she spoke in a firm, even tone. "I think your sphere has proven my resolve."

Arxad struggled to his haunches, apparently slowed by the punishing light. "I could scorch you with a single snuff, and your quest would come to an end."

The sphere darkened to gray.

"Does the crystal think you're too weak, dragon? Are you really able to produce such a flame? You have five seconds to do as I say. If you don't vow to take us to Jason, I will shatter this mind reader into so many pieces you'll be gluing it together for a thousand years." She took a deep breath and added, "One!"

Arxad stretched out his wings. "Fool of a girl! I cannot vow to take you to Jason. Not only would I betray my people, I would betray my integrity. I might not be able to find him at all."

"Two! Then vow to be my prisoner and do what I say!"

"But I do not know what you will say. How can I make such an open-ended vow?"

"Three! You said you believed in the spirit of words, not their literal rendering. You knew what I meant, and now you're prevaricating. So much for your integrity." With the sensation of hundreds of bees stinging her mercilessly, she flexed her muscles, drew the sword back another notch, and called out, "Four!"

"Very well." Arxad let out a long breath. "I vow to be your prisoner and do what you say."

The sphere stayed bright, verifying Arxad's promise.

Blinking, Elyssa backed away until the pain became tolerable. "Wallace," she said as she lowered the sword, "go tell some lies to the orb."

"Will do." Holding his arm in front of his face as he approached, he called out, "This doesn't hurt. No, not one bit."

Within a few seconds, the sphere dimmed, bringing relief to Elyssa's tortured skin. "Now, Arxad. Tell me how to get you unchained."

Arxad lowered himself to the floor again. "The task will be difficult. Someone has taken the master key that I normally keep in this room, but you will find another one in the hallway you passed through. I assume you noticed the mural that featured the Starlighter."

"I did."

Wallace pointed at the doorway. "If you're talking about the redheaded, green-eyed girl with the halo around her, and the spooky woman in black holding the dagger …" He shook his head. "I didn't see it."

"If you look closely," Arxad said, "you will see a small cavity in one of her palms. The key is inside, but once you take it, the lights in the paintings will go out. Then, you will have to negotiate the corridor in darkness."

Elyssa nodded. "That shouldn't be too hard. There are no obstacles on the floor."

"True," Arxad continued. "It would be an easy task if not for the fact that when the key is removed, the floor drops away, creating a passage to a lower floor. This is not a problem for dragons, of course. We simply fly away. Yet for humans it poses quite a threat and therefore stands as a deterrent to the curious. You see, when we constructed the floor mechanism using slave labor, the humans spread all sorts of gossip about its purpose. They created a legend that the Starlighter holds the key to a treasure deep within the Zodiac. There is some truth to the treasure story, to be sure, but that is not important now.

"In any case, Magnar was concerned about human intruders, so he compelled one slave to add a trap. If a human breaks into the Zodiac in search of the treasure and takes the key, his plunge into the hole will not end with a painful, yet survivable thump on the ground. Instead, sharp stakes embedded in the floor will impale his body."

Elyssa cringed. "Has anyone taken the bait?"

"Not a soul."

"Then why go through all the trouble to install such a complex device to open the floor? A slave who really wants to get to the lower floor can find a way to avoid the stakes. And you left the key out in the open, an obvious temptation for anyone who knows how the trap works. It doesn't make sense."

"There are other safeguards protecting what we seek to conceal," Arxad said, "and the key is a diversion. It unlocked a door that stood at the end of a once-secret passage between the Zodiac and the Basilica, but that door no longer exists. Most who know about the key think the floor apparatus was designed to hide the passage from humans, but they are wrong. In fact, you and your friend are the only humans who know about the obstacles, because Magnar killed the slave who put the stakes in the lower floor as soon as he completed the task."

A cold chill crawled along Elyssa's skin. Why was Arxad giving away all this information, especially details that made one of his fellow dragons look bad? "It's clear that we want to stay away from Magnar."

"Not me," Wallace said. "Magnar and I are best friends."

Arxad stared at the doorway leading to the corridor. "He is cruel to humans. Of that, there is no doubt. And because of that cruelty I counseled him to seclude himself from their presence. Yet his loyalty toward his fellow dragons is beyond question."

After breathing a long sigh, Arxad continued. "Magnar and I had a plan to save the dragon race from a prophesied day of trouble, and the pieces to carry out that plan are still in place. But it seems that the coming of potential rescuers from your world has caused him to forget about our plan. In recent days he has been deceived far too easily, and I suspect that he has played along with the schemes of the rescuers and the Starlighter in order to achieve a greater purpose only he knows. I have been trying to discern what advantage he might find in allowing for turmoil in his otherwise stringently controlled world, and I have been unable to come to a conclusion."

As the orb's light returned, bringing again the energy needles, Elyssa tapped her chin. "I can't worry about Magnar's secrets right now. I just have to figure out a way to get the key while avoiding getting impaled."

"I would love to get impaled," Wallace said. "You could let me go."

Elyssa patted him on the back. "Stay here and lie to the orb. You're real good at it. But if I yell for help, come running."

Pointing at his eye, Wallace grinned. "I'll keep this eye on you and use the one in the back of my head to watch Arxad."

"The wall is lined with lanterns," Arxad said. "If you are skilled enough, you can swing from one to the next and make your way back to the door."

"Jason and I used to swing from tree to tree with vines. I should be able to do it." Elyssa imagined the process. Although the gap between the lamps wasn't too big, once the mural lights went out, the darkness would make swinging impossible. "Is there any way I can light the lanterns in there?"

"You will find a torch and flint stones near a utility box at the wall," Arxad said.

"Can't you just light the torch for her?" Wallace asked. "After all, you are a dragon."

The sphere brightened, sending hot, stinging rays all around.

Wallace covered his eye. "Sorry. I mean, you're not a dragon. How stupid of me to think so."

As the light dimmed again, Arxad spoke to Elyssa in a resigned tone. "Bring the torch to me. I will light it for you."

Elyssa hurried to the wall, found a long, thick torch leaning against it, and ran back to Arxad. While Wallace mumbled random sentences about flying turtles and fire-breathing canaries, Elyssa held the rag-topped torch in front of Arxad's snout.

Arxad drew in a breath, then, exhaling slowly through his narrowed mouth, blew a fine stream of flames at the oily top. The fire caught hold of a rag's loose edge and crawled rapidly around the torch.

"Keep lying," Elyssa said as she marched away. "I'll be back as soon as I can."

Wallace gave her a hurried wave. "Take your time. I'm looking forward to being alone with a dragon who could bite my leg off."

After pulling both doors open fully, she entered the massive hallway and approached the first lantern on her left, a head-high, wall-mounted lamp that looked very much like the ones at home, except that it had no glass enclosure to protect the wick. An iron bar protruded about three feet from the wall, supporting a flat metal pan upon which the lantern stood.

As she touched the flame to the wick, the torch pushed the lantern, but it stayed in place, apparently welded to its support pan. A draft blew past, drying her emerging sweat, but it didn't affect the new flame at all. That was a mystery best left alone for now, though it explained how the lanterns could stay lit with dragons flying past.

Running with the torch and pausing to light each lantern, she tried to ignore the mental image of her body impaled on sharp stakes below. Still, her divining gifts wouldn't allow such peace. The promise of spikes delivered sharp pangs to her chest and abdomen, so real they almost took her breath away.

As flickering flames brightened the corridor, the smell of burning oil tightened her throat and coated her tongue with an acrid film. She coughed and hacked but never slowed. The situation called for haste. Who could tell when another dragon might return to check on Arxad?

After lighting the final lantern, she hurried to the Starlighter's mural near the middle of the hall, prominently displayed above and between two lanterns. Elyssa stared at the girl's brilliant green eyes, then moved to the uplifted right hand, painted in tones of pink and peach. Indeed, her palm held a dark spot, apparently a crevice, not quite within reach, even if she stood on tiptoes.

Scanning the lanterns between herself and the doorway that led back to Wallace, she gauged the distance between each pair. It would take all her strength to swing from one to the other without falling, and she would have to do it several times before reaching safety.

As she laid the torch on the floor and faced the wall, nausea simmered in her stomach. With an outstretched arm, she jumped toward the Starlighter's hand. Her fingertips touched the crevice but failed to push inside before she dropped back to the floor.

Glaring at the girl's hand, she set her fists on her hips. There had to be an easier way.

She grabbed the torch and tamped out the flames. This would reach easily, and maybe the rags would drag the key out. As she imagined the process, the key in her mind's eye dropped from its hiding place, and the floor collapsed at the same time. Could she hang on to a lantern rod to keep from falling and still catch the key?

Shaking her head, she muttered, "No way."

She picked up the torch again and leaned it against the wall, then, setting her right foot on top of its thick handle, she vaulted up to the lantern rod, shot to a standing position, and listened for any sign of failure in stone or metal. The rod bent slightly, and a cracking sound reached her ears. These supports weren't designed to hold her weight. She would have to work quickly.

She turned away from the Zodiac's inner door. At this angle, the girl in the mural seemed warped, barely recognizable. Her hand appeared to be within reach, about at Elyssa's own waist level and a few feet to the side. Stooping while grimacing at the lantern's heat, she slid her hand across the wall, feeling for the crevice. The surface wasn't as smooth as it seemed from below. Filled with tiny lumps and crags, each imperfection raised hopes that she had discovered the crevice, but her fingers found no real hole.

Leaning her body, she held to the rod with one hand while stretching as far as she could with the other. The rod bent further. More cracks sounded. Finally, her finger pushed into a crevice and detected something cool and metallic. Pinching the object, she withdrew it and pushed herself back to a stooped position.

The girl and the halo darkened. Across the corridor on the other wall, the dragon, the moon, and the hiding woman disappeared. A creaking sound echoed from one end of the hallway to the other. Beneath the flickering light of at least a dozen lanterns, the floor parted in the middle, lengthwise, from doorway to doorway, and both halves swung downward. The torch fell into the gap, and lantern light spilled into the void.

Her legs trembling, Elyssa gazed below. As Arxad had said, a matrix of sharp stakes covered the bottom, perhaps a hundred or more. Although the bed of deadly nails didn't stretch as far as either doorway in the hall above them, there were way too many for an unwary key thief to avoid.

She stood still and listened. No more cracking sounds. The rod stayed in place. She could afford to spend a little more time.

Closing her eyes, she probed the area below with her mind. It seemed that two corridors branched away. Excited particles flowed from somewhere, invisible to the eye but perceptible to Elyssa's senses. Apparently a passage led farther into the underground, where an energy source radiated.

She let her mind follow that path. The flow seemed tinged with life, as if someone had sprinkled the energy with living particles. Still, the life felt weak, as if struggling, similar to the way Arxad struggled under the glow of the sphere, a despondent prisoner who longed to be set free or else killed and put out of his misery.

Elyssa opened her eyes and slowly shifted around toward the doorway leading to the crystalline sphere, begging the rod to hold fast. The energy mystery would have to wait. She had to concentrate on survival.

Still at the sphere, Arxad and Wallace watched from the domed chamber. Wallace crept closer. With each step, the orb brightened, but he paid no attention.

"Keep lying to the sphere!" Elyssa called. "Arxad's in pain!"

"I don't care!" Wallace shouted as he approached the doorway. His words dimmed the sphere, at least for the moment. Then, standing at the threshold, he gaped at the lower floor. "Wow! Arxad was right!"

"I know. I know." Elyssa steeled her legs. The problem with jumping to the next rod wasn't so much the distance; it was the accuracy. Her foot would have to land directly on the dark metal. Not only that, her momentum would force her to jump immediately to the next rod, and the next, and finally down to the threshold where Wallace, she hoped, would catch her and keep her from tumbling into the hole. And what about the impact? With her momentum striking the rods, would any of them give way?

She made a quick count—six lanterns between her and the door. She could do this. No problem.

"Are you ready to grab me?" she called.

Wallace held his hands out. "Ready."

"Okay. Here I come." After sliding the key into her trousers pocket, Elyssa crouched, then leaped, extending a leg toward the next bar. Her foot struck it perfectly. She launched to the next one, again landing without a problem. She vaulted to the third, then the fourth. When she landed on the fifth, it bent and nearly ripped out of the wall, depriving her of a solid foundation for the next leap. With a desperate lunge, she shot forward, but her foot fell short of the final bar. As she dropped, she threw her arms upward. One hand struck the final rod and held on. Her body swung with the momentum, lifting her legs high before swinging back.

With perspiration moistening her grip, she swayed over the gaping hole and the sharp stakes below.

three

Wallace called from the doorway. "Are you all right?"

"I think so." She withdrew the key from her pocket and held it out. "I'm going to throw the key into your room. Don't bother trying to catch it. Just let it fly by and then pick it up and unlock Arxad. He can come and get me out of this mess."

Wallace stepped out of the way. "Go ahead and throw it."

Elyssa gave the key an underhanded toss, then reached up and grabbed the rod, giving herself a two-handed grip. The key struck the floor well into the room and slid along the tiles. "Now hurry. I can't hang around here all day."

Wallace snatched up the key and ran toward Arxad. Elyssa looked down. The invisible energy from below washed over her body, sending its message of life into her senses. It seemed to draw her toward it, tantalizing, almost hypnotizing. What could be down there? What was worth such elaborate security?

Grit from the wall fell into her hair. The bar bent, and her hands began to slide. As she regripped the metal, she shouted, "Wallace!"

"The key worked," he yelled back. "I'm unhitching the manacle. But stop asking me questions. Telling you the truth is a pain."

A chunk of the wall ripped out. Still clutching the lantern rod, Elyssa thrust her hand into the newly opened hole. She hung on for a second before slipping and toppling downward in a backwards somersault.

Arxad rushed toward her in full flight and snapped at her clothing. His teeth caught the end of her shirttail. Her shirt stretched, slowing her plunge. But it ripped, and she dropped again.

Clenching her eyes shut, she searched for the spikes in her mind. There! And there! She twisted her body, slung the rod downward at one of the spikes, and landed on her feet. She then sprang backwards, launching away from the bed of deadly nails and rolling onto smooth stone.

She sat up and looked at the spikes. Two were broken, snapped by the lantern rod. As she rose to her feet, she pushed a hand against her stomach. More nausea boiled, but it was a lot better than being impaled.

Arxad flew down and settled beside her. "Are you injured?"

"I don't think so." She took a mental inventory. Although her hip ached from the impact, and her hands stung, nothing seemed broken. "I'm all right."

Arxad snorted a spray of yellow sparks. "You have gone to absurd lengths to free me. I fear that I have vowed to aid a fool of a female."

"Is that so?" Elyssa brushed off her trousers and examined her torn shirt. Only a minor rip. She kept her gaze away from the scarlet-eyed dragon's stare, a stare too sharp to endure. In one way, he was right. It probably was foolish to save this ungrateful beast, but what good would it do to point that out now?

"Hey!" Wallace called from above. "Are you okay?"

"Fine, but I don't recommend my way of travel." Elyssa turned to Arxad. "When you bring him down and put away the key, how will you get below the floor level before it closes?"

"There is a delay mechanism," Arxad said. "But I did not say I would bring him down."

"No, you didn't, but I want to see where that light's coming from, so bring Wallace—"

"You are forbidden. No one is allowed to enter there, especially no human." Arxad looked at Elyssa and Wallace for a long moment, as if contemplating. "I will carry your friend down here, but only because we can use the other passage I mentioned. It will allow us to depart without Magnar's knowledge."

"Good." Elyssa crossed her arms over her chest. "I'll be here when you get back."

Arxad glared at her, his ears flattening and his eyes aglow. "If you leave this room before I return, you will prove my opinion that you are a fool." With a rapid beat of his wings, he jumped and sailed over the bed of stakes before rising in quick orbits.

Tightening her clenched arms, Elyssa resisted scowling. Receiving a tongue lashing from a dragon stung her pride, but no use getting too worked up about it. Things could be worse. She glanced at the stakes and shuddered. A lot worse.

In fact, events had played out quite well. Every dragon in town had gone on a manhunt, leaving easy access to this Zodiac place and a noble-to-a-fault dragon who promised to take her to Jason. Having dragon firepower and quick transport would make everything a lot easier. The sooner they could get out of here and find Jason, the better.

She looked up at the opening. Arxad and Wallace were nowhere in sight. Letting out a low *hmmm*, she surveyed the area again. As long as she stayed in this chamber, it wouldn't hurt to have a quick look around while she waited.

On the far side of the stakes, a high and wide tunnel led toward the energy, still soft and tantalizing. Behind her, a narrower passage led into darkness, likely the escape route Arxad had mentioned.

Limping to lighten the load on her sore hip, she made a wide berth around the knee-high stakes and headed toward the energy source. Just taking a peek while staying in this room wouldn't violate Arxad's warning.

She stopped at the entrance to the tunnel and leaned in, allowing the stream to flow across her body. About fifteen paces ahead, the tunnel bent to the right, preventing her from seeing beyond that point. It seemed that a breeze blew with the energy, as if the particles had a physical presence that brushed back her hair and made her clothing flap. Although the flow stayed invisible, it sharpened every detail in her field of vision.

She looked through the open floor above. Still no sign of Arxad. What could he be doing? Was Wallace safe? No use worrying. She couldn't fly up there to see what was going on.

Turning, she closed her eyes and probed the tunnel, but the energy seemed to create a blockade, reflecting back her efforts. The particles tickled her skin, drawing her forward, as if the source now inhaled. She opened her eyes and took a step, giving in to the call.

Just a few paces. It won't hurt to get a glimpse of the source from a distance.

As the tunnel curved, she tiptoed along the rough, stony path. It seemed that the rocks had been chiseled by hand, the work of human slaves. An image of sweating men and boys entered her mind, each one pounding chisels as their half-starved bodies flinched at the sound of cracking whips.

Elyssa scowled. Arxad was one of the whip bearers. Priest or not, why listen to a dragon who was trying to keep secrets that ought to be exposed to the light? He was the enemy, a slaver. Solving this mystery might help the ones who endured the lashes.

Her fists clenched at her sides, she marched deeper into the tunnel. Although the light from the upper floor lanterns faded, the energy guided her steps. After several seconds, a rock barricade halted her progress.

She stopped and stared at it. Although dim in the sparse light, it glowed in her mind's eye, saturated with energy, like a sponge filled with radiant water that someone slowly squeezed.

Setting her hand on the wall, she probed its surface. Using her gifts to penetrate a wall might be beyond her ability, but this one seemed porous, lacking density, as if filled with pockets of air.

She closed her eyes and dove in. Beyond the inches-thick barricade, the tunnel continued for a few feet before opening into a new chamber. At the center, a brilliant aura shone around a floating form.

Elyssa concentrated on the source. Was it a human body? Although the radiance clarified everything around it, the form itself seemed vague, as if veiled by its own halo.

Something crawled along the floor, perhaps the size of a melon, making slow orbits around the source. As she concentrated on it, the creature shifted toward her. A low buzz sounded through the wall, and a jolt sent her flying.

She slid on her back, sharp rocks ripping her skin before she came to a stop. Grimacing at the pain, she climbed to her feet and brushed her stinging hands together. The shock seemed to clear her mind. What a fool she had been! Whatever that energy was, it carried a hypnotizing draw, and it had influenced her decisions. Yet, even now her curiosity heightened. Only something alive and sentient could deliver such an alluring spell.

As she backed away from the wall, Arxad flew in and landed next to her. His wings whipped the air for a moment before settling. "Warden," he shouted. "It is I, Arxad. All is well."

Wallace sat atop Arxad's back, his mouth agape. Elyssa set a finger against her lips but didn't dare make a shushing noise.

A low growl sounded from beyond the wall, followed by two yips.

"You detected a human?" Arxad asked.

Another yip penetrated the wall.

Arxad riveted his stare on Elyssa. "Whoever this human is, he or she must be the greatest of fools to venture this far. The warnings against coming into this area are clear enough for even the stupidest among them to understand."

A series of punctuated growls replied.

"I appreciate your vigilance. And do not worry. Even if we have to use fire snakes, we will catch the intruder. Thortune will be here soon to relieve you, so be at peace." Arxad used a wing to guide Wallace down from his back. "I assume all is well with Cassabrie."

An elongated bark sounded, followed by a yip.

Wallace soft-stepped over to Elyssa and stood next to her at the wall. He opened his mouth to speak, but she slapped a hand over his lips and glared at him.

"There is no need for me to see her," Arxad said. "You know how sensitive I am to her power. Such is the priest's vocation, to answer every call for help."

After listening to a longer series of barks, Arxad stared at Elyssa again, his eyes flaming. "Yes, it can be crippling. Sometimes I wish I could offer help in a more fiery fashion, if you understand my meaning."

A laugh-like growl shot into the tunnel before slowly fading.

Arxad silently prodded Elyssa and Wallace with the tip of his wing. They marched toward the tunnel entrance while Arxad shuffled his feet, apparently trying to drown out the sound of human footsteps.

When they arrived at the stakes, the floor above had closed, and a newly lit lantern on the wall provided the only light.

Arxad shot his head toward Elyssa and spat out, "Am I to follow the commands of an idiot?"

Elyssa stepped back. Arxad's words stung worse than the sphere's light. "I ... I don't know how to explain it. I felt drawn, like I couldn't control myself. I didn't realize what I was doing until the Warden knocked some sense into me. Even now I feel it pulling me back into the tunnel."

Arxad stared at Elyssa, as if analyzing her. Soon, his expression softened. "I apologize for my outburst. I neglected to ask if you were hurt."

"I scraped my back. I'm not sure how badly." Angling her head, she tried to look. "Wallace, can you pull up my tunic and see if I'm bleeding?"

"Uh ... yeah, sure."

While Elyssa held her tunic down in the front, Wallace lifted the back. "Three long scratches," he said. "Not much blood. It's already clotting."

When he dropped the hem, she flapped the material, drawing cool air across her wounds. "I guess I'll be all right."

"Not for long," Arxad said. "Although most are hypnotized, they cannot feel the drawing force. You obviously can, and the power is too great for you to bear." He spread out a wing, blocking the energy. It seemed that particles flew over the wing and bounced off the ceiling before diving down and sweeping between the stakes, invisible to the eye, but not to Elyssa's mind. To her, they seemed to appear and disappear like embers in the wind.

She shook her head as if casting off a dream. "Does it control your mind?"

"In a sense." Arxad pushed Elyssa and Wallace toward the darker tunnel. "You asked me to take you to Jason. Let us be on our way."

She halted and set her feet. "I want to go to Jason, but not until you tell me what the energy source is. It has a mind, something intelligent."

Arxad's tone sharpened. "If you continue acting like the queen of this world, young lady, you will get yourself and Jason killed, and your quest to free your species will be destroyed." He gave her a hefty shove, forcing her to walk with him. "Let us go from this place before Magnar returns, and I will give you as much information as I can later." He stopped and gave her a mock bow of his head. "That is, of course, if Her Majesty grants permission."

Elyssa set her hands on her hips and faced the dragon. "Look, to me you're part of an evil group of monsters who brutally enslave my people—men, women, and children—and you use their backbreaking labors to help you live at ease. I am in no mood to be mocked with sarcastic labels of queen, Her Majesty, or even young lady." She pointed a finger at his snout. "You promised to do what I say, so until you prove yourself to be something more than a cowardly beast, I will decide what we do, where we go, and when we depart. Got that?"

"Add impetuous wench to that list of labels," Arxad growled. "If your brain worked as well as your tongue, we would be halfway to Jason by now."

Firming her lips, Elyssa stared into his eyes. The fire within seemed to crackle with life, slinging daggers of scorn. His words sliced through her pride. He was right. Her anger at dragon cruelty had boiled her passions to a frothing frenzy, and her tongue had fanned the flames. She had ignored her own words. *An enemy's prisoner is an ally indeed.* It didn't make sense to keep driving verbal swords into this dragon's heart.

She crossed her arms over her chest and bowed her head. "I'm sorry. My emotions got the best of me."

Arxad stared at her for several seconds before glancing back at the tunnel of light. "The energy particles surely affected your judgment." He gave her a gentle push with his wing. "Our accounts are settled. Let us go."

As they walked through the new tunnel, dimness enfolded their bodies. A single lantern mounted on one of the walls guided them forward. About fifty paces beyond the first one, another lantern illuminated the path farther ahead, as if handing them off from one island of light to another.

"Who trims the lanterns?" Wallace asked.

Arxad continued shuffling behind them, his wings drooping and his head low. "That had been my duty."

Elyssa let Arxad's melancholy statement stir in her mind. *Had been.* Obviously an indicator that he no longer expected to resume his normal activities, maybe not ever. "How many other priests are there?" she asked.

"We have seven priests, and this year I am the high priest."

"Why would the high priest take care of such a menial task as trimming lanterns?"

"A menial task is best undertaken by one who has been exalted to a high status. It reminds him of his lowly estate and who lifted him from the ashes."

Elyssa pondered his words again. They reflected a maxim she had memorized from the Code back when she was a little girl, a short time before the book was outlawed in Mesolantrum. *Humility is an elusive prize. The proud wear it as a badge, gladly reciting their sins as proof of their low estate. Yet true humility is as quiet as the silence of dawn. Its bearer waits in twilight for the opportunity to bless. When Solarus rises, the deeds of the humble man are easily seen, deeds of service that boast neither of accomplishments nor imperfections. His righteousness crowns him with a halo that requires not a single word, a crown he neither wants nor sees, yet it glows with an unspoken testimony that rises to heaven to please the master who places it upon his head.*

Wallace interrupted her reverie. "And do the other dragon priests take over these functions when it's their turn?"

"I have trimmed these and other lanterns ever since I took my Zodiac vows. Shedding light in dark places is good for my soul."

Elyssa glanced at Wallace. Arxad didn't really answer the question. Was he deflecting criticism of his fellow priests? Probably. Arxad brought back memories of Benjamin, a clergyman in Mesolantrum, the only religious leader who ever stood up to Orion and his rabid persecution of anyone who displayed gifts of spiritual insight greater than his own—witches and Diviners, Orion called them. Benjamin swept the floors of the cathedral and polished every inch of brass. Passersby always knew when he was inside, anytime the huge doors stood wide open.

Elyssa sighed. Poor Benjamin. When his sixteen-year-old daughter was sentenced to perish in the flames of persecution, he preached her innocence to everyone who would listen, hoping pressure from the populace would sway Orion. Most of Mesolantrum ignored his plea. How could anyone but a Diviner or a witch know what Megan knew? She forecasted rain and drought. She knew how many people gathered in a room beyond her sight. And the proof that chafed Orion more than any other was her demeanor when the inquisitors verbally assaulted her without mercy. She always spoke with love, never flinching, returning blessings in exchange for their evil words.

Strangely enough, Orion used this as his ultimate evidence. No normal human could resist the overwhelming temptation to counter her opponents with a blistering retort. In her trial, he demonstrated his theory, allowing one clergyman after another to scream horrible invectives, whisper subtle insults about her "supposed" maidenhood, and even insult her departed mother. Yet, through all that abuse, she uttered simple truths, sprinkled liberally with grace, while never taking her eyes off her accusers.

Her calm spirit infuriated her interrogators and played perfectly into Orion's plans. When Orion concluded in his final arguments that no one but a demon-possessed girl could act in this manner, the jurors were all too happy to sentence her to death. Apparently the light of her halo shone too brightly for their darkened eyes … and guilty consciences.

As Megan burned at the stake, Benjamin, though he wept well out of range of the fire, burned with her. He continued sweeping floors at the cathedral, withering with every stroke of his broom, and he died only a few weeks later.

"Elyssa," Arxad said softly. "You seem pensive. Are you frightened?"

As she continued walking, she looked back at him. He had not called her by name before. In the glow of the next lantern, a tear sparkled in his eye. "I am sad," she said, "as you also appear to be. What is troubling you?"

"If I explained, you still would not understand."

She stopped and turned, forcing him to halt. She wrapped her arms around his neck and pressed her cheek against his chest. "You need not explain," she said, her voice muffled in his scales. "I already understand." She pulled away and gazed into his eyes. "The only part I don't yet know is the identity of the one who died, the one whose death destroyed your faith in dragonkind."

The fire in Arxad's eyes dwindled. "Your wisdom exceeds my expectations. I apologize for misjudging you."

"Will you tell me? A mate? An offspring?"

Arxad averted his gaze and spoke in a melancholy tone. "The final hope for this world and for dragonkind, or at least so I thought at the time. Now I believe there is another, and she could well save us all."

"She?" Elyssa asked. "Do you mean Koren?"

"Come. I will explain while we are walking. We will soon reach the exit." Arxad shuffled forward while Elyssa led Wallace at the dragon's right flank. The dim path followed a gradual incline, rocky and uneven, with barely enough room for everyone to fit. At times Arxad had to duck low to avoid the ceiling.

"As a Starlighter," Arxad said, "Koren possesses abilities she does not yet understand. The last time a Starlighter appeared, she exercised so much power, Magnar feared that she could topple his empire. In fact, she very nearly did, but it would take too much time to tell that story. I had hoped that she would fulfill the call of the Starlighter, but she delayed her decision, choosing to hide from Magnar's persecution while pondering her options, and that delay proved to be her undoing.

"When Magnar captured her, he put her to death at the crystalline sphere from which you freed me. When it is used for executions, the slaves call it the cooking stake, because the victim is chained to it and slowly bakes. Very slowly. Because of Magnar's anger, he forced the Starlighter to suffer for days."

Elyssa imagined Koren chained to the stake, writhing in pain as her body cooked in the sphere's torturous light. How terrible! The cruelty of these dragons knew no bounds. As she tightened her fists, it took all her strength to keep from bursting into a tirade. "What did you do about it?"

Arxad stayed silent for a moment as they continued walking. A brighter, constant light appeared in the distance, perhaps a hundred paces away, apparently the end of the tunnel. Finally, he answered with a sigh. "I had no power to stop the execution, so I prepared for her survival. Again, my methods would take too long to describe, but she lives on in spirit, separated from her body, and if all goes well, you will meet her in the Northlands."

Elyssa relaxed her fingers. Yelling at Arxad for doing nothing to stop the murder wouldn't do any good. She couldn't possibly know how much torment he suffered while trying to decide how to help the Starlighter. Maybe he really had no choice. "Will Jason be in the Northlands?"

"That is his destination. Unless he has found faster transport, he has not had time to get there."

"Then why are we sneaking through this place so slowly? Shouldn't we be hurrying to catch up with him?"

"You are unaware of the events that delayed our arrival at the tunnel. At the moment I returned the key to its place in the mural corridor, Magnar discovered the empty chains. I flew Wallace out the main entrance, and we hid atop the roof in the shadows until Magnar exited, roaring for a cadre of dragons to join him in the hunt. I realized that he would have difficulty finding aid during this lockdown, so when he flew into the Basilica, we reentered the Zodiac and found you in your hypnotized state.

"Since Magnar likely believes that I escaped through the ceiling exit, his search will begin near the Zodiac and then spread out. Our hesitation will allow the searchers to depart the area. As I indicated earlier, this tunnel exits within a building we call the Basilica. From there, I can determine if it is safe for us to fly north."

"Does Magnar know Jason is going to the Northlands?" Elyssa asked. "Won't they hunt for him there?"

"They are already searching for an escaped assassin and now for me as well. They cannot afford to send dragon scouts into such a vast area until they are finished with other matters. Not only that, Magnar is unable to go beyond the great barrier wall, so he has forbidden all but the priests from crossing. If you knew Cassabrie's story, you would understand."

"Cassabrie? That's the name you used when asking about the energy source in the other tunnel."

"One moment." Arxad stopped at the tunnel exit. The rough floor smoothed out into marble tiles, and the walls ended abruptly, looking like a dragon-sized hole leading into another building. He extended his neck and poked his head into the new chamber. After a few seconds, he brought it back and looked at Elyssa, his voice now whisper-quiet. "Cassabrie is the other Starlighter."

"Her body is in there? Her corpse?"

"You must not speak of it. Very few know of her presence."

"So this dead Starlighter is alive in spirit," Elyssa said, matching his whisper, "and her body still emanates hypnotizing energy."

"Your discernment has improved. I am impressed."

Elyssa eyed the dragon. Was he being condescending? Maybe. He was hard to read. "How did Cassabrie get to the Northlands?"

Arxad looked into the chamber again. When his head returned, his tongue darted out and in, and his ears twitched. "I will tell you no more. We should find Jason and Koren before it is too late."

"Why the hurry? You said we should wait until—"

"Never mind what I said. Seeing this room in the Basilica reminded me of an important issue."

Elyssa tried to peek around him but to no avail. "What issue?"

"This was an antechamber that led into the incubator room where the black egg once resided. A temporary wall has been removed, so now the antechamber and incubator room have been combined. The warming jets have been turned off, meaning that the prince has likely hatched. Zena will be empowered to use her arts to destroy Jason from afar."

"Zena?" Wallace repeated. "I've never seen her, but I've heard about her. Her name is practically a curse word among us slaves."

"She was Cassabrie's betrayer." Arxad pushed through the hole and emerged into the incubator room. "Both of you climb on my back. We must fly with all speed."

While Arxad sat low, Elyssa crawled up his scales, followed by Wallace. When they settled at the base of his neck, Elyssa held the spine in front of her, and Wallace wrapped his arms around her waist. She whispered, "We're ready."

As Arxad rose to his full height and spread out his wings, she swallowed hard and added in her mind, *I think*. To their left, far across the spacious chamber, two doorways led to corridors, while to their right, the floor ended at a railing that appeared to be a place to observe something at a lower level.

With a leap, Arxad flew toward the incubator room's ceiling but quickly reversed course and retreated.

Elyssa squeezed the spine with both arms. This was rougher than riding one of Mother's milking goats. Wallace seemed undisturbed, still hanging on lightly from the back. Maybe he had ridden many goats.

"The ceiling hole is not open," Arxad called. "The other exit will be somewhat more difficult to negotiate without being seen." He flew over the railing and dipped down into a dark room, the largest one yet. With a stage, a stone lectern-like pedestal, and space for a standing audience, it appeared to be a theater, while a log fire near the pedestal and a pair of kneeling altars on each side gave it the feel of a house of worship.

Arxad leveled out and, beating his wings slowly, flew toward a set of double doors to the left.

"They're closed," Wallace whispered into Elyssa's ear.

"I see that. Maybe it opens when—"

"Hang on!" Arxad blew a stream of fire at the point where the two doors met. The flames splashed in a spray of orange and yellow arcs, and dry heat surged into Elyssa's eyes. The doors didn't budge.

Arxad wheeled around again. Elyssa slid to the side. With Wallace's help, she pushed upright and regripped the spine, bending her body down to lower her center of gravity.

Another dragon shuffled in from the opposite side of the theater and approached the fire. "The Basilica is locked down, Arxad, and I have sealed off the tunnel to the Zodiac."

"It's Magnar," Wallace said.

Beating his wings heavily, Arxad landed in a run and stopped several paces away from Magnar. He heaved in great breaths, each one punctuated with a smoke-filled snort.

"You did not keep your word," Magnar said as he drew closer. "What happened to the integrity of the great high priest?"

"I kept my word. I neither broke my chains nor lied to the crystal. I am now a prisoner of a promise I made to the young lady who rides on my back."

Magnar bent his neck and peered around Arxad, his eyes fiery. "She must be a powerful sorceress to be able to release you from your bonds and force you into submission."

"She threatened the crystal," Arxad replied, still breathless. "Unless I gave her the key and acquiesced to her demands, she would have destroyed it."

"Such are the disadvantages of a dragon who finds lying distasteful. Your allegiance to your word supersedes your loyalty to our species." Magnar lumbered to Arxad's flank and bobbed his head at Elyssa's side. "I have seen the one-eyed boy before, but you have the look of a free woman. Did you come from Darksphere?"

Elyssa set a hand on her hip. "Even if I knew what you were talking about, why would I confess to such a strange idea? And why would you ask for a self-incriminating statement? After all, I *am* able to lie."

"She has venom enough to be from Darksphere," Magnar said. "No female here would be so disrespectful. Lashes at an early age will drive that out of any wench."

Elyssa kept her stare fixed on Magnar. It was too late to change her posture to that of a cowering slave. Such a quick shift would be too obvious. Maybe confident silence would keep the truth a secret, at least for a while.

"Lift your shirt so I can see your back," Magnar ordered.

"What?" Elyssa touched the hem of her tunic. "Why?"

"To see if you bear the marks of an impertinent slave. Do as I say, or I will cook both of you where you sit."

Trying not to cringe, Elyssa held the front of her tunic. "Wallace? Will you lift it for me?"

"Uh ... okay."

The material rode up her back and a draft of air cooled her skin. She glared at Magnar. "Satisfied?"

The huge dragon took a heavy step toward her and stopped, meeting her glare with pulsing eyes. His nostrils flared. Smoke streamed out. Yet he said nothing. He just stared.

Elyssa swallowed, hoping her slow transition to the image of fearful slave would be convincing. When Wallace let her shirt fall back into place, she spoke in a conciliatory tone, her voice trembling. "As you can see, lashes have done little to tame my tongue. I am a ..." She glanced at Arxad. "An impertinent wench, I suppose. I apologize for my lack of respect."

Magnar continued to stare. Her words had no effect, apparently glancing off his armor like poorly thrown spears. Was he reading her face? Her posture? She had to block any silent communication.

She slumped her shoulders, hoping to display humility, and put on an innocent, confused-puppy expression. It would either work or enrage him, but no other options came to mind.

Finally, Magnar backed away and waved a wing. "Dismount. You are hiding something from me."

Elyssa slid down the dragon's flank and landed, bending her knees. Wallace slid down as well and stood at her side. "Any idea what he means?" he asked, loud enough for the dragons to hear.

She shook her head, watching Magnar. He appeared unaffected by Wallace's clumsy dissembling. His drilling stare returned. Did he think she was hiding something in her brain, or had he guessed that she was concealing something physical? In fact, she was doing both, but who could tell what this dragon had learned?

Magnar nodded at Elyssa's trousers. "You have pockets."

She stealthily brushed her hand across her pocket, feeling the crystalline peg's slight bulge. It was still there. "Yes. I have pockets."

"A human with pockets can never be trusted. That's why we allow only the foremen to have them in the mines. I have been looking for something from the quarry for many years, and I cannot allow a slave to sneak it past our overseers."

"You're right," Elyssa said, "but pockets are very handy for other things besides sneaking."

"Your friend Jason turned his pockets inside out to prove they were empty. I demand that you do the same."

Keeping her stare fixed on Magnar, she thrust her hands into her pockets, palmed the crystal, and jerked out the inner lining of each. "You see?" she said, trying to keep the dragon's attention on her words as she hid her hand behind the protruding pocket. "Nothing. Your suspicions are reasonable, but in my case—"

"Silence!" Magnar spat a fireball that nicked Elyssa's wrist. Bending double, she grasped her arm and cried out. The top and bottom of the peg extended beyond her concealing grip, making its presence clear.

"You do have it!" With a beat of his wings, Magnar scooted to Elyssa and extended his clawed hand. "Give it to me immediately."

She scowled fiercely, biting her lip to keep from crying. She laid the peg in his hand and turned toward Wallace. "Think of something," she whispered.

"I'll try." He cleared his throat and stepped toward Magnar. "Magnar, sir, I think that crystal isn't the one you're looking for. This one is—"

Magnar smacked Wallace with his tail, sending him sliding into Elyssa. She caught him in her arms and fell to her bottom.

"Thanks for trying," she said.

He massaged his ribs. "You're welcome ... I think."

As she struggled to her feet and helped Wallace to his, Magnar turned to Arxad and spoke in an odd language.

Wallace whispered to Elyssa. "Magnar said, 'They will have to be imprisoned until I have time to interrogate them further.'"

As the two dragons conversed, Wallace continued interpreting.

"Where will you put them?" Arxad asked. "Every guard is occupied."

"I will let Thortune guard them in the Starlighter's room. Once they are overcome, he will be adequate."

"But we cannot allow the secret—"

"The secret will die with them," Magnar said. "Once they succumb, they will tell me what I need to know, even though they are completely aware that they will die no matter what they say. Since the wench had the crystal, she must be the fulfillment of Gerrod's Darksphere prophecy."

"And if she can heal Exodus, then you must know that I oppose her execution. Whether you care about the humans or not, Exodus cannot endure unless it is healed."

Elyssa studied Arxad's eyes. He was trying to communicate something to her, knowing Wallace was translating, but it didn't make much sense.

Magnar cast a glance at Elyssa. "I will consider your appeal and delay the execution order."

"And what will you do with me?" Arxad asked.

Magnar spiced his reply with a low growl. "I know exactly what to do." He showed the crystal to Arxad. "I assume you know what this is. We will go as soon as possible."

Arxad gazed at the glittering peg. "Are you saying—"

"Exactly. Until recent times, you and I have had many journeys together. I think it is time for us to restore what we once had and embark on a new excursion."

Arxad's head drooped. "If I must."

"You must. I have no idea what we will face there, so I need an ally. I trust that you will not let me down again."

"Let you down? I told you how I escaped from the chains. I had to—"

Magnar interrupted with a sharp growl. "Stop the pretense! I know why you really killed Maximus, and I am weary of allowing this 'loyal priest' charade to continue."

Arxad lifted his head. "I returned the egg, did I not? I proved my loyalty to our ultimate purpose."

"You did, and it is time that we unite once again and concentrate on our one common cause. I will explain on the way to our destination … Darksphere."

four

"Uriel Blackstone?" Jason glanced at Koren. "That's impossible. He died decades ago."

Uriel raised a finger. "A man who is dead has many advantages, not the least of which is the fact that no one will try to find him while he goes about his business."

"What business?" Koren asked.

"To rescue my people from this accursed land, of course."

"But you … He died," Jason said. "I mean, no one has seen you in so long. Where have you been?"

"Trapped. Trapped like a rat in a cage." Uriel held a thumb and index finger a fraction of an inch apart. "I was this close to convincing one of the leaders to travel back to Major Four with me. Then he could return to tell everyone else the story. But a white dragon captured me and carried me to a castle in a cold region, where he imprisoned me. For a while, he took care of me himself, providing food and other essentials, but later some invisible spirits took his place."

"Invisible spirits?" Jason laughed under his breath. "Okay. Thank you for the interesting story, but we have to be on our way."

As Jason turned and reached for Koren's hand, Uriel grabbed his sleeve. "What can I do to prove myself?"

Jason pulled free from his grasp and looked at the old man's sincere face. He was certainly aged, but how could he be over one hundred and twenty years old? It was impossible. Still, a test would prove his story to be false quite easily. There were some things that no one on this planet could know. "If you're really Uriel Blackstone," Jason said slowly, "you could tell me how you locked the portal."

"From the Major Four side or this side?"

"Major Four."

Uriel showed Jason his hands and wiggled his fingers. "A genetic lock. Only I or one of my descendants can unlock it. I wrote it all down in a journal, hoping I could deliver it to my son, Tibalt, so he could eventually find his way here to give me help, but he never arrived." Uriel's head drooped a notch. "He could be dead by now, and I shudder to think about what might happen if that journal should fall into the wrong hands."

Jason felt his jaw drop open and forced it back in place. "Tibalt isn't dead," he said slowly. "His fingers got me into this place."

Uriel's brow shot upward. "Tibalt is here? Where?"

"He *was* here. We rounded up some of the Lost Ones, and he took them home."

Uriel clapped his hands. "Praise the Creator! My son is alive, and he has been doing my work!" He grasped Jason's arm and pointed southward. "The dragon realm is that way. Come, and we will finish my son's work ... my work ... your work."

Jason studied the old man, his face more visible now as the moon again peeked through a gap in the clouds. With his eyes glittering and his smile flexing his cheeks, he did look a lot like Tibalt. "I understand why you want to go to the dragon realm, but Arxad sent me to the Northlands to find someone who could help us."

"Arxad?" Uriel's face turned pale. "I know this dragon. He presided over a horrific execution. I witnessed it myself just before the white dragon captured me."

"Look," Jason said, sliding his sword back into its sheath. "I don't trust Arxad or any other dragon, but he did help us escape. I don't think he would let us get this far if he meant for us to die along the way."

Uriel pointed at Jason. "That's it! He meant for you to die along the way. And even if you reach the bitter climes of the Northlands, the white dragon will imprison you forever. It was only by sheer cunning and years of planning that I managed to escape. Perhaps Arxad has sent you north to get you out of his way, knowing you will either be captured or killed."

"I don't believe it," Koren said. "If you had heard Arxad's defense of my friend Natalla during her trial, you would know. He helped Natalla and me escape, and before that I lived in his home for over a year. He gets grouchy, but he is never cruel."

"And he stood by while we were getting executed," Jason added. "He's not exactly consistent."

Uriel shook a finger. "He does what is best for himself, as all dragons do."

Koren crossed her arms over her chest and glared at Uriel, muttering, "You don't know the hearts of all dragons."

"Come with me," Uriel said, pulling on Jason's arm. "We will trust only humankind and rescue every soul from this land of lies and brutality."

"How will you open the portal?" Koren asked. "We don't know when Tibalt will return."

Uriel released Jason and drew something in the air with his finger. "From this side, the portal is controlled by a row of crystalline pegs, and I hid one of them. All we have to do is retrieve it, and we'll have easy passage. Since you're from my world, maybe together we can convince the slaves to join us. They wouldn't believe one man, but maybe they'll believe two additional eyewitnesses."

"You'll never get past the wall," Koren said, nodding toward the south.

Uriel squinted at her. "Past what wall?"

Koren imitated Uriel's air art and drew with her finger. "The dragons' domain is enclosed almost all the way around by a high wall, and it's guarded constantly. No one can get in or out."

"Is that so?" Uriel gazed toward the south, though it was too dark to see beyond the meadow. "No such wall existed when I was last there."

"It's there now," Koren said, "and it's the best reason to keep heading north."

"But the white dragon—"

"We'll stay out of sight and watch for the white dragon. Even if he finds us, I know what to do." Koren's voice altered to a beseeching tone. "Please. Don't worry. We'll be safe."

Uriel hitched up his trousers. "Very well. I will go with you. I am familiar with the castle, and ..." He looked southward again, a forlorn expression sagging his wrinkled face. "I have waited many years to return. I can wait a little while longer."

Jason patted Uriel on the back. "Then let's go. It will be good to have another set of eyes. We can take turns sleeping."

As they marched alongside the edge of the chasm, Jason had to raise his voice to compete with the waterfall's constant roar. "You seem to be in excellent condition for a man of your age. You must be at least a hundred and twenty, but you look younger than your son."

"Something in the castle, I think. The air crackled with energy, and I hardly needed any sleep. I know I worked on projects of some sort, though I cannot remember what they were. Now that I am away from the energy, my mind feels dull, and memories have fled, but I suppose those projects made the time pass quicker. Whatever the reason, it seems that I never aged a day."

"Very strange." Jason looked up. Clouds again covered the moon. Misty rain swept in with the wind, dampening his cheeks. "This is strange, too. Koren tells me it never rains here, only in the mountains."

"Really? Then much has changed since I departed. In my days here, every time Trisarian rose, we would get a deluge, with lightning, high winds, and hail."

Thunder rumbled from the east, and wind began to whip their clothes. "Let's go," Koren said as she marched forward. "When the moon peeked out, I got a picture of the landscape ... I think."

"You think?" Jason waved for Uriel to follow. "The moon wasn't out for very long."

"I have a great memory," she called back through the strengthening drizzle. "And, besides, if I fall into a hole, you'll have some warning."

Holding his scabbard against his hip, Jason caught up and ran at her right. Lightning flashed in the east, illuminating her face every few seconds. She glanced at him and smiled. Her hair, its redness muted in the chaotic light, flapped against her back, and her green eyes shone. As before, they seemed to speak to him, like tiny oracles that communicated from mind to mind. *Thank you for running at my side. I want to be your partner, not your leader or your follower.*

The drizzle became a heavy downpour, and the turf transformed into a squishy blend of grass and mud. Ahead, the edge of the chasm bent to the left, leaving a wide-open field to the north. From that direction, another stream poured into the chasm, a second waterfall to join the northbound one in the depths. An empty raft sat on the nearer bank. As he passed by, Jason studied the raft for a moment, but in the darkness only logs and tie-vines were evident, no other details. Apparently someone had journeyed from the north and disembarked to keep from tumbling into the waterfall. In any case, a raft wouldn't do them any good on a southbound river.

On the western side of the river, trees came into view — shelter, at last. His father had told him that taking cover under trees wasn't safe in a thunderstorm, but standing out in an open field didn't seem safe, either. And if it started hailing, he would choose a forest covering over getting pelted by falling stones. Still, in order to get to the trees, they had to cross what might already be a rain-swollen torrent. Every option seemed filled with obstacles.

When they reached the edge, Jason studied the south-running current in the midst of pouring rain. Constant lightning flashes lit up the stream. Although it flowed swiftly, the water tumbled over rocks from one edge to the other. It couldn't be very deep.

He stood between Koren and Uriel and held out a hand to each of them. "It looks safe enough. We'll go together."

Holding hands, they stepped in. Jason cringed at the icy water but kept his body calm. No use risking that a shiver might communicate fear of this little creek. They had to keep moving.

The stream's bed proved to be uneven, forcing them to help each other out of an occasional knee-deep hole. With the thunder and the tumult of rushing water, they didn't bother to say anything more than "Up you go!" or "Watch out for that stone."

When they came within ten paces of the western bank, Koren halted. "Do you hear that?" she shouted.

"Besides the obvious?" Jason asked.

Koren's eyes grew wide and her voice almost too quiet to hear. "A roar. An enemy's fury. She has sent the waters to devour us."

"Enemy?" Jason said. "What are you talking about?"

Koren turned upstream and pointed. A long streak of lightning lit up the sky, revealing a dark wall of water rushing their way.

"Run!" Jason pulled Uriel and Koren and splashed through the stream. A deafening roar overwhelmed all other sounds. Lightning flashed again. The wall of water thundered closer. The shore lay five leaps ahead, too far to avoid the rampage. Even there, the flood would wash them away.

Jason grabbed Koren around the waist with one arm and thrashed through the stream until he found a secure boulder. "Hold on to me!" he shouted, as he wrapped his arms around the boulder as far as he could reach.

Koren held him from behind, her wrists locked at his waist. Uriel latched on to the boulder from the other side and clutched Jason's arms. Jason took a deep breath and held it.

The water crashed over them. Like a battering ram, the impact slammed Jason against the boulder, knocking his breath away. As the surge ripped at his ears and repeatedly beat his body against the rock, Koren's arms squeezed his ribs. Uriel's fingers felt like vises clamping down on his wrists.

As the flood continued to sweep by, Jason's fingers began to slip. One of Koren's hands loosened and pulled free. She held on to his arm and dug her nails into his skin.

Jason's lungs begged for air. He couldn't let go and ride the wave. They would tumble into the chasm. He had to hang on. It would slow down soon, wouldn't it?

Koren slipped away. Jason lunged and caught her wrist. Uriel grabbed his ankle, keeping him in place.

Holding on to Koren, Jason paddled in place to keep from smacking against the riverbed. He thrust his head upward. His face broke through the surface, but he couldn't take a breath. The surge eased, but not enough to keep them from being raked into the waterfall. With Uriel's grasp slipping, they would be swept away in seconds. Only one chance remained—a direct assault.

Pulling with all his might, he drew Koren closer until he could wrap his arms around her. He squeezed her body close, set one foot at the pebbly riverbed, and jerked free from Uriel. The river threw him forward, but he planted his other foot and halted the momentum, his back against the current. Now standing with his body angled, he pushed his head into the air and sucked in a breath. Koren, her face pressing against Jason's, breathed in. Water splashed into her mouth, forcing her to hack and spit.

As they both coughed, their heads knocked and their cheeks slid together. Jason strained against the flow and took a step backwards. Lightning flashed once more, revealing the waterfall, now only two steps ahead. One stumble, one slip, and they would both be dead.

He took another backwards step. The water level eased down to his shoulders. Still, with the violent surge ramming his back with frigid water, and Koren's saturated body weighing him down, his muscles ached. If they cramped, his legs would give way.

As he labored, Koren shouted into his ear. "Creator, help us! You can do it, Jason! Push!… Good!… Again!… Come on!… Yes!"

The water level dropped to the middle of his back, making the effort easier. When it fell to his waist, he lowered Koren and, taking her by the hand, turned to face upstream. They trudged against the flow, one slow step at a time. Rain poured. Wind slung their wet hair. Lightning flashed every few seconds, framing the silhouette of Uriel sitting on a boulder with his arm outstretched.

"You can make it!" he shouted from atop the boulder. "Just a few more steps!"

Jason leaned forward and pushed. Koren did the same. The current swirled through her long cape and dragged her back, but Jason pulled her steadily along. He reached for Uriel's shaking hand, grabbed hold, and rode his strong pull to the boulder.

With Uriel's help, Jason and Koren climbed to the top. They sat down heavily, their heads drooping as they gasped for breath. After coughing several times, Jason tried to speak over the sound of rushing water and pounding rain. "This isn't … the same boulder."

Uriel shook his head. "I chased after you two and slammed into this one. Since it was too late to catch you, I climbed aboard and prayed for a miracle."

"Good thing. That waterfall nearly swallowed us. I'm sure we had some divine help."

Uriel looked at the horizon, blinking as water dripped from his nose. "If this storm keeps up, we might get another big wave. No way to tell."

Koren hooked her arm around Jason's and drew close, whispering. "If Zena is behind this storm, we can probably count on another wave, or else she'll send something worse."

"What could be worse?" Jason asked.

Koren held out her hand. "Hail?" Tiny ice pellets bounced in her palm and down to the boulder.

"Okay," Jason said as he struggled to his feet. "We'd better get to the woods."

The trio climbed back into the stream and plowed through the water, now at Jason's thighs. When they reached the western bank, they hustled up a short, sandy incline and into a forest. As they moved deeper in, the lightning flashes no longer illuminated their surroundings, and the thunder seemed muted. Hailstones, larger now, fell through the branches along with huge raindrops, making cracking noises as they crunched leafy debris.

Jason spied a big manna tree with hefty limbs and guided his company that way. After settling with their backs against the trunk, Jason in the middle, they listened to the cacophony. Hailstones as big as fists crashed through the smaller branches and smacked the ground. Lightning struck a nearby tree and knifed out in tongues of sizzling white. With every pop and crackle, Uriel flinched but kept his eyes wide.

As wide-eyed as Uriel, Koren moved her head back and forth as she took in the scene. She seemed to be memorizing every element, as if storing it for a future Starlighter tale.

When his breathing returned to normal, Jason forced a tone of confidence. "So if this is the worst Zena can throw at us, we'll be fine. It can't rain forever."

"Zena?" Uriel stared at Jason, his voice quavering. "Do you mean a slender raven-haired woman with black eyes?"

Jason nodded. "Have you met her?"

"Met her?" Uriel laughed under his breath. "Let's just say that our acquaintance ended in a manner that caused us both great consternation. In a word, it was a catastrophe. She is a devil in a dress."

"Did she know who you are?" Koren asked. "I mean, that you're the man who escaped from the original group of slaves?"

"Oh, yes, indeed. That's why she was obsessed with killing me." Uriel heaved a sigh and rested his head against the trunk. "It's a long story, and it ends with Zena orchestrating the death of a lovely young lady named Cassabrie. Fortunately, I escaped in a way that prevented any pursuit."

Koren leaned forward to look at Uriel. "That's interesting. If Zena was so obsessed, why would she not pursue you?"

"As I said, it's a long story." Uriel leaned forward as well. "Koren, you resemble Cassabrie in many ways, especially your red hair and green eyes. Do you happen to be gifted at storytelling?"

She dragged a toe along the ground, her head low. "I suppose some would say that."

"If you're wondering about her being a Starlighter," Jason said, "you're right. She is one."

Uriel clapped his hands. "Excellent!"

"What's so excellent?" Koren asked.

"That you're here and not there."

When Koren and Jason exchanged puzzled looks, Uriel went on. "Well, it's rather complicated. You see, Zena is a sorceress with great skill, but her ability is limited in a strange way. She requires the power of another energy source. A Starlighter has such energy, but the girl must be bent to Zena's will in order for her to corrupt that power for her own use. Since you are on our side, you can use your abilities to free the slaves."

"What abilities? All I can do is tell stories that seem to come to life."

"Is that so?" Uriel stroked his chin. "Cassabrie had the ability to manipulate the environment around her, such as light, water, and the air. I had even seen her raise the dirt from the ground and make it swirl like a tornado as she guided it with her hands. Her images seemed to have substance. They bent when you touched them, fell when you pushed them, though they were no more physical than a dream."

Koren looked at her hands. "I guess I have a lot to learn."

"It's your potential that Zena craves." Uriel pointed at her. "You are a storehouse of spiritual power."

Wrinkling his brow, Jason glanced between Koren and Uriel. "If Zena needs a power source, how did she create that wave? Or this storm?"

"The prince," Koren said, cupping her hands as if holding something. "The prince from the black egg probably has power. That's why she could make this storm."

Uriel firmed his lips. "So the prophesied king has been born. When did that happen?"

"He was still in the egg when we left, but I think he hatched recently. I felt his presence, and he's trying to call me back."

"Your theory is likely correct. Zena is using him, but at his age, how powerful can he be? Certainly not as powerful as a Starlighter, otherwise why would he call for your return?" Uriel looked up at the dripping branches. "If only Cassabrie were here to teach you how to use your gifts fully, but wishing for ghosts is a deadly game. Seeing one likely means you have become one yourself."

"Do you have a suggestion?" Jason asked.

"Well, now that I know the circumstances, I am in hearty agreement with going to the Northlands to meet this helper Arxad mentioned. Returning to the dragon realm and risking Koren's capture could be a drastic mistake."

Jason cocked his head and listened. The competing noises had subsided, and only an occasional lightning bolt lit up the sky. "Sounds like the storm is passing. Should we keep going?"

Koren laid a hand on his arm. "No. You need rest. Sleep a while."

"I am quite handy with a sword," Uriel said, "or at least I used to be. If you trust me, I will watch over you and the young lady while you rest."

"Thank you. I appreciate that." Jason unbuckled his sword belt and handed it to Uriel. "Wake me up if Zena sends another attack."

"I don't think she will," Koren said. "I haven't heard from Taushin in quite a while. Maybe he can't find me here."

The rain ceased, but the hefty breeze continued, a warm wind that kept them from shivering. Jason leaned his head against the trunk and half closed his eyes, stealthily watching Koren. "Will you sleep, too?" he asked.

She rose to her feet and fanned out her cape. "I was thinking that since Uriel is here, we can tell his story about Zena and Cassabrie together. That way, we'll all know what happened." She curtsied toward Uriel. "Will you join me and play your part?"

Uriel stood and bowed. "It would be an honor. I did this once before with Cassabrie, and it was a thrilling experience, indeed."

He took Koren's hand, and the two walked into a clearing. They stood among leaves, twigs, and small branches torn down and scattered by the storm.

Jason rose and drew within a few paces of their makeshift stage, hoping to get a closer look at a Starlighter in action.

Koren stepped back from Uriel and, twisting her hips, made her dress and cape swirl around her. Then, she lifted her hands and began speaking in an orator's tone, as if addressing the surrounding trees as her audience.

"I am a Starlighter," she began, "and I will now tell you a tale from long ago."

five

The moon broke through the clouds and cast a glow over Koren's body. Her eyes sparkled, and her hair shone. As she glanced at Jason, she smiled, her face radiant and dazzling. Distant flashes of lightning from the opposite horizon created a backdrop of sporadic illumination, further enhancing her glorious appearance.

"Uriel Blackstone risked his life to return to Starlight. Motivated by the Creator's love, this heroic gentleman hoped to break the shackles of slavery and convince the Lost Ones to follow him to their home planet."

As if unaffected by the breeze, Koren's words echoed in the forest. She swayed as she spoke, her face displaying every emotion. She lifted her dress and allowed her legs to move freely through the leaves. Her feet stepped in perfect time with her cadence.

"Being of sound mind and guided by wisdom, Uriel first approached a leader among the slaves, one of the first children born to those who came from Major Four, a woman considered an elder among the human population though her years numbered only thirty."

A human form appeared, a woman sitting on the ground. Life-sized and semitransparent, she looked like a ghost.

Uriel dropped to one knee in front of her and spoke with passion. "You must believe me, Brucilla. I can take you to a place of freedom and safety. You will never feel a whip on your back again, nor will your children. Every drop of sweat will benefit your family instead of selfish dragons. You will labor for the cause of love rather than fear of blood."

Brucilla's lips moved, and Koren, now swaying behind her, gave the woman voice. "My mother sang of this land, but it was just a bedtime story, a tale of impossible dreams to help me and other children sleep at night. No one can fly from one planet to another. We might as well believe in brooms that sweep by themselves and chisels that dig for pheterone without the miners' hammers and the muscles that drive them."

"Come with me," Uriel said, his hands held out in entreaty. "I will show you the doorway to paradise. If you see it for yourself and spread the news, others will follow. Surely your children and your husband will—"

"No!" Koren ceased her swaying, and her tone spiked with anger as she continued speaking for Brucilla. "You know I have no husband. To the dragons I am a breeding machine who must produce a child every year, regardless of whom they choose as a father. They care nothing about dignity or the precepts of the Code. They are cruel tyrants, and if I am caught chasing after myths with you, they will be sure to multiply the welts on my back."

Koren stepped up and crouched next to Brucilla. "I will go with him, Mother."

Brucilla looked at her, alarm in her eyes. "Cassabrie?" she said, Koren again speaking for her. "How long have you been listening?"

"Long enough to see this man's heart. Perhaps what he says is merely a tale, but he believes in it, and that is enough for me. I want to learn the truth that drives him to risk his life. If there is one thing Father taught me before he died, it's that no man is quick to lie when his falsehood will draw blood from his veins."

"For a sane man, yes, but what if he is a madman? You are fifteen, too young to defend yourself. He might take you to the wilderness and—"

"He is no madman. His passion rings true, and his eyes reflect what he has actually seen rather than the tortured dreams of a wild imagination."

"But what of Zena? If you come out of hiding, she might find you, and your life will be forfeit. Your reason for solitude is noble. You still need time to make your decision about the star."

"For the sake of every slave on this planet, I am willing to take the risk." Koren straightened her body and extended her hand. "Uriel Blackstone, lead me to this doorway to paradise. When I return with news of the other world, our people will believe."

Brucilla raised two fingers. "If you do not return her safely within two hours, I will assume that you are the scoundrel that I suspect you are, and I will send six men with picks and drills to find you. When they are finished with you, there will not be a piece of your body larger than one of these fingers."

Uriel bowed. "Let it be as you say."

When he grasped Koren's hand, Brucilla disappeared. As they strode in a circle in the forest clearing, Jason took another step closer. The scene before him warped, and his mind swam within the mesmerizing tale. Koren's appearance altered. Although she still had red hair and green eyes, she seemed to be a different person. Had she become Cassabrie?

The forest melted away, replaced by a lush meadow springing with colorful flowers, easily visible in the moonlight. As Uriel and Cassabrie waded through knee-high grass, flower petals swirled around them. Cassabrie waved her arms as if choreographing their dance. Soon, the Zodiac came into view, its spires towering high above the other buildings.

Jason leaned closer. When he saw it earlier, the land-scape leading up to the dragon village wasn't this green and fertile. It was desertlike with stony ground, scrubby trees, and cacti mixed with dry, wiry grass. How could Koren have made such a mistake in her tale?

After she and Uriel sneaked into the Zodiac's front doors, they entered a corridor illuminated by a series of lanterns sitting atop iron rods protruding from the walls. A mural decorated each wall, one depicting Magnar flying between two planets with several humans on his back, and the other showing a black dragon sitting atop a hill with a host of other dragons bowing toward him.

Uriel and Cassabrie walked hand in hand on the stone floor, their backs bent as they labored to silence their footsteps. When they stopped at a second set of double doors, Cassabrie whispered, "What do we do now?"

"You tell me. Your gifts allowed us access to the Zodiac. Since we couldn't go through the portal at the mine, I am now at a loss."

"I sense the same energy here that was blocking the portal, but what do we do if we find the cause?"

"Destroy it if we can," Uriel said. "Or perhaps we will see how to neutralize it. Time will tell."

Uriel pushed one of the doors open and peered inside. Then, signaling for Cassabrie to follow, he proceeded into a circular chamber with a domed ceiling. At the center of the room a brilliantly shining sphere sat atop a crystalline column. Moonlight poured through a hole in the dome above, striking the sphere and sending radiance throughout the sanctum and back through the ceiling and into the sky.

Uriel rubbed a finger across his wrist. "The sensation is pleasant, like a soft pillow with massaging tentacles."

"That sphere is blocking the portal," Cassabrie said. "I'm sure of it."

Uriel picked up a fire poker at the wall and gripped it tightly. "I fear the ramifications of destroying it, but I don't know what else to do."

"We could wait." Cassabrie pointed at the ceiling. "If moonlight is providing the sphere's power, maybe the energy will subside when Trisarian begins to set, and the portal will be released."

"That will be too late. You heard what your mother said. We have only an hour remaining."

"Let's look for another option." Holding out an arm to block the light, Cassabrie tiptoed toward the sphere. Uriel followed, his head angled to the side to keep from looking directly into the radiance.

When they arrived, she set a hand a few inches from the surface. Like iron filings swirling toward a magnet, the glow swarmed under her palm. Cassabrie stood transfixed, now staring directly into the light. The radiance streamed into her fingers and filled her body. Her red tresses flared out. Beams shot from her eyes and pinpoints of light sprang from her pores. Yet, Cassabrie stood unmoved.

"Cassabrie!" Uriel hissed. "Get away!"

"I can't," she said in a bare whisper. "My feet … They won't move."

Uriel grabbed her around the waist and lunged backwards. They rolled on the floor, Cassabrie still emitting a brilliant aura. When Uriel helped her to her feet, the radiance surrounded her in a glowing ball as if she had been swallowed by a transparent moon.

"What did you do?" Uriel asked.

"I don't know." Cassabrie looked at her shining hands. "I feel so strange, like something hot is throbbing inside me."

Uriel stared at the sphere. "It appears that you took whatever power that thing had and ingested it."

"Then will the portal stay blocked even when Trisarian sets?"

A dragon appeared in the room, his wings beating as he hurried toward them. "What are you doing here?" he roared.

Cassabrie gasped. "Arxad!"

Uriel raised the fire poker, but Arxad whipped his tail around and slapped it out of his hand. "Fools!" Arxad bellowed. "What have you done to the Reflections Crystal?"

"Nothing!" Cassabrie said as she backed away. "I didn't even touch it!"

The sphere brightened a shade as if absorbing some of the moon's glow.

Arxad glanced at it before continuing. "You speak the truth, but something has greatly weakened the sphere, and you are wearing its radiant coat."

Cassabrie rubbed a hand down the front of her tunic as if trying to slough off the light. "I don't know what happened. It's as if I absorbed it. I didn't intend to; it just happened."

Again the sphere flickered brighter.

"Zena has touched the sphere many times, and nothing like this has ever happened. What is different about you?"

A woman materialized. Slender and dressed in black, she walked to Arxad's side. "You already know what is different about her, yet you fear to speak the truth. I have told you about Cassabrie. She is very dangerous."

Arxad stared at Zena for a moment before looking again at Cassabrie. "Are you saying that she has weakened the crystal? Has your meddling in our affairs wrought this result?"

"How little you know." Zena glared at Arxad. "We should speak no more about this in front of these two. Let them be locked away until we consult with Magnar."

Like a splash in water, the scene rippled, and when the surface smoothed, only Zena and Arxad remained.

"It is because of my arts that Starlight has survived this long," Zena said. "I have searched for this Starlighter for weeks. Since she already knows how to use the cloak, she is too powerful to contain for long. For now, it seems that her encounter with the sphere has overwhelmed her. Otherwise she would have used her tricks already."

"Tricks?"

Zena waved her arms. "Conjuring phantoms, scaring her captors, making them flee from realistic but merely gaseous opponents. I do not fear her ruses, but many dragons do."

"If this Starlighter is so powerful, then is she the fulfillment of the Exodus prophecy?"

"Can there be any doubt?" Zena ran her fingers along her black sleeve. "Now we must persuade her to refrain from her foolish notions and work with us to resurrect Exodus."

"And if we are unsuccessful?"

Zena stalked toward the wall and returned with a dagger in her grip. "Then we will terminate her, so that she doesn't continue to drain our world's power."

Arxad glared at her for a moment before offering a nod of surrender. "If that is the only option remaining."

"What other options do you think we have?"

"We can try to buy some time. Remember, since we have a Starlighter, the black egg will not be long in coming."

Zena looked at him for a moment before lowering the dagger. "What do you suggest?"

"The sphere absorbs energy. Perhaps if we tie her to it, it will be restored."

"Perhaps." Zena touched the sphere but quickly snatched her hand back. "The light stings."

Arxad set a wing near the globe. "I feel it as well."

Dragon and human stared at each other, anxiety obvious in their scowls. Finally, Arxad shuffled away from the sphere, his ears twitching wildly. "It has lost its life-giving power!"

Her body trembling, Zena stepped slowly backwards. "But … but how?"

Now side by side, the two stopped at the edge of the sphere's aura. "I can draw only one conclusion," Arxad said. "Cassabrie absorbed it."

Swallowing hard, Zena looked up at the ceiling. "Our region will be devastated. Even our climate might change."

Arxad's scowl returned, more menacing than before. "Magnar never should have listened to you. Stealing energy from the star was bad enough, but infusing the crystal was worse. You have traded blessings from the Creator for personal control and brought a curse upon us."

Zena clenched a fist and shouted. "Superstitions! Nothing but superstitions! You explain everything with spiritual rhetoric, while I speak with rationality."

"Is that so?" Curling his neck, Arxad drew his head back. "Then feel free to provide your rational solution."

As she paced slowly in front of the crystal, Zena pursed her lips. "The stinging sensation proves that the sphere no longer possesses life-giving energy, so the Starlighter will be unable to harm it. We should employ your suggestion and tie her to the crystal."

"It now carries a painful shock," Arxad said. "She will suffer during the process."

"True enough. In fact, as the sphere drains her energy, she could die. Yet, we should all be willing to permit such a sacrifice in order to gain the survival of our planet. When the black egg arrives, the Creator will send us another Starlighter."

Arxad growled. "You would try to manipulate the Creator? Does your foolishness have no bounds? There must be another way."

"Then name the alternative, Arxad. Otherwise, I will suggest to Magnar that we proceed as soon as possible. First, however, since there are other green-eyed redheads, I suggest that you test Cassabrie to see if you can learn how to identify her distinctive attributes."

"Are you saying you want to locate other Starlighters so you can kill them as well?"

Zena halted. "I am willing to sacrifice this Starlighter for the sake of our land, but we must be ready to capture and control the next one. When the black egg appears, her cooperation will be crucial. You know this as well as I do."

After glaring at Zena for a long moment, Arxad lowered his head. "I will do as you ask."

"After your tests," Zena said, "have her put on the Starlighter's vestment. She must be at full power when the absorption takes place. And let there be a public procession so that every slave will believe that Cassabrie caused any climate change that comes about."

Jason mopped sweat from his brow. This story was so real, his heart thumped. Again the air seemed to ripple, and when it cleared, Cassabrie stood with her back to the crystal, chains wrapped around her body. The domed ceiling had opened, and sunlight beat down upon her. The sphere captured Solarus's rays and reflected them into her body.

Now dressed in a white gown and a blue cloak, sweat poured down her cheeks and dampened her clothes. The cloak's hood covered her head, allowing only wisps of her flaming red hair to peek out, and her eyes sparkled with green luminescence, a bright mimicry of the pair of embroidered green eyes on the front of her cloak.

Dozens of people filed past, some looking on with disdain. A few displayed sadder frowns, while Brucilla couldn't look at Cassabrie at all. She wept bitterly as she staggered by.

Uriel sat within a few steps of the sphere, also bound in chains. Whenever Cassabrie groaned, he winced, as if sharing her pain. Soon the last human witness disappeared, and two dragons stood in front of Cassabrie: Arxad and Magnar.

Sweat no longer seeped from her pores. Her hood had fallen to her shoulders, exposing her face fully to Solarus. With her head leaning back against the radiant sphere, stringy hair stuck to her cheeks, and cracks covered her bleeding lips. She licked her bottom lip with a swollen tongue but made no sound.

"If the heat kills her too soon," Magnar said, "the crystal will not absorb enough energy."

Arxad laid a foreclaw on the chains. "She is suffering greatly. Either kill her now or let her go. Mercy demands one or the other."

"Mercy?" Magnar swiped Arxad's claw away. "If we lack the energy to keep our region fertile, then dragons will die, and they are of more value than this runt of a human."

After shooting a glance at Uriel, Arxad thrust his face close to Magnar's. "You are the one who decided to rely on the crystal rather than natural cycles, and now we are all paying the price."

"Those natural cycles brought about our loss of pheterone," Magnar replied, his cadence stilted, as if he were reading from a script. "If not for that, we would never have returned to Darksphere and enslaved humans."

"There was nothing natural about it. Fear destroyed our pheterone source, and only faith in the prophecy will restore it. You trusted in your own devices. You have forsaken faith in the Creator."

Magnar swung around and smacked Arxad in the face with his spiked tail. Arxad winced but stood his ground, blinking away blood that oozed from a cut on his brow.

Pointing a claw at Arxad, Magnar bellowed, "You are fortunate that you uttered these insults with condemned prisoners as your only witnesses. Your evil words will die with them. If not for your ability to warn the miners of coming quakes and flooding rivers, I would have dismissed you long ago."

"I prefer dismissal. I made my vow in ignorance, and I wish to be released from it."

Magnar set his snout near Arxad's and stared at him, eye to eye. "The only release from your vow is death, and you know why I cannot allow that."

Backing away, Arxad lowered his head. "Yes ... I know."

“Now adjust the sphere and your whatever it is you do, so that it kills slowly. I want every bit of energy body before she dies.”

“And what of the other prisoner?” Arxad as

“After I have interrogated him, I will let Zena kill She will enjoy that.”

“Must she? His only crime is wanting his people set free.”

“He has served his purpose,” Magnar said. “His story is preserved.”

As if summoned by Magnar’s words, Zena appeared, a dagger again in hand. Arxad and Magnar were nowhere in sight, and Uriel sat close to Cassabrie, still bound by chains.

“Have you come to cut out my heart?” Uriel shouted. “Thirteen days I have suffered under the cruel sting of this viperous globe. You will do me a service to end my life, for I will go to be with my dear family who already rest in the glory of our Creator.”

Zena’s smile seemed to crack her face. “You will not be so brave when my blade slices into your skin.”

As Zena stalked past the sphere, Cassabrie took in a deep breath and called out, “Look at me, foul sorceress!”

Zena stopped and turned. Cassabrie stared at Zena, parched hair dangling in front of her reddened face.

“What is it, Starlighter?” Zena crooned as she drew near.

Cassabrie pushed against the chains and, with a puff from her bleeding lips, blew back her hair. “What do you see in my eyes?”

na bent closer and stared. "I see the green of envy," said in a mocking tone, "envy of a woman who will ontinue to live in luxury while you die a horrific death. I see anguish that although you possess tremendous power, you are impotent. You cannot save yourself or your friend. And, finally, I see despair. You will die young, never loving a man, never holding your own baby in your arms, and never seeing the liberation of the slave race."

As she riveted her stare on Zena, Cassabrie's voice exploded with passion. "Then hear my prophecy, sorceress of the underworld:

This view of light will be her last;

Her eyes will darken, sight is past.

Unless she holds my hand in faith

She staggers blind, a hopeless wraith."

Beams of light shot out from Cassabrie's eyes and into Zena's. The blistering rays locked in place, and when they finally turned off, Cassabrie's head and shoulders slumped.

Still clutching her dagger, Zena stumbled backwards, smoke rising from her eyes. She fanned them with her hand and screamed, "What did you do to me?"

Cassabrie stood limply. If not for the supportive chains, she likely would have crumpled to the floor.

Zena charged toward her, swinging her dagger violently. "I will cut your eyes out! I swear it!"

"No!" Uriel struggled against his chains. "Oh, great Creator, send us aid! I am helpless to save her!" He jerked and squirmed but to no avail. "Arxad!"

The sound of beating wings filled the room, and a draconic shadow covered the floor. Uriel looked up. A white dragon descended from the sky. As he landed, he knocked Zena down with his tail.

Arxad flew in from the corridor. When he saw the white dragon, his wings faltered, and he dropped to the floor in a slide. He quickly scrambled to his haunches but kept his head low. “My king!”

The white dragon grasped Zena’s arm with a foreclaw and jerked her to her feet. “Begone, sorceress, before I give you everything you deserve.”

With a sweep of his wing, he pushed her away, and she vanished from the scene.

“Arxad,” the white dragon said calmly, “the happenings of late are not beneficial to our cause.”

Arxad kept his stare aimed low. “I have been unable to convince Magnar of our strategy. He trusts in powers from an inferior source.”

“And what of this Starlighter? Why did you allow her to suffer?”

“I made a vow, foolish words uttered in my youth. I am a priest in a cage, constructed with iron bars that I put in place, and only Magnar or the power of death holds the key.”

“Indeed. Your ill-advised vows have brought you troubles and heartaches.” The white dragon set a wing under Arxad’s chin. “Rise and look upon me, my faithful servant.”

Arxad lifted his head and gazed into the white dragon’s bright blue eyes. “What must I do?”

"You will continue in service to Magnar, thereby keeping your vow, but when it comes to choosing to save an innocent life, you are bound to a higher calling: that is, your vow to serve me. You can have only one master."

Arxad shuffled toward the sphere. "Then I will release the Starlighter immediately!"

"There is no need."

Arxad halted and stared at the king. "No need?"

"It is too late for her."

Arxad drew close to Cassabrie's body and set an ear next to her mouth. "Has she drawn her last breath?"

The white dragon lowered his head. "Yes ... she has."

"No!" Uriel moaned. "Oh, my dear girl!"

A single tear on Arxad's cheek glistened. "What must I do now?"

"We have discussed another of the sphere's properties before. Just as it absorbs energy, it has also taken her spirit. After I leave, examine the crystal. You will see. Let wisdom guide you from that point."

"Wisdom?" Arxad said. "I have none. I have proven it time and again."

"You have much more wisdom than you realize, but your use of it has not always been consistent. If you will let love and light guide you rather than fear, then your path will be straight."

The white dragon beat his wings and lifted into the air. After orbiting the room once at a low altitude, he swooped down, grabbed Uriel in his claws, and hoisted him into the air, his chains crumbling into dust. "I have need of this one." He ascended through the open ceiling, and seemed to float for a moment in midair. "I trust you,

Arxad," he called. "Do not fear. Do not doubt. You will need your faith, for the collapse of protection here will prevent me from returning for a long while."

With a great flapping sound, the white dragon flew away.

Instantly, the entire scene melted. Koren stood where Cassabrie had been, her blue cloak flapping in the breeze. Above her head, a white dove flew into the trees and disappeared among the branches.

Uriel sat next to Koren and let out a long breath. "Whew! You must be tired!"

Koren let her shoulders slump. "I am. I have never told such a lengthy tale, and the details have never come to life so vividly."

"Your power is increasing," Uriel said, pointing at her. "Soon you will be as capable as Cassabrie was."

Koren held a corner of her cloak between her fingers. "Did I tell it accurately? The scenes and words just flowed from my mind, so I had no idea."

"My memory is not as good as it used to be, but it seemed that every time I thought about the words that ought to be spoken next, they came to pass in one of the ghosts, though you spoke them yourself. However, I might have embellished my role a bit. I'm sure I added the part about thirteen days and the viperous globe and whatnot."

Koren smiled weakly. "Thank you for your help. It must have been a horrible experience, and to relive it again ..."

Uriel waved a hand. "It was nothing. I have relived it hundreds of times during my captivity."

Jason reached out and helped Uriel to his feet. "So the white dragon never told you why he took you prisoner?"

"He told me very little, only that he had further use of me and had to keep me alive until that time." Uriel spread his arms. "So here I am, wondering what this future use is. Since he released me, I should be doing something, don't you think?"

"You already have done something," Koren said. "Pulling us up to the boulder probably saved our lives."

"I think you would have survived without my pitiful aid. In any case, even as valuable as your lives are, I think the white dragon might have something bigger in mind. Don't you think he could have arranged a rescue in a way that is simpler than keeping a man alive for many years past his normal life's span?"

"You act like he's some sort of deity," Jason said. "He's just a dragon."

"Perhaps. Arxad certainly treated him with great respect, but I think his reverence fell short of worship or prayer. You might call it admiration or high esteem."

"Have you ever seen a dragon pray or worship?" Jason asked.

Uriel tilted his head upward. "Not that I can remember."

"I have," Koren said. "Well, heard, not seen. I have walked by Arxad's room in the middle of the night and heard him praying. Most of the time it was just mumbling, but once in a while I could make out words. He talked mostly about his mate and his daughter and asked for their safety, which confused me, because his tone made it sound like something terrible could happen at any moment."

"Did he ever give his deity a name?" Jason asked.

Koren shook her head. "None that I could hear."

Jason stretched out his arms and yawned. "Well, that story wore me out, and I was just watching. I'm sure you must be exhausted."

"I am now. I didn't feel tired while I was telling it. I almost didn't feel anything at all."

Jason walked back to the tree and sat down. "Speaking of prayer, it's about time I did some praying, and then I'll sleep a little while."

"You should." Koren untied her cloak, folded it, and pushed it behind his head. "It's damp," she said, smiling, "but so are you."

"Thank you. This will help a lot."

She stooped and kissed him on the cheek. "Thank *you* for all you did in the flood. I have never seen anyone act with such chivalry. I'll never forget it."

Jason gazed at her sincere face, barely visible in the darkness. Her kindness needed no answer. Adding anything to her words of grace would spoil the moment. He just smiled and closed his eyes. With every muscle spent and his mind awash in dizziness, sleep would come soon, so his prayer would have to be quick.

"Creator of All," he whispered, "thank you for rescuing us from the raging waters and the fierce storm. Watch over us and show us the way. Keep your protective hand over Father and Mother as they wait for us in ..."

As his words faded, images of Mesolantrum drifted into his mind. He and Adrian marched away from home—Adrian beginning his search for the Underground Gateway and he making ready to take Adrian's place as the governor's bodyguard. Their father called out, his wood-chopping axe poised on his shoulder. After all three said their good-byes, Jason's view followed his father back to his pile of wood. As soon as he and Adrian were out of sight, Father hurried into their communal home, limping on his war-wounded leg. He changed into hunting trousers and tunic, strapped on a sword and scabbard, and kissed Mother tenderly.

"I will return to you," he said, wiping a tear from her cheek. "You have my word."

"With Frederick?" she prompted.

"Either alive or with news regarding his demise. I can promise no more." He touched his nose. "I still remember his scent. Perhaps I will find traces of it yet remaining. Trust me to use every available clue to find him."

She nodded and laid a hand on his broad chest. "In *your* heart I trust, but I don't trust the men who have sent Adrian on this quest. Be wary of Drexel. I see evil in his eyes."

"I have no doubt that Drexel seeks Drexel's glory and nothing else. Yet, if we can use his self-promotion to our advantage — "

"No!" Mother covered her mouth, surprised at her own sharpness. "I apologize, my dear. I merely beg that you heed my advice. You know that my judgment of character is rarely wrong."

"I know." With an arch of his eyebrows, Father pointed at himself. "You married me, didn't you?"

She gave him a playful push. "Go on with you now. If you're not out of my sight before I can say 'Mesolantrum' three times, I'll go after our sons myself."

He bowed, then backed out of the room, his gaze still on her. "May the Creator of every world watch over us until I return. No matter what happens, you will be my first and best thought."

With the closing of the door, Jason's dream ended. Drifting toward wakefulness, he half opened one eye and peered at Koren sitting next to him. With her brow low and her stare fixed on her folded hands, she seemed pensive, concerned.

Jason closed his eyes again. Sleep. He needed sleep. He would ask Koren to share her worries when he awakened. For now, it would be better for all if he regained his strength. Who could tell what dangers lay ahead? They needed him to be ready.

Soon the images of Koren's amazing lifelike tale swirled in his mind. As the same hypnotic daze flooded his thoughts, Jason drifted off to sleep.

SIX

With his wrists bound by a rope, Randall shuffled behind the guard, dragging the chains that shackled his ankles and attached him to Tibalt, his fellow prisoner. The poor old man had sacrificed so much. After decades in the dungeon, he risked his life to help free the Lost Ones from the dragon planet, and now he faced prison again.

"I'm sorry," Randall whispered.

"For what?"

"For making you go with me to the palace."

"I'm not one to say 'I told you so,' but …"

Randall sighed. "You deserve it. Go ahead."

"Nope," Tibalt said, shaking his head. "I'm going to set my noggin' on what we did that was good. Nothing else. Just seeing the happy faces on those little ones is worth another fifty years in the dungeon."

"If you say so." Randall recalled an image of the Lost Ones they had rescued from slavery and how he and Tibalt had hidden them in various communes. Smiles reflected the joy of freedom the Lost Ones had never known before, and hugs from the children, who would no longer have to worry about dragon whips, once again filled him with warmth.

After settling the former slaves, Tibalt argued that they should go straight back to the dragon planet to help Elyssa, but Randall ached to bring his father's murderers to justice. Not only that, he had searched for his mother without any success. Had she gone into hiding? Been imprisoned? Some clues indicated the latter, so he begged for just a few minutes to search the palace. If they could figure out what Drexel, Governor Prescott's head sentry, knew and why he had conspired to kill the governor, maybe the entire conspiracy could be exposed, and his mother would be safe.

Randall strained against the rope. It loosened but not enough for him to pull free. With a sigh, he glared at the soldier leading them through the palace's marble-laden corridor as they headed toward the courtroom. This Drexel loyalist, a friend of Bristol—the palace's interior guard and murder conspirator—had spotted them sneaking into Drexel's quarters. No amount of persuading could turn him aside from dragging them to Viktor Orion, who, by law, had assumed the governorship after the death of Randall's father.

A sentry opened the courtroom's tall door and led them inside. They passed between two sets of benches, which were often filled with people when an interesting trial commenced, but this hearing had been arranged quickly and quietly. Only the arresting guard and two skinny, young clerks sitting in the front row would witness the proceedings.

On a platform at the front, Governor Orion sat behind a desk and peered at them overtop a pair of narrow eyeglasses. His piercing eyes, sharp chin, and pointed nose accentuated his stare, as if every facial feature took aim directly at them.

Randall tried to hide a shiver. If only he weren't so close. During higher-profile cases, the governor usually stood behind a podium at the side while lawyers battled verbally in front of the platform. It seemed that no one bothered with formalities today.

Orion gave the solider a shooing motion with his hand. "You may go. And take the clerks with you."

The solider attached the prisoners' leg chain to a ring on the floor, bowed, and marched back toward the door, motioning for the clerks to follow.

When the door closed with a clacking echo, Randall trained his gaze on the new governor. Was this man involved with the murder conspiracy? How could the one who benefited the most from his father's death be innocent?

Orion rose from his seat and walked to the front of the desk. Still elevated by about three feet, he stared down at Randall, his long body making him look like a perching vulture. "My guess is that your intrusion comes from a desire to uncover the conspiracy that led to your father's death. This consuming passion has caused you to throw caution to the wind and walk straight into the jaws of that conspiracy. Am I correct?"

Randall shot a warning glance at Tibalt. They had agreed earlier that he would stay quiet.

"As heir to my father's estate," Randall said, "I am also heir to his office when I come of age. Therefore I have rightful access to every room in this building. I have done nothing illegal."

"And I have not accused you of a crime, but as the legal steward of this office, I have to protect myself from the rash behavior of the former governor's son, who likely thinks I was somehow involved in his father's death. How could my guard know that you weren't here to seek revenge?"

Randall gritted his teeth. This pompous cornstalk of a man was blowing smoke, a verbose disguise. "I was going after Drexel, not you. I was trying to figure out his motivation."

"Ah, yes," Orion said, pressing his fingers together. "The passion to learn the truth has driven many men toward acts of folly." He walked to the side of the platform, strode down the three steps, and approached them, his fingers now intertwined. "I once had a similar passion, an obsession really, that pushed me to the brink of insanity at times. Now that I am governor, the responsibility of judging the acts of others has allowed me to view things from a new perspective. I was cold, unyielding, swift to condemn, and I fear that my harsh behavior has been the cause of many ills of late, including the departure of Jason and Elyssa—acquaintances of yours, I believe."

Randall nodded. There was no use hiding that information. It was common knowledge.

"So I am willing to negotiate," Orion continued. "I sent the usual witnesses away, because I wish to make a secret pact with you. I can tell you what I know about Drexel if you will go on a journey for me. I have learned that Jason and Elyssa have likely passed through the gateway to the dragon world, putting them in grave danger. I know the secrets behind the obstacles that prevent access to the portal, so you will have an easier time than they did. I want you to go there and retrieve them. Tell Elyssa that she has nothing to fear. I have given up my pursuit of witches and Diviners, and she is welcome to live a life of peace without fear of persecution."

Randall looked into Orion's eyes. This guy had to be the greatest actor in Mesolantrum. Not a hint of a lie shadowed his razor-sharp face. Still, if he knew Elyssa was gone, what could it hurt to listen? Getting back to the dragon world without new cuts and bruises would be a lot better than trying to get their raft down that wild river again.

He gave Orion a nod. "Go on."

"Drexel had Uriel Blackstone's diary, which revealed the secrets behind the obstacles. I read this diary and jotted down the procedures. If Tibalt is the real son of Uriel, you will have no trouble opening the portal."

Tibalt blurted out, "I don't believe you! My pappy was too smart to write everything down. If he lost it, then scoundrels like you might—"

"Tibber!" Randall barked. "Quiet!"

Tibalt frowned, his jaw tight, but he quieted.

Orion pulled a key from one pocket and a small knife from the other. "If you bring Jason and Elyssa back, I will grant your freedom along with information regarding Drexel's participation in the conspiracy."

Randall resisted a growing scowl. He had to display a calm negotiating stance. "I haven't been able to find my mother. A note in Drexel's room said something about her being in the dungeon, but the guard said she wasn't there."

"Ah! No wonder you are so persistent. A young man will stop at nothing to rescue his mother." Orion slid his eyeglasses lower. "I will investigate this matter and find out where she is. Perhaps my efforts will be enhanced by your cooperation."

Randall maintained his stoic stare. Orion held the ultimate leverage, and he knew it. Giving Orion a shallow nod, Randall said, "It's a deal."

Tibalt let out a *humph* and looked away.

"Very well." Orion crouched and unlocked their leg manacles, then straightened and sliced through their ropes with the knife. "I have notes in my desk, which I will allow you to read and memorize. When you return with your friends, please bring Elyssa to me so that I can offer my apologies in person."

Koren looked at Jason. His head leaned against her shoulder. Damp from rain and sweat, his sandy brown hair trickled over his ears, down his neck, and over his forehead, just long enough to reach his eyebrows. A single droplet dangled from his nose, making him wrinkle his narrow, angular face. As he twitched, his long eyelashes fluttered, and the droplet fell to his broad chest.

A gentle buzz in his rhythmic breathing rose into her ears. Finally he was getting the rest he so desperately needed … and deserved.

She let a smile emerge on her lips. Having a warrior at her side felt … well … comforting. She had grown accustomed to fending for herself while enduring her slave labors—chopping and hauling wood, slaughtering and butchering animals, harvesting honey while dodging bees—as well as looking after others less fortunate, especially Wallace, during their dreadful weeks at the cattle camp. And, of course, trying to find the truth about Promotions for Natalla began this dangerous journey in the first place. Being the strong one felt normal. Independence had long been her way of life.

And now? After being rescued from the precipice of a terrible plunge to a watery death and pulled helplessly through a raging river clutched tightly in the arms of a brave warrior, she felt …

This time the right words escaped her grasp. How did she feel? Warm? Protected? Loved? A combination of all three? Although it always felt good to be strong and independent, knowing that someone else cared enough to sacrifice for her benefit felt even better. The sensation erupted earlier when Arxad stole her and Natalla away from the trial at the Basilica, risking his own life in the process.

She reached over and slid her hand into Jason's. The skin of her palm warmed next to his. It had been exhilarating when Arxad carried her—with his claws and scales—but this was an entirely different sensation. It felt much better—warm, tender, alive. Jason was a man, not a beast; a rescuer, not a slaver. He was an equal, a friend, someone she could stand beside and battle the cruel dragons with until they both either died or walked away in victory, hand in hand forever.

She drew their hands to her lips and kissed his fingers. Such a friend had been a shadow in her dreams for several months now. Madam Orley sometimes told stories about romantic love between men and women and how so few of humankind ever experienced it. With dragons arranging most marriages, and with the masters of the breeding rooms forcing women to accept the company of whichever men the dragons chose, only a few husbands and wives enjoyed the bliss of self-chosen coupling and the lasting joy of fulfilling vows of love, sacrifice, and faithfulness.

Watching Jason had been like seeing one of Madam Orley's stories come to life, as if Madam were a Starlighter and Jason were one of the ghosts who acted out her words. His resolve shone clearly in his eyes. This young man would sacrifice anything to protect her, and he would rather die than allow her to suffer a scratch. There was no doubt about it.

Gently pushing Jason's head to keep it from falling, Koren rose to her feet. About ten paces away, at the edge of the clearing, Uriel strode slowly back and forth, the sword propped at his shoulder. He was the image of a fatherly protector, or perhaps grandfatherly. Would he, too, sacrifice his life for hers and display the same brand of chivalry? She barely knew him, but it was clear his heart beat with fervor in the world of free men. Experiencing liberty and its many blessings seemed to make men strong, desirous of protecting it for the women and children they loved. Yet, in this world, the cruel whip of slavery replaced such a heart with one of fear. Only a few brave men still exercised chivalry's lovely muscles. Perhaps some fathers still covered their daughters with a protective arm. Surely her own father did before he died.

She walked up to Uriel, her hands folded at her waist. "Have you heard any strange sounds?"

Uriel stopped and smiled. "Nothing unexpected, Miss. The wind stirs up the sodden branches, causing the fall of a cone or two, but I have yet to hear a growl or bark."

"Then is it safe for me to step into the woods for a moment of privacy?"

"I believe so." He extended an arm toward the opposite side of the clearing. "How much time should I allow before I search for you?"

"Ten minutes should be plenty, thank you." She walked past him and stepped gingerly through the wet underbrush, barely able to see vines of prickly ivy that crawled beneath fernlike greenery, which populated every gap between trees. When she reached a dark area surrounded by thick trunks that blocked Uriel's view, she stopped and stood quietly, listening to the sounds of dripping water.

Although she had let Uriel believe otherwise, it was not a bodily need that called her into seclusion, but a different yearning. Jason's courage had brought back memories of her father's nightly blessing, a scruffy kiss and words spoken with gentle passion, "I love you, little K." Yet no image of his face or form ever graced her recollections. He was like one of her ghosts, a phantom who appeared when she tried to recall the early years, but he always remained a mere shadow.

She looked up at the sky, dark and obscured by overhanging branches. Madam Orley said that Father was now with the Creator, probably looking down at her with love. Could he really see her? If she spoke to him, would he listen? If not, wouldn't the Creator take her words and pass them along?

As tears formed in her eyes, she clutched the sides of her dress and curtsied. Why? She didn't know. Very few people ever prayed anymore, such was their misery, so who could tell what might be the most respectful way to approach the Almighty? The Code said to show respect, and a meek curtsy was all she had to offer. Although she had often composed songs of prayer in the past, the act of normal conversation seemed so much more difficult, as if speaking to the Creator as one would to a friend might be ... well ... too familiar.

"Creator?" she said, her voice cracking. "I'm sorry I haven't talked to you in a while ... well, in a long while. Being a slave, I have a lot of excuses, but I suppose you don't want to hear them. If you really are the Creator of All, you probably know about them already." She brushed her foot against a prickly ivy leaf. Its sharp point jabbed her skin, feeling like a rebuke for her impertinence. Cringing, she hurried to continue.

"Anyway, I need to know what to do. Taushin has been speaking to my mind, and he says I should return to the Basilica to help him bring justice by releasing the slaves. He says he is blind and needs to use my eyes to discern truth from falsehood and justice from injustice. Of course I want to help my people, but how can I know if he's telling the truth? His words sound true, but—"

"My words *are* true, Koren."

Koren gasped. Where had that voice come from? She looked to her left. A dark form approached, a small dragon whose head rose to her own height. As with the characters appearing in her tales, this dragon was semi-transparent, a dark phantom.

"Who are you?" Koren asked.

"I am Taushin. I am speaking to your mind as before, and now that you have used your gifts to bring me here, I can see through your eyes. So much the better. Since you have asked for guidance, it is obvious that the Creator brought this about. Now we can speak as if face-to-face."

Koren stared at this odd invention of her mind. As seconds passed, it seemed to solidify and become as real as the trees around her. "Okay, so you can see through my eyes. But how did you hear what I said?"

Taushin chuckled. "I think giving away such secrets would be counterproductive, but you should consider the possibility that every image you see and every word you hear might be elements of your own imagination. Perhaps I am not real at all, and the words I speak are from your mind, not from the real Taushin who is peering through your orbs at this moment. Perhaps my words are a combination of my thoughts and your own, and any sign that I can hear you comes from your imagination." As his eyes glowed bright blue, his tone grew deep and mysterious. "And perhaps I am able to hear every word you speak and every sound in this forest. So beware what you say. Taushin might be listening."

Koren shivered. The idea that she might have conjured this phantasm and granted it sentience seemed too strange to be true. "This doesn't feel like my other tales. They have never been so real … so solid."

"Interesting," Taushin said. "Your powers are maturing. Zena told me the manifestations Cassabrie created appeared to be real, and she could manipulate them to move with the physical forces around them."

"Move with the forces? What do you mean?"

"Reach out and touch my image."

Koren cocked her head. Had he really heard her response or merely anticipated her question? She stepped slowly toward the black dragon. He still seemed to be as small as one of the younglings, though he spoke with a maturity that far exceeded other younglings she knew. Steeling herself to keep from trembling, she put her hand through Taushin's neck. "You're not solid at all," she said. "You only appear to be."

"Now concentrate. Give me a slight push and make me move with your touch. My shape and size are all your doing, so it is in your power."

Koren focused on the black dragon's scales, a crisp and detailed pattern. Reaching up slowly, she touched his neck with her finger. The surface dimpled slightly. She pushed harder, this time with her palm. His neck and head shifted in response. Somehow her mind was redrawing the dragon based on her actions, and as she repeated her push, it seemed that she could feel his body on her skin, as if the image and response fooled her mind into thinking it was really there.

She withdrew her hand. "This could be very powerful."

"Cassabrie became dangerous because of this power. She was able to conjure an army of realistic humans that were no more than phantoms. Even if a dragon blew fire on their bodies, she could make them burn in anguish as if they really felt the pain. You can imagine what problems such power could cause for dragonkind."

"Or how much it could help humankind."

"You are as wise as you are gifted." His tone became pleading, passionate. "Come to me, and I will help you learn your powers. Together we can rule the dragon kingdom and set your people free."

Koren took a step back. What was she doing? How could she be having such a deep conversation with something she created with her mind? Yet, since Taushin was communicating with her, at least she wasn't really talking to herself. Or was she? Maybe every part of this encounter originated within. Maybe Taushin wasn't really able to communicate with her at all.

Still, she had prayed for help. Perhaps the Creator sent this image as an answer to her prayer. Did he want her to go back to Taushin to help the slaves? How could she know for sure?

Koren took three steps back. "What … Who are you? Why are you here?"

The dragon bowed its head. "You have created me—perhaps you should answer your own question."

"Well …" She looked at Taushin. With his ears turned away, he appeared to be inattentive. Was he listening? Would it be safe to guess out loud why she had summoned the white dragon from her mind? "I heard Uriel talking about a white dragon in the Northlands, so maybe I created you as someone to counter the words of Taushin."

"That is a reasonable conclusion," the white dragon said. "Yet, if Taushin is really speaking to your mind, I am at a disadvantage. As the white dragon's representative, I can speak only what you know about him using the words you give him. It is you who counters him through me."

"That makes sense." Koren glanced between the two dragons. With one black and the other white, the scene sketched a comedy of sorts. Madam Orley once told a story about a child who had to make a decision, and an imp materialized on each of her shoulders. One told her the right thing to do while the other contradicted every word and suggested that she do something awful. Had Madam's story caused her to imagine this silly skit? Was she so exhausted that she had lost all sense of reality?

"Since you are the king of the Northlands," Koren said to the white dragon, "can you tell me what to do? If I return to the dragon realm and serve Taushin, will everything turn out all right?"

The white dragon let out a low chuckle. "Do you expect both omniscience and foreknowledge from me, a dragon whom you have summoned from your mind? I know only what you know, and you know the Creator through the words of the Code, so from that fountain alone must you drink."

Lowering her head, Koren took another step back. "I see."

"Your self-chastisement is all too clear," Taushin said. "You are angry at yourself for your lack of devotion to the Creator, and now you have brought this figment to lash you with a verbal whip. The only help you can receive are the trite generalities of the Code and your own limited experiences, while I offer a tangible solution to the needs of your species. Again I appeal to you. Come with me, and we will work together to set every human free."

Koren flinched. If those were her own thoughts rather than Taushin's, she truly was giving herself an emotional beating.

The white dragon extended his neck, bringing his head within arm's reach of Koren. "Your knowledge of the Code and your experiences are not trivial. They are truth and guidance, the words of liberty, and applying them correctly will provide the answers."

"Okay," Koren said. "How do I do that?"

"By comparing the elements of your dilemma to the essentials of the precepts. For example, in what manner did this dragon first call you to himself, by freedom or by slavery?"

"He put me in chains." Koren crossed her arms over her chest. "He said I had to stay in chains until I learned to love him."

The white dragon's eyes glowed amber and crimson. "And does that claim ring true?"

Koren shook her head. "Real love needs no chains. In fact, chains prove that love is absent by definition."

"You rely on dead definitions," Taushin said. "Listen to the voice of reason. Someone who fears the source of truth cannot understand it until she listens. If chains are required to keep her from escaping what she fears, then the chains are no more than an embrace, a shelter to keep the wayward from bringing harm to herself."

Koren searched her thoughts. Hadn't Taushin said something like that while he was in the egg? Maybe she had just reworded it and given this image a response. "But if I feared you, why would you force me to stay? That would be absurd."

"Really? If you found an injured animal, you would try to give it medical aid. Yet, if it feared you, it would bite and claw to keep you away. What would you do?"

Koren imagined an injured squirrel hissing at her as she approached. "I suppose I would keep it in a cage until it learned to trust me, or I would put a sedative in its water to calm it down."

"You have made my point," Taushin said. "I offer healing and liberty for the humans, but your fear of me is keeping you away. In such a case, chains, as for your animal in a cage, are a gift of love."

Koren looked at the white dragon, hoping for a rebuttal. Could he counter this twisted logic that made slavery appear to be something noble and good?

"Aren't you going to say anything?" she asked.

The white dragon cocked his head. "What do you want me to say?"

"Is Taushin telling the truth? Does love sometimes require chains?"

"Well," the white dragon said, "you know that the greatest love is borne of sacrifice that draws one to another freely. Yet, if you fear the light, if you cower in the presence of goodness, if you lash out at a helping hand, then what else can a loving benefactor do?"

Koren spread out her hands. "But I haven't done any of those things. They took me by force when I was trying to help someone else."

"Only to provide a greater service," Taushin said. "Your path was leading to destruction for yourself and your fellow slaves. Since I love you, I could not allow that."

Koren clenched her arms tightly in front of her as she continued to address the white dragon. "What if the helping hand is a deceiver? A liar? A fraud? I can't submit to chains when I have seen the cruelty of their keepers. Whips on the backs of children speak louder than the words of a dragon who purrs under the hand of a sadistic sorceress."

Taushin snorted. "Are we quite finished arguing between two mental phantasms?"

Koren kept her body aimed toward the white dragon but looked at Taushin out of the corner of her eye. She nodded. If that question came from the real Taushin, maybe he would be able to see her response even if he couldn't hear her words.

"Good," Taushin continued. "Then listen carefully. If you do not return to me willingly, then I will force you to return by threatening your friends. In order to achieve the greater good, Zena will send the next assault directly at them. If you surrender, she will allow them to go to the Northlands without harm."

"They wouldn't go without me," Koren said. "Jason is a warrior and a gentleman. He would follow me back to the dragon village and try to set me free."

"You have far too much confidence in this stranger from another world. You might be quite surprised at the choices he makes."

Letting her scowl dig deeper, Koren extended a pointing finger. "Don't you dare hurt Jason!"

A crooked smile bent his scaly face. "Come back to me, and you will have nothing to fear."

"I don't believe a word you say. Zena can't be that powerful." She looked at the white dragon. "And you're more powerful than Taushin, right?"

The white dragon shimmered, fading as he spoke. "I am unable to teach that which you do not already know. Perhaps it would be wise to search for answers from the source. Yet here is truth you have learned from the Code: Whatever is done because of sacrificial love will never be lost, and a lamb who walks among wolves for the sake of other lambs will never be forsaken, even if she dies." With that, the white dragon disappeared.

"Koren!"

She stiffened. The voice was Uriel's. "Yes?" she called back, rotating toward him. "I'm here."

"You have very little time to decide," Taushin said as he vanished.

Uriel's voice returned, coming from a dark thicket. "It has been more than ten minutes, so I decided to check on you. May I approach?"

"Certainly." Koren scanned the ground. She half expected to find dragon prints, but none showed up in the muddy grass. "I appreciate your concern, but all is well."

Uriel pushed between two evergreen branches and appeared in the clearing. He propped his sword on his shoulder and extended a curled arm. "Would you like an escort?"

Smiling, Koren slid her arm around his. "I would be glad of one. Thank you."

As they walked back, Uriel cleared his throat. "May I ask a personal question, Miss?"

She looked up at him. His eyes focused straight ahead. "Yes, you may."

"I noticed that you and Jason were traveling as a pair without a chaperone. Are you married? Betrothed?"

Koren laughed gently. "Neither. We were kind of thrown together. I guess you could say we rescued each other from the dragons, and we're traveling as a couple out of necessity rather than by choice. We have no … romantic attachment."

"I see." When they reached the clearing, Uriel stopped and looked at Jason, still sleeping against a tree at the opposite side. "He is a valiant young man, Miss. If I may be so bold, you would do well to consider him as more than a necessary companion. I have lived many years, and I have never seen someone his age exhibit so much courage, willpower, and sacrifice to save the life of another. He will make someone a wonderful husband, to be sure."

Koren's cheeks grew hot. "I … uh … I don't know what to say. That's a very personal issue."

"True, Miss. But I had to say it. All my years have taught me an important maxim. If you have something important to say, never waste a moment to get it said. Another opportunity may never arise."

Koren gazed at him again. His eyes, sad and gray, now focused directly on her. "That is a wise maxim."

Sighing, he let his shoulders slump. "I learned the lesson the hard way. I never said a proper good-bye to my first wife before she died, my second wife before I was sent to prison, or my son when I traveled to this planet on my current journey. If only I could have simply said, 'I love you' when I last gazed at them, I would have saved myself decades of mental torment while I languished in the white dragon's clutches."

Koren imagined Uriel sitting in a cage with manacles around his ankles, shackled to the iron bars surrounding him. Why would the white dragon be so cruel? Of course, Uriel's accommodations might not have been as terrible as she imagined, but any imprisonment had to mean that the dragon couldn't be trusted. It seemed that both dragon kings worked in the same way, keeping humans captive to get what they wanted.

"Thank you for telling me what's on your mind," she said. "You're right about Jason. He will make a wonderful husband. But I wonder if the Creator has something else in mind for me, perhaps something not so pleasant."

"Is that so?" he asked, his brow lifting. "Would you like to tell me about it?"

Koren folded her hands at her waist. "I'm pretty sure I have to work it out for myself." Tilting her head up, she looked again into his eyes. "All I ask is that you trust the decisions I make."

"Are you planning to do something besides accompany us to the Northlands?"

"I'm not sure yet." She reached out and took his withered hand in hers. "From what I have heard about your story, you know what it's like to be certain of something that everyone else believes to be insane."

He patted her hand. "Yes, my dear. Being alone in one's opinion, especially when that opinion is crucial to the survival of many, is the worst sort of captivity. Being certain that you are right and everyone else is wrong is a lonely island, indeed. Yet to venture off that island is a step that a man of noble character cannot take. His integrity will not allow him to sacrifice truth in order to gain acceptance from his fellow man."

Koren rubbed his knuckles with her thumb. "I see that your years on that island have given you eloquence."

"I had little else to do but formulate maxims." He lifted her hand and kissed it gently. "I am glad to be able to pass a few along to someone as receptive as yourself."

"You are very kind." Smiling, Koren backed away, turned, and joined Jason at the tree. After sitting close, she leaned her head against his shoulder and closed her eyes. Then, taking his hand in hers, she whispered, "You are a good man, Jason Masters, and you will make a fine husband, the best of husbands." As tears welled in her eyes, she bit her lip and silently added: *For someone else.*

seven

Jason blinked open his eyes. Uriel stood nearby with the sword drawn, looking into the forest, wary but apparently unalarmed. No rain fell. A breeze swirled about, cool but not uncomfortable.

Turning his head, Jason peeked at Koren as she slept with her head against his shoulder, a slight buzz in her respiration. She jerked, likely from a dream, but slept on.

Closing his eyes again, Jason settled his head comfortably against the tree trunk. As he drifted toward sleep, another vision materialized in his mind: Uriel standing with a girl in a dark blue cloak—the other Starlighter, the girl from Koren's tale.

This Starlighter held a crystalline peg in her palm, much like those Jason had seen at the portal. It glowed, creating a halo that enveloped her entire hand and continued swelling until it encompassed both Uriel and herself in a spherical aura. While they watched, mesmerized, a woman dressed in black approached from behind, a long dagger in her grip and murder in her eyes.

Jason took in a breath to shout a warning, but no sound came out. Zena drew closer, ever closer. The dagger's blade gleamed in the light. She raised it higher, ready to strike.

"Watch out!"

Jason opened his eyes and looked around. Zena was gone, but Uriel was still there, staring at him in the light of early dawn.

"What is it?" Uriel asked. "Did you hear something?"

Jason shook his head. "Sorry. It was just a dream."

"What was it about?" Koren asked, still leaning on his shoulder, her eyes trained on the forest.

"Zena was about to stab Uriel and Cassabrie."

Koren pulled away and looked at him. "Were you there, too?"

"Yes, but in the vision I couldn't do anything to stop her. I think my hands may have been tied."

"We should go." Koren climbed to her feet and reached for Jason, her face now tense.

He grasped her hand and allowed her to pull him up. As he rose, the folded Starlighter cape he had used as a pillow dropped to the ground. He picked it up and looked at the pair of green eyes embroidered at the left breast. Moisture on the threads sparkled against the deep blue background.

He shook out the cloak and held it at arm's length. "So green eyes are one of the signs of a Starlighter."

She turned to the side. As he draped the cloak over her shoulders, she nodded. "One of the signs, yes."

He smoothed out the damp creases, noting the tone in her tight muscles. No wonder she was able to hoist him to his feet so easily. "I know another green-eyed girl who has an unusual gift."

"Elyssa?" she asked, turning to meet his gaze.

Again, those green eyes sparkled. "How can I tell if she's a Starlighter?"

Koren combed her fingers through her damp tresses. "Is her hair as red as mine? When I saw her, I couldn't tell. She was soaked."

"Not so red. More like auburn. Elyssa is what we call a Diviner, but I thought it might be the same thing."

"Maybe her gift is similar." Koren averted her eyes, but not before a tear glistened.

Jason leaned to get a better look at her face. "Is something wrong?"

She wiped the tear and stepped away, fanning out her cloak. "Taushin is speaking to me again."

Uriel walked over from his post. "Does that mean Zena knows where we are?"

"Maybe," Koren said. "Let's just head north. I don't feel safe here."

Uriel extended the sword and belt to Jason. "I think you slept just under two hours. If Zena finds us, are you rested enough for another battle?"

Jason wrapped the belt around his waist. "I think so. I feel pretty good."

"Since dawn is breaking, we will be able to see danger coming from afar, but only if we travel out in the open rather than in this forest."

"Where a flying dragon could spot us?" Koren asked.

"Dangerous creatures can hide in these thickets, dear girl. We can scan the skies for dragons. One skill they lack is stealth."

"We'll stay out in the open," Jason said. "We can follow the river and walk close enough to the forest to hide quickly in case a dragon comes."

"Agreed. As a horribly unskilled poet once said, 'In my eyes, it is wise to compromise.'"

Jason grimaced. "That *is* pretty bad. Who was the poet?"

Smiling, Uriel bowed. "At your service."

"Well, Sir Poet," Jason said, laughing, "can you tell me how far it is to the Northlands?"

Tilting his head upward, Uriel set a hand on his chest, as if ready to deliver a pompous speech. "By steps a many, I marched aplenty, a pair of days in one. I slept but a little; my body's not brittle. I traveled by moon and sun."

"Okay." Jason stretched out the word. "What did that mean?"

Uriel held up a pair of fingers. "Two days is my guess, but I made it in one. I never stopped to rest. Whatever was in the air in my prison fueled my body well."

"Speaking of fuel, we'll have to find food on the way. Do you know what's edible around here?"

"I do," Koren said, her eyes scanning the brightening sky. "Please. Let's get moving. Taushin is driving me crazy."

"Okay. We'll go." After sliding the sword into its scabbard, Jason led the way out of the forest and back to the stream. The flow had settled to a gentle tumble over and around the riverbed's varied collection of rocks and boulders. The slower-moving sections appeared to be no more than a foot deep.

Staying on the forest side, they marched quietly single file along the bank, Jason in front, Uriel at the rear, all three a step or two from the water and about ten steps from the trees. The grass under their feet had been flattened, and pebbles lay scattered throughout the turf, obvious signs of a recent flood. Although wet, the ground was solid enough, very little mud to catch their sodden shoes. Each squishy step raised a multitude of odors, most earthy or moldy, yet carrying a hint of freshness, as if the rushing waters had unearthed new life.

To their right, on the other side of the stream, an endless field of taller grass waved in the breeze. Sprinkled with short bushes sporting green leaves and yellow blooms, the meadow seemed inviting, much more so than the dark woods.

Keeping a hand on the sword's hilt, Jason glanced from forest to sky to river to field. Whatever Zena had in mind, he had to be ready. Who could tell what a sorceress might be able to brew in these strange lands?

Soon, Solarus appeared at the field's horizon. A blinding ball of reddish orange, it forced Jason to squint. Every glance painted spots in his vision, and they seemed to take the shape of stalking beasts walking in the field stride for stride with them.

Shaking away the images, he scolded himself. Those were fear-induced. *Stay focused. Battle real enemies. Don't waste energy on imagined ones.*

As a dry breeze brushed their clothes, Solarus warmed their skin. Jason scanned the sky again, more carefully this time. Not a trace of a cloud marred the blue canopy, no sign of Zena's plot anywhere.

Koren pulled Jason's sleeve. "Look!"

Jason halted and followed her pointing finger to the stream. The flow had stopped. No, it had reversed. The water drifted slowly northward, its movement almost imperceptible as the breeze licked the surface.

"Impossible," Uriel said. "Gravity is not a respecter of sorcery. Not even Zena can alter it."

Jason kept his stare locked on the gurgling flow. "You reversed the river at the portal."

"That was science, not sorcery. I set up a lever that tilted the land, and the reversed flow would last only until the reservoir emptied. I didn't reverse gravity."

A snarl sounded from the field, deep and menacing.

Jason whipped out his sword. "Did you hear that?"

"I heard." Koren spread out her arms, fanning her cape. "I'll tell a tale that will summon a company of phantoms. A beast will not know the difference."

"Wait," Jason said. "Let's see what it is."

A wolf emerged from the grass and stalked toward them, almost twice the size of any wolf on Major Four. At least five more rose to join the first, each one with teeth bared and ears pinned back.

Jason waved an arm and shouted, "Leave or die!"

"Shall I take Koren to the woods?" Uriel asked.

"No one is taking me anywhere!" Koren lifted her arms, spreading out her cloak again. "I am a Starlighter!" she shouted. "Beasts of the field, approach ye not. I summon all Starlighters past and present to attend to me now."

A second Koren appeared to her left, then another to her right, both exact copies of herself standing in the same pose. Many more replicas materialized; twenty, thirty, fifty. And unlike Cassabrie and the other phantoms in the forest, these seemed solid. As she continued speaking, a chorus of Koren-like voices reverberated. "Go back to your mistress, or my sisters and I will overwhelm you."

Jason shifted away from the real Koren and stood in front of one of the copies, pretending to guard her. If those wolves attacked, confusing them might be Koren's only chance.

As the lead wolf stepped into the river, the northward flow accelerated. The wolf paused, but only for a moment. Along with three growling allies, it began a slow advance.

Jason swiped his sword back and forth. "If you devils are Zena's minions, maybe you can understand my words. If you want to keep your throats intact, don't take another step."

The lead wolf paused again. Its ears pointed upward as if listening to something in the breeze.

"Taushin is speaking to me," all the Korens said. "He says if I begin a southward march immediately, Zena will call off the wolves. She has fifty more getting into position."

Uriel pointed. "I see them. Some are crossing the stream, north and south."

Jason glanced both ways. Indeed, wolves were creeping toward the forest side of the water, perhaps a hundred paces in each direction. Yet something else lay to the south, an object floating toward them on the reversed stream. Was it the raft he had seen earlier?

"We can't fight fifty wolves," the Korens said. "They want me. Let me go south, and you two can get help in the Northlands."

Jason looked at the army of Starlighters. Which one was the real Koren? Turning and facing the wolves had made him lose track. He regripped the hilt and set his feet. "Not a chance. I'll die before I let them take you."

"But, Jason," the chorus said, "if you die, I will die, too. If I go, Taushin won't kill me. He needs me."

The lead wolf and three others splashed to the river's midpoint and halted—snarling, panting, drooling.

"Zena awaits your decision," the Korens said. "You have five seconds."

The wolves on the forest side closed in from both directions. They would arrive within those five seconds easily.

"Three seconds," the Korens announced.

The raft floated between them and the wolves approaching from the east, bouncing over rocks in the shallower areas. A voice shouted from it. "Get on! Now!"

As the raft stayed in place, defying the current, the wolves leaped past it and attacked. Jason yelled, "Uriel, bring Koren!" He marched into the wolves, slashing with his sword. Standing in knee-deep water, he sliced through the lead wolf's throat. With a backswing, he whacked off another wolf's head. Finally, he plunged his sword into a third wolf's chest, but the fourth jumped and clamped its jaws over his arm.

Something jerked Jason's sword away, and the blade swung at the wolf. Its body fell into the stream, though its head stayed latched to Jason's sleeve, its teeth embedded in the cloth.

Uriel stood in the water, panting, Jason's sword in hand. "We must hurry," he said as he sloshed toward the waiting raft.

Dozens of wolves charged into the stream from the forest side, each one dragging a passive Koren replica through the current. Breathless, Jason looked at the raft. Koren stood upon it watching her copies being hauled away. Uriel hacked at two other wolves before hoisting himself aboard.

Jason trudged toward them, knocked one of the wolves away with a forearm, and leaped onto the raft. A surge of water swept them northward. Two more wolves lunged for them. Uriel swung the sword at one and sliced into its snout, knocking it back. Jason punched the other across the side of its face. It, too, fell.

The raft glided along, too swiftly for the remaining wolves to follow. The rough water forced all three humans to sit on the wet, splintered wood, Jason and Uriel at the raft's two back corners and Koren near the front.

Jason glared at the wolf's head, still dangling from his sleeve. Its beady, malice-filled eyes stared back at him. With a quick swipe, he slapped it off into the river.

Behind them, the retreating wolves continued dragging Koren replicas southward. As before, the cloaked girls didn't struggle. Being mindless clones, they felt no pain or fear. Even as they shrank in the distance, some of the copies began to vanish like evaporating fog.

"Is the bite severe?" Uriel asked.

Jason poked a finger through a rip in the sleeve. "It broke the skin, but it's not bleeding much. I think I'll be all right."

Uriel turned the sword around and extended the hilt with his shaking hands. "Take it. I'm too jittery to hold it any longer."

"I know what you mean," Jason said, taking the sword. "That was a close one."

"That, too, but I meant the voice. Remember what I said about ghosts?"

Jason nodded. "Did you see one?"

"Heard one. Didn't you?"

"I heard someone say, 'Get on.' For a minute it sounded like it came from the raft, but I guessed it was Koren, and the water made her voice bounce somehow."

"It wasn't Koren." Uriel pointed at the logs, bound together by vines. "The voice definitely came from the raft."

"A talking raft?" Jason asked. "That's ridiculous."

"Who said anything about the raft talking? I meant the ghost. But either explanation is no more ridiculous than water flowing upstream or a raft rescuing us from sorcery-crazed wolves in the nick of time."

Jason ran a finger along a knot in one of the vines. It seemed similar to the knots he and Adrian used when they made a raft only a few months ago. "I get your point. So many strange things have been happening lately, this just seemed like another one."

"Which leads me to a crucial question," Uriel said. "If there really is a ghost, then where is it?"

"I am here, Uriel Blackstone."

Jason turned toward the voice. It seemed to come from the gap between himself and Koren, too small of a space for anyone to sit. "Who's there?"

A wisp of light sparkled, and the outline of a girl dipping into a curtsy flashed in his sight and instantly vanished. "My name is Cassabrie."

"Cassabrie the Starlighter?" Jason asked.

"The same."

Uriel trembled, a hesitant smile growing on his face. "Are you a ghost?"

"In a manner of speaking. A spirit would be a better term. Yet I am more real than the other female apparition on this raft."

Jason looked at Koren. She stared back at him, her expression forlorn. As her body faded, she said, "Trust me, Jason." Then she disappeared.

"No!" Jason pivoted and searched the field to the south. The wolves and their prey were nowhere in sight. He climbed to his feet and balanced on the rollicking raft. "Cassabrie! Let me off! I have to save Koren!"

Uriel snatched Jason's pant leg and yanked him down. "The wolves would just kill you. Then where would we be?"

"I can't stay here!" Jason clenched his fist so hard it shook. "I can't let those wolves drag her back there!"

Uriel reached around Jason's head and pulled him close, almost nose to nose. "Listen, son! Think about it! Koren intentionally let the wolves take her away. She knew we were no match for them, and she knew you would fight to the death to rescue her. The only way to save everyone was for her to sacrifice her freedom."

Jason pulled back and slammed his fist on the raft. "How can I sit here and ride to the Northlands knowing she's in their clutches?"

"It's the only way, Jason," Cassabrie said. "When we arrive, we will get the help we need. Until then, any effort would result in failure and death."

Jason looked at the source of the calm voice, a sparkle in the midst of empty air. Here was the spirit of a dead Starlighter speaking without a body, guiding a raft after reversing the stream's direction. And all of this was taking place on a world ruled by dragons.

As he unclenched his fist, he slowed his breathing. He had to calm himself and gain control. Cassabrie knew so much more than he did, dead or alive, and if going to the Northlands was the only way to save Koren, he would have to allow Cassabrie to lead the way.

"Okay, Cassabrie. You're right." After taking a deep breath, he let it out slowly. "Tell me what we'll find in the Northlands."

eight

Elyssa sat on a cold stone floor, her back against a wall, her legs extended straight in front of her, and her wrists and ankles bound by sticky black rope. With the mysterious energy source only a few steps away, the mesmerizing influence had again drawn her into a clouded reality. Was it really a human body? It certainly appeared to be.

Suspended about a foot off the floor and dressed in a white gown and blue hooded cape, the red-haired, green-eyed girl stared straight at them. With the exception of a missing finger on each hand, she appeared to be a normal human, perhaps in her mid-teens.

A circular, transparent plate had been embedded in the ceiling above her as well as in the floor below. If not for the angle creating a glare on the surfaces, the plates might not be visible at all.

Elyssa studied one circle, then the other, forcing herself to focus. About twice the size of dinner plates, they emanated a soft humming sound, as if energized by an unseen source. Could they be nonmetallic magnets that held the girl in place? At home, magnets were little more than toys for children or a means to attach notes, and none seemed capable of attracting or repelling human flesh.

A bright aura surrounded the girl's body, like a fine mist of electromagnetic particles that streamed away in all directions. As the particles passed across Elyssa's skin, the foggy sensation heightened. She felt somewhat lucid, but judging one's own mental state wasn't always a good idea. She could be completely daft and unable to recognize it.

Fighting against the influence helped, but weariness dragged her down. The few hours of sleep she and Wallace had stolen before entering the dragon's village seemed very long ago, especially with the strange energy sapping her resistance. Yet every rest brought another wave of hypnotic euphoria and with it a sensation of danger. Letting herself go might send her into an ecstatic ride of bliss from which she would never want to return.

As the shadow of Thortune, their dragon guardian, passed across her body, Elyssa shook away another cloud. She had to keep battling. Clear thinking was her only hope.

Next to her, Wallace sat in the same pose, his limbs also bound. At times, his eye seemed glazed. Poking him with an elbow usually shocked him out of his slumber, but how long would that work? He needed mental stimulus.

"Wallace," Elyssa whispered. "Stay with me. Fight it."

Wallace blinked several times. "I'm fighting, but it's like swimming in mud."

"I know. Concentrate. Think about something else."

"Like what?"

"Like how to escape. I'm thinking about biting through this rope."

"Better not," he said. "It's coated with laxie syrup."

"Laxie syrup? What will that do?"

"First, it will burn your tongue off. Then it will spread into your throat and down into your stomach. Before you know it, it'll eat holes in your gut and make you bleed to death."

"Lovely." Elyssa looked at the black gunk smearing her wrists. "Why doesn't it burn my skin now?"

"It's moisture activated, but it takes quite a bit to set it off. Try not to sweat."

"Thanks. I'll remember that."

Thortune growled. "No talking between yourselves. Magnar's orders."

"If we can't talk to each other," Elyssa said, "can we talk to you?"

"Perhaps I will allow it, if you do not become impertinent."

Elyssa nodded at the girl. "Is that Cassabrie the Starlighter?"

Thortune chuckled. "Even if I had knowledge of that creature, why would I give away such information? I am a guard, not a fool."

"I heard one of the dragons call her that. I am merely verifying it. At my young age, would I be familiar with that name and suspect who it is unless I had already heard it?"

"A good point. I will grant you that."

"Then maybe you can tell me how you avoid being affected by her influence. I can feel her dulling my senses."

"Other dragons are affected by this Starlighter, so I was selected for this duty because of my impenetrable mind."

Elyssa pressed her lips together. Probably stupid dragons were too dense to be penetrated by the particles' energy. If he really was lacking intelligence, maybe prying for more information would bear fruit. "How does a girl's dead body emanate these energy particles?"

"You have proven how little you know. She was a Starlighter. If you had any knowledge, that would be all the explanation you need."

"I realize that a Starlighter is very powerful when she is alive. But dead?" Elyssa laughed under her breath. "Come, Thortune. Either you don't really know, or you must think I'm pretty stupid."

"The second option suits me. I can see that you are trying to lure me into providing you with information. If you believe that I will comply, then you have proven your stupidity."

Elyssa forced herself to keep a straight face. Maybe this dragon was smarter than he appeared. Maybe he really had an immunity for a reason other than a dense skull.

She gazed at the girl, still lovely in spite of her ashen skin and gaunt face. How long had she been there? Months? Years? Somehow the dragons had figured out a way to preserve her body, or perhaps her Starlighter powers preserved it for her. The pulsing energy probably had something to do with it. Yet, without sustenance or a beating heart, how could her body radiate unceasing light? It seemed impossible.

"I will be back in a moment," Thortune said. "Have no thoughts of escaping. I am not leaving the tunnel." He shuffled toward the exit and spoke a strange word in the dragon language. The wall slid to the side, and after he passed through the opening, it slid closed again.

Elyssa tried to copy the word. She had heard it earlier when the dragons brought them to this place, but, as Wallace had warned, humans were incapable of creating exactly the same sound.

She leaned close to him. "Are you still with me?"

"Sort of. I can't tell if I'm dreaming or not. For a minute I thought I was floating over a river watching Jason being attacked by wolves. It seemed so real. But a second later I was back here." He opened his eyes wide. "Am I dreaming now?"

"No. You're fine. But if you really were dreaming, then you couldn't trust me when I'm saying that you're not dreaming. Right?"

"I suppose so. But if this isn't a dream, then you're thinking clearly. How do you fight it so well?"

"Practice. I was chained in a dungeon for several weeks, and suffice it to say my captors weren't the best housekeepers. So I trained myself to shut out certain input. I suppose it was a blessing that they fed me barely enough to survive." She gave him a quizzical look. "You saw Jason?"

Wallace nodded. "He was with Koren and a man I've never seen before. I think Jason said his name was Uriel."

"Uriel? Uriel Blackstone? Have you ever heard that name before?"

"No. Why?"

"I have a hunch." Elyssa focused again on Cassabrie. Could Jason be with the real Uriel Blackstone? How could that be? Uriel Blackstone would have to be well over a hundred years old. Yet the vision had to come from a source other than Wallace's mind. Had the energy particles provided Wallace with a view of something real? Could the Starlighter's body be a gateway of some kind? Maybe the particles were pieces of visual reality, and her own probing abilities could search through them to see what was going on.

Elyssa blew out a sigh. There was only one way to find out. She nudged Wallace. "Stay alert. I'm going to let the influence take me. Snap me out of it in about three minutes."

"All right. I'll try. Don't punch me if I have to hurt you to wake you up."

Elyssa smiled. "I won't. My hands are bound."

She stared at Cassabrie's green eyes, glassy, yet penetrating. Closing her own eyes, she probed the floating body with her mind. As the energy particles bathed her face, they drew her toward the source. Like a kite being taken by the wind, Elyssa let her mind go, hoping Wallace could keep hold of her lifeline.

She rushed to the pulsing light and splashed into its center. For a moment, brightness blinded her, but it soon cleared, giving way to a river. As if riding in a boat, she floated with the current. Trees rushed by on her left and a flower-filled meadow on her right, giving the impression of swift travel. No one spoke. Only the sound of tumbling water and rushing wind came through.

As the view bobbed and shifted, more of the panorama came in sight. She seemed to be sitting on a raft made of logs bound by vines. Jason sat near the back edge to the left, and an elderly man balanced himself at the right. With every bump, water splashed, and the two riders gripped the sides more tightly. Although both looked dirty and weary, they seemed in relatively good health. A bit of blood stained the upper part of Jason's right sleeve, torn at the bicep, maybe the result of a recent battle. His fist and teeth were clenched. He was clearly upset.

Elyssa studied the scene. The elderly man was likely the same one Wallace had noticed. Was this Uriel Blackstone? And where was Koren?

Jason looked directly at her and said, "Okay, Cassabrie. You're right. Tell me what we'll find in the Northlands."

"Elyssa!" someone hissed.

Jason and the older man began drifting away, and the river scene blurred.

"Elyssa!"

The bright light again blinded her. As she rushed back from it, Cassabrie's body came into view, floating between the magnetic plates.

A sharp pain in her ribs snapped her to attention. Blinking, she turned to Wallace. "That was a pretty hefty jab."

"You weren't waking up."

"Silence!" Thortune lumbered toward them and slapped Elyssa with a wing. The claw at the end caught her hair and jerked through it painfully. "I told you not to converse."

As Elyssa's eyes locked on the dragon's, something odd happened. His countenance took on a relieved aspect, as if his brief journey to check the exit tunnel had confused him, and now he had returned to normal.

As Thortune breathed the charged air deeply, she studied his heightening satisfaction. Maybe he was chosen for this task because exposure to Cassabrie sharpened his mind instead of the opposite effect. This dragon wasn't immune to the energy source; he was addicted to it. If he was accustomed to being absorbed in her power, what would happen to his mind if he could be persuaded to leave for more than a few minutes?

"In your great wisdom," Elyssa said, "did you and your dragon cohorts discuss how to provide food for us or what to do about ..." She searched for an impressive phrase. "About bodily waste elimination?"

"You will likely both be executed. It is inefficient to feed condemned prisoners."

Elyssa felt Wallace flinch. The poor kid was trying to be brave, but such a menacing pronouncement would chill anyone. "Well," she said, keeping her voice stern, "we still have bodily elimination systems to consider, and I, for one, have to use that system. I'm confident that you don't want the odor to foul the air here. Am I correct?"

"You are. We cannot allow such odors in the Starlighter's presence. But we have no facilities for humans in the Zodiac."

"The tunnel to the Basilica," Wallace said. "I saw alcoves there that will do. You can get a drone to clean it up later."

Thortune snorted, mumbling something about troublesome human habits. "Very well. I will follow you into the tunnel, so do not think you can use this as a ploy to escape."

Elyssa extended her hands. "Cut our bonds."

"What?" Thortune scowled at her. "Why?"

She faked an impatient huff. "Dragons might have no problem going around naked, but we humans wear clothing that gets in the way. I can't drop my trousers while my hands and feet are tied."

Thortune swiped a wing claw through the rope around her wrists, then through the ankle bindings. After doing the same for Wallace, he walked toward the exit tunnel. "Stay close and silent. Remember, I can kill you quickly in a variety of ways."

Her brain still awash in dizziness, Elyssa climbed to her feet and helped Wallace to his. When Thortune opened the wall, she glanced at the crevice where it had disappeared. What could she do to keep him from closing it? A distraction?

They marched through, Thortune leading the way. As soon as the dragon turned back toward the opening, Elyssa hurried ahead. "I'll see you in the other tunnel," she called behind her.

Thortune shouted, "No!" but she kept up her pace, not too fast, hoping he wouldn't think she was trying to escape and blast her with a volley of flames, but fast enough to make him give chase.

Seconds later, a stiff wind blew her hair, and a shove from behind knocked her forward. She stumbled and landed on all fours.

"Foolish girl!" Thortune said as he settled next to her. "What were you trying to do?"

Elyssa suppressed a smile. Her plan to keep the wall open had worked. "I told you I have to go."

Wallace arrived and helped her up. "She's just like that," he explained. "She does things without warning. It's hard to get used to."

"She had better alter her ways," Thortune said. "The next rash move will be met with fire."

Now walking with Thortune in front, they entered the room with the sharp stakes. The ceiling, which doubled as a floor for the corridor above, was closed, leaving the room dim. A single lantern at the entrance to the Basilica tunnel provided the only light.

Thortune slowed and looked both ways. With his ears and wings twitching, he seemed nervous, confused. When he found his new heading, a straight path toward the Basilica tunnel, they passed by the stakes.

Elyssa dropped back an extra step or two, snatched up one of the stakes she had broken, and hid it behind her. Wallace quickly shifted between her and the dragon.

As Thortune continued walking, he curled his neck back and stared at her. "What are you doing this time?"

She pushed the point of the stake into the waistband at her back and folded her hands in front of her. "Following you."

He stopped and sniffed. His eyes glazed over, and his head swayed with his neck. "You are not being truthful. I can sense it."

"Why? I *am* following you, just as I said."

"You are hiding something. Turn around."

Elyssa fidgeted. Thortune was losing his wits. If only she could delay him a little bit longer. "Turn around? Why?"

His head swayed erratically. "Just do as I say."

As Elyssa began to turn, she glanced at Wallace and tried to communicate panic with her eyes. She needed his help, and she needed it now.

"I have to go!" Wallace ran toward the tunnel. "I'll see you in there."

Thortune looked that way and roared. "Come back here!"

Elyssa grasped the stake, jumped in front of Thortune, and rammed the point into the soft spot in his underbelly. The dragon belched a ball of fire at her, but she jumped out of the way, leaving the stake partially embedded. Now staggering, he launched a weak stream of flames at her, this time swiping her sleeve.

She lunged at Thortune and, shoving with all her might, thrust the stake as far as it would go. Grasping the butt end, she jerked it back out and leaped away.

As thick fluids poured, Thortune doubled over. Elyssa ran to the Basilica tunnel, still clutching the stake.

Wallace batted sparks from Elyssa's sleeve, while both watched the scene. Thortune, gasping and gurgling, staggered from one side of the chamber to the other. For a moment, he paused, teetering. His expression twisted with puzzlement, as if he couldn't understand why Elyssa had attacked him.

Finally, he toppled over and crashed into the stakes, breaking several with his tough scales. After twitching for a few seconds, he moved no more.

Wallace's jaw dropped open. "Now what?"

"Now we go back to Cassabrie." Elyssa tossed the bloodied stake next to Thortune's body. A wave of remorse swept over her, but she shrugged it away. The dragons were probably going to kill her and Wallace. She had no choice.

"Are we going to take Cassabrie's body?" Wallace asked.

"I don't know if it's even possible, but I want to study her and figure out what's going on. They're saving her for some reason, and I doubt it's a good one."

Elyssa ran past Thortune's carcass, through the tunnel, and into the Starlighter's room. She paused in front of Cassabrie and stared at her lifeless body. With her long white dress and dark blue cloak adorning her in fine array, she appeared to be ready for travel, though she likely hadn't moved from this spot in years.

As Elyssa gazed at the lifeless visage, a similar face entered her mind, just an outline, a vague memory. Somehow, Cassabrie seemed familiar, someone she had met before. Who could it have been? Koren, maybe? They did look a lot alike.

Elyssa knelt and peered at the disc embedded in the floor's oddly angled tiles. Underneath its transparent surface, seven glowing spheres, each about the size of a small acorn, floated in a slowly orbiting circle.

She bent back and looked at the large disc well above Cassabrie's head. It, too, held a circle of tiny orbs, making it seem as though Cassabrie wore a crown.

Wallace knelt at the opposite side. "What are they?"

"I was going to ask you that." She set a finger close to the surface. A tingle spread across her skin — not strong, but enough to make her pause. "The top is so clear, it looks like it's not even there."

Wallace reached out and touched it. The pad of his finger flattened as he pressed harder. "It's there."

"Does it hurt?"

"Not much." He pulled back. "But I got those pictures in my mind again."

"Let me see." Elyssa lowered her finger, but it passed into thick liquid, as if she had poked a hole in jelled water. A storm of images flashed through her mind, so fast she couldn't recognize anything.

Digging deeper, she touched one of the spheres and plucked it from its orbit. She drew it out and set it close to her eyes. The stream of images continued, but not quite as fast. Jason and Uriel flew by, along with other people she didn't know. "This must have something to do with a Starlighter's power."

"Cassabrie doesn't look any different," Wallace said.

Elyssa stood and stepped backwards. Cassabrie's radiance flowed unabated. "I guess taking one isn't going to hurt anything, and it might help us find Jason."

"Why couldn't I put my finger in?"

She turned her gaze to the sphere once more. "I assume because you're not a Diviner."

Wallace joined her and touched the sphere. He jerked back and sucked his finger, grimacing. "Not being a Diviner is getting worse all the time."

"Don't talk with your mouth full," Elyssa said. "It's not polite."

Wallace withdrew his finger and shook it. "Should we try to get Cassabrie out of here?"

"I don't think so. These spheres might be keeping her body intact." She gave him a nod. "Let's go. As quietly as possible. Through the other tunnel and into the Basilica. We'll have to scout for an exit from there."

"So you don't have to use your bodily elimination system after all?"

"I do, but I can wait."

"Me, too, but not very long."

With Wallace leading the way, they hurried into the tunnel and followed the series of lanterns, dimmer than before. The tiny sphere's energy, now swarming like bees over Elyssa's body, dizzied her mind worse than ever. Although she fought the influence, the march through the passageway felt like a dream. The walls seemed to close in, warped and surreal, like a charcoal drawing that reshaped at a whim.

When they reached the end, they found it blocked by a flat stone. Wallace laid his palm on it and examined the gaps at the edges. "Magnar said something about blocking the exits, but there's some space here. I think I can squeeze through. Obviously he meant to stop Arxad, not a slave boy."

"Makes sense."

"What about you?" Wallace said, pointing at her.

Elyssa lifted her tunic's hem, revealing a belt tightening her oversized trousers around her waist. "I ate only dungeon gruel for weeks. I'll make it."

Wallace dropped to his belly and snake-crawled through a gap at the lower-left corner. After a few seconds, a whisper passed back through. "Your turn."

Clutching the sphere in her fist, Elyssa copied Wallace's method and slithered on her belly. After clearing the stone, she scrambled up and whispered, "Quietly now."

Wallace kept his voice equally low. "There are two open doors. I heard a dragon talking in one direction, so we'd better go the other way."

"You lead," she said, again trying to cast off the fog. "I'll follow."

As Wallace skulked toward a tall, dark archway, Elyssa shadowed him. Odd guttural sounds drifted into the room from behind her, raising prickles on her neck. A woman laughed, then spoke in a mixture of unintelligible grunts and clicks, but the name Koren came through clearly.

Elyssa wanted to pause and listen, but they had to go on. Whoever was back there wouldn't be friendly.

Wallace stopped. Elyssa joined him at the observation railing they had seen earlier. Below, in the auditorium-like chamber, a fire burned on the floor at the front of a stage near a lone pedestal, upon which an open book lay.

She looked at Wallace, hoping to avoid speaking the obvious question—how to get down. He responded with a head gesture and soft-stepped to a gap in the railing. Leaning out, he grasped a rope and brought it back with him as he straightened.

Elyssa scanned the rope, letting her gaze follow it upward. It hung from a large bell far above. She shook her head, signaling the danger.

Wallace whispered, "Don't worry." He took off his shirt, stuffed it behind his belt, and, gripping spaces between the stones in the wall, scrambled up. With the agility of a monkey, he grappled the bell and tied his shirt around the clapper, then shinnied down the rope. The bell lifted, but only a dull thud sounded.

As Wallace hung at a point just above Elyssa's head, firelight from below flickered across his bare torso. His rippling muscles glistened with sweat as he extended an arm. "All I need is your wrist. I'll carry you down, so you don't lose that sphere."

"You go ahead. I can manage."

"I'll see you there." As he slid down the rope, Elyssa glanced between him and the bell above. It wavered just enough to let out a series of thuds, like gentle knocks on a metal plate.

Still, Elyssa cringed with each knock. She looked back into the dark room. The voices had ceased. Were the speakers listening and wondering what those odd noises might be?

Finally, Wallace touched the ground and released the rope. Elyssa grasped it with one hand and pulled slowly until the clapper touched the bell again. Then, easing her body forward, she swung out over the room below. Again the bell knocked. Again she looked back. The voices resumed, now more animated.

As she loosened her grip, the rope slid through her hand. Her skin burned, but that didn't matter. Getting caught would bring far more pain.

When she reached the floor of a dim hallway, Wallace met her. She opened her hand and let the sphere's radiance wash over his face, revealing a tense jaw and tight lines in his forehead.

"I see another door. Let's go." He hurried through the corridor and into the auditorium. As she followed, she looked up. At the railing above, a pair of blue eyes emanated beams of light, and two voices conversed in the strange language.

Elyssa lowered her head and closed her fist around the sphere. Maybe the shadows would cover her, but did Wallace notice the onlookers? Would he stay quiet?

As she tiptoed along, no one shouted. The two voices continued as if unalarmed. When she reached the pedestal and book, she paused and glanced at the text. It appeared to be gibberish, but as she let her gaze rest for a moment on the page, a whisper rose from the odd words.

"If humans do not survive the plague, only dragons will remain."

Elyssa raised her brow. Now *that* was interesting. She glanced up at the blue eyes again, still in the same place. Maybe they couldn't see this far in the dark after all. She closed the hefty book, tucked it under her arm, and hurried to catch up. Then she and Wallace skulked through a massive doorway and into another dark corridor, out of sight.

He stopped and, taking quick, shallow breaths, whispered. "Did you hear those two talking?"

"I heard, but I couldn't understand."

"The dragon language. A human woman was talking to a dragon. Apparently neither one of them could see us. It's like they're both blind, because the dragon said, 'When Koren arrives, she will see for both of us.'"

Elyssa pondered his words for a moment. Was Koren really coming to this place? She pushed the book against Wallace's side so he could feel it. "I picked this up back there. Can you *read* the dragon language?"

"Some. But won't it slow us down?"

She studied the worn cover. Should she tell Wallace about the whisper? Maybe not yet. "It might be worth it."

"If you say so." Wallace pulled the book from her. "Come on. I think I know where we are." He strode toward a dim light in the distance.

Elyssa followed once again. After turning into a lantern-lit hallway, Wallace stopped and backed against a wall. "I was right. The Basilica's main entrance."

The corridor opened into a courtyard bordered at the far end by a tall fence of iron bars and a sturdy gate. "Locked?" she asked.

"Probably. Guarded, too. I see a dragon."

As she stood close to Wallace, the sphere's light particles seeped between her fingers and flowed across her skin, again fogging her brain. "Are you able to think clearly?"

"As clear as muddy water," he said. "Do you have a plan?"

"Working on one. I saw how well you climb. Can you get over that fence while carrying the book?"

"Easy, but only if that dragon isn't scorching my backside while I'm climbing."

"Okay. Get going. I'll make sure he's distracted."

"What are you going to do?" he asked.

"Trust me. Get over the top and then help me if I need it."

"Help you? How?"

"I don't know yet. Just stop stalling. My brain's already fuzzy enough."

Wallace tucked the book under his arm and marched ahead. Elyssa followed, staying back several steps. When he reached the sunlit courtyard, he dashed toward the bars and scrambled up.

"Stop!" the dragon shouted. "Stop or die!"

"Wait!" Elyssa jogged into the courtyard and headed straight toward the dragon, the morning sunrays making her squint. "Someone is trying to take Starlight!"

The dragon swung toward her, now only a wing's length separating them. "Take Starlight? What are you talking about?"

Elyssa displayed the sphere in her palm and allowed the energy to stream over the dragon. "Look. I found this. Haven't you heard about Cassabrie and these little balls that hold her in place?"

Wallace vaulted over the pointed tops of the iron bars and dropped to a gravel path on the other side.

"Halt!" The dragon shot a bolt of fire at Wallace, but he leaped out of the way and rolled on the path.

"No!" Elyssa cried. "What harm can that boy do out there? He doesn't have the Starlighter's energy. I do."

The dragon looked at her, blinking. "Are you a Starlighter?"

"Of course not. Hurry and open the gate. I'm not allowed in here."

"You must be reported ..." The dragon's speech slowed, taking on a slur. "Reported to Magnar."

"Magnar?" Wallace said as he climbed to his feet. "Are you serious? If you don't want to get in trouble for letting a human in there, you'd better let her out. Hurry!"

The dragon shook his head hard. "No! You will both stay with me, and I will investigate this matter."

"But how?" Elyssa asked. "Every human is locked down, and every available dragon is searching for the escaped assassin. We can't allow a human to remain here. You know what might happen."

"I do?" As the dragon stared at her, his eyes turned glassy.

Elyssa narrowed the gap between them and held the sphere closer to the dragon's face. The energy flowed over him, making him blink rapidly.

She lowered her voice to a whisper. "Open the gate. We have very little time."

The dragon continued staring for a moment, his head wavering at the end of his long neck. Finally, he staggered to the gate and blew a thin stream of fire at the lock. When it began to glow, a click sounded, and the gate swung ajar.

After shifting out of the way, the dragon sat on his haunches, like a silent sentry awaiting his next orders. Taking long, quiet steps, Elyssa glided past, hoping to avoid any sudden move that might jolt the dragon out of his daze.

Wallace took the hint and stayed silent. He pulled the gate fully open, giving Elyssa room to step through. As she passed by, she whispered through clenched teeth, "If you have a place to hide, lead the way … right now!"

Still walking with furtive steps and carrying the book, Wallace navigated the path toward a downward slope. The gravel crunched under their shoes, making Elyssa cringe. This had to be the slowest escape in history. At any moment the dragon might snap out of his stupor and fry them, but they couldn't break into a run. Not yet.

Soon they reached the bottom of the slope, out of the dragon's sight. Elyssa exhaled, maybe for the first time since they passed through the gate. It seemed possible that this crazy plan might actually work, but what would they do next? She had always been one to plan far ahead, so plodding forward without an idea was unnerving. The only thought that came to mind was simple: *Find Jason.* But how? Which direction? Was he even still alive?

She took in another breath and pressed on. One step at a time.

nine

Jason set his bare feet into the shallows and helped Uriel push the raft toward the eastern riverbank. The water chilled his skin and plastered his trousers against his legs. As a cool breeze raised goose bumps on his arms, he steeled himself. He had to get used to it. The cold would only get worse as they pressed farther northward.

Although he had dressed reasonably well for a chilly climate, his two layers wouldn't be enough for the conditions Cassabrie had described along the way—thick layers of snow and ice-covered streams.

He gave the raft a final shove. Whether or not his wardrobe was enough, whatever it took to save the Lost Ones, he would do it, no matter how cold the path.

"Well done," Cassabrie said from the raft. "Are you ready to walk? You and Uriel seemed to sleep pretty well while we traveled."

Jason strode out of the river and retrieved his boots from the raft. "I think so. If the wolves don't track us, we should be fine."

"I don't see why they would," Uriel said. "They got what they wanted, and tracking us at this point would be nearly impossible."

After putting his boots on, Jason looked back at the river, now flowing gently southward again. Cassabrie warned that the water to the north had surely piled up, and she couldn't push the river upstream any longer. Soon, the flow would burst into rollicking rapids and possibly flood past the banks. They would have to move well away and walk north from this point on.

After Jason and Uriel hid the raft in a patch of high grass, Jason surveyed the landscape. High ridges covered with lush trees and amber stone spilled blue waters into a valley of verdant grass. Flowers of gold, crimson, and sapphire decorated the greenery as if brushed out in curving swaths by a carefree painter. The path to the Northlands was everything Cassabrie had promised.

He checked his sword belt and nodded at Uriel. "Me in front and you in back?"

"A good plan. And what of Cassabrie? How will she travel?"

"I can walk," she said, "but not as swiftly as you can."

Jason spread out his arms. "Is it possible for me to carry you?"

"In a manner of speaking." As Cassabrie walked toward Jason, her body reappeared. When she stopped, only her arm remained visible as she reached for his shirt. "I can dwell inside you."

His top buttons began unfastening, apparently on their own, though a wispy outline of fingers flashed in front of them every few seconds.

Jason backed away. "What are you doing?"

The upper half of his chest now exposed, a blue light pulsed over his left pectoral muscle. "I need your permission of course, but— " Cassabrie gasped. "My finger!"

Jason looked down at his chest. "*Your* finger?"

A pair of hands appeared. As Cassabrie wiggled her fingers, a gap became evident where each ring finger should have been. "Two are missing. I never found out what happened to them, but I recognize the energy coming from your skin. It has to be my finger."

Jason touched the glowing patch. "I suppose it can't do you any good now."

"No, but it makes me wonder if it can do *you* some good."

"What do you mean?"

Her hand brushed against his chest. "It could make my presence within you easier to bear. Allow me in, and I can guide you silently. No one will know about your secret helper. After I have settled within, you will feel no pain. In fact, you will feel peace and comfort, and you won't have to slow your progress to wait for a plodding disembodied girl."

"Begging your pardon," Uriel said. "How do you know this to be true?"

Cassabrie's hand vanished. For a moment, she said nothing. Only a hint of a sparkle gave away her presence. Finally, her voice returned in a whisper. "Adrian told me."

"Adrian!" Jason reached for her hand but swiped only air. "Were you with him? Where is he now?"

Her voice chirped like a songbird's. "Fear not, Jason. I rescued him from death, and he is now searching for your brother Frederick. You have another purpose to fulfill, but I'm sure your paths will cross soon enough."

Making a fist, Jason glared at her vaporous lips. Anger scorched his brain. This girl was hiding something, but it wouldn't do any good to fly into a rage.

After taking a deep breath, he uncurled his fingers and spoke slowly. "Where did Adrian go?"

Cassabrie laughed merrily. "I cannot see anything beyond what you and Uriel see, so I have no way of knowing. I can only urge you to continue on your journey and do your part. If you allow me to reside within you, I can smooth the path, and I promise to do all I can to help you find Adrian when the king's purpose for us is fulfilled."

Jason searched for any hint of deception in the invisible girl's voice. When he looked at Koren, her eyes communicated so much more than mere words, but without a view of this Starlighter's eyes, detecting insincerity seemed impossible. During the raft ride, Cassabrie had mentioned the king, a white dragon in the Northlands who would help them, but she had said little else about him, only that he was good, yet mysterious.

Jason sighed deeply. What else could he do but press northward? Maybe the white dragon would be able to help them find Adrian and Frederick. No one else seemed to know where they were. And Cassabrie had been helpful so far. She seemed to have no reason to lie about residing within his body.

"Okay. You may enter. We do need to hurry."

A sparkling arm stretched toward his chest. The end pressed against the glowing patch and drilled through, raising a tingling sensation. As more and more sparkling light streamed into the patch, the glow brightened, and warmth crawled along his skin, then penetrated deeply.

Soon it seemed that his insides had caught fire. Sweat dampened his skin. He grasped his shirt and flapped the material, allowing cooler air in. As he fanned himself, Elyssa's pendant bounced at his chest.

Uriel squinted at him. "It seems that Cassabrie packs quite a punch."

"She does." Jason continued flapping his shirt. "I guess I don't have to worry about cold weather."

A soft laugh drifted through his mind, like a tinkling bell calling from within. *No need to worry, Jason. After I am settled, I will be able to regulate the warmth.*

Jason titled his head. The voice wasn't audible, though it seemed as real as any external sound. "Did you hear something, Uriel?"

The old man shrugged. "Only you jerking your clothes like your chest hairs are on fire." He peered at Jason's open tunic. "Hmmm.... Your skin's as red as a pomegranate, except for the blue light flashing and that pretty necklace."

"It's Elyssa's." Jason quickly refastened his shirt, hiding the pendant. "I think it worked. Cassabrie can talk to me without anyone else hearing her. That might come in handy."

But you will have to speak to me audibly, Cassabrie said. *I am unable to read your thoughts.*

Jason nodded. "That could be a problem."

"What could be a problem?" Uriel asked.

"That. I'll have to let you know when I'm talking to Cassabrie. Otherwise you'll think I'm crazy."

Uriel mumbled, "Maybe I already do," and marched northward, angling away from the river.

Jumping into a quick stride, Jason followed. As he closed the gap between himself and Uriel, the blazing heat eased, but soothing warmth remained. It seemed so strange. He was carrying another person inside. How could that be? Yet it didn't feel cumbersome at all. It was comfortable, even cozy, just as she'd promised.

As the soothing effects deepened, he gazed at his surroundings. Flowers of pink and purple dotted a carpet of lush green, a far cry from the tufts of thick grass and stunted trees they had left behind. Why would the dragons live in a desertlike region when this verdant beauty spread out like a sea of fertility for miles and miles? Of course, Koren's tale explained why their own region had become desolate, but why hadn't they simply moved here?

The details especially drew his attention. The flower petals seemed alive, some so long they looked like purple banana peels while others resembled tufts of blue cotton bunched in sets of five. A cool wind combed over the living rainbow and pushed the hues into a dance. As the flowers swayed, he longed to spread out his arms and sway with them, enjoying their splendor.

Jason shook his head hard. Dance with flowers? What was he thinking? It was time to march with his face set to the north, not fritter away time by ogling vacuously at the scenery. Surely exhaustion was setting in.

Now walking stride for stride with Uriel, Jason spoke up. "Any idea how far it is from here?"

Uriel let out a low humph. "Are you talking to me or that little sprite?"

"You, but either one of you can answer if you know."

"My guess is about five hours," Uriel said, "depending on how fast we travel."

Cassabrie's lilting voice returned. *That is a good guess, Jason. I pushed us pretty quickly up the river, so we might be even closer than that, perhaps three hours.*

"Three hours. That's not too bad."

"Are you hard of hearing?" Uriel asked. "I said five."

"Cassabrie said three. I was answering her."

Uriel wagged his head. "Well, excuse me for butting in."

Jason pulled Uriel's arm, stopping him. "Why are you so grumpy all of a sudden?"

"Look, young fella," Uriel said, jerking away. "I stayed locked up in that white dragon's castle for decades, and now this elfin spirit who claims to be Cassabrie comes along telling us to sashay right back into his clutches. She's twirling around in your head, putting you all in a tizzy. That doesn't make a lick of sense."

"Then why are you staying with me?"

He tapped a finger on Jason's chest. "You're my last hope. Someone has to make sure you don't fall into a trap."

"Do you have a plan?"

Uriel stared at him for a moment before answering. "Since that talking fairy dust can hear me, I'll keep my own counsel. Just make sure you ask me my opinion before you make any quick decisions."

"I can live with that."

Uriel shrugged to straighten his shirt. "Very well, then. Let's get back on track."

As they hurried onward, still angling away from the river, their legs brushed through the flowers. Lovely scents filled Jason's nostrils, again drawing his mind into a rapturous mood. If only he could stay and drink it all in.

He bit his lip hard. He had to stop this nonsense! What had gotten into him?

Jason, Cassabrie said softly. *What's wrong?*

He ignored the question. Answering her would just get Uriel riled up again. Maybe she was influencing his thinking process, causing him to take notice of details and the beauty in the world he normally took for granted, the details Elyssa always noticed. As children, even when they were as young as six, she often urged him to absorb, as she put it, the Creator's bounty.

He reached under his shirt and pulled the pendant into his palm. The symbol of a bird flying from open hands seemed so eloquent. Release. Escape. Liberty. That's what he and Elyssa had come for. That's what Uriel strived to keep. That's what Cassabrie died to bring to others.

Shaking his head, he dropped the pendant back to its place. Although Uriel was probably wrong about Cassabrie, who could blame him for being suspicious of the white dragon? It made sense to let him be skeptical. Freedom was too important to lose now.

Jason, Cassabrie said. *I understand your silence. You are very much like your brother. I will be patient and speak with you only when you wish.*

Jason nodded. She could probably detect that gesture. Questions about Adrian burned in his mind, but they would have to wait.

He kicked one of the cotton-like blossoms, scattering hundreds of floating seeds. Just three more hours.

❧

Koren dropped from the wolf's jaws and fell heavily to the tile floor. When she rolled to her back, the wolf leaped and straddled her. As he panted, hot saliva poured in a long string from his dangling tongue to her chin.

Glaring at him, she wiped her chin with her cloak and scooted back. "Keep your spit out of my face!"

As the wolf's yellow eyes focused on her, he licked his chops and continued panting.

"Be kind to Hoya, my dear, or he might leave some teeth marks on that pretty face."

Koren grimaced. Zena. More trouble, but she expected as much. Angling her head, she caught sight of the sweeping black sheet Zena called a dress as she glided across the Basilica's theater-room floor.

"Hoya!" Zena said, clapping her hands. "Return to your kennel."

The wolf backed away and loped toward the room's exit.

Koren sat up and wiped her chin again. Furrowing her brow, she gave Zena the fiercest stare she could muster. "Okay, I'm here. What do you want with me?"

"Merely what you were born to do, to fill the position you have been prophesied to take." Zena reached out a hand and helped Koren get up. Her fingers were cold and moist. "You will be Taushin's eyes."

Koren took a step back. "And what exactly does that mean?"

"You will soon see. I will summon him in a few moments."

"What about Jason? Did you let him go?"

Zena laughed softly. "I have no way to harm Jason. I have no idea where he is. It is you I can track, because Taushin made a partial connection with you. Yet, if Jason returns, we will kill him."

Koren looked into Zena's black eyes. Her comment was a setup. The wicked sorceress wanted her to ask why it was *partial*, but the reality of it was all too plain. The prince had spoken to her mind from far away. Although it already seemed impossible to escape his call, that wasn't enough. He wanted complete control.

"Since you can't find Jason," Koren said, "your sorcery is as blind as you are. That's rather a bitter potion after all you've sacrificed to be a dragon's puppet."

Zena slapped her across the face. "I can see well enough to deal with the likes of you."

Refusing to flinch, Koren tightened her hands into fists and maintained her glare. Tears welled, but she dared not wipe them. "I hope that made you feel better."

"It did indeed." Zena turned toward the open doorway. "Wait here. I will return with your new master."

When Zena disappeared, Koren glowered at the theater's perpetual fire. "Your new master," she said, exaggerating Zena's condescending tone.

She stared at the flames as they consumed a knee-high pile of logs. The crackling fire radiated luxurious heat over her body. After being dragged across a river by a huge wolf, then over a bumpy meadow, into a watery gateway at the barrier wall, and through the village on its rough streets, the hot air massaging her chilled, bruised skin felt wonderful. Now her cloak and hair would have a chance to dry, and her arms and legs could bask in warmth until her shivers calmed.

"And calm your nerves," she said in a whisper. The only way to battle Taushin's influence would be to stay strong and confident, and resting here for a while and gathering her strength in mind and body would help. Yet her heart longed to be back on the river with Jason, braving the elements for the sake of her fellow slaves.

She took a step forward, used her toe to nudge a metal ring embedded in the floor, then shifted her toe to touch an altar. The wood felt dry and rough. How many of those slaves had knelt here, drugged into a stupor, to receive a new Assignment from the Separators? How many had felt the lash of a whip when they responded too slowly to dragon demands to kneel, rise, or march?

The crack of a whip sounded. A human cry echoed. Koren cringed. Her gift created nightmares from which she could not awaken, tales of woe that would not be silent. What could she do but use every moment to end the cruelties that generated the haunting images?

Turning toward the stage, she looked at the empty pedestal to the right of the altar, where the Separators' book should be. Zena hadn't mentioned its absence, though she must have noticed.

Koren shivered. Maybe the job of the Separators was finished. With the rise of the new king of the dragons and the prophesied killing of all humans, they wouldn't have need of the Separators' book. And with the dark secrets contained on the book's pages, its keepers likely hid it away somewhere. Koren lowered herself to her knees and folded her hands on top of the altar. Dragons considered this a position of humiliation and defeat. That was perfect, exactly how she felt.

She looked toward the dark ceiling, too far away to be seen, and spoke softly into the rising warm air. "Creator of All, ever since the image of the white dragon appeared in the forest, I've been thinking about what he said. He couldn't help me much, because I know so little about him. I couldn't put words of wisdom in his mouth beyond what I already knew. He was just a phantom who responded with my malnourished understanding. And that made me wonder. I have most of your Code memorized, and I suppose that's good, but do I really know you? I follow what it says the best that I can, but is there more?"

She sighed deeply, glancing at the open doorway before continuing. "Maybe you let me get dragged across the countryside by a wolf to get my attention. Well, it worked. I'm talking to you now, and I'm willing to listen. Please give me guidance. I'm about to do something that's scarier than anything I've ever done. I'm going to submit myself to chains, to a dragon who will use me to oppress and maybe kill my own people. But if I don't, he and Zena will murder Jason and Uriel and spoil any chance they have to gather the slaves and escape to the other world. So what am I supposed to do?

"How can I serve Taushin and still be true to the Code? I can't fake allegiance. He probes my mind, but

I don't know what he can see or hear inside my head. Can I deceive him? It might be dangerous to try, and the thought of acting as his puppet is nauseating. If the prophecy is true, then his purpose is to kill every human. How can I possibly submit to such a wicked end, even in pretense?"

Tears welled in her eyes, and her voice cracked. "Creator, please tell me what to do. The Code has taught me many valuable principles, but no matter how much I search my memory, I can't find anything that applies to this situation. If you can't speak to my mind, then send the white dragon and let him tell me. You know I'll do whatever you say. Just don't let me ..." She swallowed. The words entering her mind seemed foreign, as if erupting from somewhere she had never explored. "Just don't let me suffer and die for no reason like Cassabrie did. If I must die, let my blood fall to the soil of a planet that has sent every slave safely home. Knowing that my efforts have contributed to that cause, I will die without hesitation, without regret. Even though the chains on my wrists will be pulled by a wicked being, the chains on my heart will always be in your hands."

She rose from her knees and looked at her wrists, where manacles had rubbed her skin raw. Soon those horrid things would be back. Too soon.

After a few minutes, Zena appeared at the doorway and walked into the firelight. In her bony hand, she dragged a thick chain that split into two thinner ones leading to a pair of manacles. "Hands out," she said without emotion.

Koren stretched out her arms. Her sleeves rode up toward her elbows, exposing her wrists. Zena clamped the manacles in place with a metallic click. Koren blinked. It sounded like the closing of a door that would never open again.

"The prince is here," Zena said. "I recommend that you tame that sharp tongue of yours."

Koren leaned to the side to see around Zena. The fire cast undulating light across a small dragon, perhaps a fifth of Arxad's size. Narrow blue beams flowed from his eyes and scanned the room. With his wings spread low and sweeping the floor, he shuffled slowly toward them.

"Welcome, Taushin," Zena said. "We are over here. Just follow my voice."

Koren stepped closer, her heart thumping. Although she had figured out that Taushin was blind, actually seeing the proverb come to life brought a pulse of excitement. The hatchling from the black egg did, indeed, have a handicap. How should she receive him? Maybe pretending to serve him gladly would work, at least for now.

The young dragon beat his wings, lifting himself slightly off the floor, and glided to Zena's side. His blue eyebeams swept past her and landed on Koren's face. The moment the light touched her skin, an odd sense entered her mind—something drilling in, probing. It caused no pain, but it filled her with the chill of exposure—cold air with no warm blanket to wrap around her body.

She raised her cloak's hood as far as possible, shadowing her eyes. Any amount of protection felt better than a sense of nakedness.

"Ah!" The dragon's eyes locked on her own, pushing the beams deeper into her mind. "There you are, Koren."

"I am glad to meet you face-to-face," Koren said as she dipped her knee. "Pardon me for saying so, but you told me you are blind. How are you able to recognize me?"

"I am blind visually, but I can use your eyes. Once the connection is complete, you will be my surrogate. As a Starlighter, you will serve as better eyes than I would have had naturally. You will provide a view of the present and the past."

The drilling continued. Koren turned her head away, hoping to obstruct his view. "What is your goal?"

"Freedom. I have come to provide liberty to every species."

She turned her head back toward him. "Really? Why does one of your own prophets say otherwise?"

"If you are referring to old Tamminy's doggerel," Taushin said with a laugh, "he has sung that ballad for centuries, and it has degenerated into a doomsayer's dream in the minds of dragons and humans alike. If we want to live with courage, then we should not heed the ramblings of one who cowers at every cloud looming on the horizon."

She clutched the fringe of her cloak tightly. "So what do you want me to do?"

"Your service," Taushin said in a pleasant tone, "will begin here. You might have noticed that the Separators' book is missing. Zena has confirmed that no official business has called for its removal, so we assume that an intruder has stolen it. It will do the thief little good. It is merely a record of slave Assignments along with some history that no one will comprehend. Yet some of that history is crucial for my purposes, so I will need you to conjure its contents with your gifts."

"How can I? I know nothing about it."

"Every word in that book has been spoken in this chamber. As a Starlighter, you will be able to gather the echoes from the air around you. Since this is a skill that you have not yet exercised, I will give you some time to practice."

Koren let his beams enter her mind again. It was so hard to hold him back. He was powerful, seductive. Even his call to learn a new skill sent shivers of excitement crawling from head to toe. Of course she wanted to learn. Of course she wanted to master a Starlighter's arts. But what would it cost? How could she become powerful without falling into this mind-bender's trap?

Forcing a kindly smile, Koren dipped her knee again. "Thank you, Your Highness. I appreciate your patience and longsuffering."

"*My* longsuffering?" Taushin asked. While Zena stooped and attached the chain to the floor ring, the dragon's blue eyes seemed to laugh. "Dear Starlighter, it is not I who will suffer if you are slow to learn. It is you and your fellow slaves. When I return, I will explain why their lives depend on your cooperation, and you will learn to put away your false smile and serve me with your heart."

ten

Sitting cross-legged with her back against a tree, Elyssa propped the Basilica's book on her lap. While Wallace knelt at her side and looked on, she rubbed her finger on the leather cover, feeling an embossed symbol that looked like a pair of dragon eyes, yellowed and worn, hovering above a pair of human eyes.

As her skin drew in the feel of the designs, her Diviner's sense interpreted the chemistry. The yellowing didn't appear to be a result of age. The dragon eyes were actually painted that way. The human irises had once been green, but now only a few flecks of green paint remained. The cover felt old—very old—but since she had no experience gauging the age of leather, it seemed impossible to guess how old it might be.

She kept her fingers curled around the sphere, hoping to block its influence for the moment, and opened the book to the first page. A bold title filled most of the top half, apparently several carefully shaped letters spaced into two words.

"That's easy enough," Wallace said. "Book one."

She pointed at the lines underneath, smaller letters but equally neat.

He spoke slowly, pausing as he deciphered. "This ... record ... ordered by ... Magnar the ... uh ... large, I suppose."

"Great?" Elyssa offered.

"Probably. Magnar the Great ... will be written ... to give an account ... of events as they ... hmmm ..."

"Something not clear?"

"I don't know this word," he said, pointing. "It might be their word for rain, but since it doesn't rain much, I don't hear it very often."

Elyssa mumbled the phrase. "To give an account of events as they rain."

"I guess that sort of makes sense," Wallace said.

"Sure. As events rain. As they transpire."

"That works, but if we have to read like this, it'll take forever."

"True. I was hoping this might give us some clues that will help us find Jason, but we can't afford to study it for days." She thought again about mentioning the book's whispers, but out in the daylight, the events in that dark Basilica room seemed like a dream.

Wallace pointed again, this time at a line near a lower corner. "That's a date. It looks like this was written more than four hundred years ago."

"Four hundred years! How could that be?"

"The book is awfully worn. Couldn't it be that old?"

"That's not it," Elyssa said. "Why would the Separators have a book like this for their task of separating humans before humans ever arrived? And how could the words be written so neatly by a dragon? I was guessing that a human wrote this while a dragon dictated, but now . . ."

"Now we're completely confused."

"My thoughts exactly."

Elyssa closed the book and set a finger on the lower pair of eyes. "These are human. There's no doubt about it."

"Could they have put those on there at a later time?"

She exhaled heavily. "I don't know. I just don't know."

"Would she know?" Wallace pointed at her closed hand.

Elyssa blinked. "What do you mean?"

"This might sound crazy, but I've heard stories about what a Starlighter can do, so—"

"It won't hurt to try." Elyssa shot to her feet, turned back to the tree, and propped the open book against the trunk. Then, uncurling her fingers, she let the sphere's energy flow over the text. As the particles began fogging her senses, she stared at the page. The odd words stared back at her, unchanging.

"I don't know if this is going to work, Wallace, it's just—"

"Look!" Wallace thrust a finger toward a grassy gap about four paces away. A man sat on a three-legged stool, leaning over a small wooden table and holding a quill. He dipped the point into an inkwell and began writing with great care. When he came to the bottom of the page, he stopped, as if frozen.

Elyssa reached out and turned the page. The man turned his page as well. When the paper settled, the man disappeared, and a new scene slowly took shape. It looked like a village of some kind with shops, cobblestone streets, and leafy trees lining the walkways on each side.

"This is the first story in the book," Wallace said, pointing at the page. "It starts with, 'One hundred years ago today.'"

"So this is an event that happened five hundred years ago."

"That's my guess."

"I'm going in," Elyssa said. "Turn the page whenever the action stops." She rose and walked toward the image. Holding the sphere in her open palm, she extended her arm to keep the energy flowing back to the book.

As she entered the scene, the energy enveloped her mind. She was really on the street, walking on cobblestones.

A woman emerged from a shop. Dressed in an ankle-length skirt of dark blue and a white long-sleeved tunic, she could have easily passed for a middle-class employee in Mesolantrum, perhaps a headmistress of a school or the overseer of peasant labor in the governor's palace.

The woman turned back to the shop and called out, "Timmon, come out immediately."

A small boy hopped through the doorway. "I want to look at the dragons. I've never seen baby ones before."

"You saw them. That should be enough. Dragons are workers, not pets."

After the mother and son hurried away, a man walked out from the same shop, rolling a cage behind him on a cart. Two small dragons lay within its thick bars, one reddish-brown and the other a lighter brown with scarlet tones blended in. With their necks intertwined and their bodies nestled close, they appeared to be siblings, perhaps newly hatched.

As the man drew close to Elyssa, she lifted a hand to ask a question, but he walked by without noticing, and the cart passed right through her leg.

"Okay, then," she muttered.

She followed him to the end of the street where another man stood next to an adult dragon. A collar had been fastened around the dragon's neck just below its jaws, and the man held a small, thin box in his palm. He glanced at it from time to time as he turned it over and over in his hand.

"Have they been measured for collars?" the second man asked.

The cart-pulling man nodded at the young dragons. "One needs a five and the other needs a one-point-five."

"One-point-five? Who ever heard of such a compliant dragon?"

"The meter actually said one, but I bumped it up a notch just in case."

The second man squinted at the cage. "I'll wager the red one is the five."

"He is. You'd better put the collar on him while he's sleeping. He bit the hatchery keeper so fiercely, it took twenty stitches to close the wound."

"A few jolts will set him straight." The second man pointed the box at the adult dragon and pressed a button. "Lower your head," he barked.

Grimacing, the dragon extended his neck downward and set his head on the street. The man climbed up the neck and settled on the dragon's back. "Pick up the cage with your claws, and fly me home."

The dragon grunted, obviously annoyed. The man pushed the button again, this time holding it down.

Wagging his head from side to side, the dragon moaned. After a few seconds, the man released the button. "No more back talk!"

The first man chuckled. "I suppose you'll be glad when these two are old enough to do the job."

"It won't come soon enough. But this old beast will make many fine pairs of boots, don't you think?"

"True, my friend." The cart-pulling man mopped his brow with a handkerchief and looked up at the sky, shielding his eyes with a hand. "If we don't do something about that star soon, no one will wear boots. We'll all have to go barefoot and wear bathing suits."

"Or roast to death. I hear the weapon is almost ready. If it works, we'll be rid of that scourge forever."

"Not soon enough. If I could, I would fly up there myself, tear it out of the sky, and throw it in the river. That would stop the worshipers."

"Not likely. We'd probably hear rumors about fish rising from the river and telling bedtime stories to the children."

The two men laughed for a moment, then froze. The sound of rattling paper reached Elyssa's ears, and, like a turning page, the scene warped and reshaped into a new vista, a row of five stalls with high ceilings and wide berths.

Elyssa looked around. Ambient light had diminished, indicating evening or early morning. She appeared to be inside a stable, though it was considerably larger than the stables at home. Chains and oversized manacles hung on a pair of iron hooks on the wall to her left. Against the opposite wall, a long rod with a sharp blade attached to the end leaned precariously.

Above the neck-high door of the closest stall, a dragon head appeared. As he extended his neck, his reddish scales glittered in the light of Solarus's morning rays, framing the black collar near his jaw.

He made an odd guttural noise that sounded like a call.

"Wallace," Elyssa said. "Help me out. What did he say?"

"He said, 'Are you awake?'"

Elyssa replayed the noise in her mind. It would be helpful to learn the dragon language, but this crash course might be too difficult.

Another dragon, more brown than red and also wearing a collar, appeared at the stall beyond the first one. As the two dragons spoke, Wallace interpreted, calling into the scene from his place at the tree.

"I am awake," the second dragon said.

"What are you doing?"

"It is dawn. You know what I am doing."

The first dragon snorted. "I have given up on prayers. We need to stop waiting for divine help and learn to help ourselves."

"These are not contradictory. This morning I focused my prayer on ideas for our escape. If you have received one from the Creator, I am willing to listen."

"Whether or not it is from the Creator, I do not know, but I do have a plan. I have learned to make a high-pitched noise that blocks the signal to my collar. I have practiced on our stalls' signal throughout the night. I believe I can neutralize it long enough to break free."

The second dragon's voice grew excited. "Then fly. Escape to the Northlands where the king will take you in."

"You can continue believing the myths, brother, but I will not leave without you. I swore to you long ago that nothing would separate us, and I will not break my vow."

"I appreciate your devotion." The second dragon thrust his neck out, as if to indicate his own collar. "Are you able to neutralize mine as well?"

"I will try, but if I cannot do both at the same time, I will teach you how to make the sound yourself. Once you learn, we will escape together."

Elyssa looked back. The stable door opened to another world, a forest scene where Wallace sat next to a tree. That world seemed so strange, distant and warped, an inadequate reflection of reality.

She squeezed her eyes closed. *Think, Elyssa. Concentrate. That's the real world out there. You're standing in a story.*

Opening her eyes again, she nodded at Wallace. "Keep turning the pages. I think we have a lot to learn."

Using his clawed hand, Arxad placed the crystalline peg in the central hole in front of the portal. Three tunnels at the rear of the chamber faded away, replaced by a swiftly flowing river.

"Excellent!" Magnar said, his ears twitching wildly as he stood next to Arxad. "After all these years, we will finally go back."

Arxad straightened and looked at Magnar. "Indeed, the door is open, but you must test your ability to return here before we both go in. Jason mentioned a genetic key, so I am concerned that the humans might have altered the return access."

"Yes, of course." Magnar stepped into the river chamber and turned back to Arxad. "Remove the peg. If all is well, it will take no more than a few seconds for me to open it. If I do not reappear, open the portal on your side."

Arxad wrapped his claws around the peg but left it in place. "My counsel is still to stay here. We can take Cassabrie and the stardrops and hide in the wilderness until Taushin resurrects the Northlands star. Then we can use her to restore the kingdom to you."

"Do you think Taushin will be so easily defeated?" Magnar raised a foreleg and pointed at Arxad. "You were the one who insisted on sparing Koren. If he captures her, and Zena trains her, her power will grow."

"Not beyond Cassabrie's."

Magnar snorted. "Your dream of reuniting Cassabrie with her body is beyond reason. You have visited her too frequently, and her charms have muddled your thinking."

"*My* thinking? If you think you will persuade the armies of Darksphere to come to our aid, then perhaps a muddled mind is a genetic predisposition."

"Your memory of human courage is defective. Being around those who are emasculated by slavery has caused you to forget the passion of a father or husband who learns about enslaved women and children. Trust me. The men will come, especially if I persuade them with a few illustrations of cruelty upon their citizenry."

Arxad flared his nostrils. "Do you intend to bully everyone into cooperation?"

"If necessary, but I do not know how powerful they have become, so I might have to return for Cassabrie. Her body, even without her spirit, will be sufficient to bring the humans to their knees."

Arxad thumped his tail on the ground. "We vowed to use her only if the prince proved to be a force of destruction."

"I made a vow not to use her unless necessary. I will be the judge of what constitutes *necessary.*"

"And you complain about my vows, you hypocrite!"

Billows of smoke rose from Magnar's nostrils. "Beware, Arxad. I will not tolerate insults."

"How else can I dredge the truth from you? You hide your intent. You conceal prophecies. You share what you know only when you find it convenient."

The smoke thinned, revealing sadness on Magnar's face. "I have protected you from many truths, brother. Perhaps, however, I should tell you one that will confirm my plan to conquer Taushin with whatever force is necessary."

Arxad released the peg. "Speak. I will not proceed until I hear it."

"Very well." Magnar took in a deep breath. "When Taushin resurrects Exodus, he plans not to seal the breach."

"What? Then how will it rise?"

"How is not important. Just understand that he is capable. We must go to Darksphere and mount an army to stop him."

"But he might accomplish this while we are gone. We must conquer him now. We will use Cassabrie and—"

"We cannot. He already has Koren. A dead Starlighter will not defeat a living one."

"Another lie? You said—"

"I said, 'If he captures her.' It was a hypothetical, not a lie."

Arxad blew out his own columns of smoke. "I am tired of your prevaricating. You have deceived me for the last time."

"Is that so? What do you plan to do, O mighty Arxad? Fight Taushin and Koren yourself?"

"I will retrieve Cassabrie and reunite her spirit with her body. I must. There has to be a way."

"Do not be a fool! You have tried for years. What will change now?"

"Perhaps you will not be here to stop me." Arxad pulled the peg out and stepped back. Magnar swiped at him with a wing, curled the tip around the peg, and slung it into the Darksphere chamber. Both dragons lunged for it. Just before it could slide into the river, Magnar stopped the crystal with a wing and held it in place.

The room's light faded. The river's rush grew louder as it bounced from wall to wall. Dim radiance from an unseen source provided enough light to see that the portal was now solid rock.

"You fool!" Magnar bellowed as he rose to his haunches. "Look what you have done!"

"What *I* have done?" Arxad righted himself. A rocky ceiling kept him from rising to his full height. A few stalactites hung at eye level, dripping water. "You caused this, with your rash actions and your plots. But, by all means, if you wish to deliver your usual harsh discipline, then so be it."

"Your dramatic posturing nauseates me. We have a crucial duty to fulfill. When that is complete, then I will decide what to do with you."

Arxad took several deep breaths, and with each exhale a plume of smoke rose from his nostrils to the ceiling. "Very well, but how did you leave this place when you last came? I see no exit."

"Strange," Magnar said as he looked up. "This chamber was not enclosed before. There was a hole big enough to fly through."

"We had better go back." Arxad swung around and blew a thin stream of fire to the side, illuminating the portal wall. While he kept the fire going, sporadically at times as he inhaled between bursts, Magnar scraped a claw along the wall. Soon the scratch of rock turned to the squeal of glass as he rubbed across something smooth.

"It is a window that allows a view to our world," Magnar said as he splayed his claws over it. "It will soon light up and open the portal."

Arxad continued breathing fire. The river roared on, but not loud enough to drown out his brother's growls.

"It is not responding," Magnar said. "It should have brightened long before now."

Arxad stopped his fiery jet. "Is there nothing the crystal can do from this side?" he asked, breathing heavily.

"Without holes, of course not." Magnar displayed the peg. "The treasure I have searched for all these years is now useless."

"Then our only escape is the river. Do you know where it leads?"

"I never bothered with learning the river's course. There was no need."

"Then that is not a solution. We could drown before we find an exit." Arxad scanned the room. "The light here is odd. Have you detected a source?"

"I believe the stones themselves contain a glowing agent. I don't see a path to daylight."

Arxad blew another jet of flames upward, giving light to the ceiling just inches above their heads. "If this barrier is new, then perhaps it is not thick."

"The dripping stalactites indicate otherwise."

"Only in our region. Consistent rain through limestone can create these formations quickly. We had such formations in tunnels before the rains departed."

"I remember," Magnar said, nodding. "How do you suggest that we punch a hole?"

"A combination of fire blasting and ramming, unless you have another plan."

"I do not." Magnar shot a torrent of flames at the ceiling. As the jets continued, the rocks glowed red, and the dripping water sizzled. A few pebbles broke away, but the barrier stayed intact.

After the fire eased, Magnar lowered his head, beat his wings, and leaped. His back struck the ceiling, shaking the chamber. When he landed again, causing another shake, a stalactite fell, and pebbles rained down.

Both dragons looked up. A slight dent marred the ceiling. "Progress," Arxad said, "but who can tell how far we have to go?"

"Does it matter?"

"No. I suppose it does not." Arxad lowered his head and spread out his wings. "I will try now. If it takes a hundred blows, at least we have water to quench our thirst."

"When we leave this chamber," Magnar said with a probing tone, "we will eventually have to return to Starlight. There is the Northlands portal."

Arxad glared at him. "You cannot use that portal. You would come out beyond the barrier wall and break the curse. Need I remind you—"

"No, you do not. Your fear of the Bloodless is a phobia that defies reason. We defeated them before; we can defeat them again."

Arxad returned his gaze to the ceiling. It made no sense to argue a point they had already debated a hundred times before. "We will discuss this later. For now, we should focus our energy on this physical prison and revisit your invisible barrier when we have to face it."

eleven

Koren stood in front of the firewood remains. The flames of the Basilica's legendary fire had dwindled to sparks, making it seem as though all of Starlight had lost its heart. Dark prophecies rushed to fulfillment, bringing an end to light and life. These were the blackest of days.

She touched the pedestal where the book had lain. For hours she had struggled to find some element of the mysterious history Taushin sought. Yet she had succeeded only in resurrecting mundane Assignment meetings, one slave after another parading in and out of the theater, each one staggering under the influence of the stupor-inducing drug. Again and again she had wept with the forlorn slaves and winced with each crack of the whip as it slapped across their backs.

The emotional turmoil had worn her out, but she forced herself on. One more time. One more trial before

Taushin returned might provide the clue she could use. Raising her hands, she called out, "Come to me, voices of the past, words recorded in the book. Show me the secrets I long for." A new thought spilled out of her lips even as it came to mind. "This time I ask the Creator of All to guide the secrets my way, perhaps even mysteries no one dared to record."

Arxad and Magnar appeared in front of her, nearly as solid and lifelike as their real forms. Holding an open metal box, Arxad spoke in a whisper. "These are stardrops. The energy they release gives a Starlighter her power."

Her legs trembling as she kept her hands lifted, Koren drew close and looked into the box. At least ten radiant white spheres sat within.

"Cassabrie collected these from Exodus," Arxad continued, "hoping to discover a way to resurrect it. Speaking tales from the outside did not work, but now it is too late to try my theory. Still, I was surprised to learn that material could be gathered from the star's outer membrane. It might be possible to use this information for other purposes."

Just as Magnar opened his mouth to reply, a familiar set of blue eyes appeared at the doorway. Koren waved her hand out of range of her vision, just in case he could see through her eyes, and sent the image into oblivion. "Taushin," she said as warmly as she could. "I have made a lot of progress."

Flapping his wings, he scooted toward her, apparently following her voice. "Yes, I know. I heard Magnar and Arxad from the doorway. Why did you not allow them to continue?"

Koren flinched. "I wasn't sure if it was important. When I saw you, I guess I got excited."

"No matter. I heard enough. This is exactly the information I required, and now I will be able to accomplish my goal. Dragons will live without fear of extinction, and I will set every human slave free."

"I don't understand. What is Exodus? And what did Arxad mean by resurrecting it?"

"Exodus is a star that hibernates in the Northlands, and I will awaken it from slumber."

Koren imagined a huge ball of fire rising from a polar cap, melting the snow and ice as it lifted into the air. "If Arxad and Magnar haven't been able to do it, how will you?"

"They are not the ones the Creator has chosen. Only you and I together are able to accomplish this. We will be a symbiosis—human and dragon as one. If you help me, I will help you. If you allow me to see through your eyes and give me your allegiance, I will liberate your people. Together, no one can stop us."

Koren slid back a step. *Symbiosis.* The word sounded like a death knell, a prison sentence that would never end. Since she was supposed to be his eyes, wouldn't he need her for the rest of her life?

An image of herself—gray, bent, and wrinkled—appeared in her mind, the only living human remaining on Starlight, led by a leash, the other end clutched by an adult dragon. She shuddered hard. The chains she wore while speaking to Taushin through the egg's black shell no longer chafed only her wrists; they clamped around her mind and scraped her soul.

Taushin extended his neck, closing the gap between them. "Are you ready to make the final connection? When it is complete, we will be able to accomplish what no one else could."

Koren slid her foot back again but kept her body in place. What choice did she have? Run and hide? Where? And if she did, what would become of the chance of freedom for all the other slaves? If Taushin's words began proving false, could she stop serving him then? Or might the connection be unbreakable?

"You are hesitating," Taushin said. "Is it not your desire to set your fellow humans free?"

"Yes, but ..." She didn't know how to finish.

"To demonstrate my good will, I will allow you to select one slave to be with you. Adult or child, male or female, that slave will be yours to direct in whatever way you wish."

"Petra." The name flew out before she could stop to think. The mute girl's face came to mind, sad and lonely. It was a good choice. Petra deserved to have an easier life. Koren took a deep breath and repeated the name with more conviction. "Petra. She is a girl who serves Arxad with Madam Orley."

"Very well." He aimed his head toward the railing that overlooked the theater. "Zena, bring Petra to us at once."

"I will, my prince."

Koren looked up and caught sight of Zena's distinctive black dress as she hurried away.

"And now ..." His voice softened to a seductive purr. "Lower your hood and expose your face."

A sudden burst of fear broke through. This was wrong. It was all so wrong. Trembling, Koren backed away. "No … No, I can't."

"Do not sour my good will, Starlighter. We will soon have Petra, and I know you would not want anything unfortunate to happen to her."

"Unfortunate?" Straining every muscle in her face, she spat out, "You monster!"

"No, Koren," he said in a calm, smooth voice. "I am not a monster. I am merely forcing my will upon you. Your obedience is for the good of all, and Petra is the first beneficiary."

Koren's cheeks burned. What could she do? She had to either submit or risk harm coming to Petra.

Taushin's eyes shone brighter than ever, and his tone firmed. "Now, Koren … Is your hood up?"

Her throat constricted so tightly her voice squeaked. "Yes."

"Then lower it."

Shaking, she pinched the trim near her ear and pushed the hood back. As the material cascaded down her hair, it felt like she had stripped away a shell of protection.

His beams again poured into her eyes. "Just as you lowered your hood, now you must lower your defenses. Allow my mind to enter yours, but not just on the surface. I must be at the center, for only then may I fully use your eyes and cognitive abilities. Until now I have seen only bare images, glimpses of light and the glory of this miracle you call vision. I was meant to be born blind, but only so that I can show the Creator's power through you, a humble girl who willingly serves me so that her loved ones can find freedom."

Koren blinked, but only once. The dragon's push was so soft and gentle, her eyes had already grown accustomed to the light. But should she continue to allow it? Was he really telling the truth? Setting her people free was the ultimate goal, the only goal, so it made sense to sacrifice whatever was necessary to bring it about. If she didn't give in, she would never know what might have happened. No one else could be the sacrifice. She, a Starlighter, had to do it. Her sacrifice was their only hope.

Taushin exhaled, sending a warm caress across her cheek. The breeze seemed to penetrate and enter her mind. A strange feeling crawled into her senses—an emotional cage, bars made of mental iron encircling her thoughts, a prison of the soul.

A competing sensation grew in response. Starting as an inkling of attraction, more of a mood than a conscious thought, the feeling grew into fervor. She wanted something. But what? Not food. Not comfort. Not companionship. Something deeper, stronger. Something that suddenly seemed impossible to live without.

Her chest tightened, allowing her to take in only the shallowest of breaths. Tears streamed. It seemed that flames licked her body. Battling the crazed obsession, she focused on Taushin's face and spoke through gritting teeth. "What are you doing to me?"

"Giving you what you need. Fear not. The embracing force that envelops you is holy."

Koren swallowed. This yearning to be set free from his grasp seemed as horrible as the embrace itself. It was wild, bestial, like an animal lunging at the bars of its cage. She tried to slide her feet back, but they wouldn't budge. She had to run, hide, get away from this violation of her senses as well as the unquenchable craving to escape.

As his voice continued to croon, his scaly head swayed, though his eyebeams never shifted. "Tell me a tale, Starlighter. What do you see?"

She licked her parched lips. "A tale? I have no tale."

"Look around. You will see."

Koren turned her head to the left. The logs erupted into a trembling column of flames, and a human female took shape in its midst. As the image sharpened, her identity became clear. With striking red hair and piercing green eyes, Koren's likeness appeared more sharply than it ever had in the reflection pond near her home.

As the replica stood in the flames, her eyes morphed from green to blue. Manacles clamped around her wrists, and chains weighed down her arms. Wearing a contented smile, the girl lifted her arms, dragging the chains higher, as if showing her pleasure at being bound.

"She's ..." Koren swallowed a lump. "She's happy."

"Of course. Did I not tell you that chains are necessary for love to be born? For the hatred in your heart had to be removed."

She forced out her words. "But I don't love you. I *won't* love you."

"You don't love me, to be sure. But you will. The chains you see in the flames are the ones you will wear—invisible but every bit as real. You are now mine, and you could not leave me if you tried. You would always come back ...

always. And when you learn to love me, the chains will become self-imposed, for you will not ever want to leave."

Koren stared at the poor girl. Her smile made her look like a fool, a prisoner who felt no chains. Showing them to her would do no good. Her ignorant bliss had blinded her to the reality of her slavery.

As she looked down, her real chains fell away and clanked to the floor. She rubbed her wrists—bare skin, still wearing the marks of the manacles. The bleeding and pain had ceased, but the shame of imprisonment remained.

Giving in to the dragon had exposed her. She was vulnerable, unable to defend herself against his penetrating presence. And now, chained to his will, the sensation set her conscience aflame. This was the burning desire, to be set free from his crushing embrace, to escape the shame of allowing herself to be overpowered.

She was again in chains, a prison of her own choosing—shame, utter shame. As the girl in the flames continued holding her chains aloft, the real Koren thrust her arms outward. *Break free, you fool! The chains aren't real!* As if her actions would help the imagined girl, Koren shifted her body in an attempt to move her own legs. *Run from this place! Escape this monster!*

But she couldn't. And the girl in the flames kept smiling that stupid smile. The real Koren's legs stayed put. The dragon who had stripped away every façade continued drilling his blue stare into her eyes.

She clenched her fists. Oh, to be free of this dragon's influence! To go back to Madam Orley and just be Koren, a simple slave girl who hauled olive oil and honeycombs for Arxad. She was happier then—as ignorant as a prancing lamb in the hills, but happier.

Taushin's voice returned, still calm, still soothing. "The battle is over, Koren, and you are mine. Fret not. As you exercise your gifts, you will grow stronger and more confident. I will have need of no one else."

The blue light faded. The drilling force drew back. As the flames subsided, her passion did, as well.

Koren took a deep breath and exhaled loudly. That was better. The awful feelings had gone away, at least for now. Yet was this quick sense of relief more of a curse than a blessing? Had she become so much of a slave that her shame of captivity was too easily lost?

Finally able to move, she took a step closer to him. Her legs wobbled, but not too badly. "So ... is the attachment complete?"

Taushin hesitated for a moment. "Complete enough for my purposes at this time."

"You said you won't need anyone else. What about Zena?"

"Do you think she is absent for no reason?" He laughed gently. "No, my Starlighter. You will take her place at my side. She has served our interests for a very long time, but she is old and nearly blind. She is no longer of use to us."

"But—"

"You need not worry about her. Her allegiance will triumph, and she will bow out with grace and honor. You will see."

"Speaking of seeing ..." Koren cast her gaze upon the doorway. "Can you see through me now?"

"It is a glorious sense, my Starlighter. I see the room's exit, but it is rather dark in comparison to the fire you were looking at moments ago."

Koren nodded. "You are learning about lighting differences quickly. It must be difficult taking in all this new information."

"Difficult? No. Delightful. And I will be able to see through your eyes no matter where you go. This is a union that I will never want to dissolve."

His words tightened her throat. *Never want to dissolve.* At first it sounded awful. But why? So far, being the new king's eyes wasn't too bad. Maybe they could set the slaves free after all. It wouldn't be the worst situation—to rule a free world alongside the king of the dragons, assuming he was as good and noble as he claimed to be.

As her own thoughts sank in, the chained girl flamed again in her mind. Koren shook her head hard. *No! Stop thinking like that! He's a monster! Evil! Hang on to what you know to be true! Don't let his mind influence you!*

"We are here." Above, at the railing, Zena looked on with Petra at her side. Although the fourteen-year-old slave stood almost as tall as Zena's shoulder, Zena fawned over her as she might a little girl or a cat, petting her hair with long strokes.

"Excellent," Taushin said. "Will you be able to fit her for a cloak?"

"I can have one ready soon."

Forcing herself to smile, Koren waved at Petra. With both arms pressed against her sides, Petra lifted a hand and offered a weak wave in return, but her face contorted with terror. Wearing her long work smock and tunic, she trembled and flinched with every touch of Zena's hand.

"Take Koren and prepare them both for the invocation," Taushin said. "I want them to be clean, groomed, and cloaked in Starlighter splendor."

"Will you have Koren climb the bell rope?" Zena asked. "Or are you strong enough to fly her up here?"

"Take her through the legacy passage."

Zena stared openmouthed for a brief moment. "The legacy passage?"

"She is one of us now. There is no need to hide anything from her."

"I will be down in a moment." Zena and Petra walked away from the railing and out of sight.

Koren looked at Taushin. With his neck extended as he returned her gaze, he seemed to be more mature now, even handsome as dragons go. His scales reflected the firelight, making the black surfaces shimmer like obsidian crystals. His snout displayed smooth lines without a hint of imperfection, giving him an air of nobility. Was he growing at a faster rate than other young dragons? Could that be part of the prophecy?

A door opened at the back of the theater's stage area. Zena appeared, hand in hand with Petra. "Come," Zena called. "There is a stairway here."

Petra broke free and ran toward Koren.

"Stop!" Zena ordered.

Petra halted at the center of the stage, wavering back and forth between Koren and Zena. Her face twisted into a mournful expression.

"Let her come," Taushin said. "She is under Koren's authority now."

Petra dashed ahead and ran into Koren's arms. As the younger girl wept, Koren—nearly nose to nose with her—ran her fingers through her hair. "Shhh. It's okay. You're with me now." She took Petra's hand. "Taushin has given you to me. You're no longer a slave. You have been set free."

Clutching Koren's hand tightly, Petra's lips moved from a smile to a frown, then back to a smile. Her blend of disbelief and joy was clear. How could a dragon, a member of the same species that had cut out her tongue, be the one who would set her free?

They walked together and met Zena at the door, a panel without a knob or visible hinges. Oddly enough, it was too small for any dragon, except maybe a youngling like Taushin. Why would they have such a passage in the Basilica?

When they entered, Zena picked up a lantern and pulled the door closed behind them with an attached rope. The passage, not quite wide enough for two to walk abreast, led straight ahead for about twenty paces before reaching a steep staircase leading upward.

As they approached the stairs, the lantern's light flickered on the walls' rectangular blocks, revealing crumbling mortar and faded paint of indiscernible hue. Dark lanterns sat atop iron rods embedded in the joints, spaced apart by about three steps. A hint of rust colored the lanterns and rods. Apparently moisture had once visited this passage. But where could it have come from? It certainly seemed dry now.

When they reached the stairs, Zena stopped and turned. "Take care. The steps are old and fragile. If you slip, you will likely fall."

She began climbing the stairs, raising and lowering her long legs slowly and gracefully. Petra followed and Koren trailed. With the lantern now shaded by Zena's body, the steps were too dark to study, but the evidence was all too clear. This was obviously a human passage, and it was old, very old.

She let her mind drift back to when she first tried to enter the Basilica. A cornerstone gave the date of construction: Starlight—2465. More than five hundred years ago. This passage had likely been here at that time, predating Jason's story about when humans arrived on Starlight. Had he lied? Was he simply wrong?

After about fifty steps, Zena pushed a door that opened into a square room with a low ceiling and only about four paces' distance from wall to wall, again too small for dragons. When Koren and Petra entered the new room, Zena pushed the door closed, this time using a knob. "These are my quarters. I do not know yet where Taushin will provide lodging for you, but for now you will wash and dress here. I will arrange for meals a little later."

Zena reached into a shallow alcove and began searching through a pile of material on a shelf. "While the two of you groom yourselves, I will make a cloak for Petra."

Koren spied a basin, pitcher, and sponge on a small table in one corner. "Come, Petra. You wash first so you can be fitted for your cloak."

While Petra stripped off her clothes, Koren turned away. How strange this all seemed. With Taushin able to see through her eyes, she had to be careful about what she looked at. Of course humans were little more than beasts in dragons' eyes, so the sight of an undressed slave meant nothing to them. Still, it seemed appropriate to secure Petra's privacy.

A small table stood against one wall, supporting a glass sphere on a wooden base, three stubby candles, a mortar and pestle with crushed brown fragments within, and a porcelain dragon statuette with a long tail and shining blue eyes—probably Zena's sorcery table.

As Zena knelt, measuring a section of linen material with a long tape, Koren stepped closer. "May I help you? I can sew."

Zena looked up. A frown slowly transformed into a hint of a smile, making her appearance less ghastly than usual. "Why, yes, you may. I have to cut this sheet according to the pattern and sew the pieces together, so an extra set of hands will shorten the effort." She returned to her work, her hands feeling for the edge of the material. "And a better set of eyes."

Koren knelt on the opposite side of the sheet. Zena's comment seemed melancholy rather than spiteful. In fact, she appeared to be sad, resigned to the fact that her position of service was being usurped.

As Zena pressed her finger on the tape, she leaned over, her nose within inches of the material. Koren touched her shoulder. "I'll read the measurement for you."

Zena looked up and smiled again, this time even more pleasantly. "Very well. We will divide the work according to your eyesight and my experience." Her dark eyes sparkled, a gleam Koren hadn't seen before. "Perhaps I misjudged you, Starlighter. You are not at all like Cassabrie. I think you will be an excellent servant for the king."

As Koren bent to read the tape, Zena's words sank in. They sounded like a gong—lovely in one sense, deep, clear, and penetrating, yet making her heart vibrate painfully. Was Zena mocking her? Or were her kind words a real expression of love? Either way, the statement clawed at Koren's senses. Did she really want to be an "excellent" servant for the king? Maybe. Maybe not. Koren whispered the measurement, then added, "Perhaps I misjudged you as well."

A shout erupted behind Elyssa. "I see dragons!"

The stall vanished. Elyssa spun toward Wallace, who had closed the book and was now pointing at the sky. "It's a dragon patrol, and it's coming this way!"

"Can't we hide in the trees?" she asked.

"This part of the forest isn't dense enough." He scooped up the book and waved. "Come on!"

As he jogged along a path that led deeper into the forest, Elyssa followed, dizzy from the sphere's influence. It seemed that two boys led the way, each one carrying the old book, and they both staggered, apparently also affected.

She closed her hand over the sphere and tried to focus, to join the two Wallaces into one. She would have to stop soon or else stumble and be caught out in the open.

After a few more seconds, Wallace turned left and ducked into a thicket, disappearing in the midst of leafy branches and brambles. Elyssa stopped and looked up through the gaps in the canopy. From the direction they had come, two dragons flew toward her, each one carrying something snakelike and sparkling in its claws.

Strong fingers grabbed her arm and jerked her away from the path. She stumbled into the bushes, landing on her hands and knees. Her fist held tight to the sphere, though the radiance continued to leak out. Wallace pushed fallen leaves over her hand, dousing the glow, and let out a long, quiet, "Shhh ..."

A sizzling noise, punctuated by pops and snaps, shot in from the path. Wallace flattened himself on the ground and hissed, "Stay down and don't move a muscle! Don't even breathe!"

Elyssa turned toward the sizzle and dropped to her belly. A serpentine line of shimmering orange light slithered toward her. About three feet long and two inches thick, it avoided various roots and branches as if alive and aware, though it possessed no scales, darting tongue, or any other reptilian feature.

Holding her breath, Elyssa steeled her body but kept her head up, still watching. The snake slid over her concealed hand and paused, as if sniffing her skin. She glanced at Wallace, who was lying on his back. A second serpent crawled over his face, covering his eye and nose as it continued a slow squirm down his chin and toward his chest.

Elyssa's serpent glided up her arm toward her shoulder. Its touch burned for a moment, then itched. When it reached her neck, it pushed under her collar and inched its way down her back. Every skin cell it touched set off an alarm. She needed to scratch ... now!

She bit her lip hard. *Just concentrate. Focus on the creature, not the itch.*

Closing her eyes, she probed for the serpent's mind. Did it even have one? Just as it began to slide out at her hip, she detected a weak signal—a simple, single-tracked purpose, like a call to anyone who looked upon it. *Fear me. Hate me. Kill me.*

So that was it. These serpents didn't detect movement, as Wallace had thought. They were sent to be killed. She reached back, grasped the snake by its neck, and held it aloft in front of her, looking straight at its blinking head. Still unable to locate any eyes, she continued to probe its mind, what little of it she could find. Its signal did nothing more than indicate its presence, but a dragon might be able to detect it.

After lowering it gently to the ground, she uncovered her fist, rose to her feet, and looked at the sky while scratching the unrelenting itches. Barely visible through the gaps above, a single dragon flew away from the area, apparently unaware of their presence.

"We're safe," she said.

Wallace threw the snake to the side and jumped to his feet. "The itch was driving me crazy!" He raised a foot to stomp the snake, but Elyssa pulled him back.

"No. That's what they want." Elyssa nudged one of the serpents with her shoe until it slithered into the bushes. Its sizzle had died away, and its skin had paled, allowing its features to clarify. Now it appeared to be a typical snake. "If you kill it," she said, "the dragons will come back."

"Is that a good guess or another Diviner's trick?"

"Not a trick or a guess. It's a deduction." She eyed the snake's trail. A few particles of sand glowed in the shallow rut it had left behind. "What were those snakes coated with?"

"The only thing I can think of would be mazerum."

"Wait a minute." Elyssa wagged her head. The dizziness had returned, and the look in Wallace's eye proved that he was losing his grip on reality. She gestured for him to follow, walked to a thick bush, and sat down, nestling close to the foliage. When Wallace settled next to her, she held her open hand over her fist. "Okay. What's mazerum?"

"It's a glowing dye," he said. "Once in a while, the miners find it while they're drilling, and we use it for working in the dark until it stops glowing." He cocked his head. "I saw you holding that snake. It looked like you were talking to it."

"Not really. It was more like reading its simple little mind. I think it was signaling the dragons. If you had killed one, the dragons would have known."

"Got it. Makes sense." He set the book on his lap and rubbed a finger across the cover. "I think our next step should be to go to the cattle camp."

"My mind feels drained. Do you have a plan?"

"Maybe. You see, there's a rumor going around that someone made a refuge in the wilderness for escaped cattle children. If that's true, it means the dragons have a hole in their security. I already knew it was possible to escape from the cattle camp. Not over the wall, though. Most of the children can't climb the thorny vines that cover them. There's another way, and Koren and I used it lots of times, but we always had to go back, because we didn't have a choice."

"Why not?"

Wallace shrugged. "There just wasn't anywhere else to go. If we stayed out, we would have gotten caught and killed."

"If escapees made it to the wilderness, would the dragons search for them there?"

Wallace shook his head. "The dragons use the camp to cull the herd, so they don't mind slaughtering the few who try to escape. If one or two get lost in the wilderness, the dragons probably think they'll just starve or be eaten by beasts."

"The sphere's glow hypnotizes dragons," Elyssa said, nodding at her fist, "so we have a great weapon. Since we have no idea where Jason is, and we have some idea where the refuge is, we should aim for the better target. If we go to the camp, we can get as many children out as possible, and then search for a place to hide them."

"It's not as easy as it sounds. We can't strut into the camp and point a glowing marble at a dragon like it's a spear. We might outwit a drone, but the guardian dragons will burn us to a crisp before we get close."

"Okay, you're throwing a blanket over your own idea. Did you have something else in mind?"

"Not really. I was just pointing out the dangers. I'm willing to try it, no matter what."

Smiling, Elyssa gave him a light punch on the arm. "The hero's heart. I love it."

His brow lifted. "Then you're willing to risk it?"

"Just lead the way, warrior." She tapped a finger on the book. "Do you think you can find a place to store this before we go?"

"Probably. I wish we could see more of what it has to say, though."

"It takes too long, and we have no idea if it's going to show us anything useful." With Wallace's help, she climbed to her feet, still a bit wobbly. "Let's see what we can do at the cattle camp, and then … the wilderness."

twelve

Koren stood near the front of the Zodiac's portico, facing the street—Zena on one side and Petra on the other. As she looked at Zena in her usual black, form-fitting dress, herself in her dark blue Starlighter's cloak with the hood pulled up, and Petra in a similar cloak, yet without the embroidered eyes, Koren felt a stab of dread. Their appearance probably incited many silent judgments from the lines of slaves filing into the outer courtyard, especially considering Koren's new garments.

She glanced at the sleeve of the dress Zena had provided, similar in cut and form to the old one, but black instead of white. It was also shorter, falling to her knees, just long enough to cover her short trousers underneath. With her lower legs exposed in front, her new black boots, lifted by a platform heel and laced in the back, rose to mid calf for all to see.

Closing her eyes, she imagined how she looked, a specter of a girl with green eyes shining from the darkness of a hood-shadowed face. Her silhouette drew the portrait of a traitor, the personification of evil wearing a dress and cape.

She reopened her eyes, unable to keep from cringing. The boots pinched more than just her skin; they pinched her heart. Her costume felt like a suffocating cage.

Holding the bag that once housed the black egg, Zena whispered in Koren's ear. "You have been without chains for a while, but that was in the Basilica. Now that you are outside, our trust in you will be tested. Remember my instructions. When the prince comes, you must guide him with your eyes so that he can land at your side. If he falters, his image will be tarnished. Do not allow that to happen."

"I will remember." Koren scanned the people streaming in from the various work camps—miners and labor children from the two mesas, dirty and hardened from their backbreaking tasks; rock haulers from the river, tanned and muscular, though bearing cuts from sharp edges and lashes from cruel taskmasters; log cutters from the forest, the strongest of them all, yet slouched as they displayed the sorrow of their dangerous occupation; and, finally, various house servants, mostly girls and older women. The women of childbearing years would likely appear at the ends of the lines, either as the camp helpmates, or slow to arrive simply because pregnancy made walking such a distance difficult.

Dragons flew in from every direction, some watching over the lines to make sure no human strayed, and some coming from the forbidden barrier wall, border guardians who looked every bit as fierce as stories about them portrayed.

The people, now numbering close to a thousand, pressed closer, and the dragons, perhaps a hundred or more, made a semicircle behind them. No human would be allowed to miss this momentous occasion, save for the cattle children, who, if Tamminy's prophecy proved true, would likely be slaughtered before the day was over.

Koren pressed her lips together. No, that couldn't happen. She wouldn't let it. Hadn't Taushin promised freedom? Yet he had made no mention of exactly which slaves he would set free. Everything seemed so nebulous, so uncertain. She was caught in a trap. Still, one advantage remained. Taushin needed her eyes. They would be her ultimate leverage. If he allowed even one slave to die, she could refuse to serve him … couldn't she?

When everyone had gathered, whispered voices sounded like wind whipping through dry grass. Some stared at Koren, including Madam Orley, who stood about three rows back. She neither smiled nor frowned, though the deep lines in her forehead gave away a host of emotions. She was worried, very worried.

Some onlookers watched with tightened fists and firm jaws, as if more angry than frightened. Koren knew the gossip flowing through the crowd had named her as the object of their fears. This kind of assembly was unique, as was her presence with Zena, so whom else could they blame? The cloaked redhead standing before them like newly crowned royalty was an obvious target.

Koren pinched the fringe of her robe near the embroidery and frowned. She did look like a pompous princess who had risen above her peers, supremely cocky and too proud to step down among the commoners. Any frightened grimace she could make to the contrary would be useless. Her elevated position as a dragon representative contradicted any verbal or facial disavowals.

Zena raised her arms and called out, "Dragon citizens and human servants of Magnar, the time we have awaited for centuries has finally come to pass. You have heard stories about the predicted arrival of a prince hatched from a black egg, fanciful tales of doom that would shame the most eloquent liar, but you have also heard wise prophetic utterances of a glorious new future that will soon prove to be true."

A low murmur ran through the crowd, followed by the buzz of whispered voices. Koren strained to listen, but the actual words seemed of less importance than the tone—fear and distrust. Most humans knew of Tamminy's dark prophecies, and those were likely causing the stir.

While Zena blinked at the sky, apparently waiting for Taushin to appear, Koren searched for Tamminy. There he was. The old dragon bard stood near the back of the crowd. Had he flinched at Zena's critical words about tales of doom? Were his own songs flowing through his mind—glorious for dragons but wretched for humans? Was he now ashamed of them?

She blinked and refocused on the humans—Taushin's orders. He had commanded her to scan for negative expressions—frowns, scowls, anything that might indicate a rebellious attitude. Yet there were so many. Which ones should she choose to focus on? Taushin had said that some slaves would need encouragement, so the dragons would round them up and bring them to her. As a Starlighter, she could tell them tales that might raise their hopes. Everyone would have to cooperate to bring about the desired future.

"Now," Zena continued, her voice rising in pitch and fervor, "I introduce to you the prince who has hatched from the black egg. Taushin!"

The dragons roared, some interspersing deep clucking noises, perhaps indicating their pity for the humans now that their doom was drawing near, while a smattering of applause radiated through the human crowd, most of it coming from those closest to the dragons.

A small shadow passed over the audience. Koren looked up and found Taushin high in the sky, flying slowly downward. It was time to provide a landing path. She whispered to Petra. "Stand behind me so he'll have room."

After Petra moved out of the way, Koren swept her field of vision from Taushin down to the floor of the portico, repeating the motion several times. Taushin had to compensate for the difference between her angle and his, but they had practiced successfully within the Basilica. Out in the light of day, it would probably be easier.

As if gifted with perfect eyesight, the small black dragon followed Koren's sweeping arc flawlessly. Then, with a graceful flutter, he settled at her side.

Koren looked him over. Indeed, he was growing quickly. With his body erect and his neck extended, his head was now out of reach of her hand, even if she stood on tiptoes. As he folded his wings, his jet black scales glistened in the light of Solarus, highlighting the lovely lines in his chest, shoulders, and flanks. He was truly spectacular. And for some reason, his eyes no longer glowed blue. They were now a blend of brown and black, typical of many dragons in the land.

He glanced at her, his ears twitching. That was the signal. He couldn't see her, of course, but he wanted to make pretense that he had no handicaps, at least until the proper time.

She took a step forward and spread out her arms, fanning her cloak. As she opened her mouth to speak, her arms and legs trembled. Maybe no one would notice. Fortunately Taushin had provided her with an opening script, but at some point she would have to speak on her own.

"My fellow humans," she called with a voice deeper and more resonant than she expected, "you know me as Koren, the servant of Arxad, the noble priest who has acted as your faithful intercessor throughout the generations. I learned a great deal under his gentle tutelage, including the fact that I am the fulfillment of a great prophecy. Some of you know the story of Cassabrie the Starlighter and how she failed in her quest to set you free from your captivity. She was a prophetess, not your deliverer. She acted as a forerunner, preparing you for the final Starlighter who would usher in the new king of the dragons, the prince hatched from a black egg."

Keeping her eyes focused on Tamminy, she paused for effect. Then, lowering her arms and pulling her cloak to herself to make it swirl, she added, "I am that Starlighter."

A new buzz passed through the crowd. Humans glanced at each other, whispering in confused or frightened tones. Koren waited for the next step.

Tamminy lifted his head higher and spoke above the murmurs. "The new king was prophesied to be handicapped. Yet this young dragon appears to be in good health. In fact, he is quite a fine specimen. If he is the expected king, what is his handicap?"

Koren resisted smiling. Taushin had predicted Tamminy's protest, almost word for word. Resuming her orator's tone, Koren kept her stare trained on the old bard. "Taushin is handicapped indeed, for he is blind, born without vision so that the Creator's power can be displayed more fully in him."

The crowd again erupted in whispers, louder this time. Tamminy gave their confusion a single voice. "How can a blind dragon fly? We all saw him maneuver with elegance and precision. It is impossible."

This time Koren allowed a small smile to break through. She grasped Petra's hand and pulled her to the front. "Can a child without a tongue communicate?" She turned to Petra and spoke to her in sign language, saying, "Tell us why you are happy."

Koren glanced at Taushin. He had said that no one would question this odd device, signing to Petra when she had no trouble hearing. It made for a dramatic illustration.

Petra used her hands to reply, making sure everyone could see her, just as she had been instructed.

Madam Orley spoke up. "That child can say more with her hands than most people can with their voices. Lacking a tongue never stopped her. She is saying that she is no longer a slave. Taushin has set her free."

"In the same way," Koren continued, "the new dragon king has overcome his handicap in a unique manner. He is able to see through my eyes."

As a hush fell over the crowd, Tamminy's scaly brow lifted. "I am sure we would all be edified by a display of our new king's abilities."

A murmur of agreement rose from the crowd, and heads bobbed like driftwood on the river.

Koren's smile faltered. Again Taushin had guessed correctly. Why were these people so predictable? They seemed like mindless bodies ready to be filled with any notion Taushin wished to inject.

Turning, she swept her arm toward Zena. "Tamminy, soon you will observe and believe."

Taushin lowered his neck, allowing Zena to place the egg bag over his head. With his face covered, he turned toward the Zodiac.

"Now," Koren said, again looking at Tamminy, "what do you wish to show me so that your new king can prove his miraculous vision?"

Tamminy extended his neck toward the dragon at his side and whispered in his ear. After the two conversed quietly for a moment, Tamminy again focused on Koren. He scraped a claw on the ground and lifted a small stone from the cobbled pavement.

"A pebble," Taushin called out, his voice muffled by the bag.

Tamminy tossed the pebble into the air and caught it in his mouth.

A laugh erupted from the bag. "They say that prophets sometimes speak hard truths, my good bard, but I do not think eating pebbles will enhance your songs."

As laughter spread from one smiling face to another, Tamminy spat out the pebble and joined in. "Well, Taushin, you have certainly made a fool out of this old bard, but perhaps you can explain another miracle. I have known Koren for quite some time. She has often paused to hear one of my poems. I will never forget her green-eyed stare of wonder. So could you tell us how she now has blue eyes? They shine so brightly, I am sure we all can see them."

Madam Orley spoke up again. "I can see them. She always had green eyes when she worked with me."

Koren blinked. Blue eyes? How could that be? Had her connection with Taushin changed her that much?

Taushin lowered his head and let the bag slide off. Then, turning back to the crowd, he spoke with a voice that nearly thundered. "Hear me, dragons and humans alike. You have seen for yourselves that I am indeed the dragon hatched from the black egg, your new king. I have overcome my handicap, and I am able to see through this gifted girl. The Starlighter's transformation is merely a sign that I speak the truth."

As another hush descended, Taushin lowered his voice. "Those who recognize my authority, those who help me establish a new kingdom, will surely be rewarded. And those who resist will fall by the wayside."

"It is not that I doubt you," Tamminy said. "I am merely wondering what Magnar has to say about all this. His control over this land has been complete and long lasting, so what of our allegiance to him? Although he has been reclusive of late, why is he not here?"

"Your question is just," Taushin said as he spread a wing toward Koren. "Our Starlighter will give you the answer and prove her gift at the same time."

Koren bit her lip. The final prediction came true. Now it was time for her to perform without a script.

Taushin backed away, signaling for Zena and Petra to give Koren room. "Now, Starlighter," he said. "Tell us a tale. Where has Magnar gone and why?"

❧

Jason trudged to the top of a snow-covered ridge and looked out over a shallow valley of white, sprinkled with evergreens protruding from the wintry blanket. With the ridge curving around the valley in an enormous circle and rising to mountains on the far side, the scene appeared to be a bowl filled with ice, snow, and …

Squinting as Solarus glittered on the frosty landscape, he said out loud, "A castle?"

At the far side of the bowl, an immense structure sat at the foot of a snowcapped mountain. Although ivory-colored stone covered most of the outside, something red coated the cylindrical shapes of three turrets on the top floor.

Uriel joined him on the ridge, puffing clouds of vapor. "Yes, that's the place—my prison. And, like a fool, now I'm marching right back into the icy enclave."

The old man's wrinkled face gave away his concern. Why should they trust Arxad's word that someone in the Northlands might help them? Maybe it was all a ploy to get them thrown into a prison so they couldn't complete their mission.

"We'll just have to be careful," Jason said, touching the hilt of his sword. "I wasn't planning to walk right up to the front door."

Cassabrie giggled. *Of course not, Jason. No one can get there on foot.*

Jason raised a finger, a sign he and Uriel had agreed upon to indicate he was speaking to the Starlighter within. "Cassabrie, I'm tired of playing games. Just tell me. Who is there?"

No matter how many times you ask me, I will not say. I am under strict orders.

"Suit yourself." Stuffing his hands into his pockets, Jason strode over the ridge toward the castle. With the first step down the slope, an odd sensation tickled his feet and began running up his legs. Was it dread? No. He wasn't scared, at least not much. Excitement? Not really. Exhaustion had drained that away miles ago. What could it be?

"You're feeling it," Uriel said. "I can tell."

"I do feel something. What is it?"

"The dragon. Whenever he was near, I got so jumpy I felt like hopping right out of my skin."

Jason shivered, casting some of the sensation away. Should he and Uriel duck under the boughs of the evergreens? If the dragon flew patrol nearby, it would be better to see it before it saw them.

After locating a forested area to the left, Jason strode quickly toward it. Unfortunately, he couldn't avoid making a trail in the snow, but if they could find some ice, perhaps a frozen river, maybe they could throw off any potential pursuer.

The snow grew so deep, they had to lift their arms and wade through waist-high powder. Jason cut the path, making it easier for Uriel. With Cassabrie providing plenty of body heat, the icy crystals didn't bother him at all.

Finally, the snow hardened, and they stepped up to a compacted path. With various tracks from deerlike hooves and feline paws, it appeared to be the main thoroughfare for this desolate land.

Uriel pointed. "It leads out of the woods toward the castle."

"I see. Straight into the open where we'll look like ink splotches on a sheet of white paper."

Go to the castle, Cassabrie said, this time with firmness in her tone. *There is no use wasting precious minutes. If you want help, that's where you'll find it.*

Jason raised a finger again. "You said I couldn't get there on foot."

You can't. Just go. You will see.

Rolling his eyes, Jason looked at Uriel. "Cassabrie says we should go to the castle—that we'll see how to get there."

"If you think that plan is best. I do prefer the comforts of the white dragon's prison to this exposure. We will not last long out here."

"Comforts?" Jason asked. "So that place wasn't as bad as you said?"

"It's all relative, my friend. I never said my accommodations were uncomfortable, only that I was imprisoned.

Whenever freedom is lost, even luxury becomes nothing more than overdressed chains."

"Was the dragon cruel?"

"No. Not at all. He was … well … I don't know how to describe it. Magical, perhaps. Mysterious. You would have to be with him to understand."

"Let's hope I can skip that experience." Jason drew his sword and followed the path. As they emerged from the forest, he looked up at the sky, so clear and impossibly blue it seemed unreal. No dragons patrolled the area, only a golden eagle drifting lazily between them and the castle.

After tramping silently for nearly half an hour, with Jason scanning the sky every few seconds, they reached a river capped by a coat of blue-tinted ice. He looked back at Uriel. "Did you cross this river?"

Uriel shook his head. "The dragon flew me over it and dropped me off beyond the ridge."

Jason set a foot on the ice and leaned his weight forward. It seemed solid. Yet Cassabrie had warned about not being able to go on foot. Falling into frigid water would be a terrible way to prove it.

"Look." Uriel pointed at a layer of snow over the ice. "Those tracks are from a hefty animal, and they go to the other side."

Jason walked to the river's edge, closer to the tracks. Indeed, they appeared to be those of a bear, and a big one at that. It had to weigh at least as much as the two of them combined. "Cassabrie?" he said, raising a finger. "What should we do?"

Well, what does the evidence indicate?

"That we can make it across without a problem."

Trust your gifts, Jason. They were bestowed upon you for a reason.

"Fair enough." Jason thrust the tip of the sword through the snow and into the ice. Again, it seemed solid.

"If turning back isn't an option," Uriel said, "we should proceed and announce ourselves. We will find hospitality in the castle."

"You mean the ghosts?"

"Of the friendliest sort."

"What about the dragon?"

"If he had plans to accost us, I think he would have done so by now."

A gnawing sensation bored into the pit of Jason's stomach. Their last meal had been too long ago. *Hospitality* sounded very promising. He exhaled, blowing a thick stream of white. "If you say so."

Stabbing the ice with the sword before every step, he walked ahead, setting his own feet in line with the bear tracks. With each footfall, the snow crunched against the underlying ice, but it held firm. Stories came to mind, tales of brave men on dangerous journeys who always encountered pitfalls along the way, like falling into an icy river, but the storybook heroes never had bear tracks to follow. After all, who would be insane enough to follow a bear ... in a frozen wasteland ... while being hunted by a dragon?

He grinned. Jason Masters would. Sure, he might end up facing a dangerous bear with sharp teeth and claws. That wouldn't be anything new. But at least he and Uriel would be dry.

After another minute, Jason's sword plunged deeply into the snow. Holding a hand up, he stopped. "No ice."

Uriel leaned over Jason's shoulder, so close his hot breath warmed Jason's cheek. "Is the river below?"

Jason pushed the sword deeper. "We must be past it. The snow is hard enough to walk on. The bear made it."

"I say we keep following the bear. Who can tell where a pond or a chasm might be hiding underneath?"

"True." Jason visually followed the trail. It continued straight toward the castle, now looming much closer than before. The red turrets on the third floor looked like three scarlet sentries ready to warn of approaching intruders, and the doorway at ground level, bordered by ivory columns on either side, seemed to open more widely as he watched. But would he and Uriel be guests … or someone's dinner? Perhaps the dragon kept bears as pets, which would explain the tracks heading that way.

After taking a cold draw into his lungs, he held his breath and listened. Not a sound, save for the lightest breeze brushing his ears and Uriel's clothes shifting. With only a field of white in every direction, no one could attack without warning, yet something in the air pricked his skin, an ever-so-slight gap in the breeze. Someone was near. Could the white dragon be lurking, camouflaged by the snow? The jumpy sensation crawled up his leg again, faster and more intense.

"Cassabrie," Jason whispered. "Do you see anything dangerous?"

I see only what you see, but I interpret differently. There is great danger, but I am not at liberty to warn you. The king's orders.

He spoke through clenched teeth. "The fate of the entire human race hangs in the balance, and you won't even tell me what you're seeing with my own eyes?"

No, Jason. If I tell you, all will be lost. I will say no more.

Jason kicked the snow, sending the sparkling powder flying. When the flakes settled, he glared at the castle. Now the entire structure seemed red. Was it anger? If so, what had gotten him so riled up? If that jumpy sensation took over, his training would be useless. He had to stay in control.

He took another deep breath. *Settle down. Remember your training. Don't let anything take you by surprise.* After counting silently to ten, he nodded toward the castle. "No more delays, but keep your eyes open for a dragon hiding in the snow."

As they followed the tracks, the ground dipped toward a swale, perhaps two hundred feet from front to back, before rising again toward the castle. Jason slowed his pace and peered ahead. The tracks stopped at a point about a dozen paces in front of them.

He halted just before the final track and touched it with the point of his sword. "Where could he have gone?"

Uriel looked up. "A bear with wings?"

Jason crouched and studied the marks. "They're perfectly formed. If this bear could fly, I think we'd see evidence of pushing off."

"I see what you mean. Some kind of smearing or elongation."

Jason guided the sword over the snow at a point ahead of the tracks. "Let's see how deep this is." He sent the blade plunging down, but nothing resisted the force. His momentum pulled him forward, but Uriel caught his arm and jerked him back.

Gasping for breath, Jason stared at the gap. "It's nothing but air!"

"White air, to be precise. It looks exactly like snow."

Sliding his feet, Jason edged closer, then knelt and reached down. His arm disappeared up to the elbow, but his fingers detected nothing below, only emptiness. It seemed warmer than the air above, more like autumn than winter.

He handed Uriel the sword. "I'm going to have a look." Pressing his hands near the last of the bear's prints, he lowered his head into the "snow," keeping his eyes open. Nothing. Nothing but whiteness. Yet a strong odor filled his nostrils—rotting flesh.

A sharp pain streaked across his chin. He shot back up, dabbed a wound, and looked at his finger. Blood.

"Scratched your face?" Uriel asked.

"A sharp rock, I guess, but I couldn't see anything. I smelled something dead, though."

Uriel propped the sword on his shoulder and nodded. "Then the bear fell in along with any other animal that happens to—"

Long talons reached out of the snow and clawed at Jason, ripping his pant leg. Uriel slashed with the sword and severed three wiry fingers from a black hand. A muffled scream sounded from below. The hand jerked back into the field of white, leaving behind the fingers and a trail of dark green blood.

Jason slid backwards. Another clawed hand, this one reddish, broke the surface and swiped, but it quickly submerged again. As if awakened by the others, more claws lashed at the open air. For a moment it looked like a pot of bubbling milk, but the field soon settled into a meadow of pristine white once again.

His hand shaking, Jason pinched one of the severed fingers and drew it close. Although it appeared to be a dragon claw at first, mammalian flesh covered the bone instead of scales.

He flung it away and stood again. "Cassabrie wasn't kidding when she said we wouldn't make it on foot."

"Has she offered a solution?" Uriel asked.

"No. She got huffy and decided to be quiet."

A shaky feminine voice drifted into Jason's ears. "Are you ready to cross, My Lord?"

"Ready to cross?" Jason shifted his eyes upward as if trying to see into his own head. "Cassabrie, you know we want to cross. And when did you start calling me 'My Lord'?"

Cassabrie laughed. *That wasn't me, Jason.*

"Not you?" Jason swiveled his head. "There's no one else around except whatever those monsters are, and I don't think they would—"

"I heard it as well," Uriel said.

"I am here." The trembling voice returned. "If you are ready to cross, please let us go. The moat is very frightening."

Jason located the source, a sparkle in the air that glittered a few feet above the snow just beyond the bear's final tracks. He slid a step forward. "Who are you?"

Like a wisp of light, a girl curtsied, hovering inches above the snow, and when her movements stopped, she vanished. Yet, with every word she spoke, sparks of light flew from her vapor-thin mouth. "I am a servant of the king. My name is Resolute, but I think this place is threatening to shatter my confidence. We should cross immediately."

Jason pondered the odd name. *Resolute*. With her tremulous voice, she didn't present the best image for the word.

"I'd love to cross," he said. "But how? We're not floating spirits."

"We have tested this fake snow cover," Uriel said. "I don't think it will hold a shoe, much less two men."

Resolute's hand appeared as it swept in an arc near the false snow. "My boat will carry you."

"I don't see a boat."

"Nor do you see me, but I am here."

And me, Cassabrie said. *Resolute is my friend from the castle. I can't see the boat either, but she always speaks the truth.*

"Has any other human ridden in this boat?" Uriel asked. "I do not doubt its existence, only its capacity."

Resolute touched her finger to her chin, making both appear for a moment. "Not that I have seen, but the king told me it will carry you, and his word is always true."

"And what of the creatures that lurk beneath?" Uriel's shivers made his voice shake. "Is the boat impervious to their attacks?"

"Certainly not." Resolute trembled, making her entire body visible. Still merely a faint wisp, her hair brushed against the shoulders of a calf-length dress. Her face appeared to be that of a teenager, perhaps fifteen or younger. "We have to be very careful or they could capsize the boat."

"Is there another way?" Jason asked, training his eyes on the smear of green blood.

"No," Resolute said. "This moat encircles the castle. Your only other option is to return the way you came."

Jason looked back at their path—a long furrow leading from the forest to where they now stood. They couldn't go back to the dragon realm, not without help. His mind zoomed through the field of flowers and flew into the land of the Zodiac. A wolf dragged Koren and dropped her in front of Zena, and the black-hearted witch laughed. Then Elyssa appeared in his mind. Where was she now? She would never rest in safety as long as she knew he was still in the dragon world. And knowing her, she would ignore any danger in order to find him. She personified courage.

He glanced at the trembling girl, still hovering over the moat. Resolute. Although terrified, she was here, ready to do whatever needed to be done. The name suited her perfectly.

Jason reached for the sword and pulled it from Uriel's hand. "It's time to go."

"And the moat creatures?" Uriel asked.

Jason pointed the sword at the path ahead. "Those creatures need to fear us." He marched straight to Resolute and lifted his leg. "Just guide my foot. Where do I put it?"

A shining outline of two hands grasped his ankle and pulled his foot to an invisible but solid surface. He pushed off with his other foot and stood unsteadily. The boat rocked for a moment before calming. "Your turn," he said, pivoting toward Uriel.

Uriel gave him an uneasy smile and shrugged. "Another impossible adventure. Why not?"

"Sit back here, Jason," Resolute said, her pointing finger appearing, "so he will have room."

Feeling an invisible bench with his hands, Jason sat while Uriel climbed aboard. They sank slightly with Uriel's weight, shifting and bobbing as he took a spot on the bench to Jason's left. Both braced themselves with one hand while the boat rocked.

Once it settled, Jason scanned the white surface, keeping his sword at the ready. If any claw showed itself, it would get a free manicure.

thirteen

Resolute picked up a transparent paddle and pushed against the shore. Again the craft bobbed, sending them lower into the white air. With the boat displacing its surroundings, its shape and size became apparent—an oval, no longer than a single bed and just as narrow.

Jason and Uriel slid toward the middle until their hips touched. Resolute, again trembling enough to be seen, remained standing at the front of the boat. Turning toward them, she let out a quiet "Shhh" and slid the paddle into the moat. She pulled against the thick matter as if paddling in a stream, but the surface didn't react, not even the slightest swirl. They skimmed along as if propelled by her effortless strokes.

With his sword angled toward the moat's surface, Jason peered over the side. No movement. No claws. Where had they gone? Why didn't they attack? It seemed that whenever he expected something to happen in this frozen wilderness, it didn't—no white dragon swooped down to snatch them away, no cracks formed in the river ice, the bear disappeared into nothingness, and now the claws didn't resurface. Not only that, an invisible girl with an odd name paddled them across an impossible body of snow.

Cassabrie spoke again, her voice no more than a whisper. *You appear to be troubled, Jason, but don't explain. It is better to maintain silence. Just let me tell you that this place has many more surprises in store, some that will lift you up, and some that will threaten to cast you into despair. The puzzles you encounter will challenge your mind, perhaps even your sanity. Prepare yourself. Pray for peace. Unlike Darksphere or even most of Starlight, this is a place that will not allow you to survive for long without an abiding peace in your spirit. Turmoil will be your undoing. Ponder these things now, for you will encounter sights even more unsettling very soon.*

Jason looked at Uriel. As he gazed over his side of the boat, his fingers clutched his pant legs, and his brow wrinkled, but he seemed to be handling the anxiety well. Resolute had disappeared, apparently no longer trembling.

Peace. Jason mouthed the word. The very idea made his skin bristle. How could he have peace while Adrian, Frederick, Elyssa, and Koren were likely all in trouble? Someone had to rescue them. And if he took too long finding this person who was supposed to help him, what would happen to those he loved?

Jason took a deep breath and forced his muscles to loosen. Even if his brain wouldn't slow down, maybe his body could pretend to relax. With all the potential disasters looming, who could really be at peace?

After a few minutes, they approached a sign mounted on a wooden post that read *Dock Here*. Resolute dug hard with the paddle, and the boat slid up onto real snow, almost hitting the sign. "It's safe now," she called. "Just step straight ahead. You can brace yourself on that sign if you need to."

Jason sheathed the sword and hopped out. He sank to his knees in snow, but the ground seemed firm underneath. The castle, now only fifty or so paces away, towered over him. Its front door, wide open to the frosty air, seemed strangely inviting. With the moat protecting the grounds, maybe they didn't feel the need for more security. But this was a world of dragons. What if enemies mounted an aerial attack?

After Uriel disembarked, Resolute led the way, walking on bare feet without making an impression on the surface. "Let's hurry. The king has long awaited your arrival."

Jason trudged ahead, wading through deep snow that thinned as they approached an outer courtyard. Within, lush grass grew in a semicircular skirt in front of four marble steps leading to the castle's portico. He stared at the odd spectacle, a summer lawn in the midst of winter's blight.

Resolute scampered up the stairs, crossed the portico, and glided through the doorway.

"I suppose we should follow," Uriel said.

Jason touched the hilt of his sword. "We'd better be ready for anything. I don't want to be a prisoner."

"Nor do I," Uriel said as he looked up at the turrets. "The castle fills me again with dread, and now I think I would choose a frosty death over loss of liberty. It's as though I have competing desires for the easiest form of torture, and they keep trading places."

"No time to analyze your brain." Jason strode up the steps. With his boots clicking on the portico's marble floor and Uriel's echoing behind him, they ruined any hope of a stealthy approach. No matter. Resolute had probably announced their arrival.

After passing between enormous ivory columns, Jason paused at the center of the doorway and looked inside. Sunlight illuminated the foyer, a massive chamber with a ceiling at least as high as three dragons lined up snout to tail, perhaps one hundred twenty feet. He brushed his shoe across deep scratches that marred the wooden floor. Why would an extravagant castle have such damage in its showcase entryway?

He pointed at one of the deeper marks. "A dragon?"

"The white dragon flies in here," Uriel said, using his hand to demonstrate the flight path, "and he digs his claws into the wood when he lands."

"He must come and go often."

"I wouldn't know, but I have seen one other dragon. Arxad pays a visit on infrequent occasions."

Jason pointed at the floor. "Arxad comes here? Why?"

"More mysteries. I am not privy to the conversations he and the white dragon carry on."

"Maybe not, but I'm getting the impression that you know more about this place than you've been letting on."

"Yes, I realize that, but my reticence is not intentional. Memories are returning as if summoned by the castle itself."

Resolute's arm appeared inside, beckoning a few paces away. "Come in where it's nice and cozy."

"Cozy?" Jason asked as he strode forward. "With the open door, how could it be ..." When he crossed the plane, the air instantly warmed. "Cozy?"

Uriel followed in Jason's wake. "A remarkable change."

Jason turned toward the outside and reached his hand through the doorway. Cold air bathed his skin and ran up his sleeve, as if his arm had become a conduit. When he jerked it back, the hole sealed.

He turned toward the foyer again. A giant mural covered the far wall. It looked like a throne of gold with multicolored gems embedded in the back, arms, and legs. Somehow, even without light shining on the painting, the gems glittered.

Above, ivory beams spanned a domed ceiling. Between the beams, leaded glass displayed a network of colorful spheres with a large reddish one at the center. The display tugged at Jason's memory, resurrecting Adrian's mural of the planets in their room back home.

Resolute's voice sparks appeared, drizzling over a hardwood chair. "Rest. Make yourselves at home while I tell the king of your arrival."

Uriel plopped heavily into the chair. "I assume you will allow an old man the honor."

Jason scanned the foyer, void of any other seats. "Of course."

"I might change my mind," Uriel said as he squirmed. "Whoever designed this chair knew nothing about human posteriors."

"I'll be back soon. If my master so instructs, I will return with food and drink." Resolute hurried into a passage to the left. With high ceilings and wide clearance on both sides, it seemed too big to be a hallway. Illustrations decorated either side, as if the entire room were an art gallery with frameless landscapes and portraits. A wide beam of light illuminated the hurrying girl, as if her presence drew the beam toward her.

Jason searched for the source, but it seemed to come out of nowhere. When Resolute faded in the recesses of the passage, he looked toward the opposite side of the foyer where a similar corridor stretched out into darkness. Its height and width confirmed that the castle had been designed for dragons. They could fly through these passages with ease.

A rumble vibrated through the floor. Uriel clutched the sides of his chair. "I don't recall seismic disturbances while I was here."

"I don't think it's seismic." Jason followed the sound. It seemed to be coming from the mural wall. Squinting at the throne's sparkling gems, he walked toward the painting, his eyes level with the seat of the huge ornate chair. As he drew near, the wall began to slide from right to left, creeping along inch by inch.

Reaching his fingers around the hilt of his sword, he leaned to the right to catch a glimpse of what lay beyond the wall. A shining vapor flowed through the gap. With a bright head about the size of a fist and a long, shimmering tail, it looked like a slow-moving comet. As if swimming against a current, it undulated through the air, and when it reached the doorway and penetrated the barrier, it shot out and disappeared.

As the gap expanded, another vapor appeared, and another, then five in succession, each one following the same path, though not always at the same speed. One brushed Jason's face as if caressing his cheek. A whispered voice, feminine and frightened, breezed into his ear as it passed by: "It happened so quickly, I didn't know what to do."

Then the vapor hurried to the doorway and vanished into the white landscape outside.

Jason stared after it for a moment before shaking himself out of a trance. "Come with me," he whispered, waving at Uriel. He set his shoulder against the wall and peered around the edge. Uriel stood behind him, making no sound as they both moved with the receding wall.

As Jason's eyes adjusted to the room on the other side, a floating cloak came into view, as if worn by an invisible person. Dozens of shining vapors continued to flow, each one wiggling toward the door. When the wall reached the halfway point, it stopped with a loud thud. The cloak drifted closer and spoke with a soft voice. "You will need to wear this if you wish to see the star."

A wisp of a girl appeared, clutching the cloak's hood in her shining hand. As she walked, her body shimmered in and out of visibility. Taller than Resolute and perhaps a year or two older, she paused and faded away. "I was told to bring one person to the star. I see now that we have two visitors. Which one of you is Jason Masters?"

As Jason stepped into the open, another vapor swept past, and a masculine voice called out, "Don't go! The danger is too great!" With two tail thrusts, it rejoined the others and continued toward the door.

Jason watched it disappear. What might that vapor be afraid of? Should he heed its warning?

Turning again to the girl, he gave her a quick bow. "I am Jason Masters."

"Uriel Blackstone," Uriel said, also bowing. "What is your name?"

Still holding the cloak, she curtsied, becoming visible with the motion. "I am Deference."

"Deference," Jason repeated in a whisper. "You mentioned a star. What is it?"

"We call it Exodus."

Jason waited, but Deference said no more. Instead, she guided the cloak toward him, her arm appearing then fading when he made no move to take the garment.

Uriel drew close to Jason and whispered, "Who needs the sword more desperately—the young man following a ghost or the old man standing alone in the haunted castle?"

"I'll let you choose." Jason set his hand on the sword belt. "But I'm not sure how effective it will be if ghosts attack."

"An excellent point," Uriel said, waving a hand. "You keep it. I do not wish to frighten any timid spirits."

Jason clasped Uriel's arm. "Godspeed."

"I shall await your return." Uriel glanced around, his brow bent low. "Unless, of course, that white dragon shows up. I have a bone to pick with him. If I make him too angry, you might find a pile of Blackstone ashes waiting for you."

"Then discuss the weather until I come back." Jason spoke again in the cloak's direction. "When will we meet your king?"

"Our king will join you at his pleasure." Walking slowly, she closed the space between them and extended the cloak again. "Raise the hood and pull it over your eyes."

Jason took the sleeveless forest green cloak, wrapped it around his shoulders, and fastened its bronze clasp, two halves of a five-pointed star that joined to complete the design. As he drew the hood up, he searched for the elusive girl.

"Does the cloak fit?" she asked. "If not, I might be able to alter it, though it would take a while. I'm not exactly a seamstress, but I will do what I can."

"It fits. Don't worry." He pulled up the hood, tugging on the front edge to draw the material over his eyes. Although the fabric was thick and black, the light in the newly opened chamber allowed him to see through it fairly well. "I met Resolute earlier. How did you come about these … uh … descriptive names?"

"Do you find my name troubling? If so, I can change it. I have been offered other options."

"Don't change it," Uriel said. "Your name fits you better than the cloak fits Jason, and it seems to have been tailored precisely for him."

Her fingers appeared, wringing nervously. "I could choose Peaceable, but Marcelle thought Deference was the better option."

Jason's heart thumped. "Marcelle was here?"

"Indeed. She came by the Northlands portal. Didn't Cassabrie tell you?"

"No," Jason said, mentally glaring at Cassabrie. "She didn't."

Deference disentangled her fingers. "Well, then I suppose I shouldn't have mentioned it."

"Uriel Blackstone?" Resolute had returned and now walked slowly toward them. "The king wishes for you to come with me. He wants you to help him with a new invention. You will be served a bounteous meal when you arrive."

"A new invention," Jason repeated.

"Yes," Uriel said with a sigh. "Another returning memory. Since I am skilled at mechanics, I constructed a number of devices while imprisoned here. It seems that dragon anatomy is not well-suited for nimble work, and he wished to introduce certain aspects of Major Four technology to the dragon realm."

"How many devices did you make?"

"I can hardly remember that I did any at all, but I assume I could accomplish quite a bit in seventy years. I remember something about a pair of plates that would make something hover between them, but it is a vague memory."

"Come," Resolute said with a firmer tone. "The king awaits."

"I suppose I have no choice." Uriel gave Jason a nod. "Good luck, young man. It has been a pleasure."

"I'm sure we'll meet again," Jason said, but he regretted his words. How could he make such a promise? He didn't know if either of them would survive until evening.

After Uriel and Resolute departed, Deference waved an arm. Again each part of her body appeared as it moved. "Come with me. We will descend a long flight of stairs with no railing, so please be careful." She turned and strode into the light.

As Jason followed, new questions begged for answers. What was the Northlands portal? Where was Marcelle now? Had she come with Adrian?

He gritted his teeth. Too many questions and too few answers. Maybe Deference would be willing to give more information when they reached this star, whatever it was.

With that hope bolstering him, he peeked around the edge of the hood to see his surroundings. The stairway, consisting of rocky steps no more than two feet wide, was really a downward-angling ridge with sheer drops into blackness on each side. To his left and right lay open space, dark except for flickering lanterns attached to cliff faces far away. The steps, uneven and craggy, felt unstable, as if any one of them could break away and send him plunging.

The shining vapors streamed up from below, giving brief views of the darkness, like pulsing candles in the night. Another slowed as it came upon him and swirled around his head, whispering as it blew through his hair.

"The guardian dragon shot a river of fire at the boy. He burned in agony while his companion watched in horror."

Then it broke away and continued its upward flight.

Jason stopped and watched the whispering vapors fly past. It all seemed like a strange dream. Everything around him warped, as if displayed through curved glass.

"Jason," Deference said, "the storytellers will hypnotize you if you let them speak."

"Storytellers?" he repeated, barely loud enough to reach his own ears.

A tingly feeling spread across his fingers. Deference's sparkling hand had slid into his. "Use your other hand to hold the hood closed, and come with me. One step at a time."

He grabbed the hood and pulled the edges together. Deference drew him forward, though her touch felt more like buzzing numbness than flesh and bone. With each new stair, he set his foot down carefully, but after a few successful steps, he relaxed and trusted her guiding hand. The feeling of dreaminess passed, and with the new clarity the recent revelations stormed back into his mind.

"So," Jason whispered, "why didn't you tell me about Marcelle?"

"What did you say?" Deference asked.

"I'm sorry. I'm talking to Cassabrie."

"Oh, I am the one who is sorry. Please converse, and don't mind me. Just keep walking, and we'll be there in a little while."

Cassabrie sighed. *Jason, I have not been given leave to tell you certain things. The king doesn't want you to be distracted from your purpose.*

"My purpose? How could knowing about Marcelle distract me?"

Perhaps this stairway is a fitting illustration. The king has a path for you to follow, and you need to focus on his guiding hand and not be concerned about your surround-

ings. If you learned about the paths of others, you might try to cause them to intersect before the proper time.

"Do you mean everything I'm doing has already been decided beforehand?"

Not at all. You could easily stray from the path, far too easily, and never find the end. Yet the ultimate purpose will be fulfilled. If you don't accomplish what you have been called to do, the king will find someone else to do it.

"So if I die ..."

The king will raise up another warrior. Of course, many more slaves could suffer in the meantime, so it's best for everyone if you stay on the path.

Jason looked through the hood at Deference's shimmering glow. "I feel like a game piece that can be sacrificed at any moment, a pawn being played by someone I can't see."

Her voice grew quiet and sad. *I know that feeling far better than you do. I am a pawn who made a choice, and I was taken from the board.*

Jason stayed silent for a moment. He couldn't contradict her poignancy or add anything profound. "Well, even if I make the choices in the game, what good is it if I can't see beyond the squares I occupy?"

Why is that important? Her voice regained its strength. *The one who created the board sees every square. Isn't that enough to know?*

"So does the Creator move the pieces or just watch them move on their own?"

I am not wise enough to know that answer, but I suspect that he moves some and watches others. You are free to make your own decisions, unless you get in the way and endanger the outcome of the game.

Jason glanced over the side of the stairway. "And that's when your piece gets removed."

If necessary. Or perhaps your piece will stand and watch from the side.

Jason nodded. Irrelevance. That would be a fate worse than death.

If you die fighting for justice, she continued, *or you die because you get in the way, or you die of old age after standing outside the battle, you still die. The end is always the same. The pieces go back into the box, or maybe worse. Might the useless ones be thrown into the Creator's fireplace? That is an end I wish to avoid at all costs.*

Yet, think of it. Perhaps, just perhaps, the Creator puts his martyrs on the mantle. Oh, Jason, that's where I want to be. Can you imagine it? The Creator walks by and admires his handiwork, perhaps even speaks to me, and we laugh about the silly worries I had when I faced my execution. Pain? Disappointment? Loneliness? All fleeting, all in the past. And we enjoy the warmth of his love together. The joy is unspeakable!

Jason continued marching down the stairs. More glowing vapors breezed by, some wrapping around his head, but the hood prevented their whispers from penetrating. It seemed that the barrier made Cassabrie's words bounce in quiet echoes. This joy, was it unspeakable? Not really. Just foreign. The Code said to seek justice and free the captives. Obey the Creator, yes, but chat with him while sitting near a fireplace? Laugh with him? What an odd concept.

"We still have a long way to go," Deference called. "I hope you're not getting weary."

"No. I'm fine. I'm wondering about the climb back up, though."

"I wouldn't worry about that if I were you. Whether or not you return will be up to the king."

Jason halted, letting her hand and the hood slip from his grasp. "Whether or not I return?"

Deference stopped and stared at him. Only her outline stayed visible, and even that began to fade. "Don't worry, Jason. I merely meant return by the same path. There are other means by which one may leave Exodus." As the parade of vapors, now surrounding them in all directions, continued their upward flow, she laughed. "I apologize. I didn't mean to stoke the fires of fear. If you are frightened, I will let the king know. Perhaps he will allow you to leave right away."

Jason pushed back his hood fully. "No. Don't do that. I just have to be careful. I'm in a strange place, you know."

"Of course, Jason. No one is suggesting that you are cowardly. I certainly wouldn't."

"Then maybe I shouldn't be led by the hand. Maybe I shouldn't show any sign of fear of these … whatever they are."

"I call them storytellers. The king calls them whisperers. In any case, it is not cowardly to protect yourself from harm and trust someone who knows the way. Sometimes the most courageous act is to accept help from those who are most capable of providing it."

"Cowardly," Jason said. "I wish you'd stop using that word."

"If that is what you wish." When Deference resumed her downward march, she lifted her dress slightly, revealing bare feet that seemed to stay an inch or so above the steps. With every footfall, a tiny splash of sparks filled the gap, as if igniting some kind of energy field between this spirit and the reality of stone.

While Jason pressed on, Cassabrie hummed a sweet tune, inserting lyrics now and then about twinkling stars and never-ending light, how they guided navigators and inspired poets. In the song, a child snatched a star out of the sky and put it in a jar. She kept it in her room so she could be inspired and never feel lost.

As the vapors continued brushing by and leaving behind fractured stories, their words seemed to hang in the air while Jason concentrated on Cassabrie's song. Her tale was pretty and touching, but it wasn't real. It was pure fantasy. Astronomers knew that stars were giant balls of burning gas, too distant for anyone to reach and too hot to grasp. Nobody could keep one in a jar.

Finally, Deference reached a landing and pointed to Jason's right. "You will find a tunnel in that direction. When you get to the end, you will have arrived. But I would put the hood up if I were you."

Jason looked in that direction. The storytellers streamed from a dark hole about fifty paces away, flying out of the darkness like bats from a cave. "Aren't you coming?"

"Oh, no, Jason. I am not permitted in the Exodus chamber. It is not my time yet."

Jason measured her words. Not her time? That usually meant someone's death. Was the room that dangerous, and wasn't she already dead?

"Besides," Deference continued. "I have other duties to attend to. I am taking care of an old man who wandered into the Northlands and fell through the ice. He nearly drowned before the king plucked him out of the water and flew him to our castle. The poor man suffered from a terrible blow to the head as well as hypothermia."

"That's too bad," Jason said. "Is he healing?"

"To a point. Today has been worse than yesterday, so I want to hurry back and tend to him."

"Of course you should. I'll be all right."

"It was good to meet you." Deference lifted her hem and scampered up the stairs, light and fast, unaffected by gravity.

Jason took a deep breath and walked toward the tunnel's entrance, about a hundred feet away. With his head still uncovered, the whisperers swirled around him, one after another, each leaving a verbal puzzle piece.

"So Magnar went there by himself. Arxad stayed behind."

"My name is Shellinda, sir. What is yours?"

"I don't have time for such trifles. Leave it there and be on your way."

"I heard his name. Frederick. He protects four of the cattle children there."

Jason turned and snatched the vapor, but it passed right through his fingers. "Where?" he shouted as it streamed away. "Where is Frederick?"

Dizzy again, he blinked, trying to ward off the hypnotic effect. *Don't listen to them. Just ignore them. It's the only way to battle the influence.*

With his back against the flow, the whisperers struck his cloak and streamed around him. Their words flew by so quickly, he couldn't string them together. It seemed that they cared to pause only when they could see his face.

He turned again and marched right into them. "Talk to me, Cassabrie. Help me fight them."

Of course, Jason. I know you can do this. Just focus on my words and ignore their cries. She hummed for a moment before continuing. *I first knew there was something different about me when I was five years old.*

He reached the tunnel entrance, ducked his head to get under the arch, and continued with a long stride, keeping his head low. Hundreds of vapors drifted by, some pausing to drop a comment, and the barrage of words split Cassabrie's monologue into pieces, making it impossible to concentrate.

My hair was so red, the other children pointed fingers at me and—

"Arxad will not help you now. You will die without mercy."

My green eyes added to the effect.

"Bring the old bard to me. The song must be altered. I will tell him what to say."

So when the Separators decided to allow the Traders to sell me—

"You are not the first human on Starlight, Uriel, but what will you do with that information?"

Jason trudged on. Wave after wave of vapors flew by, and dozens, if not hundreds, of disconnected tales spun in his mind, triggering the dizzying effect once again.

Although he tried to remember the familiar names and how they applied, even they fell into the churning mix of confused thoughts.

With so many pulsing lights flashing in his eyes, seeing where he was going became impossible. He held a hand out in front. His fingers were barely visible as they groped for obstacles. How strange it seemed that light could be as blinding as darkness. Who could ever approach this star without being given a reason, especially without preparation for the onslaught of hypnotizing messages? Any unprepared person would surely turn back.

After several more seconds, he exited the tunnel and entered another massive chamber. The flow of vapors halted, as did the whispers. Cassabrie quieted. It was like walking into a cathedral—on the outside, the buzz and bustle of people going about their business never ceased, but one step past the tall doors, and a hush descended. Could this be such a holy sanctuary?

About ten paces ahead, a transparent sphere hovered above the floor, perhaps fifteen paces in diameter. At eye level a few feet to his right, streams of radiance flowed from the surface, starting out invisible and slowly beginning to glow as they drew farther away. When they reached a point beyond where Jason stood, they burst into light, shaped themselves into the comet-like vapors, and swam into the tunnel.

Like rain dripping down a sheet of glass, clear liquid streamed around the surface and collected at the very bottom of the sphere. A steady drip fell from the base to the floor about two feet below. Each drop sizzled on contact and transformed into vapor before disappearing into cracks in the rocky surface.

Jason smacked his lips. Yes, the telltale bitter film coated his tongue. It was extane. So that was how the gas entered the planet's mining veins.

Looking up, he followed a long, chimneylike channel that opened to the sky far above. Maybe that was the way those whispering streams escaped when the wall at the entry foyer was closed.

He stared through the sphere's surface. Inside, another sphere floated. Multicolored and about the size of a wagon wheel, images of dragons, humans, and their surroundings flashed on its surface at high speed, too fast to take in the details. As if feeding itself with each new image, the central sphere grew until a layer peeled off, spewed out, and formed into one of the light streams.

As a new stream broke from the surface, Jason studied the point of exit, a hole the size of his palm, jagged, as if ripped open by a projectile that slammed into it from the outside. Reaching out, he set his hand a few inches in front of the hole. A prickly flow warmed his skin. Light gathered underneath, tickling his skin, while some bounced back into the star. For a moment, the star seemed to lift higher as if buoyed by the influx, but the heat grew too intense to continue the experiment.

Jason drew back. His palm, now red, itched terribly. As he scratched, the whispers continued, but too many and too jumbled to understand. The dizzying effect died away. In fact, an unusual sharpness cleared his mind, like sunlight breaking through a fog.

"Cassabrie," he whispered, still sensing the holiness of the place, "do you feel anything?"

Oh, yes, Jason. I feel alive. Energized. There is power here that I can't describe.

"Deference called this star *Exodus*." He stopped scratching, though the itch continued. "What do you know about it?"

Quite a lot, but yet again, I cannot tell you all I know. The king gave the star its name, and he let me come down here, but no one else. He said I needed to bathe in the flow from the star's heart until I was ready for my journey.

"What journey?"

I'm sorry, Jason, but that is the tale I cannot divulge.

Jason frowned. How many times would she echo that useless reply? "Tell me. When you died and came to the Northlands, did you have your Starlighter powers?"

Not for a long time, but they returned.

"Before or after you started bathing in the energy here?"

After. I assume that's why the king sent me here.

"That's my guess, too." Jason eyed the whispering "heart." It continued to swell and deflate, much more rapidly than any real heart, and it altered at times from its original spherical form, to ovular, to a variety of amorphous designs, once nearly splitting into two kidney-like shapes. "What's it doing?"

It takes on many forms and has a language of sorts. I think the shape indicates its mood, because when it's a sphere I hear happy whispers, and when it twists into a tight coil, I hear sad and tragic ones.

"I hear whispers, but I can't understand them like I did back there."

I understand them. They call out to me. Some laugh. Some weep. Their stories fill me with empathy. When I was in this chamber, I sometimes laughed or wept, as if I had been with them when their story took place, and as I grew stronger I created the forms of the whispering wounded right here in this room so I could see them.

Jason imagined Koren standing with them, twirling her cloak as the whisperers came to life. "Starlight," he murmured. "This is the fuel of a Starlighter."

Yes, Jason. And Exodus is our heart.

fourteen

Randall knelt, pressing down one of many dead flowers that littered the landscape. Once yellow and supple, they were now browned and crumbling after succumbing to the poison Tibalt had concocted in preparation for their journey back to the dragon planet. The plants' fragrance could no longer render them unconscious as it had during their previous visit.

Randall combed his fingers through the grass while Tibalt stood at his side. "If Orion is telling the truth, the door should be right around here."

"That's a mighty big if," Tibalt said. "Trusting Orion is like trusting a lion. They both have teeth that will bite. If we find out he's lyin', we'll both soon be cryin', and we'll wish we had kept out of sight."

Randall grimaced. "That's a terrible rhyme, Tibber."

"Maybe so, but I don't trust him. And I noticed you didn't want any part of Orion's liver berry potion."

"That's true." Randall recalled reading Orion's notes. They offered a concoction of bitter herbs and rotten liver berries to counteract the flowers, but simply eliminating them was much easier. "Now if we can just find the door handle. It should be a metal ring."

A burst of fire shot through a crack in the turf. Randall fell back, then scrambled up and yanked out his sword. When the flames subsided, something thudded near his feet, shaking the ground.

Tibalt backed away. "Maybe riding that river wouldn't be so bad after all."

"Nonsense," Randall said, pointing at the ground. "The portal chamber has to be right under us. Whatever is down below would be there no matter which way we went."

Another thud sounded. A wooden door flung open, revealing a square hole.

A deep voice sounded from underneath but without any intelligible words.

Tibalt drew a sword of his own. "That didn't sound like any human I ever heard."

"Dragon language," Randall whispered. "I heard Yarlan use it."

Tibalt lowered his voice to match. "What do we do?"

"Position yourself on the other side of the hole and do what I do. We'll lop his head off." Randall knelt close to the opening and readied his sword. Tibalt did the same on the opposite side.

More draconic words erupted from below as well as the sound of beating wings. Then, a scaly head popped out. With twitching ears and bugged-out eyes, it looked around frantically.

Randall and Tibalt swung their blades, but the dragon dropped down just in time.

"Missed him!" Tibalt said. "You've seen him before?"

"I don't think so, but they all look alike to me."

"Humans!" another deep voice shouted. "We mean you no harm. Kindly refrain from using your weapons against us."

Randall mouthed "we" at Tibalt, who just shrugged.

Keeping out of fire-breathing range, Randall yelled into the hole. "How many dragons are down there?"

After a moment of silence, the dragon replied. "If we are two or twenty, would that matter? We merely request a safe exit from this place."

Tibalt cackled. "Well, I know twenty can't fit down there. Maybe three, four at the most, if you squeeze together like cats on a cold night."

"Why should I let dragons loose in this world?" Randall asked. "The last time you came, you stole some of our people and enslaved them on your world."

"We have come with terms of peace."

"Peace? Do those terms include bringing back all our people?"

"Every one of them."

Tibalt shook his head fiercely. "They will ask a high price. Be sure of that."

"It can't hurt to find out." Randall leaned a bit closer. "What do you want in exchange?"

A new pause ensued, this one longer. "If they're taking this much time," Tibalt whisper shouted, "they're making it up on the fly."

Finally, the dragon called again. "Taushin is a newly hatched dragon in our world, and he has great power that he will use to destroy your people who are enslaved on Starlight. I am a priest there, and I have come with the former dragon king. We want to wrest control from Taushin, but we cannot yet do so. We are convinced that we have no hope but to appeal to you for aid."

"Ah!" Tibalt said, raising a finger. "A power struggle. The new king kicks out the old one, so the old king gathers an army to fight back. A classic tale, indeed."

"How are we to know you're telling the truth?" Randall called. "Once we let you out, you could kill ..." He looked around at his lack of army. "Us all."

A sigh rose from the hole. "We are only two, so your armies are likely sufficient to conquer us. I have nothing to offer to ensure my pledge, only my word as Arxad, the high priest of Starlight, that I will not harm you in any way, and I will do everything within my power to bring about the return of your people to your world."

Randall stared at Tibalt. They both mouthed the dragon's name at the same time. Natalla, one of the girls they rescued from the dragon planet, had sung the praises of Arxad every chance she could. He had defended her nobly at her trial and rescued her and Koren from certain death, risking his own life in the process.

Randall stood and pushed his sword into the ground near the edge of the hole. Cutting a wider opening would take time, but they could do it. "I need one more promise from you, Arxad."

"If it is in my power."

"My father was the governor of this land, and he was murdered by someone who hopes to rule in his place. In the meantime, that usurper has installed someone else until he completes his plan."

"Then you are Governor Prescott's son," Arxad said.

"You knew my father?"

"Yes, but not that he was murdered. He and I were negotiating sending the gas you call extane to our world, hoping for a way to free your people. It is a long story, but, as is obvious now, the deal was never completed."

"I see."

Tibalt pointed at Randall. "I can read what you're cooking up there in that head of yours. I say do it."

He looked at the old man's wild eyes. "Are you sure?"

Tibalt waved his sword, letting his voice rise. "First I'll help you corral these dragons. Then I'll go and help Jason and Elyssa. One man alone is a better sneak than any other number."

"Are you contemplating a rescue mission?" Arxad asked. "If so, you should know we have no way to open this portal."

"But we do!" Tibalt shouted merrily. "Yes, indeed!"

Randall elbowed Tibalt's ribs. "Quiet! Don't give away our secrets."

"It is no secret that humans have access," Arxad said. "Their appearance in our world is proof enough. Our coming here is similar proof that we possess the means to enter your world, a crystalline peg that opens the portal from there to here."

"That seals it," Randall said. "If I let you out, in exchange I want you to help me restore order here. You will also give us the peg so we can come and go as we please."

After yet another pause, Arxad replied with a quiet "Agreed."

*

Koren stepped forward, giving herself plenty of room in front of Taushin, Zena, and Petra. She stared out over the hundreds of wide eyes, each one following her every move. Telling tales from the past was hard enough, but revealing mysteries going on at the present time? That required more than a perfect memory and a glib tongue. She needed her gift more than ever.

After pulling her hood over her forehead, just enough to allow the shadow to accentuate her eyes, she fanned out the cloak and gave it a dramatic spin. "The prince asks where Magnar has gone. The great king of the dragons, whom many of you have never seen, has been little more than a mythical character in stories handed down in whispered words from guarded lips. Did he rescue us in another world where we were brutally tortured? Did our ancestors ride on his back as he flew through the skies to this place where we could pay back his kindness with labors that would save dragons' lives? Or did he steal us for selfish motives? Maybe he was a king who would soon lose his kingdom if he could not produce the pheterone that could save his own scaly hide."

She paused, allowing the questions to sink in. Then, bending her knees, she stalked toward one side of her makeshift stage where Magnar now stood, semitransparent and scarlet-toned, but not as large as his true form.

Koren stopped and swept her cloak in front of him. "Here he is, my fellow humans. The dragon who rules. The dragon who rescues. The dragon who rides between the worlds. Let us see what has become of him."

Another dragon appeared next to Magnar. With tawnier scales and slenderer form, he appeared to be a much younger version of Arxad. Koren looked into his eyes. There was no doubt about it. He was Arxad. This tale would reveal history, not a current event. Yet perhaps it would connect to the present somehow.

Magnar spoke, but his words sputtered as if passing through a screen. Angling both palms toward him, Koren concentrated. He was speaking in the dragon language. That much was clear. She had to force his voice to grow and project over her audience. If they could just hear him, no one would have any trouble translating.

Finally, his speech clarified, and Koren backed away.

"We have no choice," Magnar said. "We must kill every one of them."

Arxad thumped his tail. "Not the children. Some are not infected yet."

"And how do you know this? Because they exhibit no external symptoms? Are you willing to start a new colony with infected stock? Sending the eggs along with the genetic instructions is the only answer."

"But when the children hatch," Arxad said, "who will protect them until they are old enough to understand the instructions? Who will teach them to apply the alterations? Who will ensure that the recessive gene survives until it is ready to combine with another? And when that generation is created, who will bring a specimen back here to repopulate the world?"

"We will have to share those roles. May I suggest that you are better suited to protect the eggs and the young offspring?"

Arxad nodded. "I agree."

"And I will be the judge of when we should bring them back here."

"Silence!"

Koren spun to the rear. That was Taushin's shout. As the two dragons faded, she blinked at the prince. "What's wrong?"

"I asked for Magnar's present activity, not ancient history."

A new buzz passed through the crowd, dragons and humans speaking their own languages in frenzied whispers.

"Aren't you interested in this information?" Koren asked.

"Zena has provided all the history I need to know. What you were showing us will not benefit the dragons and humans here. It will cause only confusion."

Koren clenched her teeth. This story would clear up confusion, not create it. Magnar and Arxad seemed ready to reveal the mystery of the humans' presence on Starlight, apparently telling a tale that merged all the legends into a coherent history. Why would Taushin try to hide it?

Zena laid an arm over Petra's shoulders. "Concentrate, Starlighter. If you cannot show us Magnar's current activity, show us his most recent history."

Koren glared at Zena. The black-hearted witch's pretentious show of affection sent a clear signal—obey or Petra will suffer.

"I ..." She cleared her throat to combat a squeak. "I will try."

When Koren raised her arms again, the crowd fell silent. Mystery thickened, and no one stirred.

After going through her usual tale-telling motions, Magnar and Arxad appeared again, this time standing in front of a line of crystalline pegs embedded in the floor. Once more the voices warped, and only a few words penetrated the constant interference.

"After all these years, we will finally go back," Magnar said in the dragon language.

Arxad responded in a garble, finishing with, "Hide in the wilderness until Taushin resurrects the Northlands star. Then we can use her to restore the kingdom to you."

"Do you think Taushin will be so easily defeated?" Magnar asked.

More garbled words spewed.

"Do you intend to bully everyone into cooperation?" Arxad asked.

As scratchy sounds veiled the conversation, Taushin shuffled closer, his ears standing up straight.

"If necessary," Magnar said.

Again, noise overwhelmed the conversation. This time the dragon images flickered in concert with the interference.

"Go back," Taushin shouted. "Make him speak again! I must hear Magnar's treacherous plan!"

"I'm trying!" Breathing heavily, Koren focused on Arxad and Magnar. Concentrate. Sharpen the view. That was probably within her power. But go back and retell the tale? Was that even possible?

The scene jumbled, warped, as if the two dragons battled. The interference spiked. Jagged lines fractured the image. Then, in a splash of light, it disappeared.

As a bead of sweat coursed down Koren's cheek, she turned slowly toward Taushin. His eyes burned a purplish hue. With a growl, he mumbled his words, too low for the crowd to hear. "Turn to the others, so that I may see them as I speak."

Swallowing, Koren pivoted on her heels. She let her gaze sweep across the blank stares, imagining Taushin's angry eyes looking through her own. Were hers just as fiery? Maybe so. But the people gave her no indication. They had already been entranced by her hypnotic power.

"As you witnessed," Taushin called out, "Magnar has departed to a secret hiding place that the Starlighter cannot reach. He and Arxad desire to usurp me and destroy my plans to release every human on the planet."

Koren boiled inside. She wanted to shout, "He didn't say that," but the words died in her throat. It did sound like Magnar was planning a rebellion. But Arxad?

"As you saw for yourselves," Taushin continued, "even Arxad is in league with the traitor. If he returns, I trust that anyone who sees him will report it to his dragon master immediately. Yet we have nothing to fear. We have the Starlighter, who will monitor the traitors' schemes so that your future liberty is assured. She will continue to be the mediator between humans and dragons, and her power will be a sign to you that the age of free humans is about to dawn."

Koren wanted to look at Zena and Petra, but she had to keep scanning the audience until the dark prince's sermon ended. His scheme had grown crystal clear. She would continue mesmerizing everyone while he spoke, ensuring that his version of truth penetrated their minds and locked in place. Not having sight, he seemed immune to her tale-telling dance and the images she conjured, though he could see them through her eyes.

She let out a quiet sigh. What could she do? Watch for Arxad and warn him? Dare she risk Petra's safety? Of course, trading one life to save hundreds made logical sense, but the thought ripped a hole in her heart. Might there be a way for her to save everyone?

Finally, Taushin finished his speech and dismissed the crowd. Koren stood quietly on the top step, watching the dragons and humans stream away.

"It is time to go," Zena said from behind her. "I'm sure you must be exhausted after that ordeal. I can draw you a warm bath, and you can—"

"No, thank you." Koren kept her stare straight ahead. "May I stay here and think a while?"

"Of course. Petra and I will make preparations for you."

Koren nodded. Of course Petra had to go. She was the anchor that kept Koren from running away.

Taushin sidled up to her and whispered, "I must go as well. Zena will guide me. Just remember, I see what you see. No matter where you are, with Zena's power I am able to find you."

When the sound of his dragging tail faded, a new draconic voice whispered from the side. "Starlighter, gaze not this way. Even if you must pluck out your eyes, cast not those shining jewels upon me. The sake of every dragon and every human in every world depends on your deference to my command."

Koren looked in the opposite direction. The newcomer spoke in a lyrical cadence, and his odd choice of words made his identity clear. "Tamminy?"

"Yes. It is I, the ancient singer, the bard who is blessed to see beyond mortal vision, yet cursed to sense an ill wind before it arrives. Such a wind is mounting on the horizon, and you carry its portending odor. Taushin sees through you, I know. The blue in his blind orbs flashes, and your eyes echo the light, like thunder chasing a lightning bolt. As a verdant meadow fades in a scorched land, your green eyes have tasted the fury, and they are withering. They are taking on the color of coldness, the color of death. Yet, when you resist, I see the sparkle of life return. Flashes of green signal that hope remains. You are able to overcome."

Koren blinked. A battle in her eyes? They burned a little, but wasn't it from lack of sleep? "How did you pay such close attention? Everyone else was hypnotized. Weren't you?"

"I know secrets, Starlighter, old secrets, mysteries lost, and mysteries locked away. Your gift is a buried treasure that has been unearthed, and those who look upon it with greed in their hearts are captured by its allure. Few are those who are immune to the call of hidden knowledge. They long for a taste of its magic. For some, it is a fresh flavor on their gossiping tongues, a tale that elevates them over a neighbor, a cheap and passing pleasure. For others, it is a door to advantage. In the race between men or between dragons, the one who holds the gems of history will surely bypass the ignorant competitors. Only a few are immune—prophets, who see beyond the glitter to the heart of wisdom; the blind, who see nothing but feel the power of knowledge; and fools, who perceive neither wisdom nor knowledge, and even the glitter bounces off their glazed eyes."

Koren drank in his poetic words, very nearly swaying to his rhythmic delivery. "Okay. I think I understand. What do you want to tell me?"

"Your countenance betrays you. You serve Taushin by force. I perceive an invisible collar around your throat, bonds that choke your freedom of will. Your friend, the mute waif, is a hostage, and love for her is a barbed hook that keeps you from running. Your freedom is a sham. You are still a slave."

Keeping her head turned, Koren nodded. "Do you have a solution?"

"There is only one who can give aid to both humans and dragons, the only one who cares for both with equal weight. He is an intercessor, a lover of truth and justice, a defender of the defenseless."

"Arxad? It looked like he was leaving with Magnar. Didn't you see it?"

"I saw beyond his exit to the world of humans. Arxad did not leave of his own accord. He was bound by oath to Magnar. To a dragon of integrity, such a chain surpasses any material restraints. He is also bound by love, for he knows what Magnar craves—dominion, oppression, and lust for bowed backs—and Arxad's love of liberty is a passion that conquers all other loves."

"What will he decide to do?"

"I cannot see the future, fair lass. I merely sing the Creator's songs. I do see, however, a war raging within Arxad. He longs to be here to guide the hatchling's rise to power, for history teaches that a young king is a river. Such a river can be channeled into a reservoir that quenches the thirst of those he rules, but without the stones of wisdom on each bank, the river can flood and destroy all it was designed to nourish.

"I believe Arxad hopes to return as soon as his chains allow. But he must honor his principles and restrain the madness of the former king. So, for now, Arxad is Magnar's shadow, and he will stay with his brother until his chains are broken."

"His brother? Magnar and Arxad are brothers?"

"Twin brothers. Rare are they, for most dragonesses lay but one egg during each cycle, and even then, perhaps half never hatch. In my long and tiresome lifetime, I have never known of twin eggs hatching, apart from these two, and they are as different as Starlight and Darksphere—in color, in caution, and in character."

Koren imagined two younglings, one reddish and one tawny, nestled together in the midst of two shattered shells. They appeared in front of her, ghostly in aspect as they slept. It seemed impossible that Arxad was ever so small. He had always been Master, Lord of the household, not a defenseless youngling.

As she took a cleansing breath, the image faded away. "What can you do in the meantime?" she asked. "What can *I* do?"

"For your part, you must not completely succumb to Taushin's influence. Eventually Arxad will return, and you must be of sound enough mind to rebel against Taushin in order to help Arxad. But first we must take care of the speechless lamb, or else your love for her will be too great a chain."

Koren pictured herself shackled to Petra. Tamminy was right. Her love for Petra was an invisible chain, and Taushin would always keep it in place. "What do you have in mind?"

"Taushin's coronation will take place this afternoon in the presence of the Separators. When he is officially king, he will be in position to do as he pleases, and I expect that he will use your power to impose his will." After a brief pause, Tamminy added, "Dark forces are hastening to possess you, child. You must escape with all speed."

A shiver ran up Koren's spine. "I know, but how can I escape? Can you help me?"

"Meet me in the theater room in one hour, and bring Petra with you. Of course, you will have to get away from Taushin and Zena and, again, avoid looking at me. So you must be clever. If, on the other hand, they happen to fall asleep, we will be able to converse eye to eye."

"That's not likely. Not in the middle of the day."

"We'll see about that," Tamminy said.

Koren forced down a painful swallow. "One hour. I'll be there."

fifteen

Elyssa jogged along a narrow path, following Wallace, who now carried a sword. Earlier, he had stowed the book in a cart used for hauling stones. After laying a blanket over it, he covered the cart with branches and fronds and hid it in a dense part of the forest. He then went home where he borrowed a shirt and retrieved a sword one of the slaves had hidden long ago. A number of legends had arisen concerning where it came from, but few dared to talk about actually using it. It seemed a pitiful weapon when compared to the firepower of a dragon.

As they hurried toward the cattle camp, Elyssa clutched the glowing sphere, trying not to lose her battle with dizziness. Concentrating on Wallace's feet helped, though the constant jiggling incited a bout of nausea.

A few minutes later, he slowed to a halt at a vine-covered wall. A waist-high wooden box with a padlocked lid stood nearby, apparently a storage unit of some kind. While taking deep breaths, he turned to Elyssa. "This is the cattle camp. Now I just have to find the hole Koren and I used to sneak through. I'm sure we're close. We always used this food bin to mark the spot when we returned in the dark."

"A food bin." Elyssa touched the roughened top. "For the cattle children?"

Wallace nodded. "Locked tight, though. The dragon guard holds the key."

Elyssa glanced at the hand that held the sphere. "Perhaps we can find a way to get that key. Not only will the children likely be hungry, but I'm starving as well."

"If they're eating what I did when I was in there, it's nothing *you* would want to eat."

She caught the emphasized *you*. "What do you mean?"

Shrugging, he directed his gaze at the base of the wall. "Nothing, really. I just suspect that you're used to better food than we eat. Compared to us, you're royalty."

Elyssa flinched. Royalty? Arxad had already accused her of acting like a queen. Was she being too bossy? Too self-assured? Since she was so thin because of her stay in the dungeon, Wallace couldn't possibly think she was well-fed. He must have had a different reason for calling her royalty, maybe her penchant for skipping steps. She needed to be more careful.

She looked at the ground. "Let's keep moving."

Shielded above by arching branches, he bent low and scuffled through the undergrowth, pushing his finger through the gaps in the vines to test the blocks of stone at the bottom. After testing three blocks, he stopped. "Here it is."

While Elyssa stooped next to him, he pulled a few thorny vines to the side, braced his feet against a root, and pushed a knee-high foundation stone with his hands. As he grunted, his face turned red. "It's not as loose as before. I guess it hasn't been used in a while."

Elyssa knelt close and added her weight. The stone slowly gave way, leaving behind a low hole, perhaps two-feet square. Elyssa lowered her head to the opening. Since the stone was still in the way, wiggling through while continuing to shove would be quite a chore. "This won't be easy."

"It's loosened up now," Wallace said. "We're stronger than Koren and I were back then. We should be able to do it."

Elyssa began unfastening Wallace's sword with one hand. "You go first and push it the rest of the way. When you're clear, I'll reach your sword through."

Wallace grinned. "You remind me of Koren. She wasn't shy about telling me what to do."

Elyssa tried to return his smile, but it wilted. His remark felt like yet another jab at her queenly behavior.

Wallace dropped to his belly and, digging in with his elbows, crawled through the opening. After nearly a minute of muffled grunts, he called from the other side. "I'm clear."

After passing the sword to him, she belly-crawled through the hole. When she reached the other side, he pointed with his sword and nodded. "That way."

As they jogged into the wall-enclosed landscape, Wallace slightly in front, Elyssa measured the area with her mind. The vine-covered wall extended both ways about a mile and curved to form an ellipse. The opposite wall stood about a mile and a half across the way, easily visible over the flat expanse of pebbly terrain and dry grass. The dead body they had seen from the top of the wall during their last visit was now gone.

A few trees dotted the area, but only a sparse collection of leaves hung on each one. They seemed as starved as the cattle children likely were. Elyssa rubbed her thumb and finger together. Water ran somewhere nearby, likely the stream they had seen from the wall earlier, but it wasn't in sight now.

Wallace explained the children's duties. As she had seen in the mesa, the pheterone miners cut out stones, and mining children piled them on rafts and sent them floating on the stream. When the raft entered the cattle camp through a gateway in the wall, the cattle children collected the stones in pails, and, as the raft floated along, they hauled the stones to the stream's exit from the camp. There they dumped the stones back onto the raft, and it departed through another gateway.

Elyssa fumed. *Pure evil.* The dragons designed this useless labor as a way to strengthen the toughest children while killing the weaker ones. These human beings were lower than cattle in the dragons' eyes.

Soon the stream came into view, flowing left to right. Dozens of children milled about between the water and a ten-foot-high mound of dirt. They appeared to range from about three to maybe ten years old, walking aimlessly as they looked up at the sky with dull, vacant expressions. Smeared with dirt and blood, nearly all had narrow, bare chests, and the older ones wore ragged short trousers while the younger ones wore loin cloths or nothing at all.

With only two skinny trees separating her from the pathetic little slaves, a strange sense of exposure made Elyssa shiver. While she spent years in relative luxury, these half-naked children suffered in cruel bondage, lacking food, suffering lashes, and uselessly hoisting stones half their size, day after day after day with no hope for release from their torture.

Elyssa slowed to a halt, laid her arms over her chest, and wept. As she watched the suffering playing out before her eyes, suddenly she was the naked one. In all her dungeon daydreams about this journey to the dragon planet, the slaves had been smiling, grateful, even awed at her heroic feats. But this …

Stripped of the pride that she would be a valiant rescuer, shame replaced her snobbery. With her soul undressed, it seemed that every emotion spilled out with her flowing tears.

Wallace stopped and looked back at her. "It breaks your heart, doesn't it?"

"And a lot more." She wiped the tears with a thumb. "Let's get these kids out of here."

A small girl, maybe six years old, ran toward them, staying quiet as she glanced several times at the children behind her. When she arrived, naked from the waist up and just as dirty as the others, she whispered, "Have you come to take us out of here?"

"Yes," Wallace said. "How did you know?"

"A woman swore that she would rescue us." The girl pointed at Elyssa. "She's about your size, only her hair doesn't go past her shoulders, and she's more muscular."

Elyssa imagined a more toned version of herself. The only picture that came to mind was the sword maiden anyone in Mesolantrum would think about if given the same description. "Was her name Marcelle?"

The girl's brow shot up into her jagged bangs. "So she *did* send you!"

Elyssa looked at Wallace. "Marcelle is one of the believers from back home. I knew she was trying to get here, and she fits the description." She laid a hand on the girl's sun-bronzed shoulder. "What's your name?"

"Erin. But only my friends call me that. Most of the bigger ones just call me Dirt Squirt."

Elyssa tried to smile, but the girl's pathetic visage made it impossible. Her hair, braided into a matted, dirty rope, swung like a mongrel's tail across her back, brushing at least five whip marks, two still red and angry.

"Well, Erin," Elyssa said, swiping at another emerging tear, "we *are* here to rescue you." She looked up at the sky. "Are any dragons around?"

"One. He said everyone else is locked down, so we don't have to work. Now we're all just waiting for food, but it might take a long time, because most of the dragons are busy hunting for someone." Erin's face contorted into a worried frown. "Could they be hunting for Marcelle?"

"I don't know, Erin." Elyssa stooped in front of her. "Can you help me get everyone organized? We should leave right away."

The girl turned toward the other children. "Some might trust you, but not all will. Whenever we try to escape, someone gets cooked. Thad burned just yesterday."

A boy writhing in flames pierced Elyssa's thoughts, but she quickly pushed the image out. Crying again wouldn't help. "Don't they all have to come? If any stay behind, won't they risk getting the same punishment Thad received?"

Erin nodded. "But I've been thinking about it. I have a plan."

Suppressing a grin, Elyssa looked the girl in the eye. "What's your plan?"

"Just follow me and watch." Erin strode back to the group, her arms rigid at her sides.

Elyssa and Wallace followed several paces back, though still within earshot. When Erin rejoined the others, she pointed at the two would-be rescuers. "Since the dragons are busy," Erin said, "we're supposed to go with them to get food."

One of the older boys eyed Wallace suspiciously. "Why does he have a sword?"

Erin shrugged. "The dragons are gone, so I guess he's supposed to protect us."

"Why did they tell you and not the rest of us?"

Tilting her head upward, she pointed at his nose. "Listen, you can stand here all day asking questions, but I'm going to get some food." With that, she marched toward Wallace and Elyssa, using the same tight-armed gait, but a smile wrinkled her lips as she drew closer.

Behind her, the older boy waved his arm. "Come on. Let's see what Dirt Squirt's up to."

As the children began to fall into line, a boy near the back pointed at the sky and shouted, "Nancor is coming!"

Elyssa hissed at Wallace. "Quick! Hide your sword! I'll see what I can do to confuse him."

While she opened her hand, a big dragon closed in, his wings beating fiercely as he slowed his body for landing. Adding a roar to the whipping wind, he touched down and trotted to a stop. "Who are you?" he shouted.

The children backed away from Elyssa and Wallace, staring with wary eyes. While Wallace held the sword behind his back, Elyssa stalked straight to the dragon and held the sphere close to his snout. "I am Elyssa. We have never met before."

Nancor blinked several times. "Why are you showing me that shining stone?"

She fought the influence. It was strong, but she had to win. "It's a gem of some kind. I heard dragons crave them, so I thought you might like to see it."

As Elyssa waved her hand back and forth, Nancor's head swayed with it, and his voice slowed. "It is an odd specimen."

She glanced back at Wallace. He crept toward the dragon, the sword still hidden behind his back. This time he had figured out her plan without hearing all the steps, but would it work? Dizziness flooded her senses. She couldn't keep the sphere exposed much longer, but she had to make sure he was fully hypnotized.

"Yes, it is rare, I think." Elyssa took another step closer. "Tell me, how many children have you killed while on guard here?"

"I have not counted. They are vermin. Not worthy of the time it would take to keep track."

"Can you guess?"

"Perhaps twelve. Usually the weakest ones. They would die anyway."

Now within breathing distance of the dragon's nostrils, she spoke in a chant-like cadence. "Keep looking, dragon. Drink in its beauty. Absorb its energy."

Nancor stared at the sphere, his eyes completely glazed over, but he said nothing.

"I think he's ready." Backing away slowly, Elyssa looked at Wallace. "If I leave with the sphere, he might snap out of it."

"Well, I can't hold that thing."

"Let's try this." She set the sphere on the ground. The moment it touched, it began to sizzle and throw off sparks.

"Uh, oh." Wallace waved an arm. "Get out! Quick! He's blinking."

She turned and bolted toward the children, staggering as she ran. She set a hand on the two closest shoulders and whisper shouted, "Come! Everyone! Now!"

As she herded them toward the hole in the wall, she listened for Wallace but heard nothing. She resisted the urge to look back. Maybe he was delaying as long as he could to make sure everyone got out safely before he risked a stab. If he merely awakened the dragon from his stupor and couldn't deliver a fatal blow, this escape attempt would end before they reached the wall. Then again, maybe the dragon had killed him.

When they arrived at the wall, she stooped next to the hole. "Erin, be brave and go first. I'll come through last."

"I think going last is braver." Erin dropped to all fours and scooted through the opening. Then the others followed in single file. Elyssa stayed in her crouch, urging each child to scamper in as quickly as possible. Most scooted along the dry soil without a sound. A few of the youngest children cried, but they responded to Elyssa's soothing words.

Finally, after the last child crawled through, Elyssa stood and allowed herself a glance toward the stream. Wallace ran toward her, his sword drawn. When he arrived, he showed her the blood-stained blade. "That's one dragon who won't be bothering children anymore."

She gazed toward the stream. A dark lump marred the otherwise flat terrain. It seemed odd to feel remorse over the death of a murderous slaver, but the feeling swept through her all the same. This rescue mission had now become a bloody, life-and-death reality.

"Go ahead." Wallace nodded at the hole. "We can't keep them waiting."

Her arms trembling, Elyssa elbow-crawled through the hole again. When she emerged on the other side, one of the bigger boys grabbed her wrist and helped her rise.

"Thank you." She motioned for everyone to huddle low. Putting on a confident expression, she whispered, "Everyone must stay quiet. Nancor won't bother us, but the other dragons still might."

She looked back at the hole. Still no Wallace. While she brushed her elbows clean, she made a quick count of the cattle children. With their wide eyes staring at the trees, their bare skin exposed to potentially prying eyes from above, and their emaciated frames painting the portrait of starved war refugees, they seemed more pitiful than ever.

When she finished counting, she mumbled the total. "Forty-one." How could they get this many children to the wilderness without being seen? And what if the younger ones made too much noise?

Wallace emerged from the hole and skulked to their huddle. "So far, so good."

"What took you so long?" Elyssa asked.

He lifted a key, pinched between his thumb and finger. "I went back and found this. Nancor had it embedded between two scales."

She glanced at the dozens of emaciated bodies surrounding her. "The bin?" she whispered.

"That's what I'm hoping, but we can't have a riot. Take them to the forest while I see if this works."

Elyssa rose and, pressing a finger to her lips, spoke to the children in a hushed tone. "We're leaving this place now, but we have to be very quiet until we get where we're going."

A little girl, barely more than a toddler, held a hand against her belly. "Is there anything to eat there?"

Elyssa pushed her fingers through the girl's tangled black hair, and glanced back at Wallace. He had unlocked the bin and thrown open the lid. "We will eat soon. I promise." Then, taking the girl's hand, she bent over and walked into the undergrowth, wading through thick heather and ducking under low branches. She glanced behind her from time to time to check on the rest of her newfound brood. Although exposed to the prickly branches, they pushed through the obstacles, apparently ignoring the minor scratches.

When she found a clearing that was relatively well-covered by the trees above, she sat and motioned for everyone to gather as close as possible. Sometimes scanning the sky for dragons and sometimes gazing into the eyes of the children, she waited. A sense of calm prevailed. The children seemed more awed than anxious. The closest two girls, both about five years old, petted Elyssa's long sleeves while trying to catch her attention with their big brown eyes.

After another minute, Wallace, once again shirtless, bustled into the clearing, his shirt bulging in his hands. He let his stare pass from child to child, his one eye looking like an oracle of doom. "Only the quiet ones will be able to eat," he said in a dread tone as he passed around what looked like stale hunks of bread.

As each child grabbed a two-fisted helping, the bread flew to his or her mouth. Soon a chorus of eager chewing filled the air.

"So," Wallace said as he handed a smaller morsel to Elyssa, "I assume you have a plan." He added a smile. "You're the queen of skipping steps, right? So you've probably already led them to safety in your mind by now."

"Maybe." She pulled her knees up to her chest and hugged them close. Wallace hadn't emphasized the word, but *queen* stood out all the same. Yet, since it wasn't directed at her forsaken pride, it didn't hurt this time. To this point she had been the queen of plans, the solver of puzzles. Sure, a dozen ways to parade these children through the forest without being seen had crossed her mind, but each one had ended in a dark fog. With no knowledge of the land or how the children might react to the circumstances, how could she have an idea how to proceed?

Allowing a smile to emerge, she gazed at Wallace's sincere face. It would be better to let the warrior lead the way. "I think you should do the planning."

Wallace drew his head back. "Again?"

"It worked out last time." Elyssa took a bite of her bread. Yes, it was stale, but it tasted like a royal feast.

"Well ..." Wallace looked back toward the food bin, then deeper into the forest. Splaying his hands, he showed them to Elyssa. "I'll take ten at a time along with a load of food. That should be a small enough group to keep from being seen. Two will be older boys, two others will be a pair of the youngest children. While you wait here, we'll go as fast as we can into the wilderness. I'll carry the smallest all the way, and the older boys will help the others if they get tired. When we find a safe place, I'll come back for another ten and more food."

"Wallace," Elyssa said, grasping his forearm, "that's a great plan."

"Thank you. Do you see any holes in it?"

"Only if one of us gets caught, but who can predict that?"

As a shadow passed over, they both looked up at the sky. A trio of dragons flew in a triangular pattern, apparently heading toward the village.

Wallace lowered his voice further. "They might be bringing the search closer to home."

"If we take too long, can you find your way to the wilderness in the dark?" she asked.

"Probably. The elders say the forest in that area is more dangerous at night, but we can manage."

"If the children don't get frightened."

Wallace looked at the huddled group as they continued to gnaw at their bread, apparently oblivious to their wretched states. He let out a long sigh. "I don't think you'll have to worry about that."

She followed his line of sight and found one of the older boys. Turned to the side, his profile cut a sharp portrait of pain. A burn scar covered most of his head, leaving only tufts of hair near the top; reddish stripes lined his frame from bony shoulder to hip; and a scar dug a gouge out of his cheek. From fire, to whip, to claw, this boy had suffered every blow a dragon could deliver. How could he now be frightened of an escape from his cruel captors, no matter how dark the night?

Elyssa slid her hand into Wallace's and pulled it close. "I'm not worried. We'll get them there, one way or another."

"So now that I've seen this star," Jason said, "what am I supposed to do?"

Cassabrie replied in a more somber tone than usual. *Discern. Understand. What you learn here could well be the difference between success and failure, between life and death.*

He scratched his wrist. The itch was spreading. "But what is there to learn? These pictures are too fast, and the whispers fly by before I can figure out what they're saying."

That mystery remains for you to unravel. If you fail, then you will be safe here until it is time to send you home to your world, but you will not play a role in the emancipation of your people.

He laid a hand over his eyes. "Okay, okay, let me think." As darkness flooded his vision, thoughts roared through his mind, every bit as quickly as the images flashed on the heart of the star. The planet—Starlight, a world of tyranny and woe. Storytellers—Starlighters, able to replay the tales of the past, whether seen or unseen. This pulsing sphere—Exodus, sending out streams of whispered thoughts in radiant energy that filled Cassabrie with power.

This place, deep in the heart of the planet, housed the source of power—the star that gave light to the storyteller, the whispers that became tales, the energy that poured out in passion, as if the planet itself cried for its tragic story to be heard.

Jason opened his eyes. "It's weeping," he whispered. "It's calling for someone to …" He closed his eyes again and listened to the whispers. Now breathy words filtered in, each one striped with sorrow.

"Will this toil never end?"

"Freedom is a hopeless dream."

"The disease is incurable."

"Our chains will never be broken."

As hundreds of grief-stricken cries swirled in his mind, heat spread across Jason's skin. A tear dampened his cheek. Clenching a fist, he reopened his eyes and stared straight at the star. "Exodus is calling for someone to destroy it."

Jason! Cassabrie's voice spiked. *Are you sure?*

A flood of words, some unbidden, spilled from mind to lips. "It is pure anguish. It was born of sorrows, and its purpose is to weep for an end to the grief and suffering that its own downfall has caused. It absorbs every tale this planet creates and sends them out again for Starlighters to hear and retell, but the Starlighters' songs have not reached ears that were able to respond." He took a deep breath before adding. "Until now."

Cassabrie gasped. *I don't know what to say. I thought the king brought you here for another reason.*

"Is something wrong?"

It's just that ... Her voice washed away.

"You're wondering what will happen to you if your energy source is destroyed."

A bare whisper replied, *Yes.*

As more whispers filtered in, new words formed on his lips. "That story has not yet been told. The future is a blank page."

Then we don't know what will happen to me.

Jason shook his head but said nothing.

So how will you destroy it?

"I suppose by doing what I was going to do anyway. Free the slaves. That should stop the sorrow."

Then why did the king want you to see this?

"To let me know how much my actions might cost. Freedom for them might mean ..."

Death for Koren.

He nodded. "And maybe for you."

I'm already dead, Jason, but who can tell what will happen to my spirit? When Arxad captured my essence just before my body perished, it was by accident. The king told me what happens to a Starlighter in such a case. If not for the Reflections Crystal, my spirit would have been trapped between worlds, a wandering ghost, unable to communicate in this realm and unable to enter the Creator's glory.

"For how long?"

Eternity, I think. Cassabrie broke into a gentle lament. *An eternity of separation from my Creator would be worse than a thousand deaths chained to the cooking stake.*

"I have never heard of such an existence. It's not mentioned in the Code."

No, it's not. But you have heard of the Netherworld.

"Of course. The place where rebels against the Creator perish forever."

Is the torment of eternal loneliness any better?

"I suppose not." Jason looked at the heart of the star. It had twisted into a coil. "So that's where you would go if Exodus is destroyed."

I don't know. As I said, this revelation is new to me. I thought the king brought you here so you could learn to be a Starlighter. He said one of the rescuers has similar gifts.

Jason nodded. "That would be Elyssa. Not me."

Silence ensued for a moment, interrupted only by Cassabrie's sighs. *Now that I understand the king's purpose, perhaps it's time for me to come out. I need to reenergize.*

"That's good. I imagine you—"

Good? Cassabrie seemed surprised. *Wasn't my presence a benefit?*

"It's not that. I just got confused with your voice inside my head."

Interesting. I thought you might react differently.

Jason almost said, "Don't be offended," but the words stuck in his throat. That would be stupid. She was already offended.

Since we have been together for so long, she said, *my departure from your body might hurt quite a bit.*

He straightened and flexed his muscles from his shoulders down. "I'm ready."

As if infused with the outside air, an icy chill erupted within his chest and radiated outward. The glowing patch on his skin burned. Swallowing a scream, he tensed every muscle in his body. It seemed that a dagger blade of pure ice had plunged into his breast and embedded in his heart. The itching intensified, and the skin on his palm began to peel.

A ray of light poured from underneath his shirt, rising past his face and then flowing toward the floor, where it collected and shaped itself into a human form. Consisting of pure radiance and taking on the curves of a young woman, she seemed fragile, as if a touch would shatter her visage into a thousand pieces.

The frigid sensation tempered. Jason relaxed and let his shoulders droop. He scratched away loose skin on his palm but more remained.

"I survived another infusion." With her hands folded at her waist, Cassabrie smiled meekly. "I am glad of that."

He set a finger over the glowing skin patch. It was warm to the touch. "You mean there was doubt?"

"Every moment I am away from the star, I lose power. I was strong when I left here, but I have expended much energy during my journey." She spread out her arms and basked in the radiance. "Now I will gather strength until I must leave again."

As the streams of whispered tales washed over her, the light in her frame brightened. Beginning with the top of her head, the glow dripped down, as if poured in liquid form. Her hair turned from white to red, and with every inch the radiance traveled, the light took on material reality. The skin on her forehead turned bronze, darker than most people in Mesolantrum, and her eyes shone green, twin emeralds that matched Koren's exactly. Soon, the flow covered her entire body, creating a young woman dressed in a white gown and wrapped in a sleeveless blue cloak.

Cassabrie took in a deep breath and let it out slowly. "Ahhh! That feels so good!"

"You're ..." Jason took a step closer. "You're solid."

She offered a sad sort of smile. "Only while I'm here. If I take three steps backwards, I will become a ghost again."

Jason gazed at her lovely face, so radiant, so filled with mystery and intrigue. Again words slipped out before he could stop them. "You're beautiful."

Her smile broadening, she curtsied. "Why, thank you, young man. And you're quite a handsome warrior."

He closed the gap between them and lifted her hand. A missing ring finger blemished its delicate shape.

"I have another one just like it," she said, showing him her other hand. "Zena's doing."

As the patch on Jason's chest throbbed, he opened his shirt. "You already know where one of them is."

She reached out and touched it gently. "I have been a part of you all this time. You were immune to my indwelling."

"Immune?"

"Any other host would be hypnotized by me, as would all who experience the fullness of my power."

Jason longed to ask more about her powers, but they had been in the star chamber so long, the extane might already be affecting his body. "So now we have to go out and rescue the slaves. If Koren gets back to Major Four, maybe she'll survive. Maybe she will—"

"Oh, Jason!" Cassabrie leaped forward and wrapped her arms around him. "Jason, I don't want to be alone forever! Don't let that happen to me!"

As hot tears dampened his shirt, he returned her embrace and patted her back. "You could go to Major Four with us. We'll ask the king."

He felt her head shake against his shoulder. "He told me I can't survive there for more than a day. My Starlight energy would run out, and then I would be trapped between the worlds." Her voice rose to a new lament. "Oh, Jason, don't let me go there. I don't want to be a lonely ghost. I want to live. I want to breathe. I want to … to …"

"To what?" he asked gently.

Her arms tightened around him. "To hold the people I love."

As her tears continued to warm his skin, Jason rubbed her back. He had to help her, somehow, no matter what.

"Maybe it will be all right. Maybe the star wants to be destroyed ... I don't know ... metaphorically. Transformed to something else. Change it from a weeping star to a rejoicing star."

Cassabrie pulled back, still grasping his arms. "Do you think so?"

As he looked into her eyes, sparkling and lovely, guilt washed over his soul. He had no idea how to answer. He had thrown out the option as a wild guess. Lying to her wouldn't help her now. "I don't know, Cassabrie. I just don't know."

She embraced him and pressed her cheek against his chest. Again tears moistened his shirt. After breathing a sad sigh, he kissed the top of her head and just let her cry. After all she had been through, she deserved a chance to pour out her grief. She was right about so many things, but one statement couldn't be more wrong. He wasn't immune to her. She had captured his heart, but he didn't care. She hadn't hypnotized him with a Starlighter's charms; she simply showed him love. And that was enough.

sixteen

Her hands clutched tightly behind her, Koren paced the theater room floor. Finally free of the hated boots, her bare feet padded quietly on the hard tiles.

Each time she pivoted to reverse direction, her cloak fanned out and spun freely. What was taking Tamminy so long? The one-hour span had passed several minutes ago. Showing up late might ruin everything, especially when Taushin or Zena could wake up at any moment. For some reason, both decided to rest. Of course, Koren encouraged a nap, saying that they had slept very little lately, but she didn't expect them to comply. It was all so strange, almost as if Tamminy had prophesied their drowsiness.

As Koren passed by the log fire and empty pedestal for the twentieth time, she looked once again at Petra sitting atop the altar with her hands folded on her lap. Dressed in her gown and cloak, she flashed a series of hand signals that communicated alarm. She had heard something, maybe the sound of dragon wings beating the air.

Koren scanned the area near the open doorway. Nothing so far. Petra's hearing had always been acute. She even claimed to hear the garden plants calling for water, a high-pitched cry that she said reminded her of a squeaking wheel.

A few seconds later, Tamminy flew in and landed on the theater stage. As he folded in his wings, he walked to the front edge and looked down at Koren and Petra. "Since you are looking at me, I assume the prince slumbers."

"Zena has a dragon statuette that indicates Taushin's state," Koren replied. "The eyes weren't glowing, so I knew he was asleep."

"And Zena?"

"She's also sleeping. It was really odd. They both became so sleepy they couldn't keep their eyes open."

"Excellent. My potion worked."

"Some kind of poison?" Koren asked.

"Zena is too wise to allow poison to pass through hers or Taushin's lips. I added a natural sleeping agent to their cups. I fear that it won't last long."

She looked up at the railing that allowed a view of the theater room from above. Fortunately, Zena had cleared out Magnar's quarters, so Taushin now slept far enough away from the incubator room to be out of earshot. "You'd better tell me what your plan is."

"Very well." Tamminy's ears bent back, and his eyes turned from red to purple, a sure sign of worry. "I assume you are aware of the difficulty in escaping. Zena and Taushin will use what you see to track you down."

Koren nodded.

"I could take Petra away, but I would not be able to find a safe refuge for her on this side of the great barrier wall. When Taushin subdues the kingdom, no one will be able to shelter her."

When he paused, she nodded again. Obviously he wanted to know that she understood each step in his thinking, but the deliberate pace was maddening.

"There is only one place that Taushin would not be able to find her."

"The Northlands?" Koren prodded.

Tamminy bobbed his head. "As a former high priest, I would likely be able to get past the guards at the wall if I were flying alone, but certainly not with Petra riding my back. Even if we used deception and I carried her in my claws as a prisoner, they would know there is no reason to transport a human beyond the wall."

"I understand. Go on."

"At least no living human."

Koren's voice pitched higher. "What do you mean?"

"I have watched Arxad prepare the promoted slaves. You might not know this, but he removed their spirits and sent them to the Northlands for safekeeping."

Feeling suddenly hot, Koren fanned her face. This flood of new information was almost too much to take in. "Arxad did that?"

Tamminy nodded. "I can do the same for Petra. Although her body will be dead, her spirit will be very much alive, yet invisible to all but the most perceptive.

Then I can transport her dead body and living spirit without interference from the guards."

"That sounds terribly dangerous."

"Dangerous? Certainly more dangerous than sleeping in the comforts of Arxad's cave. But those days of peace have passed, and I can assure you that her alteration will be safer than wandering through the wilderness should she try to escape alone, safer than the calamities Zena would cast upon you if you should try to escape together, and certainly safer than what Taushin has in store for her if she stays here."

"Will you be able to put her spirit back into her body when she gets there?"

"Arxad had a theory ..." His brow bent downward. "It is not a certainty that it will work."

"Not a certainty," Koren whispered as if echoing. She looked at Petra. Her fingers had intertwined, and she squeezed them tightly. "What do you think? Do you want to take the risk?"

Petra pulled her fingers apart and formed her reply so quickly, Koren could barely read it.

"You don't have any choice?" Koren asked.

She nodded, her chin taut.

Lifting a hand, Koren caressed Petra's cheek. "I'm so sorry for getting you involved in this. It's all my fault. I should have figured out what Zena and Taushin had in mind."

Her fingers now moving more slowly, Petra spelled out her reply, looking straight at Koren with tear-filled eyes.

Koren read the symbols. "I forgive you." Those simple words felt like a soothing balm.

She turned back to Tamminy. "How much time do we have to decide?"

"Perhaps an hour, but certainly no more. The sleeping agent is not strong. I have no way to predict how it will affect Taushin, so I prefer to do the extraction as soon as possible."

One word froze in Koren's mind. *Extraction*. It sounded terrible—painful and permanent. And it would be far worse than pulling a rotting tooth. This extraction would end in death with no guarantee for reversal.

She looked again at Petra. The girl's expression hardened to fierce determination. She believed. She trusted. Her eyes reflected the flaming logs, an appropriate symbol for the courage pouring forth, courage beyond her years.

Yes, she was willing to sacrifice, but for what purpose? Walk willingly into death's jaws in order to escape death? It didn't make sense. There had to be another way.

Firming her chin, Koren shook her head. "I won't let her do it."

Petra's eyebrows arched, and her fingers flew. "If I go to the Northlands with Tamminy," her hands said, "they can't use me to force you to do anything."

"No!" Koren hissed. "I can't allow it."

"I suspect you have an alternative plan," Tamminy said.

"We will escape together. If I keep my eyes closed, Taushin won't see where we are. Petra can be my eyes."

"A bold yet dangerous option. Eventually you will have to open your eyes."

Looking down, Koren nodded. "I know. Maybe I can find a safe place for her by then."

Tamminy extended his neck and sniffed her bare feet. "A lengthy journey is likely, so you will need footwear. Will you be able to get ready without awakening the prince or Zena?"

"I think so. We sneaked out a little while ago. We can do it again."

"If I could fly you to a safe refuge, you would have a great advantage, but the patrols are still out because of the lockdown. Even if I carried you in my claws, I could not explain why I am transporting living humans."

"Then could you cause a distraction somewhere so we can escape on foot?"

"I am not accustomed to creating excitement, but I will think of something." Tamminy stared at the fire, apparently deep in thought. After a few seconds, he drew in a deep breath and looked at Koren. "Do you know the passageway to the Zodiac's lower level?"

Koren nodded. "We found it while exploring the Basilica. Zena told us what it was, but she wouldn't let us go in."

"Now you will enter. Meet me there as soon as you are ready. I must reveal a secret that Arxad and Magnar have kept for a very long time. It is possible that what you see will save your entire race."

Koren reached for Petra's hand. "Then we will go there as soon as we're ready."

"To increase the odds of success, allow me to take Petra to the Zodiac now. If anyone questions me, I will say that she is a promoted human who must be prepared for the coronation banquet. This way, if you are caught as you collect your travel items, I can proceed with the secondary plan, to extract her spirit and carry her to the Northlands."

"What happens if the ruse doesn't work? Will you come back here?"

Tamminy looked at the burning logs for a long moment. The flames had settled to inch-high firelets. "If I encounter trouble on the way to the Zodiac, I will return here in great haste, and I will attempt a distraction while the two of you escape. That means that you should wait here for a short time, let us say until the theater flames die away, to be sure that we arrived safely. At that point, you may go to your room with all stealth, finish your preparations, and join us at the Zodiac."

"Suppose I'm caught," Koren said. "How long will you wait for me before you extract Petra from her body?"

"No more than a half hour. After the extraction is complete, I must have time to transport her body past the barrier wall before she is discovered to be missing."

Petra snapped her fingers, then signed, "The plan is good. I will go with Tamminy. I would rather die than be the reason you do what the dragons say."

"Okay, Petra," Koren said, "I get the picture. Death is better than bondage."

She helped Petra rise and embraced her warmly. "Try to be brave. If I don't see you at the Zodiac, I will see you in the Creator's palace in the sky."

Petra kissed Koren's cheek and formed a familiar symbol, the fingers of one hand curled into the other's, with her knuckles pressed into the heel of the opposite palm.

"I love you, too, Petra." Koren pulled in her lip. If she tried to say another word, she would cry for sure.

After Petra climbed onto Tamminy's back, the two sailed through the doorway and out of sight.

Koren stood alone. The crackling fire made a clicking sound — a clock of sorts, an odd timekeeper. Soon it would die down to embers, and the guard dragon would bring it back to life with another slave-hewn log or two, but not before she had already embarked on the most dangerous journey she had ever taken.

Sighing, she sat on the altar and stared at the dwindling flame. It seemed so symbolic. Humans were little more than logs in a fire pit. The dragons seemed happy to let them provide warmth, serve a purpose for the benefit of those who punish them with flames, and then let them burn to ashes. Other slaves would come along and take their places.

Koren buried her face in her hands. *Don't despair! Concentrate!* But too many mysteries swirled in her mind, and they seemed to multiply with every passing moment. What did Tamminy want to reveal that might help save the human race? What untested method could Arxad employ to reunite Petra's spirit with her body? It was all so confusing!

Peeking between her fingers, she watched the fire — smaller, quieter, cooler. It wouldn't be long now. Shaped like arrowheads, the yellow flames swayed in an imperceptible draft, as if waving at something above.

Koren looked up at the Basilica ceiling. Nothing but blackness met her eyes. Was that really how life worked? Humans toiled, suffered, and waited for relief, praying and hoping that someone more powerful than they would reach down from the heavens and help them. Yet so many times it seemed that no one was there, just a void where prayers drifted into the darkness and died without ever being heard. Who could listen to the laments of broken men, desperate women, and starving children for so many years and not be moved to bring solace to those in bondage?

And if no one in the heavens listened, what was life worth?

Koren drew her head back from her hands and studied her callused fingers, the signature of a slave. Born in servitude, traded as if chattel, she now risked her life to make sure others avoided the same fate. Did it really matter? At the end of it all, everyone dies. If the Creator didn't care about their pain, would he rescue them from this world and restore them in a better place? Was there a heavenly Northlands, a land of eternal peace and comfort? Was there even a Creator at all?

Again covering her face, Koren wept quietly. Maybe it was all a myth. Maybe the Creator and his palace in the sky was a dream conjured by desperate women who wanted to believe in happy endings to their tragic tales, or by broken men who longed for rest for their weary bodies. Everyone, even Arxad, had deceived her for so long, who could know what was true and what wasn't?

Finally, the last firelet gave up its useless prayer and sank into the wood. Koren rose and jogged silently to the hidden stairway at the rear of the stage, guided by a single lantern on the back wall.

She pulled the lantern from its bracket and picked up the flint stones sitting in an attached tray. After opening the hidden door, she tiptoed up the ancient stairs, paused at the top, and blew out the flame, stuffing the stones in the waistband of the trousers under her dress. Now in complete darkness, she set the lantern down and pushed the door to Zena's room. The hinge let out a low whine, prompting her to stop the swing. She waited, listening. No sounds. Total silence was likely a good sign.

Koren squeezed through the narrow opening. With a map of the room in her mind, she padded forward. Zena slept on the bed to her left. The conjuring table stood to the right, but with the dragon's eyes dark, Zena's collection of sorcerous oddities sat invisible. Straight ahead lay the storage cubbyhole where Petra's half-length trousers waited along with a new pair of sandals Zena had provided. They would be essential for rugged travel, certainly better than bare feet.

Koren reached the alcove and crouched, probing the darkness with her hands. It seemed that eyes drilled into her back, but the chamber remained silent.

Ah! The trousers. Now for her boots and Petra's sandals.

A grunt sounded from Zena's bed. Koren froze.

"Koren?"

She stayed in her crouch, perfectly silent.

"Koren, are you still here?"

Again feeling for the sandals, Koren whispered, "Yes, Zena. I hope I didn't disturb you. I'll try to be quieter."

"It doesn't matter. I have to get up for Taushin's coronation."

"You still have time. Go ahead and sleep. I'll wake you."

"Thank you." Zena yawned. "I am impressed that you stayed. I was concerned that you would use my swoon to do mischief."

Koren blinked at the darkness. She wanted to scream that holding Petra's life in the balance was a cruel motivator, but it didn't make sense to continue the conversation. If Zena would just go back to sleep, everything would be fine.

After a few seconds of silence, Koren continued her search. Her finger touched a sandal. The other sandal and her boots would be lined up, making them easy to stack and collect.

Slowly, carefully, she picked up sandals and boots and gathered them into her arms. So far, so good. Perfectly quiet. She covered all four with the trousers and wrapped them into a bundle. Then, sliding her hands underneath from each side, she picked it up and rose in one motion.

She turned, stopped, and waited. The blackness seemed to throb. Her heartbeat and a rush of blood thumped in her ears. Nothing stirred. She raised a foot and set it softly a pace away. Now to glide out of the room and—

The dragon statue's eyes flashed on. Bright and pulsing, the beams painted two blue ovals on her chest. A voice thrummed in her mind. *Koren, I see my statue. That means you are in Zena's room.*

She responded with an intentionally exaggerated nod, a movement Taushin could detect.

I want you to come to my chamber. The more time we spend together, the more certain will be our bond. Using Petra to induce your obedience is not something either of us wants to continue. Am I correct?

Focusing on the dragon, Koren nodded again. Looking at the rest of the room would reveal Petra's absence.

Do you agree to submit without this threat hanging over you?

She kept her head still. Would lying be the right move? Agreeing too quickly might arouse suspicion.

I see that you are hesitant. I understand. Come to me and we will discuss it further.

She drew another map in her mind. Getting to the Zodiac to meet Tamminy and Petra required going through the incubator chamber first, but sneaking around the labyrinth of corridors between Zena's room and that chamber, all without a light to guide her, might be impossible. Now she had an excuse to take a lantern. She gave him yet another nod.

Very well. We will be together in a few moments. The dragon's eyes faded but stayed on.

Koren reached through the stairway door opening, picked up the lantern with her free hand, and tiptoed into the corridor leading to the incubator room. After setting the lantern on the floor, she lit it and quickly turned it to its lowest setting. Then, keeping her eyes focused upward to avoid looking at her bundle, she picked up the lantern again and hurried on.

Staring straight ahead, she followed the corridor and turned to the right, then back to the left before scrambling up a short but steep stairway that ended at the incubator room. Now well away from Zena's quarters, she set the lantern down and adjusted the flame to allow herself more light.

Brightness flooded the spacious chamber, illuminating the passage to the Zodiac on the far side where a large stone blocked the entrance. She quickly averted her eyes toward the ceiling. The hole was closed, the normal position when the incubator fountains were off.

She turned to the right and focused on a much larger doorway, the dragon-sized corridor leading to Taushin's lair. As she shuffled toward it, she repainted the image of the Zodiac escape route in her mind. The stone left a sizeable gap between itself and the wall, proving that it had been placed there to prevent a dragon from using that route, but was the gap large enough for someone her size to crawl through?

Still moving slowly toward Taushin's abode, she imagined herself running to the Zodiac passage and sliding through the gap. How long would it take for him to figure out where she had gone before pursuing her?

She reached the new corridor and paused, her back to the Zodiac passage. The time had come. Her mentally drawn map had better not fail her now.

Closing her eyes, she blew out the lantern, but it slipped in her hand. The flame burned her skin, and she let it fall. In the midst of its clatter, she dashed toward the Zodiac passage, tracing the route on her map. With one arm free now, she reached out a hand, slowing as her instincts told her she was drawing near. With darkness prevailing, she opened her eyes, but that didn't help at all.

Her fingers touched stone, then the gap. Lying on her stomach, she shoved the bundle through and squeezed herself in sideways, wiggling as she inched her way forward. After a few seconds, her shoulders wedged. Trying not to grunt, she pushed her feet against the floor. No help. Without a sliver of light, it seemed impossible to know which way to squirm.

She reached ahead and grasped the far side of the stone. Gritting her teeth, she jerked her body forward and into the clear.

A thud sounded. Koren gulped. She stared toward the incubator room, trying not to breathe.

"Koren?"

Zena's voice. Taushin must have alerted her that his precious Starlighter hadn't shown up, or maybe the lantern falling had awakened her. A light passed from left to right, filtering through each gap along the way.

Koren inched back, just enough to avoid it. How close was the lantern? Zena might be shining it from across the room or from just a step away. Yet, she couldn't have seen anyone squeeze through the hole. Her eyesight was too poor, and it had been dark then.

Dark then?

Koren clapped a hand over her eyes. How stupid! Taushin could see where she was!

Since it was too late to fool them now, she lowered her hand from her eyes and peered through the gap. Lantern light drew closer. Zena was coming.

Scooping up her bundle, Koren dashed along the corridor's descending tunnel. Air billowed her cloak, pulling against the clasp at her chest. As light from behind faded, her path grew dark, treacherous, but she couldn't stop, and she couldn't turn back. Chains awaited—horrible, heavy chains.

Maybe she could get to the Zodiac fast enough for Tamminy to fly them to a hiding place. Maybe she and Petra could wait in safety until their pursuers gave up.

As darkness enveloped her, she slowed her pace. Her cloak settled around her body, weighing down her shoulders. It wouldn't work. Not with Taushin watching. She couldn't possibly keep her eyes closed for that long.

Foolish girl, Taushin said in her mind. *You cannot hide. The Zodiac will offer no sanctuary. Arxad is not there to protect you.*

Koren pushed his intruding thoughts away. She had to keep him out and guard her own thoughts. So far he seemed to be unable to hear her spoken words, and since he had asked questions earlier, he still couldn't read her mind, at least not easily.

Soon, a light appeared in the distance. She broke into another dash. Since they knew where she was, it didn't matter what she looked at now, with one exception. She had to be ready to protect Tamminy.

She closed in on the light, an opening into another chamber. Placing her hand a few inches in front of her eyes, she looked down at her feet and slowed to a quick march. "Tamminy!" she called. "Are you there?"

"Here, child."

Keeping her shield in place, she scanned the floor. A dragon's body appeared to her left, sprawled across the stone in a pool of liquid.

She gasped and jerked her head away. "It's … it's—"

"Thortune," Tamminy said. "I do not know who did this. It is a tragedy, but it actually aids our cause. He would have questioned our presence here."

As Koren turned away from the carnage, she caught a glimpse of Tamminy's shadow ahead and to her right. "They know I'm trying to escape and which way I went."

"We have some safeguards that will slow them down," Tamminy said as his shadow shifted and disappeared. "Still, we should hurry. Come with me."

A hand slid into Koren's and squeezed her fingers gently.

Koren adjusted her shield enough to see Petra's bare feet sticking out past the bottom of her cloak. "Lead the way."

Pulling gently, Petra guided her along a stony floor and into a darker area. Koren longed to explore with her eyes, but any glimpse of Tamminy could mean a death sentence for him.

After a short walk, Petra paused, tugging Koren to a halt beside her. Ahead, Tamminy barked out a draconic word that meant *sanctum*, easy to recognize but impossible for a human to repeat. A grinding noise sounded, and a brighter light illuminated the floor. After taking several more steps, Petra stopped next to Tamminy's shadow. Again Tamminy said something, this time the dragon word for *refuge*. The grinding returned. Koren glanced back in time to see a wall sliding closed.

"I will now step out of the way so that you may behold this sight," Tamminy said. "Fear not that Taushin will behold it with you. With Arxad gone, he would eventually find her."

"Her?" When the shadow drifted to her left and disappeared, Koren opened her eyes. A shining girl floated between the floor and ceiling. Dressed in a Starlighter's gown and cloak, she radiated streams of effervescent light. Her red hair flowed around her as if blown by a gentle breeze, and her green eyes sparkled.

Koren felt her jaw dropping open, but she couldn't help it. "Is …" She swallowed. "Is she Cassabrie?"

"She is. We cannot stay long. Although I am more immune to her powers than others, I should not risk over-exposure. I assume that you are impervious, but Petra will likely succumb in a few moments. She is not in danger, mind you, but in a dizzied state she will not be able to ride on my back."

"Is Cassabrie dead?"

"Quite dead. When Magnar had her executed, Arxad removed her spirit and took it to the Northlands, where she likely resides even now."

"Then why doesn't her body deteriorate?"

"That is the most important part of the secret. If you will look in the ceiling above her head and at the floor beneath her feet, you will see the power that keeps her body whole."

Koren walked toward Cassabrie slowly, reverently. The dragon password was appropriate. This place felt like a sanctum, similar to the sacred spring at the edge of the wilderness where a few slaves sometimes gathered to pray. Since it was too far away to visit very often, she had been there only twice. Yet the peacefulness of the place returned easily to her memory, as did its beauty. The water in the deep pool was so clear, it seemed invisible.

Kneeling, Koren looked at the floor under Cassabrie's dangling feet. A circular disc had been embedded in the midst of the irregular tiles. About twice the diameter of a human head and as transparent as the sacred spring's water, it displayed an array of brilliant spheres arranged in an incomplete circle, each sphere no bigger than a fingertip.

She counted them out loud, ending with an emphatic, "Six."

"Six?" Tamminy said from behind her. "There should be seven."

After counting again, she set her finger over a space in the circular arrangement. "It looks like one is missing."

"I fail to see how that is possible. Arxad has waited many years for someone who could use these to carry out his plan. The floor panel is designed so that none but a gifted human can penetrate the surface, and an ungifted human would burn terribly if he or she held one of the spheres for more than a moment."

"What did he want me to do with them, and why didn't he tell me about them?"

"Arxad and Magnar have long battled over the best way to save this world and its dragon inhabitants. When Arxad rescued Cassabrie, the white dragon in the Northlands provided this ingenious device, which no one can dismantle without self-destruction. We have not the time for me to explain the details, but the stardrops you see come from a hibernating star that dwells within this planet. The energy from that star gives a Starlighter her power, so Cassabrie's body stays whole as long as she is in their presence. Arxad believes that if a Starlighter ingests one of these, she will have immense power, enough to put an end to the plans Taushin has in store."

Koren looked at Petra. She stood against a wall, one hand over her eyes, resting her head back as if dizzy. The effect on her was rapidly taking hold. Asking more questions would further delay them, but Koren had to know more. "What is Arxad's plan?"

"I am unsure. Arxad kept the details of his theories to himself, but I am sure he hoped to prevent Taushin from training you in your gifts. Once Taushin had you under complete control, he would use you to rule all of Starlight and perhaps even Darksphere. Magnar knew about Cassabrie's presence here, but once she was in place, he could do nothing about it except post a guard who would keep you or anyone else from coming near her."

"Where is that guard now?" Almost before the words slipped out, the image of the dead dragon broke through. "Never mind."

She refocused on the shining, pearl-like spheres. "It doesn't make sense. If I ingest one of these, how could I defeat Taushin's plans to use me? I can't fight myself."

"I did not say if *you* ingested it. I said if a Starlighter ingests it. Arxad hoped to resurrect Cassabrie."

"Oh. I see." A surge of remorse flooded her mind. Arxad's plan was to use Cassabrie to battle the wicked Koren, if she should turn to evil. "So why are you showing me now?"

"To give you the opportunity to stop Taushin's plans before they begin. Since one of the stardrops is missing, we have to hope that removing another will not seriously imperil Cassabrie. I want you to reach in and secure one for yourself. Yet, take heed. This theory has never been tested. Swallowing one of these would surely kill a normal human, but since it energizes Cassabrie, we believe the theory is sound."

Koren looked into her mind's eye. The image of herself tied to the Reflections Crystal appeared. Magnar wanted her dead to keep Taushin from using her. That part now made sense. And Arxad was willing to let him kill her, probably because he understood the danger and couldn't do anything to stop him. Maybe if she had died, Arxad would have rescued her spirit in the same way he had saved Cassabrie's.

"I think I understand, but there are a lot of holes in your explanation."

"To be sure," Tamminy said, "and I know not how to fill them. So you must choose based on what you know, but if you decide to take a stardrop, do so now. Our time is running short."

Koren touched the disc's surface. It seemed rigid at first, but as she pressed harder, her fingers passed through. She reached farther and pinched one of the stardrops. It sizzled, throwing off tiny white sparks. Warm to the touch, she rolled it between her thumb and finger. Heat penetrated her skin, and a glow spread up her finger toward her hand. It felt good, like a luxurious bath.

She pulled the stardrop out, rose to her feet, and set it on her palm. The glow spilled over her hand and spread to her wrist, coating it with a blissful warmth.

As she backed away from Cassabrie, the glow continued slowly up her arm. The heat infused her muscles with energy. This stardrop would make her powerful indeed.

A flying dragon burst through the entry wall, crashed into Cassabrie's body, then bounced back as if thrown by the dead Starlighter's radiance. It quickly righted itself and, stretching out its wings, took on a battle stance, its head swaying as it scanned the room.

Tamminy's ears flattened. "Shrillet," he growled through his teeth. "You are not welcome here."

"I require no welcome," Shrillet said. "I do only Taushin's bidding. Everyone must come with me immediately."

Koren eyed the dragon. Its high-pitched voice and silvery color identified it as one of the barrier wall guardians—powerful and keen of eyesight—a female, to be precise.

"But first ..." Shrillet held out a metal box in her claw, extending it toward Koren. "Put the stardrop in this. Taushin says it must be protected."

"You dare not," Tamminy said. "If he possesses it, all is lost. This she-dragon cannot hold it herself, so you have the advantage."

Shrillet took a step toward Koren. "If you disobey, I will kill you."

"Return it to the floor panel!" Tamminy shouted. "Hurry! You are too valuable to kill."

Koren leaped for Cassabrie, but Shrillet swung a wing and slapped Koren's face, knocking her backwards. The stardrop slung away and rolled on the floor in front of Petra. It sizzled wildly as if casting off layers of radiance.

Petra staggered to it, picked it up, and juggled it between her hands, her face blazing with alarm.

Shrillet stalked toward her, fire spewing. "Put it in the box!" she roared.

Petra thrust the stardrop into her mouth and swallowed, staring at the she-dragon defiantly. Her face contorting, Petra's jaw shot open. From the back of her throat, she let out a rasping scream.

"No!" Koren yelled.

Tamminy burst forward, knocked Shrillet to the side, and wrapped Petra in a wing, covering her mouth. "Stay back!" Streaks of fire shot from his nostrils and splashed against the she-dragon's face.

Shrillet shook her head hard, then glared at him, unfazed. "You are too old, Tamminy. You cannot defeat me."

Petra's head lolled to her shoulder. She collapsed over his wing, and her mouth dropped open, spilling drizzles of sparks to the floor.

Tamminy drew her close to his body. Breathing heavily, he matched Shrillet's glare. "Perhaps I cannot defeat you, but I can do this." He lifted a back claw and grasped Petra's cloak. Then, dragging her, he squeezed through the hole Shrillet had made and disappeared.

Shrillet screamed, "You cannot escape!"

As she flexed her legs to give chase, Koren dove for her tail, grabbed it, and hung on. The dragon swung her tail, slinging Koren from side to side and slamming her into a wall. On the back swing, Koren rammed into Cassabrie and bounced back to the floor, but she kept her desperate grip in place.

Koren closed her eyes, grunting at the pain. How could she possibly keep hanging on? Had the stardrop made her arm that strong? Whatever the cause, she had to keep Shrillet from chasing Tamminy. Nothing else mattered.

Shrillet looked back at Koren, her head swaying with her wobbly neck. As Cassabrie's energy continued to flow, the dragon blinked several times and shifted her weight to keep from falling. Finally, she lifted her tail, Koren still attached, and slapped it against the floor.

Koren's forehead smacked the stone. Pain throttled her spine. Barely able to see, she released the tail and laid her cheek down. The surface was rough and abrasive, but she couldn't lift her head even an inch.

After teetering to each side, Shrillet toppled over and crashed next to Koren, shaking the floor.

Koren grimaced. More pain ripped through her body. Darkness flooded her vision. As consciousness fled, she whispered, "I'm sorry, Petra. I'm so sorry."

seventeen

Cassabrie pushed back from Jason and brushed away her tears. With the star's radiance still washing over her, she seemed more alive and solid than ever. "I need to tell you another reason for your coming here. The king wants you to collect some energy from the star and take it to someone who sorely needs it."

"Who?"

"Does it matter? You need only know that he will die unless you take it."

Redness tinged Jason's vision again. "Why does this white dragon want to test me? If he's so wise, doesn't he already know what I would do?"

"No, Jason. When unfamiliar duress is introduced, the future choices of a free man cannot be known, not even by the man himself or by those who watch over him."

"You and your puzzles." He looked toward the stairway. "Deference mentioned an old man who nearly drowned. Is he the one?"

Cassabrie's tone sharpened. "I heard. She should not have told you."

"Why not?"

"I should not reveal even that. Just be willing to help the man."

"I'm willing. But why did the king ask *me* to do it? If the man needs help, couldn't someone else have done it long before I got here?"

"The king knows of your immunities. You probably noticed that something in the air has affected your body."

Jason scratched his palm, again peeling away skin. "I noticed. It's not too bad."

"If not for my finger in your chest, it would be much worse. This proves that you are the only one who can do this. As a spirit who can affect the physical for only the shortest of times, I cannot carry anything very far."

"Okay, I'm convinced." Jason turned to the star. "So how do I do it?"

"Like this." Cassabrie formed her hand into a scoop and dipped into the outer surface of the sphere. She extended her cupped hand to Jason. At first, it appeared to be empty, but it then filled to the brim with a milky liquid that began to glow. After a few seconds, it congealed and shrank until it formed into a glittering ball the size of her thumb's knuckle. "Hold out your hands."

Jason formed his hands into a cup. "We call it a stardrop," she said as she rolled the ball into his palms. She then backed away a step, her eyes wide as if watching for a miracle.

The ball of light sizzled on his skin. It stung badly, but not so much that he couldn't hold it.

"Does it hurt?" Cassabrie asked.

He nodded. "Quite a bit. But it's okay. Just show me where to take it."

She pulled his hood up over his head. "Follow me. Quickly." She glided toward the stairway, passing into the whispering streams of light.

Glancing between the stardrop and the Starlighter, Jason followed, his hood falling back with each step. Cassabrie's body slowly melted. Redness dripped from her hair and fell to the ground like drops of blood. Blue and white streamed from her clothes and spilled into stretched-out pools along her path, shining bodies of liquid that quickly evaporated into puffs of sparkling fog. Soon, she was a spirit again, perceptible only as a wisp of moving light.

As before, the voices brushed by, now streaming from behind. With his back to them, they didn't pause to offer their hushed words. Still, seeing them whisk past and knowing they each carried a story, he half wished they would collect and let him in on the secrets they held. Their knowledge seemed to be a vast treasure scattered into millions of pieces—the wealth of kings, raining down in copper coins.

When they reached the stairway, Cassabrie hurried up the steps. Jason paused at the bottom and let his gaze wander up the hundreds of narrow, uneven stairs climbing out of sight and into the darkness above. The stardrop grew hotter. He rolled it in his palms to keep it from scalding his skin.

Cassabrie stopped a dozen or so steps up and looked back, fading as she spoke. “Is there a problem?”

“Deference said there were other ways to exit.”

“She spoke the truth. There are other paths.”

“Well, climbing all these stairs isn’t my idea of an easy route.”

“It is not easy, but it is necessary.” Sparks from her mouth again gave away her position. “Come. I assume the stardrop is getting hotter.”

“It is.” Jason rolled it into his right hand and used his left to open a pocket in his trousers. “I’ll just put it in—”

“No!”

Jason jumped back. Cassabrie’s outburst seemed like an explosion.

“I should have told you earlier. The stardrop will burn your clothing, and it would quickly deteriorate.”

He set the ball near the fringe of his cloak. The material immediately began smoldering. “Okay. So much for that.”

Cassabrie appeared again, scurrying up the stairs. Jason launched himself upward, careful to keep the stardrop safe. At first, the climb seemed easy, in spite of his tired legs. The sword, still at his hip, clanked now and then against the stairs, but it was too important to leave behind. Who could tell when he might need it?

After a hundred steps, his muscles burned, yet not as much as the spherical spitfire in his hand. It felt like it was drilling a hole in his palm. In fact, the peeling skin smoldered as it melted away, raising the odor of scalded flesh.

He stopped and rolled it out onto a stair. "I need to put it down for a minute until—"

"No!" Cassabrie bolted down the steps. "Pick it up! Now!"

Jason pinched the ball and set it in his palm again. It dwindled, emitting arcs of light until it disappeared.

Cassabrie let out a harsh sigh. "It can't touch the stone or it will deteriorate."

"Why didn't you tell me that before?"

"Because I told you to carry it. I didn't expect you to put it down."

"Isn't there anything that will hold it?"

"There is a certain kind of metal that can, but it doesn't exist in the Northlands."

"But it's too hot. I can't hold it."

"You have to. Alaph thinks you can do this, so I—" A lightning-fast hand covered her voice sparks.

"Alaph? Is he the white dragon?"

The sparks resumed. "Please don't tell him I told you. He has ... an obsession, I suppose, with names. I don't know any other way to explain it."

"Don't worry. I won't say a word." He looked at the spot where the stardrop left a burn mark on the stone. "So what do we do now?"

"We'll get another and try again."

"But it's so far. Can't we go one of the other ways?"

She pointed at the stairs. "This is *your* path. Do not think the path you're on is the most difficult when you haven't experienced the other options."

Jason looked up the stairway. With no end in sight, judging how hard it was seemed impossible. He let out a quiet sigh. "If you say so. I'll give it another try."

They retreated together and, after scooping another stardrop, began ascending the stairs again. This time he never stopped, never slowed. He just concentrated on taking one step at a time while trying to ignore the awful pain. Now it would be better if the voices whispered their story segments into his ears. At least they would take his mind off the scalding little demon in his hand.

Cassabrie's voice drifted down from above. "Would it help to concentrate on the man to whom you are delivering aid?"

"Yeah. Good idea." Jason imagined an old man lying in bed. His face was vague, and a thin sheet covered his body, trembling as he shivered. Jason glanced at the stardrop. Maybe it would bring him warmth no other medicine could provide. Alaph probably knew how to make a potion out of it that could—

The stardrop's heat suddenly spiked. Jason winced. As hot as burning coals, it tore into his skin.

"Ow!" He dropped the ball and rubbed his palm against the cloak.

"Jason!" Cassabrie scrambled down the stairs. "Why did you drop it?"

"Because it was hot!" he snapped.

"I know it's hot, but now you'll have to start over again."

"I can't. This is insane. No one can do it."

"Don't you want to help the old man?"

"Of course I do." He showed her his hand. The whispering streams passed by, drawing streaks of light across his skin. A raw spot blistered the center of his palm. "Can't you see it's impossible?"

She stepped down to his level, making herself visible for a moment. A firm scowl bent her features. “Is it?”

Jason took a deep breath, forcing himself to calm down. “Look, Cassabrie, we’re not even halfway there and it nearly burned a hole in my hand. What do you expect me to do?”

“I expect you to do what the king called you to do.”

Jason looked away, resisting the urge to roll his eyes at the ghostly girl. With the lives of hundreds of slaves at stake, she wanted him to play a game of hot potato while Elyssa and Koren risked their own lives in the midst of dragons and wolves.

Cassabrie slid her hand into his. It tingled, not quite physical but enough to let him know she was there. “Come with me.”

Her pull felt more like a mental impulse than a tug. As she hurried up the stairs, he ran alongside. Her cloak flowed behind her, and her legs, bare from the calf down, churned, never slowing, never tiring.

After at least a hundred steps, Jason began puffing. He couldn’t give up. Not now. Not when they were finally leaving this place.

When they reached the top step, he stopped and let out a long breath. “What now?”

“You will meet the man you are called to heal.”

“Will he be angry that I didn’t bring the stardrop?”

“Angry? That’s probably not the word for it. But *you* will be.”

Before he could ask what she meant, she marched ahead. Jason followed, once again entering the foyer where he and Uriel had first come in, but the old man had not returned.

Cassabrie breezed into the corridor to the right, and Jason joined her, the sword now hanging low at his hip and scraping the floor. He hiked up his belt and tightened it in place. If he were ever to meet the white dragon, looking like a warrior might help in more ways than one.

As Cassabrie strode through the spacious corridor, Jason angled his head to check her expression. Since she was only a moving outline of light, reading her face proved difficult. With her lips pressed in a tight line, she seemed upset, perhaps disappointed. He had let her down.

They passed under a high arch and walked into a smaller chamber, dim and quiet. It seemed that light from the corridor was unable to penetrate the archway, leaving them in a room that felt like a cemetery just before nightfall.

Cassabrie stopped, and, except for her cloak flowing in a slight draft, she disappeared.

Continuing with slow, cautious steps, Jason walked onto the new room's floor, a network of twisted vines and branches. About a hundred feet long and fifty feet wide, and with tall trees lining the walls to the left and right, the room looked like a small jungle. The floor bent slightly as he pressed his foot down, but it seemed stable.

"Explore," Cassabrie said as she gave her cloak a gentle swirl. "You will find what you have been called to save."

Jason walked to the first tree on his left. As he drew closer, another object came into view. It looked like a bed with someone lying under a blanket, motionless and quiet. Jason stopped at the side of the bed and waited for his eyes to adjust. Soon, the occupant became clear, an old man with deep wrinkles and watery eyes. With a large leathery hand, he rubbed his bulbous nose, smearing his finger with mucous.

He coughed hard, bringing up more mucous, but he swallowed it back down.

Jason forced himself not to cringe.

"Did you bring it?" The man's voice sounded like a deep gargle, pain-filled and tortured.

Jason looked at his burned hand. Now the wound seemed miniscule. Showing it to this man and explaining his failure would make him sound like a whining child.

He lowered his head. "No. No, I didn't."

"I see." The man heaved a sigh. "The white dragon said as much, but I hoped for better."

Jason's cheeks flushed hot. "The dragon thought I wouldn't bring it?"

"He said you were a fine young man, but ..." He hacked up another phlegm ball and spat it into a cloth in his hand. "But you lack a crucial quality."

"What quality?"

"He didn't say. I assume it's none of my business."

Jason averted his gaze. How could he look this man in the eye? He had failed. But how could he have succeeded? The dragon had given him a test beyond his abilities. It wasn't fair.

Clenching his fist, Jason fumed. *Not fair?* What a childish thought! Fair or not, he failed an important test, and that was all that mattered.

He slid his wounded hand into the man's grip. "I'm sorry. I'm very sorry. If there is anything I can do—"

"Get the stardrop." The man jerked his hand away and pointed above his face. "Put it there, and I will be healed."

Jason looked up. The tree wasn't a tree at all. It was a tall, elongated man with spindly arms. With his eyes closed and his face expressionless, he appeared to be asleep or perhaps dead. Just above Jason's eye level, one of the tree man's arms extended over the bed, his hand open as if checking for rain.

Reaching up, Jason touched the tree man's skin. Rough and segmented, it felt like bark. In fact, the man was completely covered with bark, concealing any anatomical details and making it appear genderless rather than male. Yet, with two clearly defined arms and legs as well as humanoid facial features, it definitely wasn't a normal tree, although its roots stretched out in a complex network, creating the room's floor.

"The stardrop goes in his palm," the old man said. "That's all I know. The dragon said the tree would do the rest."

Jason looked again at the man. Of course he needed the stardrop. Of course he needed to be healed and get out of that bed. But the stardrop would just burn another hole. It was impossible.

"Again, I'm sorry," Jason said as he backed away. "I wish I could help, but I just can't."

"Can you not?"

Jason spun toward the new voice. A white dragon towered over him, his sleek ivory neck supporting a hoary head of smooth shiny scales.

His legs trembling, Jason took a step backwards. He almost coughed out the dragon's name, but at the last moment, he sputtered, "The ... the king?"

Alaph lowered his head to Jason's eye level. His ears pointed straight up, rotating as he spoke. "More than a mere guess, I assume."

"Cassabrie ..." Jason's voice squeaked like a rusty hinge. "Cassabrie said you wanted me to ..." His thoughts fled away.

"Ah, yes. Cassabrie, the Starlighter, the talebearer, the conjurer of images that make her stories come to life."

Nodding, Jason kept his stare locked on Alaph's blue eyes, so different from the dragons in the south. Should he say something else? Alaph hadn't asked a question. Maybe he could ask his own now. "I was wondering something. Arxad, a dragon in the ..." Again his words failed him. Alaph's eyes seemed to drain his thoughts.

"I know who Arxad is. Feel free to pursue your question. Do not let my presence intimidate you."

Jason cleared his throat. "Arxad said we ... that is, Koren and I ... could find someone here who could help us free the slaves. Might that be you?"

"I am able to help. Yet I am not the one to whom Arxad referred."

Jason offered a courteous head bow. "Then please, sir, would you tell me who that is and where I can find him?"

"Certainly." Alaph turned and, using his wings, half walked and half flew toward the far side of the room.

Jason followed. He glanced back at the old man, but in the dimness he had faded to a shapeless mass.

Another tree and bed took shape on the left, but no patient lay there. This place seemed to be a hospital ward, with perhaps four beds on each side.

Alaph stopped at the farthest bed on the right, apparently oblivious to the branches bending under his weight. A man lay there, and a humanoid arm extended over him with its palm begging to be filled.

Before the man's features became clear, Alaph blocked Jason with a wing. "This is the man to whom Arxad referred, but I fear that he is not well enough. In fact, he will likely not survive the night. I pulled him out of icy water, and he had sustained a head injury that has caused severe swelling. Only a stardrop can help him now."

Jason leaned to the side but caught only a glimpse of Deference carrying a suction bulb to the bed. "Deference mentioned him. Who is he?"

"I will answer your question if you will answer mine."

"Okay. I'll try."

"You wish to know the identity of this patient. Will you kindly tell me the identity of the first patient you visited?"

"You mean his name?"

The dragon nodded. "That will be sufficient."

"Uh …" Jason ran the conversation through his mind. The man never spoke his name. Cassabrie had said the white dragon had an obsession with names, so his question wasn't too surprising. "I'm sorry. I don't know."

"Did he refuse to tell you when you asked?"

Jason shook his head. "I didn't ask."

"Interesting." Alaph blinked at Jason and cocked his head as if confused. "Since you did not tell me the other man's identity, I will not tell you who this man is. Yet I think you will be able to guess if you ask other questions that still prick your mind."

"You can read my mind?"

The dragon brought his head directly in front of Jason, close enough to send twin streams of cool air across his cheeks. "I do not read minds, but I know the primary reason you journeyed here. Once you admit this, you will have taken your first step toward the answer you seek."

Jason stared at the strange dragon. His blue eyes and cool breath made him appear to be a member of a species other than that of the southern dragons, but his delaying tactics were just as annoying. "I came here to rescue the slaves and take them back to my planet."

"I said *primary*. That is your *secondary* reason. If not for your primary purpose, you would not have come at all."

"If you mean finding Adrian," Jason said, "I didn't even know he was here until after I arrived."

"But you did not even believe this place existed at first. What changed your mind about coming here? You are not such a fool that you cannot discern your own purpose."

Jason thought back to the critical event, the moment he identified Frederick in the Courier's tube. Then and only then did he finally believe in the existence of this world, and seeing his brother planted the slave-rescuing obsession.

Sighing, Jason nodded. "I see what you mean. I came here to rescue my brother Frederick. That's why Adrian came, too."

"Ah! Good! Now tell me, whom else do you know who might be similarly motivated?"

"Well, my father, of course. He was so upset about losing Frederick he didn't even want to say good-bye to Adrian when we left the commune. But he's got a bad leg, so he could never ..."

The words died on his lips. An image came to mind, his last encounter with his father, that afternoon he and Adrian left home. His father had said, "I wanted to tell you something," but he never spoke it. Had he wanted to speak a message other than good-bye?

The dream Jason had in Koren's presence returned, the visions of his father saying good-bye to his mother. A Starlighter-influenced dream?

"My father!" Jason pushed the dragon's wing aside and leaped toward the bed, the twisted vines bending and cracking under his weight. After four long strides, he stopped at the bedside and quietly drank in the sight. His father, Edison Masters, lay there with his eyes closed. His chest moved up and down in a steady rhythm, but a gurgle accompanied his respirations. The suction bulb, an aspirator, lay near his neck. Deference's fingers appeared as she rolled it back and forth nervously.

Jason laid his hand on his father's forehead. It was hot, much too hot. "Father," he whispered, "can you hear me?"

"He has been unresponsive for several hours," the dragon said. "I fear that he will not survive long. Deference has tried every appropriate medicine at our disposal, but his condition has only deteriorated."

"There has to be something we can do. Is there a hospital anywhere? I'll carry him on my back if I have to."

"Well, there is a cure that never fails, but its accessibility ..."

"What is it? Where is it? I'll get it no matter where it is!"

"I am afraid you have already deemed that impossible."

"Impossible?" Jason stared at the hand of bark that hovered empty over his father's dying body. "The star-drop."

"Yes. Placing one there would surely cure him, but it is too great a task. In any case, his time is short. Even if one were to travel to a place where an appropriate container exists, he would be too late. In fact, I believe only moments remain."

Edison's chest stopped moving. As his mouth fell open, a spasm lifted his body. The gurgle altered to a choking rasp.

"He can't breathe!" Jason shouted. "What do I do?"

Deference picked up the aspirator. "I will try to clear the airway!"

"I'll get the stardrop!" Jason jumped away and ran. His foot broke the floor and plunged through, burying his leg in the vines up to his hip. Thrusting his body forward and clawing at the woody matrix, he jerked himself out and scrambled on all fours until he reached the hallway's solid floor.

Cassabrie helped him to his feet. "Shall I join you?"

"Can I make a stardrop with my own hands?" he asked as he cast off the cloak.

"Yes. Just do what I did. But it will burn you more than it did me."

"I don't care." He stripped off the sword and sprinted through the corridor, pumping his arms and legs. No time to give Cassabrie a reason. Wasting a single second could cost Father his life.

When he reached the open throne wall, he burst into the stream of whisperers and galloped down the stairs. Their voices entered his ears, but he shook them away, not allowing the words to pierce his mind.

Time seemed to stretch out. How long would it take to get to the bottom? His legs ached, churning so quickly he nearly slipped off the stairway a half-dozen times. Finally, the bottom came into sight, and he leaped over the last three steps. He dashed through the tunnel and slowed to a halt only inches in front of the brilliant star.

Gasping for breath, he dipped a cupped hand into its surface and withdrew the milky substance. It felt like fire. He clenched his teeth and marched back toward the stairs as he watched the radiance congeal. Every second brought more pain—burning, tearing, torturing pain. When it finally shaped into a ball, he broke into another run and raced up the stairs.

The stardrop scalded his flesh, forcing him to switch it to his other hand. As it began sizzling in the new hand, he blew on the wounded one. Smoke rose from a bloody raw hole in the center of his palm.

Jason cried out. The pain was horrible, the worst he had ever endured. But it didn't matter. Only his father mattered. He would live. He had to live.

As he ran, he continued switching the stardrop from hand to hand, each time blowing on the empty one. The holes grew deeper, three or more in each palm, and the odor of burnt flesh assaulted his nostrils. He flexed his hand, hoping to get more air into the wound, but clotted and singed blood cracked and flaked off, allowing new blood to flow freely.

Above, only darkness met his eyes, and one step after another. No stopping. He couldn't stop, no matter what. Again his legs ached. Cramps knotted his muscles. Sweat poured, dampening his tunic.

Finally, the open wall came into view. Letting out a scream, he bounded up the last steps, wheeled around the wall, and again sprinted through the corridor. In the distance, Cassabrie's cloak flowed at the entryway to the next room. Her hands became visible as she called out, "I'll take it the rest of the way!"

"I've got it!" Jason ran past her, but his first step into the room broke through the floor and buried his leg past his knee. He reached to drag himself out again, but he couldn't open the stardrop hand, and when he wrapped his trembling fingers around a vine, new pain shot through his arm. His muscles cramped. He couldn't move.

Cassabrie glided up to him, her hand open. "Give it to me, Jason! Hurry! I will save your father."

"I'll take it to him!" Jason extended his bloody hand. "Help me out!"

"Don't be a fool!" Cassabrie shouted, her arm shaking. "Give it to me!"

Deference cried out, "He's not breathing! I can't clear the airway!"

"Okay! Okay!" Jason pinched the stardrop and set it gently on Cassabrie's palm. "Hurry!"

While Cassabrie ran to the bed, Jason used both hands to pull himself out of the hole. As he climbed to his feet, he glanced at Alaph, who stood on the far side of the bed, sitting on his haunches as if casually watching a performance. Now treading lightly, Jason hurried to his father. Cassabrie stood on the mattress, staring at the stardrop she had already placed in the tree's hand.

The ball began to shrink, deteriorating as it had before. The sparks burned through the bark, making the hand glow. Soon the radiance collected at the bottom side of the hand and began to drizzle over Edison's head. Like tiny snowflakes, the white crystals coated his face. As each one touched his skin, it erupted in colors—yellow, orange, red, purple, and blue—before turning white again.

Edison gasped. His body heaved. Then, after sucking in a deep breath, he settled into an even respiration, without a hint of a gurgle.

After climbing down from the bed, Cassabrie leaned over Edison and collected the crystals. She turned to Jason. "Show me your wounds."

Jason held out his hands. Cassabrie spread the crystals over the bloody holes and pressed them together, palm to palm.

As he cringed at the ripping pain, smoke rose from the narrow gap between his palms. Radiance from within leaked out and spilled over his skin, adding to the light surrounding Cassabrie's touch.

Slowly, the pain eased. When the smoke cleared, Cassabrie released the pressure. "Let's see how they look."

Jason spread out his hands. Although caked with dried blood, they looked fine, not a trace of a burn. He gave Cassabrie a smile. "Thank you. They feel perfect."

As he brushed away the blood, he stepped up to the bed and looked at his father, still breathing easily, then at Deference's hand petting his father's arm. "How is he?"

"Let's see if he'll wake up." Deference's hand moved to Edison's forehead and stroked it gently. "Mr. Masters. Edison Masters. It's time to wake up."

His eyes still closed, Edison sniffed deeply. "I detect a familiar scent. Dreams of my son have leaked into the air."

"Father," Jason said. "Open your eyes."

Edison's lids snapped open. "Jason? Son, is that really you?"

Jason clutched his father's hand. His smile tightened his face so much, he could barely talk. "Yes ... yes, I'm here."

His father sat up and looked around the room. "We're in the dragon world. Not at home. This is the same castle, the white dragon's castle, where the dragon brought me after I fell into the river. All the legends were true, and I wasn't dreaming."

A nervous laugh heaved from Jason's chest. "They're all true."

"Why are you here? You're supposed to be Prescott's bodyguard."

"It's a long story, a story I can tell you while we're marching back to the dragon village. We have to rescue the slaves, so we'd better get going."

"Yes, of course." Edison threw off his sheet, revealing a cotton nightshirt that reached only to his knees. "It seems that my caretakers have also taken my clothes."

"They have been laundered," Deference said. "I will make sure they are ready for your journey." She backed away and ran toward the main corridor.

Alaph extended his neck, bringing his head close to Edison. "Your journey will end in failure if your son accompanies you." The dragon's blue eyes flamed as he spoke. "You are quite healthy now, so you will do better alone. Jason has proven that he is not prepared."

"Not prepared?" Jason said. "I got the stardrop, didn't I? It nearly burned through both hands, but I got it."

"If you think that qualifies you, then you are as deficient in wisdom as you are in maturity. Nearly every step you have taken since you have been here has proven your lack of readiness."

"What do you mean? I worked so hard. I traveled so far. I suffered so much. What else should I have done?"

Alaph spread a wing toward the bed in the far corner. "You might want to ask the man over there what else you should have done. You could address him by name had you bothered to ask him for it. Yet now he is unable to answer. He is a body without a soul."

Jason stared into the dimness. The bed was a shapeless shadow with only a lump to indicate the man's body. "I ... I tried to bring a stardrop to him, but ..."

"But what? It was impossible?" Alaph curled his neck and brought his face directly in front of Jason's. "Was the stardrop hotter the first time?"

Jason averted his eyes. "No. I guess it wasn't."

"I thought not."

"But he wasn't my father. Shouldn't I work harder to save my father than I would to ..." Even as he asked the question, it seemed like the most foolish he had ever asked. He couldn't finish.

"To save a stranger?" the dragon asked.

Jason shoved a hand into his trousers pocket and stared at the nest of vines at his feet. "I suppose so."

The dragon's tone and cadence shifted to that of a fiery prophet. "You were willing to burn in flames for your father, but you would risk no more than a bee sting for a stranger. And now you expect to rescue hundreds of strangers from peril far greater than any you have ever faced, challenging dragons who can inflict far more pain than that tiny drop of starlight ever could. If you have run with tortoises and lost the race, how will you fare against jackrabbits? Unless the measure of your passion matches the magnitude of your purpose, you will fail, and your failure may well drag everyone into the pit with you."

Every word penetrated Jason's mind like a thrusting sword. Alaph had struck true. There could be no retort. For now, he just had to lick his wounds and confess. Nothing else made any sense.

He looked Alaph in the eye. "I agree with you. I didn't try hard enough for the stranger, and now I know better. What can I do to prove myself?"

"You have already proven yourself, that you are inadequate for the task. I will send you home and—"

"No!" Jason shouted.

His father and the dragon drew their heads back, but neither said a word.

As a new wave of heat flooded Jason's cheeks, he stood tall and kept his voice firm. "I'm sorry, but I can't ... I *won't* ... go home without Elyssa. I brought her here, and if I know her, she came back looking for me. Maybe I do try harder for my family and friends, and maybe I'm not ready to risk my life for strangers, but I know this: if I leave now, I would be the worst traitor—the worst coward—who ever pretended to be a hero." Grasping the hilt of his sword, he squared his shoulders. "I will not go home until I'm sure Elyssa is safe."

Alaph glanced at Edison, then turned back to Jason. "Very well. Your appeal is reasonable, so I acquiesce to your demand. I expect that you will have more opportunities to prove yourself, so I will be interested in reports I hear about you. For now, I will take your father so that he can retrieve his clothes and obtain a proper weapon."

Jason looked at the floor again and nodded. Questions lined up to be asked: Who was Alaph? Why was he here? Why didn't he go south and help the slaves? Even if he had to stay here, what advice might he have? Yet, with his failure still stinging, he couldn't bring himself to ask the questions quite yet. A more urgent task called.

"I'll be back in a minute." Jason soft-stepped across the creaking vines toward the old man's bed. Cassabrie joined him, now visible as she glided at his side.

"It is too late to ask his name," she said.

"I know. I just want to pay my respects." He looked down at the roots, imagining a grave plot in the woody network. "Where do you bury your dead?"

"There is no such place. No one ever dies here."

Jason peered at her as he walked. She stared straight ahead, as if her statement were the most normal in the world.

Alaph flew toward the main corridor, carrying Edison on his back. Jason's hair and clothes flapped in the ensuing breeze, but Cassabrie kept staring without a flinch.

"What do you mean no one ever dies here?" he asked. "This man died, and my father nearly died, too."

"Your father didn't die, so my statement still stands. As for this man, you will soon see what I meant." When they reached him and stood at the bedside, she faded from sight. Jason looked at the man, curled in a fetal position, facing away. A blanket covered his body from the shoulder down, revealing only his head of gray hair.

Cassabrie's voice broke the silence. "This man did not die."

"But Alaph said—"

"Shh!... *The king* said he was a body without a soul." Her cape appeared, twirling as if whipped by a wind. The lump in the bed disappeared, blanket and all.

She looked up at Jason. "He never had a soul."

Jason's volume rose to a near shout. "You created his image?"

"I did."

"This was all a trick?"

"Not a trick. A test."

He pointed toward his father's bed, his arm trembling. "What about bringing the stardrop? Was that just a test? Would my father have died if I hadn't brought it?"

"He would have died, to be sure. Getting the stardrop was absolutely essential to save his life. But it also worked as a test, and a revealing one at that."

Jason forced his voice lower, but he couldn't stop a growl from filtering in. "You said no one dies here. If he would have died, how can it be true? I could easily have failed. That thing just about burned holes through my hands."

"I have learned not to ask such questions. Hypothetical queries that defy what I know to be true are a waste of time. You did not fail, so your father lives. The fact remains as true as ever. No one dies here."

Jason glared at the empty bed. Cassabrie had been in on a plot to test him all along. Sure, everything worked out all right. His father survived, and he did learn a lesson, but at what risk? Why hadn't they just told him the truth?

"It's not difficult to read your countenance, Jason. You feel betrayed, and I understand. I could tell you that the king commanded my actions, but even if he had merely requested my participation, I would have agreed. If you don't understand why, I cannot help you. Explaining would turn refined gold into useless dust."

Jason nodded slowly. Her soothing tone massaged away his anger. She was right, of course. The burning stardrop would forever be etched in his memory, and the pain of his failure would never allow him to forget the value of a stranger. That was how true tests worked. The one to be stretched needed to be ignorant. No one ever reaches beyond his perceived limits without a fire beneath his feet.

"We'd better go." Jason glanced around the dim room. "Will Uriel be joining us?"

"The king will have need of him for quite some time. Perhaps he will join you later. For now, his purpose lies in the Northlands."

"What purpose?"

"Jason ..." Although she remained invisible, her voice carried a smile.

"Okay. Something else I don't need to know. I suppose I shouldn't ask why the king held him here for so long."

Her shaking head appeared for an instant along with her lovely smile. "The king will provide you with supplies and take you and your father to a point where you should be able to breach the wall."

"Just the two of us? What about you?"

"I am going to Darksphere. I am needed more there than here."

"Is Elyssa there?" Jason asked. "Is she's safe?"

"Although I have withheld much information from you, if I knew the answers to those questions, I would gladly tell you. Yet, seeing that you initially set out to find Frederick, I think she would likely search for you in the Southlands wilderness. Her guess might be that you would eventually travel there."

"That makes sense." Jason looked at the blank space where Cassabrie stood and imagined the red hair, green eyes, and beautiful smile he had seen in the star chamber. For some reason, Koren appeared in his mind, the living Starlighter who needed his help far more than this spirit one did.

He reached out and caressed where her cheek ought to have been but felt nothing. Then a gentle grip surrounded his wrist and guided his hand. When his palm touched the tingly field, her face appeared, a bare outline, but visible enough.

"I am a better man for meeting you. Thank you for everything."

Her smile shone brighter than ever. "Perhaps someday we'll meet again."

They stared at each other for a moment, but a sudden noise broke the silence. A dragon flew in and dropped a limp body from its claws. The body rolled a few feet, its arms, legs, and cloak flopping. A dozen paces away, the dragon crashed and cut a swath in his wake. Branches cracked. Vines snapped. When he came to a stop, the floor sagged with his weight. Now wedged between rows of sharp wooden spears, he squirmed, sinking through the splintered growth with every twitch. Gasping, he cried out, "Help the girl!"

"Hold still!" Jason shouted. He leaped for the girl's body and scooped her into his arms. As he hurried to the bed, he looked her over. Warm to the touch, she was pale and still, dressed like a Starlighter but without the characteristic red hair. Somehow her skin glowed as if illuminated from within.

As he laid her on the bed, he searched for Cassabrie. "Take care of her! I'll try to help the dragon!"

"I'm here!" Cassabrie's hands appeared, pushing up the girl's eyelids. "Go!"

Jason dropped to his hands and knees and crawled across the bobbing floor. As he neared the dragon, he called out, "Try not to move!"

With a loud sigh, the dragon settled and laid his neck across the floor, pointing his head toward Jason. Blood poured from a puncture wound between two scales at a point just behind his front leg, and one of the broken branches pierced his neck just above the base.

Jason stopped within reach of the dragon's snout. "We're going to get you out of this. I'm not sure how yet, but just stay calm. We'll call for the white dragon. Maybe he'll know what to do."

He coughed through his reply. "Please ... Take care of the girl. I think ... something has ... punctured my heart ... There is no hope for me."

Jason scooted closer and touched the dragon's neck. "Who are you?"

The dragon spoke in a whisper, allowing his words to flow more easily, though blood trickled from his nostrils and mouth as well. "I am Tamminy, the bard who once sang prophecies for Magnar. The girl's name is Petra."

"Why are you here?"

His voice lowered even further, forcing Jason to lean close. "She swallowed a stardrop, a piece of inner starlight. She did not survive."

"She's dead?" Jason looked back at the girl. "Cassabrie?"

Cassabrie's head appeared, shaking sadly. "She is warm, so I thought she was alive, but she isn't breathing, and she has no pulse."

Jason imagined swallowing a fiery hot stardrop and feeling it burning down his esophagus. It must have eaten away Petra's organs. Why would she do such a thing?

He turned back to Tamminy. "Why did you bring her here?"

The dragon lay still, his eyes closed.

"Tamminy?" Jason set his ear close to the dragon's snout. No sign of breathing. He looked again at Cassabrie. "He's gone."

"Why would he bring a dead girl here?" she asked. "This is a place of restoration, but we don't bring people back to life."

"Maybe he thought that since no one ..." He couldn't finish the thought. It might have sounded like he was ridiculing Cassabrie's claim that no one died here. Obviously that was true no longer.

He laid his hand on Tamminy's head. "So what do you do with a dead dragon?"

"Or a dead girl." Cassabrie's voice cracked as she cried out. "So much death, Jason! So much darkness! When are we going to bring an end to this madness?"

"I don't know, Cassabrie." He pressed his lips together, trying not to lose control. "I just don't know."

A faint wisp of light shimmered atop the dragon's back. Jason tried to focus on it, but it vanished as quickly as it had appeared. "Deference?" he called.

No one answered.

"What is it?" Cassabrie asked.

"I saw something, a spark of light. I thought it was Deference." He returned to his hands and knees and crawled slowly that way. "If I can just—"

"No, Jason! Let me." Cassabrie ran from the bed and scrambled up Tamminy's side. She waved her hands, keeping her location visible—halfway between the base of the neck and the beginning of the tail. "Where did you see it?"

Staying on his knees, he straightened and motioned with his hand. "A little to my left, your right."

Cassabrie shifted, her arms still moving. Then she crouched and reached out. "Don't be frightened. I won't hurt you."

Another girl came into view, sitting and pushing back with her feet, but she said nothing.

Both girls stopped and faded from sight. "What's your name?" Cassabrie asked.

The other girl stayed quiet.

"We need to get off Tamminy's back. If he falls through the floor, we will fall with him, and it's a long way to the soil that feeds the roots of the healing trees."

A pair of hands joined, and the bodies of two girls appeared as they walked down the dragon's side to the broken floor.

Cassabrie led the new girl to Jason.

"Petra?" he asked.

Trembling, she nodded and dipped into a clumsy curtsy.

Still kneeling, he bowed his head in return. "Is that your body in the bed?"

She glanced at it briefly before giving him a stiff nod, her lips tight.

"Why don't you speak?"

She touched her lips and shook her head.

"I see," Jason said. "You have no voice?"

She shook her head again and made a grunting sound. She opened her mouth and pointed inside, but her head disappeared, preventing him from seeing what she was trying to show.

"I think I understand," Cassabrie said. "Someone cut out her tongue. She has a voice, but she can't form words."

Jason winced. What kind of sick, twisted demon would do such a thing? "I'm so sorry to hear that."

Petra waved a hand of dismissal, then touched Jason's shoulder and pointed at the bed.

"Okay," Jason said, rising carefully to his feet. "Show me."

Petra led him to her dead body and set her fingers on the lips.

"You swallowed the stardrop," Jason said. "Tamminy told me that."

Petra nodded. She traced the course from the lips to the stomach and slowly spread out her fingers.

"I get it," Cassabrie said. "The stardrop is in your stomach and spreading light and warmth through your body."

Nodding again, she grasped the front of the dead body's dress and drew her hand forward as if pulling out a thread.

Jason glanced between the spirit girl and the dead body. Seeing the dead girl and her look-alike ghost side by side was truly bizarre. Since neither one could speak, it seemed impossible to figure out what was going on or what to do next. Sorting it all out through nonverbal signals would take forever.

Cassabrie gestured with her hands. "I think I understand. Arxad takes the spirit out of a promoted human and sends it here, but this time Tamminy did the transporting. That means Arxad isn't available for some reason."

Petra nodded vigorously.

"I heard that Tamminy was the high priest before I was born," Cassabrie continued. "He and Arxad were friends, so maybe Arxad taught Tamminy how to do it."

For the next several minutes Jason and Cassabrie took turns asking Petra questions and guessing the meaning of her signals. It seemed that Tamminy had to conduct an emergency extraction of Petra's spirit because the stardrop she swallowed was about to kill her. Arxad was gone, but she had no idea where. She swallowed the stardrop to keep it away from another dragon, and she hoped to be brought here. Why? That part was still unclear, but they did learn that Koren was supposed to swallow the stardrop. On this point, Petra was adamant.

Cassabrie laid her glowing hand on the dead girl's stomach. "So there's a stardrop somewhere in there."

"Why doesn't it just burn a hole right through her and fall out?" Jason asked.

"I don't know. Darkness maybe? Moisture? Acid?"

Jason imagined the ball of light sitting in her stomach, its ability to burn flesh somehow dormant while its power to emit light and heat continued. "If Koren needs to swallow a stardrop …"

Cassabrie's eyes grew wide. "We have a way to get one to her safely." She then clenched her eyes shut and shook her head. "You can't take a dead girl's body all the way back to the dragon village. It's morbid. It's impossible."

"Impossible?" Jason repeated, letting himself smile. "I don't think I'll ever use that word again."

"I also learned that lesson, perhaps too late. As the king has told me, an impossible task requires only a possibility not yet imagined. But I haven't imagined a solution yet."

"Well, if we encase a stardrop in something that mimics the conditions inside Petra's stomach, we could take it with us."

Cassabrie's voice sparks flew. "So we need to make a container of flesh, something dark, wet, and acidic, but I think it would have to be tougher than Petra's stomach if you want it to survive the journey."

Jason nodded toward Tamminy's body. "Will dragon flesh do?"

eighteen

Elyssa sat under a dense forest canopy. The liberated cattle children surrounded her, some sitting quietly, some standing and looking around, and a few sleeping in the undergrowth—thick ferns with mushrooms of various sizes poking through the gaps. The long journey had exhausted them. After traveling several miles, often hiding under trees and then making dashes through clearings or across shallow creeks, they had climbed steadily to a higher elevation where the moist ground and lush foliage gave proof of frequent rain.

Sitting close, Erin touched Elyssa's shoulder. "I hear rustling."

"I heard it, too. Shhh ..." Looking toward the sound, Elyssa gripped Wallace's sword. It was probably Wallace returning from a search for water, but she had to be ready to fight, if necessary. The children had warned her of the strange beasts in the area, and they jumped at every sound.

A dragon-like head poked out of the bushes, small and low to the ground. With blue eyes and a darting tongue, it looked directly at Elyssa and slithered out a few inches before stopping, revealing a long neck, but its body remained hidden in the brush.

She stood slowly, picking up the sword as she rose. "Children," she said softly as she waved a hand, "don't be scared. Just move as quietly as possible to the other side of the clearing."

Gasps and muffled squeals accompanied the sound of shuffling children. Elyssa kept her gaze locked on the head. She lifted the sword higher. Could she decapitate the creature with one blow? With a head the size of a dog's, how big might the rest of it be?

Just before she swung, the creature darted back and disappeared. Elyssa leaped toward it but too late to strike. She caught sight of it as it stole away in the underbrush. Running on at least fifty pairs of short legs, it looked like a huge reptilian centipede, maybe a hundred feet long, easily big enough to kill and swallow one of the smaller children.

Wallace broke into the clearing, cradling four-year-old Phanuel in his arms. "I saw it," he said, breathless. "Is everyone all right?"

"We are. How is Phanuel?"

"Better. I found a creek." He laid the boy in the ferns and knelt beside him. "I bathed him in it. I think the fever's breaking."

"That's good news." Elyssa looked up at the sky. No dragons had appeared since they entered the wilderness, and with twilight approaching they would likely stay undetected. "Should we make camp here or start our search for the refuge right away?"

"Make camp. This is a good spot to create our own refuge. I can take a search party out tomorrow to look for an established camp, and we can keep sending parties out until we find it. I saw fruit trees, and the creek has fish, so we'll be fine for quite a while."

"Except for the beasts," Erin said.

"Well," Wallace said, taking Erin's hand, "I don't think we need to worry about them, not with Elyssa and me on guard."

Elyssa handed Wallace the sword and searched his expression. It didn't take a Diviner to figure out that he *was* worried about the beasts. In fact, his pale cheeks indicated more. She leaned close and whispered, "You saw something else?"

He took her elbow and pulled her to the side. "Nothing like that snake with legs, but maybe something worse." His chin taut, he looked into the branches above.

"What, Wallace? Tell me."

His expression grim, he stared at her. "Birds."

She almost laughed. "Birds? You mean winged creatures with feathers?"

He nodded, again searching the branches.

"How big were they?"

Still looking up, he made a circle with his fingers, indicating the size of some of the mushrooms at their feet.

This time she couldn't hold back a chuckle. "I'll be sure to watch for the sparrows."

"Don't make light of them." He glanced at the children before lowering his voice further. "Down at the creek I saw about a hundred of them attack a deer. They stripped it to bones in just a few seconds and then flew away carrying his empty hide intact. It was the scariest thing I've ever seen."

Elyssa gulped. "That'll give you nightmares."

"No kidding." Wallace pointed the sword at one of the older boys. "At night and when we go on searches, we'll need Dylan and others his size to take turns with us guarding the camp."

For the next hour, Elyssa, Wallace, and the children cleared their campsite of undergrowth and built a roaring fire. When they finished, Solarus had set, leaving them in twilight as the children filed back to the clearing, tossing newly collected firewood on a pile.

The fire swelled, crackling and popping. Sparks flew into the rising smoke and faded in the dying light. With a ring of children gathering around, Elyssa crouched next to Wallace and patted his knee. "Soon we'll have our own wilderness refuge. It's really shaping up."

"Everyone did a great job." He kept his eye on the smoke. "I hope we're not signaling any predators or pursuers."

"I don't think we have any choice." A cool breeze filtered down from the higher elevations. Elyssa rubbed her fingers together. "Rain is coming."

"Rain?" Wallace lifted his brow. "I was wondering if it might, but …"

"Is there a problem?"

He nodded at the children. "Where are we going to put them all? I don't think anyone wants to sleep in a mud puddle."

Elyssa looked beyond Wallace at the heap of sticks, vines, and ferns they had removed from the clearing. She imagined a lattice of sticks tied together with vines and covered with interlaced ferns. These makeshift lean-tos wouldn't be watertight, but they would help.

She reached across Wallace and pulled a long vine over his lap. "Let's get to work."

⁂

Lying on her back, Koren blinked. A thin haze coated her vision. Daylight filtered into the room from a hole in the ceiling far above. But what room?

As she turned her head to look around, a terrible ache stormed from ear to ear. Letting out a quiet moan, she lifted her hand to massage her forehead, but something pulled back, and a clinking sound reached her ears. She lifted again, bringing her hand into viewing range. A manacle clasped her wrist, and a chain led away toward the floor. Boots again dressed her feet and calves, perfectly laced to the top. The crumpled heap of fabric that had served as a pillow turned out to be her cloak.

The recent events trickled back into her mind. Stardrops. The she-dragon. Being slammed against the floor. Petra and her glowing face, poisoned by the stardrop's energy.

She took in a slow, trembling breath. Tears welled. Was Petra dead? Tamminy had said a normal human couldn't even hold a stardrop for long, and swallowing one was surely fatal. And what had become of Tamminy? Even if he escaped, he would always be a fugitive.

Blinking again to clear her vision, she turned to search for her captors. Zena stood near an opening to a corridor. Instead of her usual black dress, she wore a gown of white, similar to the dress Koren once had. With her arms crossed and a frown sagging her face, Zena seemed ready to shout an insult. Yet her words carried across the room like a mother's plaintive call. "Koren? How are you feeling?"

Koren raised her burdened hand and rubbed her forehead. "I have the worst headache."

Walking toward Koren with her usual provocative swagger, Zena gave her a sympathetic smile. "It's no wonder. You have bruises from your hairline down to your chin."

"How can you see well enough to know?"

"I have ways to receive temporary clarity of vision."

Koren forced herself to a sitting position. Now the chamber became clear. She was back in the incubator room, her ankles and wrists chained to a ring embedded in the floor, a familiar position. The manacles and chains, however, seemed different. Instead of the usual black, these were dark brown and rusty, and the metal stung her skin slightly as it shifted with her movements.

She tried to scowl at Zena, but her headache wouldn't allow her brow to furrow. "Do you know what happened to Petra?"

Zena, now within reach, pushed her fingers through Koren's hair and stared with her vacant black eyes.

"Shrillet was unable to find Tamminy. We don't know where he took Petra."

Koren glanced away. She wanted to cry, to wail, to lament Petra's death, but now was not the time. Allowing Zena to watch would pollute her grief. It would be like allowing an unrepentant murderer to comfort the relatives of his victims.

She looked through the ceiling hole. It appeared to be evening. Taushin's coronation had already taken place—he was now the king. Soon he would hatch his plans and force her to help him dominate the planet.

A tear dripped to Koren's cheek. Then, like a geyser, sadness pushed from somewhere deep inside and burst through. She covered her face and wept bitterly. "Poor Petra! Why did you do it? Why did you—"

She pressed her lips together. *Keep quiet!* Peeking between her fingers, she snatched a quick glance. Zena crouched next to her, staring blankly. She probably knew that Petra had swallowed the stardrop, and she likely figured out who plucked it from the floor, but had she and Taushin guessed Arxad's plan?

"When your grief ebbs," Zena said with a soothing purr, "I will take you to the new king's throne. There you will learn how you will serve him willingly."

Tears still streaming, Koren picked up a chain and shook it. "Willingly?" The rattle punctuated her question with a sarcastic bite. "What do you know about *willingly*?"

"I see that you are recovering your hostility. Your grief is short-lived." Zena withdrew a slender key from her dress pocket and unfastened the chain from the floor ring. Then, wrapping the links around her hand and wrist, she stood and pulled Koren up with her. "You have proven your unwillingness to serve in freedom," Zena said, her purr changing to a low growl, "so until you come fully under Taushin's control, this chain will be your ever-present companion."

Koren scowled in spite of the pain. "I will *never* serve that monster willingly! Petra is dead because of him!"

"It is your fault that Petra died." Zena began walking toward the door, forcing Koren to stumble along behind her. "Taushin had nothing to do with it."

Koren looked back. Her cloak still lay on the floor. She longed to rush back and put it on. It always made her feel better—covered, protected—especially now, dressed in black with her booted legs exposed.

Zena passed through the doorway to Taushin's lair. As Koren walked two steps behind her mistress, light from the ceiling hole behind her faded, replaced by weak flames burning within diminutive wall lanterns, each one no bigger than her hand.

Koren kept her gaze low to avoid the light. Although dim, the rapid flickering seemed to pound at her skull like a miner's chisel. If Taushin had really entered her head, maybe he felt it, too. That was some consolation.

After reaching the end of the corridor, they entered a new chamber that was perfectly square and at least twice the size of the incubator room. The ceiling rose to perhaps three times the height of the average human, not the usual dizzying level found in the domed rooms, though a hole in the ceiling provided light and a way for a dragon to come and go.

On an elevated platform at the far end of the room, Taushin sat on his haunches behind a dining pedestal. "Come, Starlighter. Join me in a meal. I hear that you have eaten nothing in quite some time."

Koren pressed her hand against her stomach. It felt empty but not hungry. In fact, nausea simmered, probably a sign of a concussion.

"Go!" Zena shut the door to the passageway and stood in front of it. Dropping the chain, she nodded toward Taushin. "Do not keep the king waiting."

Koren shuffled forward, keeping her head low. With her arms weighed down by manacles, she dragged the chains across the floor. The clopping of her boots echoed, sounding like the drumbeat of a funeral march.

The tiles looked nothing like the oddly angled ones in other dragon chambers. The squares resembled the shape of the room, with perfectly cut edges and finely polished surfaces.

When she reached the platform, she climbed two steps to the top and looked up at Taushin. He pushed the pedestal to the side and reached out with a wing, as black as ever but now bigger, fuller, and obviously more powerful.

Koren lowered her eyes again. Looking at him heightened her nausea. If not for him, Petra would still be alive.

A strange sight caught her attention: four brackets embedded in the floor where the pedestal had been, too widely spaced to act as a frame for the pedestal. What could they be?

She looked up. A mural covered the wall behind Taushin, displaying a chair with an ornate wooden frame and a padded seat. How strange it seemed! No dragon could sit in it. It had obviously been designed for humans.

Taushin's eyebeams struck the front of Koren's dress, dancing on the black material like two active fireflies. She raised her hand to brush them off, but the manacles weighed her down once again, squelching her futile desire. He seemed to want to draw her focus to her clothing so that he could view it for himself.

"As you can see," Taushin said, "you now wear black, while Zena wears white. You have taken her place in my service."

Koren glared at him, saying nothing.

"Petra is dead. Jason is far away where he can offer no help. Tamminy can never return, if he is alive at all. Arxad has betrayed you and departed this world." He extended his neck and breathed a flow of hot air across her cheeks. "You are alone."

Spasms rocked her body, sobs threatening to emerge. She fought to hold them back. She couldn't give this devil any satisfaction.

"And now," he continued, drawing his head back again, "I hear from Zena that you wear black and purple bruises on what was once a lovely face. Your failure shouts from your very skin. Everyone has abandoned you, even Jason, the great warrior who would follow you here no matter what the risk. Where is he now?"

She glared at him. He didn't want an answer. He wanted a broken Starlighter. He wasn't about to get one.

"So," he continued, "seeing that you have no alternative, will you now submit and help me rescue every dragon and human on this planet?"

Breathing heavy, shallow breaths, Koren spoke through clenched teeth. "I don't believe a word you say. You are filled with venom. You were born to kill. You live to witness suffering. I will die before I help you."

Taushin shook his head slowly and released a soft clucking sound. "I hope you do not regret your hasty words. Such vows are bravely uttered but rarely kept." He waved a wing at Zena. "It is time. Bring the witness."

Nodding, Zena opened the door, slipped outside, and closed it behind her.

Taushin paused for a moment while the door's echo died away, then, using a wing, he pushed a hunk of meat from the pedestal.

Koren watched it fall to the floor. Still clinging to the bone, it appeared to be the thigh of a goat. She had seen enough of them in her butchering chores to recognize it.

"At one time," he said, "the bones of humans littered the floor of this chamber. Magnar, whom you seem to honor more highly than you do your new king, consumed many girls your age from this very pedestal, and he scattered their bones as a testimony to his power."

As Koren imagined the sight, bones appeared all around. Magnar stood at the pedestal gnawing the arm of a girl, tearing flesh from the limb. She closed her eyes and jerked her head to the side.

"I see that your Starlighter powers have not diminished, and I do not blame you for being repulsed. My own hatred for such cruelty incited one of my first orders as king, that all Promotions cease, and that people be told the truth so they would understand the depths of depravity to which their former king had sunk. A new day has dawned, and when I resurrect the Northlands star everyone will be set at liberty."

"So ..." Koren slowly reopened her eyes. The bones had vanished. "So the people have been told?"

"They have, and although they naturally reacted with disgust at the news of Magnar's wickedness, their revulsion quickly turned to joy at the prospect of freedom. They also know that you must provide the insight I need to resurrect the star. You are their only hope, yet you stubbornly stand as the only obstacle."

Koren lifted her arms again, making the chains clink. "*You* are the obstacle. Your cruel ways prove that you aren't really doing this out of love. You're just trying to manipulate me."

"Your presumption is the real obstacle. Your lack of trust in me is not based on anything but your self-assured idea that I should not use force to bring about my purposes. Even the Code you cherish details events in which the Creator did the same, leading wars against hate-filled nations in order to achieve his goal of freedom for those he loves."

Koren crossed her arms over her chest, intentionally shaking her chains in the process. "As if you are wise enough to decide who should be forced."

"The accusation of a hypocrite," Taushin said, pointing at her with his wing. "You claim to know that you should *not* be forced. Are you so arrogant as to think that you should never be compelled to comply with the Creator's wishes? When your perceived goals and methods for attaining those goals are not the same as those of a greater power who sees and knows much more than you do, are you above chastisement and correction?"

Koren glanced away. His verbal blow had struck its target. She had no answer.

Taushin's tone altered to that of a plaintive cry. "The whip-scarred cattle children, hungry and wasting away; the miners, broken and weary of draining sweat and blood; the unwed mothers, forced to procreate with men unknown; and hundreds of other slaves cry out for you to help them unlock their chains. Yet you stand here complaining about your own chains, which were put there in order to end your stubborn resistance to a higher calling, a purpose that you cannot possibly view from your lowly position or understand with your finite perception."

The dragon's speech flooded her mind. So much of it was true. She was lowly. She was finite. She didn't understand everything. It seemed that his arguments washed away every possible objection, but one truth stood tall in the flood. It could not be altered, no matter what. As if slogging against the tide, it rose to her lips and leaked out in slow, measured words. "Love … needs … no … chains."

Taushin's head shot closer. "The presumptuous one holds fast to her proverb. She lives by maxims, ignorant of exceptions that every rule allows. She is a slave to her own legalities, and yet creates an exception for herself by resisting an authority she is commanded by the Code to obey. As it says, 'Be in subjection to authorities, for the Creator places them on high ground to do good and not evil.'"

She lifted her arm, heavy and tired, and pointed at him. "If the Creator made you king, and you really do good and not evil, then you could release the slaves at this very moment. I call on you to outlaw slavery, liberate my people from their bondage, and . . ." She took a deep breath. Closing her eyes, she shouted, "Tear down the cattle camp walls, and let my brothers and sisters go free!"

A smile inched across Taushin's face. "My dear girl, you have again proven your misunderstanding of me. To think that I wouldn't free the neediest of all your people is an insult to my character and purpose. At the very moment I took my place as king, I ordered the immediate release of all the cattle children. They are free and in the company of people who will take care of them. Yet I cannot release the others until I resurrect Exodus. We need the miners and their support labor to survive, and they will not work unless we force them. Surely you understand that I must help my own kind survive, so the liberation of the remaining slaves waits on your decision."

Koren slid back a step. It seemed that every objection had already been countered. Taushin was either the most calculating fraud in history, or . . . he was telling the truth. "How can I know the children are free? Can you prove it?"

"A fair question." He aimed his call at the door. "Zena, you may bring her in."

The door swung open. Zena walked in, followed by Madam Orley.

"Come, good lady," Taushin called, "and stand next to Koren."

Wringing her hands as she looked around the room, Madam ambled on her short, stocky legs, giving Koren a hurried glance. Her nervous smile indicated excitement mixed with terror. She stopped at Koren's side and dipped into a shallow curtsy toward Taushin. "What may I do for you, Your Majesty?"

"All I ask is for you to bear witness to the truth. What did you see at the cattle camp when Zena sent you there?"

"Empty, sire." She glanced at Koren again. "Not a child remained."

"And the food bin?"

"Open and empty. The children likely had quite a feast."

"Very good. Thank you." Taushin turned his head toward Koren. "Is the evidence sufficient?"

"Maybe." Koren lifted her arms as high as she could. "Will you allow me to resurrect this tale so I can see it for myself?"

"By all means."

"I am a Starlighter ..." Her voice felt weak, feeble, and her head pounded once again. Without her cloak, could she do this at all? "I call upon this tale to make itself visible, to reveal the secrets of the past so all can see the truth." The chains dragged at her arms. This would have to be a short tale. "The cattle children, tortured and tired, forsaken and hungry, emerged from their walled prison and found sustenance."

The food bin appeared in front of her. A boy bent over the edge, gathering bread from within. His head stayed low in the bin, making it impossible to see his face, but since he wore no shirt, and scratches blemished his skin, he had to be a cattle child. After a moment, however, he withdrew with an armful of loaves and began wrapping them in a shirt. One-eyed and wary, his identity became clear.

"Wallace!" The moment she called out his name, the image vanished. Reaching out for him, she shuffled forward, but the chains again dragged, halting her.

"Do you now have sufficient proof?" Taushin asked.

She stared at the floor where Wallace had stood. Although he looked older than the last time she had seen him, his face showed the same courage and nobility he had always displayed. "I saw no cattle children. Only Wallace."

Taushin spread out a wing. "Then please continue. Find them. Eliminate your doubts. Ease your mind."

Koren nodded. Although the pain was horrible, she had to know the truth. "Wallace," she called, lifting her arms again, "show me what you did with the bread. Surely you collected it for others. Where are the cattle children?"

Another image appeared, this one more transparent than the last. A misty veil fogged the scene, likely because of her weakness. Wallace scraped flint stones together over a pile of wood while Elyssa and at least twenty poorly dressed children rushed around a forest clearing, pulling up ferns and vines and tossing sticks to the side. Elyssa stopped and crouched next to Wallace. Her voice garbled, she said, "Soon we'll have our own wilderness refuge. It's really shaping up."

Koren let her arms fall. They were too heavy to keep in the air. Like a mist fleeing in the wind, the images streamed away.

Taushin extended his neck and drew his head close. “Are your doubts vanquished?”

“I don’t understand,” she said, looking at him. “Why are they in the wilderness? Why can’t they go home to their families?”

“Some are orphans without a home. Others must be protected from dragons who wish to secure free laborers. Not all dragons have submitted to my authority. They see me as small and easily controlled. This is another reason I need your power—to assert my authority and break their addiction to laziness and slave labor.” He took in a breath and spoke with tenderness. “Starlighter, I hope this act of good faith on my part will be sufficient to prove my intent. I have now done all I can. The rest is up to you.”

Madam Orley laid a hand on Koren’s shoulder. Although the touch felt like a bee sting, she tried not to flinch. “He speaks the truth, Koren. Everyone is waiting for you to do what he asks so we can all be set free.” Her kind expression became stern. “Don’t let us down. Don’t be stubborn about this.”

With the pain growing, Koren pulled away. She looked at the old woman. Her eyes displayed worry, fear, hope. Koren’s mind swirled as she stumbled through her words. “You don’t understand … You can’t understand. I can’t do … I mean … I won’t …”

Finally, she turned to Taushin. His blue beams drilled into her eyes, and his thoughts forced their way into hers. *Submit or suffer.*

As if summoned by the dragon’s words, a stinging sensation erupted on Koren’s arms, beginning at the manacles and running to her elbows and shoulders before sizzling like fire down her back and into her legs. Pain followed—searing, pounding pain that knifed into her bones and through her skull. Her head throbbed, worse than ever. It seemed that her brain expanded, pushing against her skull as if her head were about to explode.

She dropped to her knees and pressed her hands against the sides of her head. The torture was unbearable—stabbing, drilling, splitting. If it didn't stop soon, she would ...

The thought vanished, replaced by an echo of her earlier words, *I will die before I help you*.

Gritting her teeth, Koren pounded a fist against the floor. It wasn't right. No one should be forced to suffer so much. Why would the Creator allow it? If she was right to resist this so-called *authority*, the Creator should protect her. Shouldn't he? But he wasn't. He just let her suffer the most horrific torture this cruel beast could deliver.

"Mercy!" She lifted both hands toward Taushin and sobbed. "Mercy! Please, have mercy!"

The pain eased. The stinging retreated to her wrists and ebbed to a mere tingle. With her arms still raised, Koren stared at one of the manacles. A streak of rust smeared her skin as the iron cuff slid toward her elbow.

Had she been wrong? Could she really refuse him to the point of death? Maybe not. Maybe she was willing to serve Taushin if given the proper persuasion. Maybe she *was* too stubborn to understand, and, like a squirrel in a cage, she needed to learn that her captor meant no harm. And, besides, how long would it be before Taushin found another innocent loved one to hold over her head?

"Rise to your feet, child," Taushin said. "Perhaps you are now ready to help me resurrect the Northlands star and set your people free. Say you are mine, and I will believe you."

Koren stood upright, her legs wobbly. A ray of light from the ceiling hole cast a shadow behind her, a dragon-shaped shadow that undulated with her shaking body.

A new wave of nausea boiled. Was that what she had become? A dragon in human garb? No! It wasn't true! The connection wasn't complete! Breathing heavily, she stared at Taushin and summoned her strongest voice. "I am not yours!"

"We shall see about that." He angled his head toward Zena. "Please escort Madam Orley back to her home. Give instructions to all slaves and dragons that no one is to go outside until further notice. When I gain the Starlighter's cooperation and resurrect the star, there is a potential for danger. When the danger passes, I will let everyone know."

"As you wish." Zena grasped Madam Orley's elbow and guided her to the door. Madam looked back at Koren, her eyes filled with terror, but she said nothing.

When the two exited, Taushin again focused his beams on Koren, slowly shifting them toward one of the manacles. "Now, Starlighter, it is time for a little more gentle persuasion."

When his beams struck the manacle, the horrible pain ran up her arm again, this time with twice the force. She fell backwards. Jolts of energy shot from head to spine to hands to feet. She writhed, twisted, squirmed. Her jaw locked open. Screams poured out. Her lips strained to form words—halting, panting, breathless cries. "Help … help me! Oh … dear Creator … help me!"

The pain suddenly eased. Tingling numbness radiated through her limbs. Her body felt like a wet shirt, heavy and stuck to the floor. Did the Creator answer her prayer? If so, what did his answer mean? On the other hand, maybe Taushin stopped the torture after hearing her prayer, hoping she would be fooled into thinking the Creator intervened. Either way, continued resistance meant further agony, not only for herself but maybe also for Madam Orley.

As memories of Petra's dying screams entered Koren's mind, she let out a long breath. She couldn't let this monster threaten another innocent soul.

Slowly, ever so slowly, she rose to her knees, her chains rattling again as they dragged. With tears flowing, her lips barely moved as she whispered, "What must I do?"

nineteen

Again wearing the cloak he received at the Northlands castle, Jason tightened his sword belt and let a hefty coil of rope slide off his shoulder. He checked a small leather pouch dangling from his belt. The stardrop's container was still safely inside.

The belt seemed a bit tighter than before. One of the white dragon's servants, a young male phantom, had provided a generous meal consisting of a yellowish potato mash and boiled greens, unfamiliar but quite tasty. Since the boy worked only in the palace kitchen and knew nothing about the food's origin, and since the dragon didn't join them for the meal, where and how the plants grew in that land of ice remained a mystery.

Later, as they departed, the dragon met them at the vestibule for a final exhortation to free the slaves. He didn't, however, provide food for the journey, warning them to travel with as few burdens as possible. The Creator would give them what they needed.

Looking up, Jason scanned the evening sky. To the north, Alaph flew away, nearly invisible as he gained height and distance.

"Are you ready, son?"

Jason turned to his father, who strode toward him on two healthy legs, spry and vigorous.

"I'm ready." Jason set a hand on the barrier wall. Alaph had said that he could no longer travel beyond this point, so leaving them on this side was his only option. This spot, however, allowed them their best opportunity to enter. Here, a one-thousand-foot stretch rose only half as high as the rest of the wall. Much work remained, promising that many more stones would float downriver for use in later construction.

Edison picked up the rope and began fashioning a loop. "We'd better hurry."

Nodding, Jason searched the top of the wall for a protruding rock. Alaph had also said the wall's guardians would be distracted, but not for long. It seemed that events in the village had forced some to abandon their posts.

"I see a good anchor hold," Jason said, pointing up.

Edison twirled the loop and cast it that way. It flew above the rock before draping perfectly around the target.

Smiling, Jason clapped his father on the back. "You haven't lost your touch."

"Let's see if I can still climb." Edison tugged on the rope. It seemed secure. "I am heavier, so I will go first. If I can make it, you certainly can."

Edison grasped the rope with both hands, set a foot against the wall, then climbed hand over hand, using his feet to push upward on jutting stones, his sword clanking along the way. When he reached the top, he looked down, visible only from the waist up. "Hurry. I think I see a dragon."

Using the same method, Jason scrambled up and jumped down to a stony path that separated the north and south parapets. On the southern side, a dragon flew parallel to the wall, too low to be seen from the north. As Jason and his father peered over the southern parapet, the dragon suddenly changed course and headed toward them, elevating with each flap of its wings.

"It spotted us." Jason grabbed the rope, still attached to the stone on the northern side. Letting it slide through his hands, he leaped to the top of the southern parapet and rappelled down, his cloak billowing. When his feet struck solid ground next to a cart filled with stones, he drew his sword and shouted, "Dragon! I'm down here!"

The dragon shifted again and dropped toward him, fire shooting from his mouth. Jason dove behind the cart. The flames splashed on the stones and flew over his head. The dragon landed and stalked toward Jason, its wings beating madly as it spewed another storm of fire.

"Up here, dragon!" Edison leaped down. Slashing with his sword as he fell, he clipped one of the dragon's wings and severed a claw.

Screaming, the dragon swung its tail and slapped Edison against the wall, ripping his sword from his hand. Jason leaped out and charged. With a lunge and a thrust, he drove his blade into the dragon's belly, twisted it sharply, and jumped toward his father who now sat at the base of the wall, dazed.

The dragon staggered and blew a flaming tempest. Jason whipped the cloak around and covered himself and his father. Heat shot through the material but no flames.

Another scream sounded. Jason peeked out from behind the cloak. The dragon lay on its side, its legs stroking and the sword's hilt protruding from its belly. He leaped to his feet and turned back to the wall.

"Father," he called breathlessly, "are you all right?"

Wincing, Edison pushed against the ground as he rose. "Never felt better, but I can't say the same for that dragon. That was much easier than I expected."

Jason grasped his father's wrist and pulled him the rest of the way. "We were lucky. He was one of the weaker dragons. I've killed one just like him before."

"Interesting." Edison nudged the dragon's tail with his boot. "If the weaker dragons are guarding the wall, the events in the village must be serious, indeed."

Jason retrieved his sword and wiped it clean on the dry grass before placing it back into its sheath. "The carcass will signal our presence, so we'd better get going." He pointed toward the southwest. "The village is that way. I wasn't on the wall very long, so I'm not sure, but I didn't see any obstacles between here and there. Pretty much a wasteland of rocks and a few miserable-looking trees. While we were on the white dragon's back, I saw a dense forest about ten miles away, so that might be the wilderness Cassabrie mentioned. Both Frederick and Elyssa could be there."

“Agreed.” Edison grabbed the rope and gave it a snapping jerk. A wave of slack shot up the line, freeing it from its anchor. “So which will it be, son? The village to find Koren or the wilderness to find Frederick and Elyssa?”

His father’s weathered hands reeled in the rope as he kept his eyes on his work. Although Jason had already explained images Cassabrie had revealed about Koren’s and Elyssa’s respective troubles, his father hadn’t uttered a word about it. He rarely spoke of anything until the need arose.

“The village is closer,” Jason said. “I suppose it makes sense to help Koren first.”

His father’s brow lifted, though his gaze stayed locked on his hands. “The enchantress calls to you, does she? More fervently than the cry of a lifetime friend?”

“Enchantress?” Jason shook his head. “That’s not it. I’m thinking logistics. Koren’s just closer.”

Edison hoisted the coil of rope onto his shoulder. “I’m just making sure. My journeys to this point have taught me not to trust even the most innocent-looking eyes.”

“Well, I’m not enchanted, if that’s what you mean.”

“Is that so?” Edison looked Jason in the eye. “No one who is enchanted ever realizes it.”

Jason studied his father’s countenance, the face he wore every time he hoped to teach something serious without spelling it out—steely eyes peering from under his brow like a pair of warning lights. It would be better to acknowledge the counsel than to protest again. “I understand,” Jason said. “I’ll be careful.”

Stepping back, Edison nodded at Jason’s belt. “Better check the stardrop.”

Jason reached into the pouch and withdrew a pliable ball, a piece of Tamminy's stomach sewn to form a sac. About the size of a small apple, it felt like the skin inside his mouth, moist and warm. The stardrop provided its own heat, but how long would the sac stay moist and keep the stardrop intact? He placed it gently back in the pouch. "I think it's fine."

"Good." Edison looked up. "Is that a dragon?"

Jason followed his line of sight. A small dragon flew from the direction of the village, heading north. A human rode on its back, red hair and a blue cloak flowing in the wind. Although it seemed to be too small to carry her, the dragon flew straight and true as it crossed over the barrier wall to the west. No guardian dragons approached to ask why he carried a human northward. Maybe they had new orders to allow any dragon to pass.

"Koren?" Edison asked.

Jason nodded but said nothing. He couldn't tear away from the sight—the radiant hair shining in Solarus's waning rays, the blue cape blending with the surrounding sky, and the black dress and boots, nearly invisible against the dragon's equally black scales. Strange, though. She was barefoot earlier and wore a white dress. Where could she be going? The Northlands? And who was that dragon? Taushin?

"Still not enchanted, son?"

Jason spun toward him, blinking. His quick turn made Elyssa's pendant slide on his chest. He withdrew it and laid it on his palm, showing the side with the bird enclosed in a pair of hands. "No ... no, not really. Just thinking. I guess we can't follow Koren."

"Well, I'm thinking that since the wilderness is so far away, we need to get going. Darkness approaches and we have a long way to travel." Edison picked up his sword and flexed his fingers around the hilt. "I must say I prefer this course. If your assumptions are correct, your brothers might well be in the wilderness."

The sparkle in his father's eyes, the rippling muscles in his neck, and the sturdiness of his stance were beautiful to behold. Although still gray-haired and somewhat wrinkled, the warrior of days gone by had returned.

Jason pulled up his cloak's hood and glanced at the pendant again before sliding it back in place. "I prefer this course, too."

Edison pointed his sword straight ahead. "Shall we find your brothers and lead the Lost Ones home?"

Jason withdrew his own sword. "With pleasure, Father. With pleasure."

As darkness enveloped the campsite, Wallace tightened a knot in a vine holding a lean-to together. "I think it'll hold."

"Good." Elyssa set another lean-to against a tree and pushed it under a branch, wedging it in place. After giving the shelter a good shake to test its sturdiness, she brushed her hands together. "Now we can finish mine."

A hefty gust rushed down through the branches, bringing with it a smattering of rain. Wallace held out a hand. "You were right."

Smiling, Elyssa rubbed her fingers together. "My skin never lies."

"Everyone to the shelters," Wallace called, clapping his hands. "Smallest at the center. Biggest on the outside for protection."

Elyssa and Wallace parceled the children out to the lean-tos, two to five children under each, depending on the sizes of the bodies trying to squeeze in. After everyone found a place, Elyssa propped her unfinished shelter against a tree, and Wallace helped her wedge it firmly.

The rain strengthened into a downpour. Elyssa ducked underneath her lean-to and pulled Wallace down with her. They sat close, just out of the straight-line deluge. Still, gaps in the unfinished covering allowed steady drips to leak through here and there.

Wallace shook water from his hair. "It's like Angler's Falls out there, only a lot bigger."

Shielding her face from the flying droplets, Elyssa laughed. "What are you? A puppy?"

"I can be a puppy." He let his tongue hang out, panting. "How's that?"

She gave him a gentle slap across the elbow. "Stop it, silly boy."

He pulled his tongue back in. "If you say so. I'm supposed to be with Phanuel."

"Wait!" Elyssa grabbed his arm. "His fever's gone. He'll be fine for a while. Just stay until the rain stops."

As he stared at her, Elyssa took in his youthful features. Since he had worked so hard and fought so bravely, she had almost forgotten about his real age. It made sense for him to be a silly boy now and then. It might do her some good to let herself be a silly girl, but it just didn't seem right, not now, not with so many dangers lurking.

She held out her hand under a leak and caught a few drops. "It looks like we'll get pretty wet."

"That's fine with me." A wide grin stretched across his face. "I've seen rainclouds in the mountains, but this is the first time I've been under them."

"So *that's* why you got so excited. Will the children be scared?"

"Don't worry about them." Wallace pointed at the shelters dotting their campsite. Arms protruded, palms up, and a few heads emerged. Blinking and giggling, some of the younger children came out and danced in the midst of the watery cascade.

"That looks like fun," Elyssa said.

"And I'm not going to miss it." Wallace slid out and stood in the pouring rain. He grasped a little girl's hands, and the two swayed, splashing in the puddles and laughing merrily. "Come out and join us!"

She shifted toward the edge, then stopped. Her heart raced. Every part of her body longed to rush out and dance. It was so beautiful! These children had suffered for so long—lacking nourishment, enduring heavy burdens, hoping for the kiss of love but tasting only lashes. Now they celebrated freedom. With full bellies and liberated legs, they danced in the joy of heaven's blessings. Like birds set free, they spread their wings and tasted the fresh air of a newly cleansed world.

Birds? Elyssa pulled back and set a hand against her chest. Her pendant was gone, of course. She had left it at the mesa entrance, hoping to signal Jason that some of the slaves had been set free. Some—not all. Yes, these cattle children were now free, but hundreds remained in places they didn't want to be, bearing burdens they didn't want to lift, taking partners with whom they cared not to . . .

Sighing, she settled back against the trunk. Finishing that thought was far too painful. No, she couldn't dance. Not yet. Not until she led the very last slave through the portal to Major Four. Only then could her heart join in the celebration.

Again she felt the spot where her pendant always used to rest. Had Jason found it? If so, did its presence make him guess that she would never leave this world without him? She imagined him marching across the same terrain they had recently traversed, trudging through forests and crossing streams, her pendant dangling at his chest as he hurried to find her. If he knew she was still on this planet, he would never give up. They had been friends far too long for him to do otherwise. Love would guide his path.

She closed her eyes and listened to the lovely sounds—rain tapping on the shelter, wind whistling through the leaves, embers sizzling in the drenching curtain of water, and laughter ebbing as the dance of freedom gave way to exhaustion.

Sitting in the dark while waiting for the end of a storm brought back a memory—another evening, a different young man, a distant planet. She and Jason had rested under the shelter of an uprooted tree, watching for pursuers who threatened their lives. Although only days separated her from that night, it seemed long ago. What was

Jason really doing now? Was he even alive? Maybe he was a prisoner with Koren.

She imagined the two of them sitting in a dark room, similar to the dungeon cell she had occupied for weeks. The picture raised conflicting feelings, both sorrow and comfort. Although Jason sat in prison, at least he had a friend, someone to talk to while he waited for release or escape. At least loneliness wouldn't vanquish his will to survive.

A twinge of envy pricked her emotions, but she brushed it away. His comfort was more important than her own. Having Koren with him was a blessing. Still, sadness leaked in as her thoughts drifted to her own dungeon imprisonment, where she sat in chains hour after hour, day after day, without any friends, until she finally amused herself by inventing one. *Phantom*, she had named her. The wisp of a girl appeared in the midst of Elyssa's loneliest night, two weeks after she had arrived. Elyssa guessed her Diviner's gift had conjured Phantom as a way of coping with worries about her parents and the possibility of execution should Orion find her.

With her mind again in the present, Elyssa settled back against the tree trunk. As the thrumming sounds continued, calling her to slumber, she closed her eyes. Her mind sketched the dungeon cell and her own form sitting in one corner. Soon she drifted into the scene and took her place within the iron fetters.

Alone in her own filth, she clasped her hands together and looked up at the darkness. As tears streamed, she wept through her words. "Creator, I don't know why … why you're letting me rot here. All I did was … snoop through Prescott's files. I did it to find the Lost Ones, not to steal anything. And Orion thinks I'm a witch who conjures up whatever she pleases. He thinks I'm a menace to be burned. But I'm no witch. I'm just Elyssa. I sense things no one else can. That's not conjuring. I'm just reading the details of your glorious world. I understand a language others cannot."

She wiped her nose on her sleeve, smearing something malodorous above her lip. Grimacing, she prayed on. "I don't think I can stand it here much longer. I need help. Could you send Jason to find me? Adrian? Anyone? Even if I could just have someone to talk to now and then, someone who could let me know that you haven't left me to suffer alone, I would—"

"You would what?" A ghostlike image approached, no more than a light-filled outline.

Blinking at the feminine form, Elyssa scooted back an inch. "Who are you?"

"A friend," the young woman said.

"Did I . . . conjure you?"

She laughed gently. "You might say that. You called me here, to be sure."

"I knew my Diviner's gifts were getting stronger, but this is really a surprise."

A barely visible smile turned her lips. "Being able to create images that look real isn't as strange as you might think."

Elyssa waved a hand, rattling her chains. "How would you know? You're just a figment of my imagination."

"If you say so." For a moment, the girl disappeared. Then the skirt of her gown twirled with light, making her visible again. "I cannot stay long, but I am glad to keep you company for a while."

"Okay ..." Elyssa drew out the word. It seemed so comical that this imagined friend appeared to have a mind of her own. "What shall I call you?"

"Well, my name—"

"I know," Elyssa said, raising a finger. "Your name can be Phantom. That fits you perfectly."

"If that pleases you." Phantom disappeared again, leaving them both in darkness, though a few sparks trickled from where her mouth had been. "You are lonely. Would you like to hear a story?"

"Sure. Why not?" Elyssa rested her head against the dungeon wall. "I'm not going anywhere."

Phantom appeared again, her arms of light spreading out as she twirled a glowing cape. She swayed back and forth as if guided by the cadence of her words. "A long time ago in a distant world, a star hovered in the heavens. Not a normal star, mind you, a dwarf so small that it could easily fit in Governor Prescott's palace. And, unlike the fiery giants that paint the night sky, this star—Exodus, by name—brought far less heat, not enough to scald the residents of the land, but enough to cause problems for some.

"Exodus emitted a life-giving gas, though only one race on that world benefitted from its properties. The other race saw no purpose for the star. They saw only that it made the air hotter whenever it came by. Members of this race viewed it as an annoyance, but those of the first race worshiped the star because Exodus drifted from place to place in the sky as if it possessed a mind of its own."

As Elyssa listened, she let herself become absorbed in the tale. The world Phantom painted with her words appeared. Exodus hovered in the sky, a white ball emitting streams of light. A multicolored nucleus pulsed at the center, like an animated heart changing its hue with every beat. Forests and villages covered the landscape, along with people walking from place to place, every item as solid as herself.

A human riding a dragon materialized. Elyssa squinted at the pair. How strange! Why would her mind conjure such a beast? Had her obsession with the Underground Gateway infused her unguarded thoughts with draconic images?

"Those who did not benefit from the star," Phantom continued, still swaying, "fools that they were, imagined themselves wise enough to alter the natural course the Creator had designed, thinking that a hot day meant something more than yet another passing of Exodus, that perhaps continued exposure would bring lasting harm. So these blind guides devised a way to diminish the heat Exodus provided."

The dragon flew toward the star. The human riding its back lifted a dark spear in one hand and, when he drew within range, flung it at the star. The spear pierced the surface and plunged into the heart. Exodus spewed white vapor that rained across the land. Like a deflating balloon, Exodus zipped away, slowly sinking in the sky as it raced toward the horizon.

As Phantom's swaying slowed, the scene dissolved. Darkness again prevailed. "Sadly, the gas Exodus provided diminished over the years, threatening the very existence of the race that counted on its presence for survival. And the fools who devised the weapon unleashed a curse, for as the wounded Exodus flew to its hiding place in the Northlands, it emitted a disease-bearing wind that manifested itself soon afterward.

"Spreading cancerous lesions across the skin, the disease consumed the stricken, and they perished within days. As victim after victim contracted the plague, it became clear that only a few younger members of that race were immune, at least for a while, apparently protected by a genetic shield. Although the scientists among them were able to isolate the gene and understand its properties, every susceptible creature died before a cure could be found. Only one hope remained for the surviving children. The members of the other race, the victims of the insane plan, showed the children mercy. Yet even these children eventually succumbed, and this loss proved to be a greater problem for the merciful race than they first realized."

Phantom sat next to Elyssa, disappearing as she settled. "I have to go now. If I am able to return, I will tell you how one race preserved the genetics of the other race and repopulated the world with their progeny. Until then, in the event that I cannot return, I leave you with something you must remember. Only you have the gifts that will enable this knowledge to be applied."

Phantom shifted her body and knelt in front of Elyssa. It seemed that dust from the dungeon floor flowed into her glow, giving her solidity and color. Her face clarified. Her hair transformed to stark red. Her eyes shone green. "Someone will soon try to resurrect Exodus. If it is raised without sealing its puncture wound, it will unleash the disease once again, and every member of the race of fools will perish, save one. Only you remain genetically protected, and only you are able to safely seal the wound."

As she vanished again, two final words echoed: "Only you … Only you …"

Elyssa jerked herself awake. That face! Those eyes! Leaning forward, she stared into the darkness. The rain has ceased. The wind had calmed. Only her bare whisper interrupted the silence. "Cassabrie!"

She felt the space next to her. Empty. "Wallace?" she whispered.

Shifting to hands and knees, she crawled from her lean-to, then rose to her feet, peeling her damp shirt from her skin as she looked around. Three moons shone through the branches, illuminating the other lean-tos in the clearing. The sounds of a rain-washed night reached her ears—gentle snoring, water dripping from trees, the occasional click of a falling cone. All was well.

"I'm over here."

Elyssa turned to find Wallace sitting, his back against a tree. With wet hair plastered over his empty eye socket, his clothes soaked, and a sword resting on his lap, he looked like a soldier who had just battled a sea monster.

She knelt next to him. "Couldn't sleep?"

"I decided to take first guard duty. The other boys deserve a good night's rest."

She pushed the hair away from the socket. "If anyone deserves a rest, you do."

"It's all right. I never sleep well. I get nightmares."

"Want to tell me about them?"

"Not really." He looked away. "Too personal."

"I understand." She slid her hand into his. He flinched but didn't pull away. "I had a dream I need to tell you about."

He nodded, keeping his head turned.

For the next few minutes, she told him about her dungeon experiences, Cassabrie's visit, and the story she revealed. By the time she finished, Wallace was staring at her, his jaw partially open.

"Do you know what that means?" he asked.

"The humans were the ones who didn't benefit from the gas, so they—"

"Not that. I mean the conclusion. You have to find the star and seal it."

"I know," she said, still kneeling, "but I wanted to see if you agreed before I mentioned it."

"I agree. And you'd better start as soon as you can."

"What will we do with the children?" Elyssa asked. "They can't fend for themselves."

"They don't have to. I'm not leaving them." He passed the sword to Elyssa. "You're going to need this more than I will. I can make a new weapon."

She stared at the blade. "Are you saying I should go by myself? All the way to the Northlands?"

"You can't be two places at once, and I can't go with you."

Rising, she gripped the hilt tightly. "I suppose there's no choice. And I should probably go as far as I can tonight."

"And sleep during the day." He climbed to his feet and nodded toward one of the lean-tos. "Don't worry about the children. I can take care of them."

"I know," she said blankly, still staring at the sword.

Wallace unfastened his belt and wrapped it around Elyssa's waist. He then took the sword from her hand and pushed it into the homemade leather sheath at her hip. "I'll never forget what you taught me."

Shaking herself out of her stupor, she gazed at his face. As his one eye gleamed in the moonlight, he appeared to be older, taller, not the puppylike slave boy who had to tilt his head up to look her in the eye. "Taught you?" she asked.

"You called me a warrior, and you gave me confidence that I could lead the way. That's why I know I can take care of these children."

"You're right," she said, nodding. "I have confidence in you."

"And now that you have the sword, I'm passing the same words back to you." After taking a breath, he laid a hand on her shoulder, his voice now a whisper. "I can't follow you, Elyssa, but you can still lead the way. It's up to you to save the planet from the disease."

She wrapped her arms around him and held him close, his wet clothes against her own, chilling her skin. As tears welled, she whispered with a trembling voice, "We will meet again. Maybe here. Maybe at a better place."

"I hope so." He drew away, his eye sparkling. "Go. And don't look back."

"Good-bye, Wallace. When we meet again, I will dance with you. I promise." She kissed him on the cheek, drew the sword, and marched into the forest.

Retracing their path, she hacked at protruding branches with the sword. When she reached a point far from his view, she stopped. As she imagined Wallace's face, an urge to look back nearly overwhelmed her, but she kept her gaze straight ahead. A moon-dappled forest lay before her, and somewhere beyond the trees, maybe beyond the barrier wall, Jason might be standing under the same trinity of moons. Perhaps he, too, had gone to the Northlands in search of her.

Taking a deep breath, she resumed her steady stride. "I'm coming, Jason, ready or not."

twenty

Tibalt lifted a key ring. "Found it!" he called, jingling the keys. "Told you I would!"

"Shhh!" Randall jerked the keys away and brushed the ring on his tunic. Since the night Jason tossed it into the forest, rain and mud had coated it with a layer of silt and debris, but not enough to conceal it from Tibber's stubborn search.

As clean metal appeared, the surface gleamed in the moonlight. "Now we can unlock the dungeon."

Tibalt's gap-toothed smile emerged. "I'll tell the dragons."

"Tell them to keep hidden until I give a signal. I don't remember if the back entrance is big enough for them to fit through."

"We'll watch from the forest." Tibalt followed a leaf-strewn path for a moment before angling away and slinking into the darkness.

Stepping quietly, Randall followed the path to the dungeon's back gate, an iron frame with heavy oak bars. He inserted the key, disengaged the lock, and swung the door slowly open, hoping to keep any rusty hinge from squealing. If only they could get the dragons in without anyone noticing, they would be safe for the time being.

With the gate now wide open, Randall mentally measured the clearance. Arxad would likely fit without a problem. Magnar, the larger of the two, might have difficulty squeezing through the gate, but once inside he could negotiate the maze well enough to find a deep hiding place.

Randall turned and looked at the forest. Out there in the midst of the trees, two dragons waited, ready to fulfill their offer of help—or potentially burn him to a crisp. He could trust Arxad, or so it seemed. Arxad appeared to be trustworthy as he gave advice about how best to approach their plan of ridding Mesolantrum of the usurpers. Magnar, on the other hand, gave him chills every time his eyes pulsed in response to Arxad's suggestions. The bigger dragon had stayed quiet, though rumblings in his throat communicated hostility, at least in Randall's mind.

Taking a deep breath, he nodded. They couldn't wait any longer. With a dead father to avenge and a mother missing, he had to take his chances.

He waved an arm over his head. Seconds later, Tibalt emerged from the forest, followed by two dragons. Although Tibalt skulked like a cagey rat, the dragons, their scales shimmering in the moonlight, looked like a dazzling art display. If anyone happened to glance their way, their plans would be ruined.

Randall waved frantically. Risking a little more noise was probably better than leaving them exposed for too long.

Tibalt ran toward the dungeon. Arxad and Magnar flapped their wings, lifting their bodies into a skittering glide. When they arrived, all four stood at the open gate and peered through.

"Tibalt will go first," Randall said, "and lead the way as far into the maze as you dragons can go. When you're settled, he'll come back, and we'll lock you in. You'll enjoy the atmosphere. It's drenched with extane."

"Pheterone," Tibalt said as he walked into the dungeon. "That's what they call it."

"Right." Randall looked at Arxad, then at Magnar. "After I scout the goings on, I'll come back with a report and a plan. I'll also bring food and water."

"That is acceptable." Arxad ducked his head and entered.

Magnar grumbled. "Except for locking us in. Willingly stepping into a prison is not my idea of a wise plan."

"It's to keep others out, not to keep you in." Randall shook the wooden bars. "With a couple of blasts of fire and your strength, you could escape easily."

"A reasonable answer." After eyeing the bars for a moment, Magnar shuffled to the opening, collapsed his wings, and pushed past the frame, then turned back and cast his gaze on Randall, his eyes flaming more vibrantly than ever. "Heed my warning. Do not underestimate our abilities. If pheterone is indeed rich in the air, no army capable of fitting into this corridor will be able to withstand our flames."

"Warning well taken, Magnar," Randall said as he closed the gate. "I'm hoping your increased strength will benefit us all."

Tibalt squeezed between the dragons and pressed his face against two bars, his nose protruding through the gap. "I will open the portal tonight," he said, wiggling his fingers. "No sense in risking getting caught in the daylight."

"I agree." Randall reached between the bars and gripped Tibalt's shoulder. "May the Creator guide you to Jason and Elyssa. I know you'll help them."

Tibalt's smile returned. "Well, I'll be a bug-eyed potato! Of course I will. And I'll look for you in the governor's chair when we come back with the Lost Ones."

"So be it."

As Tibber led the two dragons into the depths of the dungeon, Randall wrapped his fingers around one of the bars and watched the darkness close around them. The old man had plenty of spunk, but could he really do much good in the dragon world? And how could the son of the dead governor unravel the twisted plot that stole his father's life? Drexel and Orion were so crafty, maybe they had already thought about dragons coming here to stop them.

Randall licked his lips. Even from so far away, a bitter film coated them. Could that be the reason the dungeon was flooded with extane, to bait the dragons? Might they be walking into a trap? Magnar didn't seem to know that using his fire would ignite the entire maze, which could easily cause a collapse. Yet warning him might raise trouble as well. Magnar wouldn't take kindly to the idea that his most powerful weapon would be useless in the dungeon.

Sighing, Randall turned toward the portal. It lay far beyond his vision, past the trees, across two streams, outside the barrier to the forbidden zone, an underground gateway that allowed passage for both good and evil. Now he and Tibalt played a daring game of gatekeeper, allowing two of the slave traffickers through. It felt like giving free passes to a pair of demons and providing them room and board while they plotted disaster.

As he stared at the treetops, clouds passed across the moon, darkening the night. Appropriate, to be sure. It seemed that Solarus, the moon, and every star had turned their backs, as if not wanting to witness the results of his foolhardy plans. Yet perhaps the Creator still cast a caring eye their way. They would need it. To bring Jason, Elyssa, and the Lost Ones home to a free Mesolantrum would take a miracle.

Jason crouched behind a rock and peered around its side. A little more than a stone's throw away, the dragon village lay in silence, darkened on this cloudy night. Even the spires of the Zodiac, which had sparkled in the sunlight and shone with a silvery glow late into the evening, were now dark. One moon peeked through a gap in the overcast sky near the horizon—Pariah, the crater-riddled dwarf. Alone in the dismal blackness, it shone just enough light to provide a view of the quiet gathering of deserted buildings.

Sliding his sword back into its sheath, Edison emerged from behind Jason and stepped into the open. "I see no reason to hide like mice from a cat. There is neither man nor beast anywhere in sight."

Jason rose and joined him. "I saw a lantern in a window, but it blinked off in a hurry."

"I saw it, too." Edison inhaled deeply. "I smell the odor of two men. They are close by, perhaps watching in fear. Something has frightened the humans in this place, but why are there no dragons present?"

Jason sniffed the air. With the land so dry, nothing registered, not even a hint of must or mold. "Let me know if you smell a dragon."

"Will do. The scent of the one we killed is not easily forgotten."

Jason squinted at the Basilica. When his captor flew past that building before, a huge dragon guarded the front entry, but now even that sacred place had been abandoned. "I don't like it. Having no dragons around at all is very ..."

"Suspicious?" his father offered. "As if something terrible is about to happen, and the dragons took off?"

"Something terrible? Like what?"

Edison shrugged. "I thought you might have an idea. But when I see chickens cowering and their captors flying the coop, it makes me think the coop is about to go up in flames."

"I get the picture." Jason withdrew his sword and strode toward the Zodiac. "Let's go. If any dragon stayed around, it would be Arxad."

They hurried into the village and crossed the Zodiac's empty portico. After pushing open one of the heavy front doors, they continued a quick march through the corridor. Radiance flowed from the wall murals, providing enough light to illuminate the path. A girl painted on the right-hand wall stood within a semitransparent sphere, her hands uplifted as if supporting the sphere's shell.

Jason slowed to a halt and stared at her, taking in her familiar green eyes, red hair, and ivory face.

"Do you know who she is?" Edison asked.

"Cassabrie," Jason whispered.

"Ah, yes. I see the resemblance now." Edison pulled Jason along. "Let's compare notes about her later. I doubt that this painting will tell us what we need to know."

When they entered the Zodiac's inner courtyard, Jason slowed his pace. The crystalline sphere at the center pulsed, throbbing like a light-pumping heart. Even from where he stood, at least fifteen steps from the crystal, the light particles stung his skin.

Edison held up a hand, shielding his face. "What is that thing?"

"I have heard it called the Reflections Crystal and a cooking stake. If you touch it, it packs quite a wallop, but I know how to shut it off. Speak the first lie that comes to mind."

"Let's see.... I'm not nervous about being here."

The radiance dimmed, but only enough to dull the sting.

"I guess you're just kind of nervous," Jason said. "We'll have to do better than that."

"All right. I see how this game works." Edison squared his shoulders and spoke with conviction. "I am ashamed to be here with my son."

The sphere instantly turned black, leaving them in darkness.

His cheeks warming, Jason patted his father's shoulder. "Good job. Too good, really. But it should come back on soon." Remembering the clear path between himself and the crystal, he strode forward and stood next to its column. As it slowly brightened, he scanned the area. A thick chain lay on the floor, one end attached to the column's base and the other to a loose, unlocked manacle.

Edison lifted the manacle and sniffed the metal. "Human and dragon scent."

"Both? That doesn't make sense. Zena chained Koren to the crystal. I never saw a dragon touch the chain."

"The inner part smells strongly of dragon." Edison dropped the manacle and stared at the brightening sphere. "What would it mean if a dragon was the most recent prisoner?"

"Dissension in the ranks," Jason said. "A power struggle."

"A wise deduction. I think we can assume the dragon who has been friendly to our cause was the prisoner."

"Probably. Any other clues?"

"Only that the human scent is blended with something familiar, a lye soap from back home, I think."

Jason forced a straight face. "What year was the soap made?"

"I can't tell that much, it's too faint—"

"Father," Jason said. "I'm joking."

Edison's brow lifted. "Oh, I see. It's hard to tell when I'm concentrating."

"I'll be serious, then. Look at this." He extended his arm. The brightening sphere highlighted the newly healed skin on his palm. "Smell the wrist. I think the star-drop might have stripped the scent on my hands."

Edison sniffed Jason's wrist. "Ah! The same lye soap. It has been a while since you used it, but traces are there."

"Elyssa and I washed with lye soap at the lumber shack when we were running from Bristol and his dogs."

"So I'm detecting your touch," Edison said. "Interesting. I thought I would have known your scent."

"You would have. I never touched the manacle. Only the chains."

"So that means …"

"Elyssa was here." Jason nudged the chain with his foot. "She released Arxad."

"Another good deduction." Edison raised a shielding hand. "Is it time for another lie?"

"I think we got the information we need." Jason pinched the sleeve of his father's tunic and pulled him back. "Let's go."

After retreating through the main corridor, Jason and his father stopped at the edge of the Zodiac's portico and looked out over the desolate street. Three moons now shed light on the land, making the dragon realm visible. The village boundary ended at a downslope that led to an expansive plateau where two lonely mesas outcropped in the midst of a desert landscape. Mountains created the final backdrop, and dense forests painted their slopes dark green.

Jason nodded toward the distant trees. “Elyssa’s out there somewhere. I know she is. We have to find her.”

“I agree wholeheartedly,” Edison said, “but my nose isn’t sensitive enough to track her. I’m not a bloodhound.”

Jason lifted Elyssa’s pendant and rubbed his finger across the liberated bird. “We’ll find her, or I’ll die trying. I won’t leave this world without her.”

⁂

Holding a stardrop in her closed hand, Koren stood next to Taushin in front of a great castle, shivering in the shadow of one of its red turrets. A wide door lay open, as if the master of this enormous house awaited visitors, or at least expected no intruders. With an empty chair sitting in the middle of its huge foyer, the place seemed to open a pair of arms and invite her in.

For years she had longed to visit these Northlands, and the sight of the colorful meadows sweeping beneath her as she rode Taushin’s back resurrected memories of her favorite daydreams. Simply finding that this place, this land where Solarus never set, was more than a myth had been exhilarating. Her dreams of meeting the great king of the dragons might finally be realized, but arriving at the doorstep brought reality crashing down. She had come not as a guest but rather as a darkly dressed stranger who might do more harm than good.

As a breeze kicked up, she pulled her inadequate cloak closer to her body. Although she had put on an extra shirt under her dress, the wind tore through every layer. “Should we just walk in?” she asked.

"You will walk in," Taushin said. "I will remain here. The king of the Northlands would not be pleased with my presence."

"Why is that?"

"He holds Exodus hostage. As long as it remains in his control, he can keep this land locked in ice, for if Exodus were to rise again, the polar cap would melt, and he would lose his kingdom. He prefers this little scrap of a kingdom over all else, including the lives of every dragon on Starlight. Even though he realizes that Exodus is the source of pheterone, he jealously guards it within these walls."

Koren eyed Taushin. He kept his stare aimed straight ahead, blind as always. All the legends had portrayed the Northlands king as good and noble, so hearing this dark usurper saying the opposite wasn't a surprise. "What am I supposed to do?" she asked.

"Exodus resides somewhere inside. Find it. Since you are a Starlighter, it cannot hurt you. Walk into its core and embrace its heart. Speak the words it bleeds, the tales it begs to have told. As you relate the stories, you will infuse it with your passion, and it will rise from this place."

"Is it possible to walk into a star? Won't it be blazing hot?"

"Exodus is not a galactic star. It is what you might call a celestial angel, a guiding light that the Creator assigned to this world. The citizens of the planet labeled it a star, even though they knew that the twinkling dots in the heavens were very different. Although it was somewhat hot centuries ago, Exodus sustained a wound in its outer membrane, and it lost its heat. That wound likely still exists, so you should be able to enter through the breach and approach the core. It would be reasonable, however, to use your gifts to create an image before you proceed. Perhaps you will gain some insight as to where it rests."

Koren fanned out her cloak and raised her arms. Cold wind again assaulted her body, knifing through the black dress. Her teeth chattered, shaking her words. "Come to me, Exodus. Show me your heart. Allow me to see the pain of your wound."

Ribbons of light flowed from the open door and streamed toward her. As they passed by her ears, each one whispered a brief sentence or two.

"Look! My skin! Something is eating it away!"

"There is no cure, my love. We are both going to die."

"What once protected us from harm has left behind an evil curse. We should have listened."

Koren looked for the source of the whispering light. Inside, a wall on the opposite end of the foyer had slid halfway open, and the streams poured through the gap in single file.

"Show me, Exodus," she continued. "Fallen star, rejected angel, bringer of the curse, show yourself to me."

The streams began gathering between her and the doorway and coalesced into a sphere of light nearly as large as the entry. A central body took shape at its core, flashing multicolored images so quickly that none stayed long enough for her to recognize. To the right, head high, thin vapor flowed through a small hole.

Keeping her eye on the hole, Koren walked in that direction. She laid a hand over the opening, covering the entire breach with her palm. "Once I get inside, how do I patch it?"

"You need not patch it. Telling the stories from the inside will cause Exodus to rise and again become Starlight's guiding angel."

"And it will regain its heat?"

"I detect that you fear burning. You need not. As long as the hole remains, heat will escape, and the same hole will provide you a way out once the star is again in the sky."

"Okay," Koren said slowly. "That sounds easy enough, but what benefit do you get out of it?"

"Adulation from the dragon populace. With the infusion of pheterone, all will realize that I am, indeed, the prophesied king. While I resided in the egg, the Creator endowed me with this knowledge. I alone know how a Starlighter can resurrect the star, and now I reveal the secret, a prophecy hidden from other dragons, even Tamminy. Once your will is set to raise Exodus, a crown of light will appear within the star. Take it. Wear it. Only then will you have the ability you need to accomplish this task. It is the crown that gives you the ability to hear Starlight's tales, a spiritual receiver that collects the planet's joys and woes. After you have accomplished this, we will end slavery throughout the world, and I will rule Starlight for centuries to come."

A whispering stream broke away from the sphere and swirled around Koren's head, leaving words in her ear with each orbit.

"If the hole is … not sealed, Exodus … is still wounded. The reason for its fall … must be removed."

Then, the stream plunged back into the sphere in a radiant splash.

Koren cocked her head at Taushin. "Why would we resurrect Exodus without sealing the hole? Wouldn't it just sink again?"

"Eventually. It would stay aloft long enough to prove who I am and to infuse the atmosphere with pheterone."

"How can you be sure? What if it sinks while everyone is watching? That would ruin everything."

Taushin closed his eyes, saying nothing for several seconds. Koren held her breath. The wait seemed unbearable. Her question was certainly reasonable.

Finally, Taushin let out a sigh. "I have been trying to protect you from an awful truth. I still have hope that Exodus will fly long enough to allow me to free your people, but if it sinks, our plans will sink with it."

"What is the awful truth?"

"There is a way to ensure success. It is the reason I had you take a stardrop from Cassabrie's chamber, and it is what I learned when you replayed the conversation between Magnar and Arxad in the Basilica. Once you get inside Exodus, you can seal the hole with the stardrop."

Koren opened her hand and stared at the shining stardrop. "But if I seal the hole from the inside …"

"You would not be able to escape," he said. "You would succeed, to be sure. Exodus would rise, it would fill the air with pheterone, and dragons would never again require the services of human slaves."

Koren closed her hand. The image of the star evaporated, and the streams of light dispersed into the air. "You're saying I would be trapped in there until I die, aren't you?"

"Here is the heart of the awful truth." Lifting his head high, Taushin spoke with passion. "You would neither be trapped nor would you die. Instead, you would become the guiding angel of Starlight, the destiny of an obedient Starlighter. As you will learn when you tell the tales from within Exodus, humans originated here and were relocated to Darksphere, a planet so named because it possessed no hovering angel. The reason a Starlighter is born is simply to assume this role. Cassabrie refused and therefore perished. You, Koren, were born to take her place, the savior of dragons and humans alike. Now you may take your place as a star in the sky, a watchful angel who forever tells the Creator's stories to every soul in the world, dragon and human alike … if they will listen."

After inhaling deeply, Taushin returned to his normal tone. "Your other option is the one I offered initially. Attempt the resurrection without sealing the hole. Perhaps we can accomplish our purposes without your sacrifice."

Koren blinked at him. It seemed that an avalanche of revelation had stormed over her—the names of both planets, her own label as a Starlighter, the purpose for her birth, the reason Taushin imprisoned her, choosing chains instead of persuasion. If she had known these terrible options in advance, she would likely have taken Cassabrie's choice, refusing cooperation. Who would take either option? Eternal imprisonment in a sphere of light, hovering over a thankless planet, endlessly telling its populace tales they would likely ignore? Would trying instead to inflate a broken balloon make any sense? Even if it worked for a while, what would happen to the dragons' pheterone supply later? Should she even ask this question? Taushin might not answer truthfully anyway. Maybe if she cooperated for now, she could buy enough time to get the slaves home regardless of what Taushin planned for the dragons' survival.... Maybe.

"I see that you now understand," Taushin said. "You know more than Cassabrie ever learned. In fact, you are a worthier angel candidate than she, for you are not only more powerful, you have demonstrated a willingness to sacrifice for others, a stark contrast to Cassabrie's stubborn selfishness."

"Sacrifice," Koren whispered. It seemed so long ago that she and Natalla memorized one of her favorite verses in the Code. As she pictured Natalla listening to her read from the ancient book, the words streamed back into her mind. *You will recognize love when you see someone sacrificing himself for the sake of a pauper.*

She had explained to Natalla that the cattle children were surely paupers, and she finished the lesson with, "Someday I'm going to find a way to help them. Someone has to." While it was true that the cattle children were now free, were the other slaves any less valuable?

"I cannot hear your thoughts," Taushin said, "but your struggle is clear. My advice, again, is to attempt the resurrection without sealing the hole. If it fails, then perhaps you will have the opportunity to try again. Why sacrifice? Why risk harm to yourself when it is possible to gain what you long for without it? With your power, I am sure you can keep the star aloft long enough for me to get the slaves out. In fact, when you come down, perhaps every single one of them will already be gone. Surely success without sacrifice is to be greatly desired. To be eternally trapped while your liberated friends celebrate their freedom without you would be the greatest of tortures, would it not? Yes, you would feel some joy ... temporarily. But what about after a hundred years? A thousand years? Ten thousand? After every rejoicing slave is dead, you will be hovering over a thankless land, forever and ever. Your sorrow will never end."

Koren studied his face. With his blue eyes shining brightly, it seemed impossible to check for any hint of deception. Could he be telling the truth? If so, maybe it made sense to try it the easy way first. What could it hurt? If it failed, she could then opt to seal the hole. At least she could push the horrible decision back, if not eliminate it.

As her fears subsided, her cloak blew to the side, exposing her booted legs. With Solarus shining, the dragon shadow again painted the ground next to her. She lifted an arm and looked at her wrist. An abrasion still reddened her skin, the symbol of Taushin's cruelty.

Her own voice entered her mind, passionate tones echoing after each punctuated word. *Love ... does ... not ... need ... chains!*

How could she trust this beast, this mad dragon who would torture and maim? Yet hadn't he told the truth about the Code? Hadn't the Creator forced his will upon those who rebelled against him? Didn't they require chains?

And his explanation about the names of the planets and the purpose of Exodus all made sense. Maybe she had to be chained and dragged here in order to understand what she had to do.

"So," Taushin said, again casting his beams on her, "there are no chains here. What is your decision?"

⁂

While facing a great throne and a seated white dragon, Cassabrie swayed, making her dress and cape visible. With a wide seat and a gap in the back for his tail, Alaph's ivory chair was obviously designed for a dragon's anatomy, and he seemed comfortable as he looked on, his ears erect and his eyes trained on a semitransparent image between him and Cassabrie—Koren standing in front of the door with Taushin.

"That is enough," he said. "It is time for you to go."

Cassabrie lowered her hands and waited for her cape to settle. "We didn't hear her answer."

A gentle laugh rumbled in Alaph's throat. "I think she will change her mind several times before she settles on a final decision, so hearing her first reply might satisfy your curiosity, but it would not be conclusive."

"Even so, she paused for so long. What was she waiting for?"

Alaph looked at her, his blue eyes clear and sharp and casting no beams that might hide his intent. "For wisdom."

"Will you provide it?"

"If she asks ..." His expression suddenly turned morose. "Her knowledge of the Code is a valuable treasure, to be sure, and it will be a great light to her path, but ..."

"She needs to ask the Creator," Cassabrie finished. "Will you tell *me* if Koren should resurrect Exodus? *Should* she seal the hole?"

"So many questions!" Alaph breathed a stream of icy vapor. "You heard the dilemma. You experienced it yourself. Perhaps you should be asking your questions to a mirror."

Cassabrie grinned. "Not so, good king. I wouldn't be able to see myself."

Alaph let out a roaring laugh. "Well done, Starlighter. You have bested me, so I will answer one of your questions. Choose well."

"That's easy. When Jason was in the star chamber with me, he said that Exodus wanted to be destroyed. Is that true?"

Alaph stared at her blankly. "How interesting. Jason's wisdom might be greater than I gave him credit for."

"Then it's true?"

"It is true. Do you remember what I told you about a Starlighter's fate if she were to be trapped between worlds?"

"Yes," Cassabrie said. "It is the most horrific existence imaginable."

"Then imagine this. A Starlighter lives within every such star. When Exodus moved freely, the Starlighter lived in ecstasy. It is not the lonely existence Taushin described. It is really an escape from the tortures of this life and a journey into the true Northlands. This Starlighter did not even realize she was confined. Listening to the Creator's voice and repeating his words for all to hear was the greatest existence possible. She was in pure bliss and in his presence always. There is no greater joy."

Cassabrie trembled with delight. "And now?"

"Now she is in torment. She cannot hear the Creator's voice. For all these centuries she has suffered, still learning the events of the world and still sending them forth again as she weeps. As if wedged between the worlds, she is trapped, and the torture is unbearable. She wants to die and be with her Creator."

"Can she die?"

Alaph nodded. "If Exodus is destroyed."

"Then Starlight will have no pheterone or guiding angel."

"True, but there is another option. She could be replaced by another Starlighter."

Cassabrie stared at him. Alaph's simple declaration meant so much more, but she dared not ask another question.

"Let us move on to other matters." He shifted down to the floor and spread out his wings. "You cannot help Koren at this time, but there is someone who needs you."

"You told me I was going to Darksphere again," Cassabrie said as she climbed up his tail to his back, "but you never said whom I would be helping."

"Someone who will face a threatening situation very soon. I will take you to the portal now."

"The Northlands portal?"

"It is the only one I can reach. I still cannot pass beyond the wall."

Cassabrie sat straight on Alaph's back. Without a spine to grasp, she had no way to hang on, but being a spirit had its advantages. Nothing could knock her from this perch. "I'm ready."

As Alaph flapped his wings and rose slowly into the spacious throne chamber, Cassabrie looked out the window they would soon fly through. A field of white lay before her, like a blank page waiting for an author's pen. It was better this way, not knowing what was in store. The tale was yet to be told, and as the ink began filling the page, she would witness every stroke, memorizing each detail. Someday the people of Starlight and Darksphere would need to hear this tale, and she would be ready to tell it.

Enjoy this sneak peek of *Diviner*, the third book in the Dragons of Starlight series.

one

Koren stood at the brink of a precipice and stared into the darkness below. Only inches in front of her black boots, a stairway descended sharply into the seemingly endless void. The rocky steps appeared to be hundreds of years old — narrow, crumbling, without rails or even walls — bare, sculpted stone jutting downward into the chasm before being swallowed by the eerie darkness.

Floating a few feet above the stairs, globules of vaporous light streamed toward her, each one stretching out like a comet — a shining head of shimmering radiance followed by a glowing tail. Wiggling like tadpoles, they seemed to swim in the air, and as the first one passed by it orbited her face, brushing her skin with a tickly buzz.

A soft voice emanated from the light, like a whisper from afar. "Has Exodus caused our pain? Will it ever return?" Then, after a final brush against her cheek, the stream flew toward the wall behind her, a sliding barrier that someone had left open, as if anticipating her arrival at the Northlands castle.

The streams flowed through the opening, some pausing at Koren's spot at the top of the stairway before joining the escaping herd. The rush sounded like a crowd of people hurrying by, with only snippets of their private conversations reaching her ears as they passed.

"If the genetics are pure, we can force the recessive to survive."

"I will take the eggs to Darksphere. The children will have a dragon for a father."

"Find the escapees. No one will leave Starlight alive."

Clutching the stardrop she had taken from Cassabrie's sanctum, Koren raised her hood, shielding her ears from the barrage of splintered sentences. She stepped down and shifted her weight forward. Although the stony material crackled under her boot, the stair held firm. Then, fanning out her cloak, she walked slowly down the stairwell. Ahead lay the darkness of the unknown, a dizzying descent into a river of visible voices.

Koren pressed on. She had no choice. Somewhere in the castle lay the fallen star, Exodus, and Taushin, the new king of the dragons, had compelled her to locate it—without detection. He waited outside, leaving her to pass through the empty foyer and explore the castle like a burglar.

Her mind's eye drifted beyond Taushin, across the Northlands' snow-covered landscape, southward to the lush, fertile valley where she had left Jason Masters, her new friend from the world of humans, a young man her own age who had tried to rescue her. So much had happened since she had allowed herself to be captured to save him from the sorceress Zena's pack of wolves. Where was he now? Dead? Captured? Had he returned to his own planet and forgotten all about her?

Koren heaved a deep sigh. No, Jason would never desert his quest. She had to push away these dark thoughts. Jason was a warrior. Somehow he would have found a way to survive, to go on, even if he had to retreat to the south. One way or the other, he didn't appear to be anywhere in the Northlands vicinity.

As light from the world outside faded behind her, Koren slowed her pace. The never-ending streams of light illuminated the area just enough to allow a view of the dangers—a deep plunge into nothingness on each side and crumbling narrow steps ahead, seemingly more fragile in the dimness. The slightest misstep could send her tumbling into a bone-breaking crash or hurtling over the precipice.

The stairs went on and on. Doubt stirred. How could a star have burrowed into a castle's deep cellar? Yet some instinct drove her on. The whispering streams had to come from somewhere, making the chasm a likely place to search, even if it was not the safest.

The whispers continued, quieter now but still audible in spite of her hood.

"The Starlighter is alone and forsaken. She wants to die."

"Fear not the loss of life. Fear the loss of the eternal. For life can be restored. Once lost, the eternal can never be found again."

Koren kept her stare on the steps in front of her, marching to the beat of an inner rhythm. The fleeting statements seemed to beg to be put together, like puzzle pieces or perhaps threads in a mysterious mosaic. If she concentrated, maybe she could weave them into a coherent story, but so far the big picture eluded her.

As her legs began to shake from exertion, a solid foundation came into view, an expanse that looked like the floor of a cave. A few paces in front of the final stair, a solid wall blocked forward progress. The chamber appeared to be wide open to the left, but it was too dark in that direction to see what might lie in wait. To the right, the whispering streams flowed from a cave opening in another wall.

Taking a deep breath, Koren strode to the right, her gaze fixed on the cave. The pulsing lights funneled through the entrance, thick and frenzied, like radiant bats fleeing their daytime abode. She lowered her head and pushed through the barrage, trying to ignore the flurry of chaotic whispers.

Light appeared ahead, growing brighter and brighter until she reached a massive chamber where, just out of reach, a glowing sphere hovered a foot or so above the floor. As she crossed the threshold into the room, the whispers stopped. All was quiet. Ahead, about twice the span of outstretched dragon wings, the nearly transparent ball of light trembled, as if shaking in fear.

A flow of radiance erupted from a point on the surface and shaped into new whispering streams before swimming into the tunnel behind her. At the sphere's lower extremity, liquid dripped to the floor, sizzling on contact.

Vapor rose briefly before being sucked into narrow crevices zigzagging across the stone surface.

Koren eyed the vapor-producing liquid seeping into the ground. Pheterone. The miners back home found it in veins that likely originated from this spot.

She peered through the star's curved wall. Inside, a smaller ball of light, about half the size of the entrance to Arxad's cave, floated at eye level. Images flashed on the surface, changing every second—a red dragon, a cattle child, a stone worker with a cart. Each image acted as a layer on the sphere that peeled off in a pulse of light before shooting out as one of the vapors.

Koren touched the edge of the streams' exit point, a jagged hole nearly as big as her hand. As a new stream poured out, the flow warmed her skin. The light filtered through the gaps in her fingers and gathered behind her into yet another tadpole-like projectile.

Mentally, she ran over what little she knew about this star that wasn't a star. Taushin had called it "a celestial angel," referring to the sphere as a guide given to this planet by the Creator. Unbidden, his words rose in her mind. *The citizens of the planet labeled it a star, even though they knew that the twinkling dots in the heavens were very different. Although it was somewhat hot centuries ago, Exodus sustained a wound in its outer membrane, and it lost its heat.*

As another trickle of warmth leaked from the wound, Koren uncurled the fingers of her other hand, revealing the stardrop she had carried so far. The size of a large knuckle, the sphere glowed with white light.

Her mission was to enter the sphere through the hole and tell Starlight's stories from within. The light energy should cause Exodus to inflate and rise again. It would then release pheterone, infusing the atmosphere with the gas the dragons required to survive and eliminating the need for human slaves. Her people could finally shake off their chains and return to their home world, Jason's world.

She stared at the pulsing sphere in her hand. One problem spoiled this scenario. If the hole remained in the sphere, Exodus would eventually sink as it did before, and what they had gained would eventually be lost. Only one alternative seemed to be foolproof. She could enter the star and use the stardrop to seal the hole from the inside. She would become the guiding angel of Starlight—her destiny as a Starlighter, according to Taushin.

Again his words returned to her mind: *You may take your place as a star in the sky, a watchful angel who forever tells the Creator's stories to every soul in the world, dragon and human alike ... if they will listen.*

If. And if they did not, her sacrifice would be for nothing. For there would be no way out ... ever.

As if waging war in her mind, Taushin's counterargument reverberated.

Why sacrifice? Why risk harm to yourself when it is possible to gain what you long for without it? With your power, I am sure you can keep the star aloft long enough for me to get the slaves out. To be eternally trapped while your liberated friends celebrate their freedom without you would be the greatest of tortures. Yes, you would feel some joy ... temporarily. But what about after a hundred years? A thousand years? Ten thousand? After every rejoicing slave is dead, you will be hovering over a thankless land, forever and ever. Your sorrow will never end.

Koren shook her head, trying to sling the competing thoughts away. No matter what she decided to do later, she could do nothing from outside the star. Maybe when she entered the sphere a new secret would be revealed that would make her decision an easier one.

She pushed the edge of the hole to one side. It stretched easily. As if in response, a low moan sounded from the inner sphere. She pulled again, stretching the gap and pushing her head and torso inside. Another wail of pain, longer and louder, echoed throughout the sphere's inner cavity.

She slid all the way inside and allowed the pliable skin to ease back into place, leaving a slightly larger hole than before. This time a gentle sigh drifted from wall to wall.

Koren stood on the curved floor, angling her body to keep her balance. "Is someone in here?" she called.

Her own words bounced back at her, repeating her question several times before fading.

A voice emanated from the small inner sphere. "Who are you?"

Koren let her boots slide down to the bottom of the floor. As she approached the source of the voice, she spoke in a soothing tone. "My name is Koren."

"Koren?" The images on the sphere's surface stopped, freezing at a portrait of Koren pulling a cart filled with honeycombs. "Koren the Starlighter who works for Arxad?"

"Yes." She reached a hand toward the sphere, feeling the energy flowing from the speaking ball. "What is your name?"

The flow diminished. Then, as if deflating, the sphere contracted, growing taller in proportion to its width. It formed into the shape of a girl, and the colors in the portrait spread across her body—red into her flowing hair, green into her eyes, and blue into a cloak that matched Koren's. Only her dress remained white. Finally, every detail crystallized. She seemed as human as any young woman on Starlight. It was like looking at a mirror … with one exception.

Koren looked down at her own clothes. Although she wore the Starlighter's cloak, the black dress Zena had forced upon her covered her body from neck to knees, and the equally black boots adorned her feet, tied at the back to mid calf.

The girl stared, her expression curious, yet sad. With her hood raised, she tilted her head to the side and spoke softly. "Why are you here, Koren?"

"Uh …" Koren glanced back at the hole. The question felt like a challenge, a rebuke. It would be easy to retreat and slide out, run away from this responsibility … too easy. "I'm here to try to resurrect Exodus."

"It is impossible," the girl said with an ache in her voice.

Starlighter

Bryan Davis

What if the Legends Are True?

Jason Masters doubted the myths that told of people taken through a portal to another realm and enslaved by dragons. But when he receives a cryptic message from his missing brother, he must uncover the truth and find the portal before it's too late. At the same time, Koren, a slave in the dragons' realm, discovers she has a gift that could either save or help doom her people. As Jason and Koren work to rescue the enslaved humans, a mystic prophecy surrounding a black egg may make all their efforts futile.

Talk It Up!

Want free books?
First looks at the best new fiction?
Awesome exclusive merchandise?

We want to hear from you!

Give us your opinions on titles, covers, and stories.
Join the Z Street Team.

Email us at zstreetteam@zondervan.com
to sign up today!

Also—Friend us on Facebook!

www.facebook.com/goodteenreads

- Video Trailers
- Connect with your favorite authors
- Sneak peeks at new releases
- Giveaways
- Fun discussions
- And much more!